OCTANE

OCTANE

A Novel

Theresa McNeice

TreesTales Publishing

ISBN 979-8-9917194-2-1 (hardcover); ISBN 979-8-9917194-1-4 (paperback); ISBN 979-8-9917194-0-7 (ebook)

TreesTales Publishing, Hudson, Massachusetts

T T 1 2 2 7

Cover Design by Dissect Designs

Manufactured in the United States of America

First Printing: 2025

Publisher's Cataloging-in-Publication Data

Names: McNeice, Theresa.
Title: Octane : a novel / Theresa McNeice.
Description: Hudson, MA : TreesTales Publishing, 2025.| Summary: A young woman, abused as a child, longing for a world free of anger and   pain, encounters a clandestine government operation also seeking to eliminate aggression.
Identifiers: ISBN 9798991719421 (hardcover) | ISBN 9798991719414 (pbk.) | ISBN 9798991719407 (ebook)
Subjects: LCSH: Abused women – Fiction. | Aggressiveness – Fiction. | Man-woman relation-ships – Fiction. | Friendship – Fiction. | Loyalty – Fiction. | Forgiveness – Fiction. | Rain forests – Amazon River Region – Fiction. | BISAC: FICTION / Nature & the Environment. | FICTION / Romance / Action & Adventure. | FICTION / Women.
Classification: LCC PS3613.C54 O28 2025 | DDC 813 M--dc23

DEDICATION

To Jim
for all your love and unending support

PROLOGUE

YEAR 1985

S HE TRIED TO SNEAK past the open door, but to no avail.

"Girl … I hear you out there. Better get your scrawny behind in here if you know what's good for you." Impatient and cruel, the voice beckoned from within the windowless room.

Her tiny feet stood glued to the parquet, struggling against the evil vortex eager to suck her in—but she dared not disobey. Girl knew her place. The fact that she was six years old bore no influence on her treatment. She answered when he called and did as she was told.

"Yes, Father," she said, her words automatic.

"Now see here, Girl, I'm about to teach you an important lesson," he said, his massive body blending in with the desk and his face cast as disembodied, glowing green in the dim lamplight. She stood before him, her eyes fixated on his crystal shot glass and the stream of bourbon filling it; his eyes fixated on her, this meek creation of his, with contempt.

"If you see something you want in this world, you take it. Hear me, Girl? Strength … success is built on strength." He swigged his shot and poured another. "Your mother would tell you otherwise—mindless babbling about kindness and charity—but I'll not have you believing such bull. Smarten up, Girl," he said, his voice lashing out like a whip. "Do you think kindness made me a Senator?"

She knew better. He had not one kind bone in his body. She let his rhetorical question slide.

"People respond to strength, Girl. They want a leader who's strong, unafraid of hard decisions, not some weak-kneed bleeding-heart afraid of his own shadow." He forced his chair back and stood.

Girl retreated a step, her heart beating double-time.

A rack of rifles stood along the wall. His brutish fingers massaged the smooth backbone of each until, satisfied in his selection, he lifted the Winchester from its mount.

"Strength leads to power and power leads to control," he said, steadying his aim on a mounted buck's head. "But control is only maintained through strength. A vicious circle, Girl." He pulled the trigger. A bullet exploded, tearing into the stuffed specimen, the injury an added insult.

Girl's breath sucked in and her eyes blinked wild, the blast ricocheting in her ears.

"If you're strong enough, success is there for the taking," he said. His chest puffed like a cock as he stood admiring his handiwork; she shivered in place like a mouse about to be pounced. "I intend to make you strong, Girl! Never let it be said that Senator Eugene Pendleton sired a weakling." Then he swung the nose of his rifle at Girl's head and pulled the trigger—the empty chamber clicked.

***

The parquet lay cool beneath her body, but the air hung hot and heavy, rife with the smell of gunpowder. When she came round her eyes saw nothing at first, only the filtered green light emanating from her father's desk lamp. He was gone, his hovering presence absent from the room. She lifted her head, her little fingers reaching behind to rub the rising lump. And then she saw them—those dreaded deer heads mounted upon the walls, their dead eyes reproachful of yet another doomed soul. She wanted to look away but couldn't. Her father need not be present to exert his hold over her; this room was his surrogate and, once entered, her will was no longer her own. It had always been this way for Girl—a prisoner without chains in a room without locks. If not her father's cutting stare to hold her in place, those reproachful eyes, dozens of them, did so from upon the walls—sightless eyes looking right through her as if she were a ghost, trapped and doomed to wander this room for all eternity.

Someone called in the distance. Girl registered the voice, but fear had silenced her. Footsteps fast approached. And then the voice came close … a gentle whisper in her ear. Tender fingers, stroking her hair at first and then her face, took grasp of her little hands and eased her to her feet. The two inched their way out, their footsteps a synchronized shuffle defying the room's clutches.

Out in the hallway the high noon sun pierced the column of arched windows. The blinding rays brought Girl round like smelling salts. "Hurry," the voice urged in her ear, "quickly now, up the stairs." An insistent hand pressed the small of her back forward. Reflex took command as she ran up the steps, her refuge just beyond the landing. Stepping inside, she slammed the door shut behind her. And just as she had done many times before, Girl turned the lock and slumped to the floor, panting.

Ever since Girl could remember, her mother's art studio had been a haven from her father, its smells of turpentine and oils the scents of safety. And from the room's rooftop perch she would look out beyond its lofty windows and imagine the wooded estate below a world different from her own and the life she lived there that of someone else—a game she played to escape reality—a game she would play her entire life.

Her eyes darted about the room drinking in her mother's paintings, one by one searching them out for comfort, a piece of her mother still here with her as she sat with ear to door and heart pounding, listening. Because whether it came sooner or came later, it always came—the inevitable rampage. But never was Girl to leave until her mother came for her. And this time would be no different.

When it began it was as if in a dream, muffled shouts within the manors far reaches, escalating to the booming crash of objects toppled. And then the worst of it. The screams. Girl covered her ears and hummed. Always a melancholy tune that brought tears tumbling from her eyes. Or was it the screams. And when it became unbearable, she squeezed her ears tighter and hummed louder.

Eventually, the house went quiet. She listened with ear to door once more for those familiar footsteps ascending the stairs. She listened for the voice—the voice that read her bedtime stories, the voice that said, 'I love you', the voice that spoke her name, Roxanne. She knew that voice in a crowd. She knew that voice in a whisper. It was the only voice she trusted.

And when, at last, it came from beyond the door the voice, though weary, fought for normalcy; and the woman who entered, though battered, stood tall before Girl, her smile radiant and spirit unbroken. It would be years before her mother's sacrifice would come to bear. But for now, Girl's instinct triggered, and taking tender hold of her mother's hand, led her back into the room, back to safety—back to her imaginary world.

PART ONE

Six Years Later – 1991

TreesTales Publishing

1

—.—

THE BLIND

August 19, 1991

S HE WAS GASPING FOR air, her lungs ready to burst, but she kept on running—running for her life through the thicket of the backwoods. Over her shoulder the thud of footsteps kept gaining on her, closing in. The pounce sent her flying spread eagle onto the forest floor with no air left in her to scream.

He rolled her over, the warmth of his breath and its reek of alcohol blanketing her face. "Wake up Girl," he slurred, backhanding her. "Time for the hunt!"

She knew this man whose eyes bore into hers—the tormentor of her dreams … and now her living nightmare.

Roxanne Pendleton just woke up to the worst day of her life, her father looming over her. It was useless to run, she knew, there was no escape—there never was.

Up to this point, at the awkward age of twelve, this defenseless child has struggled to keep from falling apart, though no one would blame her if she did. Her friends call her Roxy. But to a father denied of a valued son she answers, when called, to Girl. People say Roxy is the spitting image of her mother in her youth, a welcome compliment; but she considers herself fortunate to have inherited only height from her father, his sole redeeming quality. And while her life in rural Connecticut as an only child of the powerful United States Senator Eugene Pendleton and his philanthropic wife Rose has been one of privilege, it has never been one of bliss. At the Pendleton Estate love has never filled the rooms of their elegant country manor, only fear, with threats and beatings a common occurrence, though not always dished out in equal portions to mother and child. Each night the horrific tales are purged upon the pages of Roxy's journal, bound and locked away in a drawer—under wraps ... but never gone.

Some people marry for love, and some marry for love of money. At an early age it became clear to Roxy where her parents' marriage stood. The story of their meeting is neither romantic nor random. Roxy's mother, Rose Maxwell, a young and very beautiful descendent of one of Connecticut's wealthiest families, met her future husband on a hot June day at the races. The year was 1978, the place New York. It was the Belmont Stakes, and Rose's father, Maximilian Maxwell, had entered his thoroughbred into the last of the Triple Crown races. Eugene Pendleton, having plotted his scheme well, finessed his placement within earshot of Rose's father, wherein the young con artist boasted to onlookers of his generous wager—a sizable chunk of his life's savings staked to win on Maxwell's thoroughbred, a horse with forty-to-one odds. Overhearing Eugene's bravado, a flattered Maximilian struck up a conversation with the smooth-talking shammer who, soon enough, secured not only the elder's ear but a seat with the family for the race. It mattered not to Eugene that his pick ultimately failed to win and that his personal wealth was lost, because the cunning trickster had just scored the biggest payoff of his life—the esteem of the Maxwells ... and a ticket to the family's fortune.

Rose has spent her entire marriage to this man in survival mode—her two passions, painting and philanthropy, providing some sanity and separation from her dysfunctional home life. Rose likes to say that "God works in strange ways" regarding how she ended up on the philanthropic-art-world road. But it is vexing to Roxy that her mother's much-sought-after paintings had their origination as forms of therapy, questioning why God, if there is one, couldn't have spared Rose her misery in the process. But Rose claims it is those very inner feelings reflected in her paintings that have made them so popular and for that she has Eugene to thank. Her attitude irritates Roxy at times; but that's the thing with Rose, despite all that she's been through she still manages to look on the bright side, her compassion limitless, especially when it comes to her daughter and the charitable causes closest to her heart.

Eugene, on the other hand, embodies all that opposes Rose's goodness, riding the political wave to his success as a U.S. Senator on the coattails of her personal inheritance. Senator Pendleton is a man who demands attention—from his family and from his political associates. His stature, both in physical appearance and political power, looms over all who stand in his presence. Intimidation seeps from his pores as natural as sweat. And when he is inclined to imbibe too much alcohol, he can become the meanest son-of-a-bitch on the planet.

One may question why Rose would choose to endure such treatment, but divorce has never been an option for Eugene and Rose Pendleton. Eugene made this perfectly clear when her lawyer attempted to serve him papers. Suffice it to say her lawyer, adequately threatened, dropped her account like a hot potato, and Rose's two black eyes put an end to such further thoughts.

And though most of her bruises hid well beneath makeup and clothing, the ones that didn't went unquestioned, Rose's excuses seemingly plausible enough to dissuade further examination. Truth be told, Roxy felt people wanted to believe her mother's explanations and simply put to rest the uncomfortable subject.

But as Roxy grew older and became a competing target with her mother in the crosshairs of her father's rage, she became acutely aware that the art of cover-up required more than cosmetics and clothing to hide the hurt. She ingested medicine to dull her mind, but the painful memories failed to numb. She prevailed upon the written word to strip her demons bare, but the unforgivable truth did not set her free. She engaged in mind games, playing illusory characters on an imaginary world stage, only to have the final curtain slam down with the reality of life at home.

And the sad reality of life was that Eugene had no place in his heart for either his wife or daughter—his two true loves being hunting and drinking, and not necessarily in that order. Personally, Roxy detests killing for sport; but to Senator Eugene Pendleton, the more deer heads mounted on the walls of his study the better. And it wasn't enough for him to have one hunter in the family; he insisted Roxy learn to fire a rifle as well, despite her condemnation of killing. But her condemnation was secondary to the fact that she was born a girl, and that was precisely the reason he insisted. His resentful desire—to mold her into someone she was not, to strip any inkling left of her identity, to make her like him—overruled.

★★★

For days on end during this summer's heat Eugene would march Roxy out into the backwoods of their forty-acre estate for target practice until she could hit the bull's eye with regularity. Knowing what mastery meant, Roxy intentionally misdirected hits trying to postpone the inevitable. Yesterday, when her father caught on to her stall tactics, she became the target of his rage and the recipient of a rifle butt to her head.

Then, following an evening of drunken stupor, Eugene passed out in his study, his head prostrate on the desktop alongside an empty bourbon bottle. He awoke as mean as ever this morning, forcibly awakening Roxy from her sleep and summoning her to the hunt as if she were a young warrior about to make a right-of-passage. Once again, he marched her out into the backwoods, deeper than she'd ever been—the air hot and heavy with the smell of oncoming rain, the sky ominous with darkening clouds and the wind picking up speed. The whole situation left her wishing she was still under her bedcovers and that this was all just a bad dream.

Dressed in fatigues and thick-soled boots, a spare rifle hitched over one shoulder and the barrel of his own finding purchase in the cavity of his daughter's back, Eugene administered occasional pokes to nudge her along. Roxy had literally rolled out of bed and into the woods dressed in her night shirt. Her lack of footwear, along with her father's inebriated condition, prolonged their already slow pace over the notorious New England terrain of rocks and roots. Walking was an attempt in futility, as she would no sooner raise her eyes to gaze about her than she would stumble; and with eyes lowered to the encumbered ground, she became disoriented. It was a case of damned if I do and damned if I don't, her anxiety surging with each fresh affliction to her bloodied feet.

It was mid-morning when they came upon the blind—a curved wall of stones undulating knee to chest high, its jagged facade creeping with moss. Eugene made her crouch within its shadow, her rifle positioned atop the stones, while he settled onto a small, nearby boulder, rifle resting across his lap and a flask of whiskey by his side. They remained in this way for what seemed an eternity. And thus began the long, tortuous wait.

The taking of a life, any life, was sickening to Roxy. How could she possibly kill an animal? She had never even killed an ant when one ventured into their house. Roxy's mother, Rose, would have her coax the tiny, uninvited guest into a drinking glass for its prompt release outside, back to nature. Rose believed people extended their own lives by extending the lives of all living things; it was part of her philosophy to "let live and live." She had a lot of personal beliefs like that. Once, when she was in her flower garden painting a rose, it struck Roxy as coincidental that the rose was not only her mother's favorite flower but her name as well, and Roxy said as much. "No dear," Rose replied, "there is no such thing as coincidence in this world." It got Roxy to thinking. If there are no coincidences and everything has a purpose, then what possible reason was there for her life—this life? Crouching behind the wall, her legs as shaky as her nerves, Roxy doubted in the existence of a Divine Plan and wondered if she wasn't just some random victim who'd lost out on the luck of the draw.

***

As was her habit when she awoke, Rose tuned in to her favorite radio station. This morning's regularly scheduled program was soon interrupted by an emergency broadcast: A powerful hurricane barreling up the Atlantic Coast had changed course and was now on track to hit Connecticut—predicted landfall, noontime. Rose turned off the radio, hurrying out to buy the staples necessary for hunkering down during the storm. Eugene was still asleep, as it were, in his study when she left, and Roxy in her bed. By the time she returned, they were both gone.

Frantic, having discovered two rifles missing from Eugene's collection, Rose acted on instinct, heading straight for the dreaded backwoods. The deeper she ventured into the forested estate the stronger the wind gusts blew. Tree branches flailed like protective arms as she steered clear of their reach and fought a path forward through the mayhem. Above her, blackened skies tore open, letting loose a vengeful rain. But it wasn't the extreme elements buffeting her that frightened most, it was the memories now flooding back from the all-too-familiar path she was on. Still, she would not be deterred, knowing exactly where she must go.

Rose had always done everything in her power to protect Roxy from her father, often placing herself between them in his path of rage. One such time when Eugene turned his anger from Roxy onto Rose, he sought out her punishment in the form of hard labor. At gunpoint, Rose was forced to rebuild the crumbling blind. Using only her bare hands and with great effort, she lifted the toppled stones and replaced them one by one, rebuilding the wall in the summer's oppressive heat. Her delicate hands, cut and bruised, did not heal for weeks. Her explanation to everyone—she had stumbled in her rose garden. Rose had thought the memory of that day was buried for good, swearing never again to step beyond her garden's edge into the backwoods; but now, not even a hurricane would keep her from returning to the blind. She had to save her child.

***

When Heaven's full fury finally waged war in the skies above them, Roxy knew they were amid something more than a typical summer storm. Her father had not heeded her earlier pleas to return to the safety of their home. There had been no reasoning with him, his whiskey intake having obliterated his mind of all common sense. He was a man possessed, not only by the alcohol but also by the kill. He would not hear of leaving until she had done the deed they came to do. Now, as pandemonium broke out all around them like an infectious disease, Roxy realized that nothing short of a miracle would guarantee a safe passage home.

The crazed winds howled like warring beasts. Had it not been for the blind serving as a buffer, the arm of the tempest would have surely whisked her leaf-like across the forest floor. Her body shuddering, she hugged the wall. All around, pine trees thrashed, and limbs snapped. Diagonal sheets of rain showed no mercy, power-washing the earth and drenching her to the bone. Roxy honestly didn't know what frightened her most, the storm or her father. She had lacked the courage to run and now she was trapped like a cornered animal.

Then it appeared. Her father spotted it first, Roxy's gaze following his through the deluge. A regal buck had leapt into their periphery. Crowned with its many-tined antlers, the buck held its head high amid the chaos. It stood still in quiet defiance, facing down the raging storm like a courageous king readying to do battle.

The rifle jab to her thigh brought reality roaring back. Roxy turned from the buck to face her father. His voice, smothered now by the deafening rains, spat out the silent command: "Shoot!" Roxy froze. And then everything seemed to happen in slow motion. Grabbing her shoulders, he shook her to take aim; but Roxy's arms fell limp by her side, unable to move. With his face contorting in rage and his eyes searing hers, he hoisted Roxy from her refuge, her body dangling like a soaked rag doll in his powerful vise-grip before slamming her down against the wall's jagged facade. Pain shot up her spine as she crumpled into the muddied mire, her tears melding in with the pelting rains. Her father's drunken tempest seemed even more emboldened by the hurricane's fury. Kneeling over her, face to face, her head wedged between his brutish hands, he thrust it repeatedly against the stone wall. Screams escaped Roxy's mouth but were hurled back at her with the wind for no one else to hear. Everything went black.

***

Eugene slumped to the ground, blood trickling from the back of his head into the swirling rivulets where he lay.

Rose dropped the stone from her hands and collapsed over her daughter.

Roxy's consciousness faded in and out along with the image of her mother's face, etched with fear. She could feel her mother's chest heaving as Rose drew her in, a protective cocoon encasing her in a moment of hope. Neither one observed the massive shadow rearing—until it was too late.

In a helpless daze, Roxy was relegated to watching as Eugene ripped her mother out from her arms and flung her to the ground, stomping her. Rose fought the valiant fight, latching on to his leg, biting it. The affliction fed the angry beast even more, his boot lashing out like a dragon's tail whipping her delicate ribs. Anguish spilt from Rose, her body writhing in the mud-soaked earth. Crawling to all fours she attempted righting herself, but not before Eugene's boot found its footing on her backside, flattening her like a pesky bug. Instinctively, Rose curled into a ball seeking protection; but Eugene's aggression was undeterred, delivering a jolting shock with another massive kick to her side.

As her mother lay there, bleeding and broken, and as her father stood over her, rage seething from his being with each blow he continued to strike, Roxy's hand felt something smooth upon which it rested. Her fingers wrapped its familiar shape and, struggling, she drew it up onto her lap. With great effort, hands trembling, she raised it up. Her father caught the movement, turning his head. A lightning bolt lit the sky. Their eyes locked. Roxy pulled the trigger.

A simultaneous crack of thunder obliterated the gunshot. Suddenly they were strewn in evergreen, a surprising shelter from the storm. The hurricane reached its crescendo, felling trees and upturning roots with abandon all around them. It seemed like the end of the world. Her consciousness waning, Roxy lay numb in her skin. If there was meaning to her life, damn if she knew it then. To die this way somehow seemed fitting; she would die as she lived—in fear.

★★★

Quiet … absolute quiet jerked Roxy awake. Her eyelids snapped open, pine needles dangling like snowflakes on her lashes. She brushed them away. Back throbbing and skull pounding, she crawled out slowly from under the branches. Nothing stirred. Not a bird in the blue skies above. Only stillness … complete stillness. Where once the forest stood was now an unrecognizable clump of debris, a distorted world. A chill ran through her, and then the reality of what had seemed like a nightmarish dream registered full throttle in her brain. "Mother!" she screamed. A muffled moan erupted from beneath the entangled brush. Adrenaline pushed Roxy into feverish motion. Scrambling, she thrust aside the storm's refuse entombing Rose and, kneeling beside her, caressed her mother's loving face within her hands.

Through her tears Rose smiled her remarkable smile and whispered, "Roxanne … my darling Roxanne."

Mother and daughter basked in each other's embrace weary and worn from survival; but the welcome respite was but a brief interlude before Rose had time to take things in. She reeled in a panic, "Your father … where is your father!"

Fear inhabited Roxy's body like an unwelcome spirit. *What have I done?* she thought. And although she could not bear to look, Roxy felt driven as in a trance toward the mounded mass burial of tree remains and the body of her father.

He was dead. There was no doubt about it. The pine tree had hit Eugene squarely before coming to rest upon the blind, its tentacle branches splayed protectively over Roxy and Rose. Maneuvering carefully and with great trepidation, she stepped between limbs, pushing aside branches nearer his body for closer examination. That was when a ray of sunlight pieced the darkness of the brush and, like a boomerang, refracted off something shiny, catching her eye. Call it what you will, a coincidence or an act of God, but there in the tree trunk, lodged in its bark, the remnant of a bullet jutted out before her. At that moment a shroud lifted from Roxy as if exorcised, but her heavy heart knew with absolute certainty that she would never be liberated from the undeniable truth—she had shot to kill her father.

"We must go," Rose said, her voice resolute, "the eye of the storm will soon pass from us." With arms wrapped about each other's waist and shoulder, the two moved as one through the wasteland before them.

***

Tragedy has a way of uniting people; but Roxy and her mother always shared a special closeness, an unbreakable bond. Rose also had a special bond with God. She believed fear was a lack of faith, and Rose's faith was strong. She trusted they would be brought out of the wilderness through the eye of the storm, just as the Israelites had safely passed through the parted Red Sea. And so it was. Moments after mother and daughter crossed the threshold into Rose's beloved garden, the winds and rains returned with all of God's fury.

***

Journal Entry, August 19, 1991:

Today there was a hurricane—Mother and I survived.

Mother believes she was forced to rebuild the blind because God, in his infinite wisdom, foresaw this day coming; and that one should always accept life's hardships with grace, because there is a reason for everything.

Mother also believes in guardian angels. I guess she's failed to notice ours haven't been around for a while. But if there are such things as angels on Earth, then mother must surely be one, because today she saved my life.

Father died in the hurricane.

Mother says to forgive his lowly soul because he did not know what he was doing. And so I wonder, knowing exactly what I was doing ... who will forgive me?

PART TWO

Six Years Later – 1997

TreesTales Publishing

2

THE NEIGHBORS

Friday, August 15, 1997

THERE WAS SOMETHING ABOUT the young man next door. Rose felt it from the moment she first set eyes on him—the day she and Roxy moved into their new Victorian home in Cambridge, Massachusetts. Amid the chaos of the workmen unloading their furnishings from the moving van, Rose noticed the young man's occasional glances their way as he busied himself with watering the flowers lining his walkway. Whenever she'd attempt a wave hello, he'd avert his eyes. From her vantage point, he appeared to be close in age to Roxy, now eighteen, and she wondered if he, too, would be going off to college come September. The excitement of the move to a new home in a new state and a new life for both mother and daughter had Rose caught up in a euphoric frame of mind; but there was something in the boy's demeanor, something more than shyness, that caused her to pause and take notice.

"Mother," Roxy called out from the veranda, "the movers want to know where to place the sofa."

The sound of her daughter's voice yanked Rose back from her thoughts. "Coming," she practically sang as she ran up the steps, once again delighting in the task at hand.

The young man looked up from his watering to watch the pretty lady hurry into the house, only to find his glance met when Rose suddenly turned her head before ducking inside, a warm smile directed his way and a 'gotcha' look twinkling in her eyes. Caught in his own game the young man smiled back, surprised at how good it felt.

****

The summer night air was warm and muggy. It was eleven o'clock on a Friday evening and Roxy, unable to sleep despite her tiredness from the day's move, lay awake on her bed, restless. She thought about Connecticut. Her mother had been in no hurry to move after her father's death, wanting her to experience a normal life with friends and school. Though for Roxy it was just one more Academy Awards performance for her mother's sake; she knew her life would never feel normal. But soon college rolled around and with it a time for transition. So her mother settled the estate and bought the new house in Massachusetts, looking forward to a fresh start. Roxy had to admit that she liked her new home and that it felt good to finally leave Connecticut. But she knew she'd be kidding herself if she thought the move would end the nightmares still frequenting her dreams—even her medicines couldn't do that.

Roxy tried to share in her mother's excitement but couldn't quite shake the apprehension that got under her skin whenever she thought about college and the prospect of being on her own. Well, not completely on her own—there was the matter of her roommate. Roxy tried to picture how she looked. The information from school had said her name was Megan O'Malley. *Irish no doubt with a name like that,* she mused. *Probably has strawberry blond hair … petite for sure … Irish women are petite. I'll tower over her,* she brooded. But it was more than height that worried Roxy. She was afraid that Megan wouldn't like her, would find her strange when she woke up screaming in the night.

The ever-increasing rev of an engine bearing down the road suddenly filled the still night air, unleashing Roxy from her dread. Headlights bounced off her darkened bedroom walls and then disappeared as the vehicle slowly turned into the neighbor's driveway. Her curiosity peaked, and not wanting to awaken her mother in the next room, she slid from her bed and tiptoed across the oak-planked flooring to an opened window. Her vision, illuminated by a streetlamp like a spotlight onto a stage, funneled through the darkness and onto the neighbor's driveway. There, a vintage '69 Corvette convertible had come to a stop, its headlights squelched. When the driver's door opened and a very tall man struggled out from the low-rider sports car, all Roxy could picture was her neighbor transformed as Fred Flintstone in his stone-aged vehicle, his long legs protruding through the floorboards. She laughed out loud. In the darkness the man paused, turning toward the sound. Wide-eyed, she ducked behind the bedroom curtain, hand over mouth. Seconds later, heart still in her throat and inching curtain aside, she peeked out at the tall man now retiring into his home for the night. In the muggy darkness she tip-toed back to bed, sprawling face-up onto the damp sheet. Her reeling mind soon settled in with her tiredness and, despite the relentless efforts of her nightly demons, a smile crossed her face with her last conscious thought—the juicy prospect of her widowed mother dating the man next door.

***

It was a glorious Saturday morning. A rainstorm had passed through during the pre-dawn hours taking the mugginess along with it. Roxy's bedroom curtains bellowed on the fresh breeze like clothes on a line. She stirred from her sleep, the smell of chocolate wafting up from the kitchen and filling her nostrils with its sweetness. It took a few seconds for her waking brain to register the new surroundings and to cast her nightly demons back into their coffin—the daytime now her domain and the sun her crucifix. She stretched with a yawn, her long slender legs swinging off the bed. In the light of day, the stack of unpacked boxes stood on prominent display. Saving that ungrateful task for later she quickly bypassed them, bounding from her room and down the stairs, her nose on the trail of the mouth-watering scent. Today, she knew, would be introduction day with the new neighbors, freshly baked cakes in hand—that was Rose's way of doing things, seizing the moment before someone else had the chance.

Humming a cheerful melody, Rose stood frosting the last of several layer cakes now lining the kitchen counter like hats on a shelf. At the sight of her mother Roxy came to an abrupt stop, hanging back to appreciate the moment, knowing that it would be times like this she'd miss most when off at college.

As if on cue, Rose turned with a smile. "Hey, lazy girl, it's almost ten o'clock. I thought I was going to have to wake you," she said, tracing one last swirl of confection with her knife before setting it down onto the counter and wiping her hands on her apron. "Ta Da!" she said, holding up the delectable work of art with a flourish. And then, as if reading Roxy's mind, added, "Don't worry, I made one for us as well." Roxy's grin said it all as Rose handed her a plate with a hefty slice on it.

As Rose watched Roxy relish her first bite, her heart felt a pang of longing for her daughter who hadn't even left for college yet. She felt sure that the adjustment would come slowly for them both but was as equally sure they needed time apart. After all, Rose reasoned, she wouldn't be here forever, and Roxy needed to learn how to cope without her. Besides, Rose was anxious to resume her own interests as well. Still, she couldn't help but feel like a part of her was missing already, even as her daughter sat before her.

Roxy's brow furrowed.

"Mother," she said, "what if my roommate and I don't hit it off? I mean, we may have little in common to talk about."

"Nonsense, dear," Rose reassured her, "you forget that the two of you are writing majors. That alone should keep you two gabbing for hours."

Roxy wanted to believe her. It was just that the wait was killing her, too much time to sow self-doubts. She just wanted to get it over with—meet Megan and size one another up. But when Roxy looked at her mother, her heart ached at the thought of leaving her. "I guess we have that in common," she said, feigning agreement, not at all as confident as her mother that one shared interest could foster a friendship.

"You'll just have to wait and see," Rose said.

Yes, wait and see, Roxy thought. *People spend half their lives waiting.*

Rose removed her apron. "Eat up, darling," she said, "mustn't keep the neighbors waiting."

No, mustn't keep them waiting.

***

Standing in front of the wood-paneled door like two doves perched on a birdhouse stoop, mother and daughter waited expectantly as it slowly opened to the bell's beckoning call. There in the colonial's grand entry stood a tall, handsome man in his late thirties, the slightest of gray sprouting at the temples of his thick, dark hair. His wide, captivating smile was nearly overwhelming; but what caught them completely off guard were his eyes, the color of the deepest ocean, drawing the women into their mysterious depths and drowning them in bottomless blue waters.

"Why hello," he said, glancing from mother to daughter.

Undone by this unexpected vision, the two women were rendered speechless.

"I'm David Bennett," he said, stepping up to fill the awkward void. "And I have the pleasure of meeting… ?" He extended his hand.

The pent-up words burst from her lips. "Rose … Rose Pendleton," she said, her voice an embarrassed quiver, "your new neighbor." Juggling the plate of freshly baked cake, she freed her hand and took hold of his. She noticed his firm yet tender grip and his hesitation to let go while their eyes remained engaged. "And this is my daughter, Roxy," she said, breaking from his gaze.

"My pleasure, Roxy," David said as he took her hand into his. "You share your mother's beauty."

To her horror, Roxy could feel the color of her cheeks changing like autumn leaves.

"I hope you like chocolate cake," Rose said, quickly offering up her confection to David while her daughter's discoloration continued to grow.

"My favorite," he said, "but shouldn't I be the one welcoming you to the neighborhood?"

"Not if you know my mother," Roxy blurted, regretting it instantly, not meaning to embarrass her.

"Well, I don't know her yet, but I'd certainly like to get to know her," he said, locking eyes with Rose once again as he took ownership of the cake, his hands lightly brushing hers.

Rose felt her body tremble, goose bumps running up her arms. She wasn't used to such feelings, not since she was a schoolgirl. It wasn't like her to get so flustered.

"Please … come in," he said, holding the door aside.

Roxy bounded in before her mother could politely decline, leaving Rose little choice but to follow.

"May I offer you both some coffee?" David said. "Perhaps we could sit and get to know one another over this scrumptious-looking cake."

Rose hadn't planned to stay beyond the initial introductions. And she certainly hadn't come looking for a relationship, but here she was an unintended victim of this remarkable man's charms. She knew where that had gotten her once before. But as she was about to tell David they couldn't possibly stay, the front door burst open.

Arms loaded with groceries, a young man entered the foyer full throttle. He managed to stop just short of the visitors, but not before the contents of his bags shifted, causing a minor spill. "Oh, I'm so sorry. I should watch where I'm going," he berated himself, embarrassed as he bent to retrieve the run-away apples, his manicured mane spilling over his brow.

"Ladies, I'd like you to meet my little brother, Nick," David said with a mischievous grin as he stooped to further muss the teen's hair.

Rose recognized Nick instantly as the young man watering the flowers. He was a good foot shorter than David and of a leaner build, a good deal younger as well, so much so Rose thought he could be David's son. "I believe we met yesterday," she said, "well … not formally introduced, but we did smile at one another."

"Did we now?" David asked, half teasing half curious, his eyes floating between the two.

Nick stood back up, the fugitive apples re-captured and bagged, his hair disheveled, and his embarrassment growing by the minute.

"It's nice to formally meet you, Nick. I'm Rose Pendleton," she said, smiling, her hand outstretched.

Nick shifted both bags to one arm and shook her extended hand. "Nice to meet you, too, ma'am," he said.

His ocean-blue eyes captured hers. *Just like David's,* she thought, releasing his grip and trying not to stare. "Please … call me Rose," she said.

"And I'm Roxy. Let me give you a hand with those groceries," the teen said, snatching a bag from Nick's grasp before he knew what hit him. Then, just like a ship's captain she barked the order, "Lead the way."

Nick obeyed with relief, knowing a retreat to the kitchen was a retreat from further embarrassment. "Right this way, miss."

"Oh please, none of that miss stuff. Just call me Roxy," she said, tailgating Nick into the kitchen and leaving Rose in the lurch.

"Quite a take-charge young woman, isn't she?" David said grinning, his eyes following Roxy's departure from the room.

"Since the day she was born," Rose replied, the kitchen door closing on her daughter's backside and panic rising in her sudden abandonment.

With cake in hand David crossed the foyer, the echo of his heels on marble tiles causing Rose's chest to tremor. He deposited the confection onto an antique lowboy and, turning, flung open a set of French doors with seamless fluidity. "Shall we?" he said.

Rose felt trapped. But she swallowed a feigned excuse to flee and summoned herself forward with a long, deep breath.

The living room had a comfortable, manly appeal, furnished with soft leather seating. Scattered floral arrangements of woodsy eucalyptus scented the air. And off to one side another set of French doors lent a remarkable garden view, filling the space with an abundance of natural light. But none of this registered with Rose. Her attention was focused elsewhere.

David took notice. "Amazing, aren't they?" he said.

"Incredible …" she exhaled.

The magic of the oil paintings displayed about the room pulled Rose from one large canvas to the next, her eyes widening with each new experience.

"They seem to have an effect on people," David said, deftly taking her arm and leading her into the room.

"Who painted them?" she asked.

"Nick. He has a gift."

"Are there others?"

"No, he hasn't painted in six years—not since the fire."

Just then the two teens emerged from the kitchen, Roxy talking animatedly—something about Fred Flintstone—and giggling. David couldn't help but notice how she made his brother smile.

"We were just discussing your Corvette, David," Roxy said, a knowing glance directed toward Nick. "I don't believe I've ever ridden in a sports car, let alone a convertible. It certainly must catch the ladies' eyes."

"I don't know about the ladies' eyes," he laughed, "but it certainly is fun to drive; and there's nothing like the feel of the wind in your hair as you zip along the highway—it's exhilarating."

Not as exhilarating as your smile, Roxy thought.

"I'd be happy to take you and your mother for a ride sometime," he said.

"That'd be fantastic!" she squealed, the words spilling out before her mother could reply.

Suddenly, Rose felt flush, the room spinning and a need to bolt. "Thank you both so much for your hospitality," she said with as much grace as she could muster, "but it's getting late, and we really must be going … we have other cakes to deliver this morning."

"I assure you, ladies, the pleasure was all ours; but I must admit, I'm envious of the neighbors," David said, his eyes penetrating hers.

Forcing a smile, Rose tore from his gaze and turned from the room, anxiety's grip tightening her chest. "I hope you both enjoy the cake," she said, the strangled words escaping her throat as she passed the sweet confection on their way out.

"We will, thank you," David said, a hint of disappointment in his voice.

Breathless, Rose took hold of Roxy's arm and retraced their steps to the door.

"I'd like to return your kindness," David said, ushering the women out onto the portico. "Is tomorrow a good day for that ride? Say around noon?"

Roxy turned with a smile. "Perfect!" she said, descending the brick steps, her mother in tow. "We look forward to it!"

Retreating arm in arm down the flowered walkway, Rose managed several deep breaths before leaning into her daughter's ear and exhaling, "Darling, what just happened?"

Roxy grinned.

"Why Mother, we have a date."

3

CHURCH DANCE

Girl Flashback

"*A* DATE? *WHAT DO you mean a date!" Eugene snarled, having eaves-dropped on a private mother-daughter conversation. He advanced on the women. "And you know I don't approve of dances ... a complete waste of valuable time."*

Twelve-year-old Girl stood her ground, so close to her father the spittle escaping his lips showered her.

"It's not a formal date, Eugene, just a small church dance," Rose assured. "All her friends will be there."

"I determine what constitutes a date, formal or not," Eugene barked. "And who exactly is this date? Not the son of one of your sanctimonious do-gooders."

"He's the minister's son ... Aaron Shepherd," Rose said, her voice righteous.

"Of course," he sneered, "with a name like that. No matter. I can't abide wasting time, not at a dance or with a damn preacher's son."

"I can go alone, father" Girl proffered, hopeful.

"Go alone," he spat, turning on her. "So that you and your young proselytizer can rendezvous later on the dance floor? You take me for a fool, Girl?" Eugene snapped, incensed at her treacherous audacity. And then his ugly brain hatched a deceit of his own. "No," he said, his mind reeling, "you'll go ... but with a suitable young man of my choosing." And then he spoke the beastly words, "You'll go with Rodney Taft."

Girl's heart sank. Rodney Taft. He couldn't be serious. Next to her father, Rodney was her second worst nightmare—a brawny, thirteen-year-old predator who had tried to have his way with her—not to mention the son of George Taft, a wealthy campaign contributor conveniently tucked in Eugene's back pocket.

"I'll call his father now," Eugene said, his voice victorious as he headed for his study. "A fine young man, that Rodney," he said, "a fine young man."

A fine young man, indeed, Girl mocked in silent indignation, her nerves shaken and body nauseous. A wealthy young man, too. If only the minister's son came from money. No matter, *she thought,* he'd still be a minister's son.

★★★

Of course it was raining. And why shouldn't it be? Girl's hopeless spirit had all but called for it. In truth, she was glad it was raining. Why waste a starry night on a date with the likes of Rodney Taft.

The church hall was decorated with balloons and streamers, the lights set to a respectable dimness. A teen band was cranking out a fully amped version of 'Old Time Rock and Roll' while a congregation of youngsters looked on, the evening still too young for any self-respecting kid to dare be seen dancing, at least not until the cool kids hit the floor.

Girl did not want to be here—at least not with Rodney. The two had kept their distance ever since his chilly reception when he called on her at the Pendleton household. Not once did he look her in the eyes, though he met her father's full on and shook his hand in earnest. Not once did he exchange a word with her in the car ride to the church, though he engaged in thoughtful conversation with her mother. But that was fine with Girl. After all, at their last meeting the two hadn't exactly parted on good terms. Dire terms would be more accurate. 'Don't ever come near me again' terms would be exact.

No sooner the two entered the church hall had Rodney headed for the refreshment stand, obtained a single cup of soda and then made his way into the restroom. When he emerged a minute later, he passed by Girl and her friends without so much as a glance and took a seat along the wall, where he sat for the rest of the night, content in drinking alone.

It was at that moment, from across the room, Girl caught Aaron Shepherd smiling at her. A slow melody began to play. He headed her way.

"May I have this dance?" he asked, his palm offered. No one was dancing, but Girl didn't care. The couple stood regal on center floor, eyes locked and

bodies embraced, swaying to the music. People murmured and stared, but not in Girl's world. She was now a liberated princess rescued by her daring prince charming. All else failed to exist except for this castle's ballroom and the couple's long-sought union—at least until the stroke of midnight.

As for Rodney, he showed little notice of the events around him. And after several trips to the restroom, he fell asleep in his chair, bothering no one—no one except a chaperone who noticed the comatose boy and tried stirring him awake. Soon it became apparent something was wrong. Dreadfully wrong. Shouts for help went out. The lights came up and the crowd thronged. Girl's heart hammered her chest as she and Aaron looked on. The ambulance arrived within minutes and whisked Rodney away. The festive mood had turned somber, and with the siren still blaring in the distance, the dance was called to an official end.

★★★

Here it comes, *Girl thought, alone in the car with her father, her knuckles white as she clung to the door's handle. She had hoped her mother would have answered her call for an early pickup, but luck was never on her side. How was she to explain what happened? It wasn't her fault, but she knew well enough she would be blamed. Blamed for the flask of vodka hidden in Rodney's jacket, blamed for his multiple libations freely ingested though surrounded by parent chaperones, blamed for not noticing the liquor on his breath. But clearly, it was partly her fault, wasn't it? She had ignored him all night. Never once tried to check up on him. True, she hated his guts after what he had tried to do during their last encounter. She recoiled now at the thought, and at the thought that her father had done nothing, had let Rodney escape unscathed. Perhaps he considered the support of Rodney's father more important—George Taft's money backing his re-run for a senate seat more consequential. Even now, the thought of herself pinned up against the wall of her father's darkened study with Rodney's warm breath in her face … her hands fighting his grip as he reached under her skirt … she wanted to puke. She didn't want to think about what would have happened had not her father entered the room. Rodney had backed away, flustered, then mustered some excuse about rejoining his parents in the dining room, dinner guests that night at the Pendleton Estate. Guests. Girl could still hear Rodney whispering the words in her ear, "This is how guests return a favor." And yet when she made to expose the indecency perpetrated upon her, she was silenced.*

Silenced with a warning to never speak of it again. The matter was closed. Rodney's character as 'a fine young man' was not to be impugned, and she was to remain mute, even to her mother.

But to Girl's relief, the entire ride home went without verbal lashing. In fact, not a word was spoken. But when they pulled into the garage and she made to get out, her father reached over and grabbed her arm. Girl froze. She watched him reach into his coat pocket, retrieve his whiskey flask, unscrew its cap and raise it to his lips. "Boys will be boys," he said with a vile smile, and then tipped his head back and took a long, lavish swig.

4

— · —

THE DATE

Sunday, August 17, 1997

Nᴏᴛ ᴏɴᴇ ᴛᴏ sʟᴇᴇᴘ in, Rose sat out on the veranda nestled into a white, wicker rocker ready to catch the sunrise. A shawl wrapped about her shoulders to ward off the early morning chill, she sipped her black coffee as she rocked in a steady rhythm, exhilarated just to be in this place at this time. Her now deceased husband had once decreed that her future was not her own; but the only future Rose had ever envisioned for herself was one that didn't include him. Of course, the particulars of accomplishing that she had left up to God.

As the sun cast its first rays out from the horizon, Rose found herself welcoming its warmth into her being and, with it, all the possibilities that a new day brings. In the growing dawn, she made herself a promise. For as long as she lived, no man would ever control her again.

"Good morning, Mother," came the whisper from behind as Roxy bent to kiss her mother's cheek. "Beautiful sunrise," she said, plopping down onto a wicker chaise, bundled in a cotton blanket.

"Why, good morning darling. Yes, it is quite beautiful," Rose whispered back before once again fading into the stillness.

Framed in the soft morning light, Rose was a striking beauty at thirty-six years of age. Her warm hazel eyes and soft auburn hair spilling over pale silken shoulders could hold fast an admirer's attention. *It's no wonder a stranger could fall in love with her at first glance,* Roxy thought as she studied her mother's perfect profile and considered the man next door.

"So," she said, breaking the silence, "what do you think of David?"

"Who dear?" Rose replied.

"You *know* … David Bennett, our next-door neighbor?"

Rose knew, of course, but it was a path she was disinclined to take, especially now when her spirit was in such a restful state.

"Oh yes … David," she said. "He seems nice enough."

"Nice enough!"

"Shish!" her mother hissed into the quiet morning air, "voices travel."

"Mother," Roxy said under her breath, "it was quite obvious the man has the hots for you."

"Roxanne Pendleton!" Rose exclaimed, surprised and then embarrassed by her own outburst, her eyes darting quickly about the neighborhood. "We hardly know one other," she resumed in a hushed, dignified tone.

"Mother, live a little for once. You've earned the right to have some fun. You must admit he is very handsome."

"Perhaps," she said, "but I'm not ready for a relationship."

"Who said anything about a relationship? All I'm saying is give yourself a chance to enjoy life for a change, one step at a time … starting with today's date."

Today's date: a ride in a Corvette, top down with the wind in her hair and a man handsome enough to be on the cover of Esquire behind the wheel. Rose fretted she'd never get through it with her heart racing as fast as the speedometer on the highway. No—she wasn't ready for this.

"You don't have to decide now," Roxy said, as if reading her mother's mind, and then adding her favorite mantra, "just wait and see."

Rose exhaled audibly as her body cradled back into her chair.

Roxy ventured on. "So … what do you think of Nick?"

Nick. Although she couldn't quite put her finger on it, Rose had a feeling she was missing something, but her answer steered clear of her angst. "Oh, he seems like a nice young man, well-mannered … and from the looks of it, he enjoyed your company," she said, her tone insinuating more than friendship.

"Mother … he's gay," Roxy deadpanned.

Rose turned to face her daughter.

"He told me right off … probably didn't want us to start out on the wrong foot."

"Well, I suppose not," Rose said, considering the many layers of the young man's mysterious veneer. "Did he happen to mention his paintings?"

"Paintings? What paintings?"

"His oil paintings … in the living room … how could you have missed them?

Roxy shook her head. "I guess I was too caught up in the moment."

"They were incredibly moving," Rose said, and falling captive to her thoughts, an uneasy expression settled onto her face.

"Mother, what's wrong?" Roxy asked, her fingertips alighting Rose's forearm.

"Something David said … about Nick not painting in six years … since the fire."

"Fire? What fire?"

"I don't know. Just as I was about to ask, you and Nick came out from the kitchen."

In their brief time together, Roxy had felt a connection to Nick, some part of him reflecting back a part of her; but at the time she shook off the uncomfortable feeling, not wanting to think about it. Now, under the blanket, her body shivered in recollection. "No one leaves this world unscathed," she said, voicing her thoughts out loud.

Rose looked over at her daughter, recalling the day she was born and holding her swaddled in a blanket, so innocent—and now here she was eighteen years later cocooned on the chaise, her innocence sadly replaced by life's harsh realities. Rose reached out and clasped Roxy's hand. Together, eyes closed and faces now fully embraced by the rising sun, mother and daughter drank in the warmth of a new day—and all its possibilities.

★★★

"He's here, Mother," Roxy called out from the front parlor. She had been planted on the settee by the stained-glass window for the last half hour, her image obscured to passersby outside while her view, although distorted, was direct to the street.

For the whole hour before, she had fretted over an appropriate outfit, emptying her closet and dresser drawers of the contents she had just unpacked, negating hours of laborious effort in just minutes.

It's no use, she thought, scowling at her reflection in the mirror, mounds of clothes shifting like sand dunes under her feet, *nothing looks right.* Roxy had long ago accepted her height as an intractable blip in her gene pool, but it was impossible to see herself as beautiful—her self-esteem bruised along with her body as a child. Back then, pretending to be someone she wasn't had come easily when self-preservation hung in the balance; but after her father's death, still, she clung to hiding in the conjured personas of her mind from the demons of a painful past, and worse … from the guilty little girl who pulled the trigger.

Today, the broken eighteen-year-old stared at her reflection in the mirror and thought, *Who am I?* The answer was instantaneous: a glamorous actress riding off into the sunset with David, convertible top down and onlookers gawking, pondering the mysterious woman riding shotgun. Inspired, she slipped into a white linen dress, gathered her long, auburn mane into a chignon at the nape of her neck and wrapped a red silk scarf loosely about her head. Disguising her hazel eyes with a pair of Foster Grants, Roxy glanced in the mirror and smiled. The look was sheer Vogue.

Walk slowly, she thought as the bell rang, not wanting to appear too eager. She took a deep breath at the door and turned the knob.

David surpassed her expectations.

"Hello Roxy," he said, smiling seductively, his bronzed six-foot-six frame outfitted in white Polo shirt and shorts dazzling in the sunlight. Roxy fought to maintain her grown-up facade and to quell the butterflies in her stomach.

"Why, hello David, so wonderful to see you again. Please, come in," she said, stepping aside to allow his passing, his aftershave lingering on the air.

"You look lovely," he said, his eyes fully taking her in as she closed the door behind him. A blush flooded her rouged cheeks.

Stirred by his proximity … his scent … his words, Roxy floated like a bubble on air, climbing higher and higher—until David's eyes looked up and fell upon her mother.

For the last half hour Rose had remained noncommittal, entertaining her 'wait and see' attitude to the very end. Roxy had no idea what to tell David, uncertain whether her daughter-mother pep talks would work.

No words were needed.

Standing at the top of the staircase Rose was a vision of loveliness waiting to be swept off her feet, like Scarlet O'Hara in Gone with the Wind. From the moment David turned and caught sight of her, his eyes never left her, didn't want to leave her. She took his breath away. As Rose made her dramatic descent, it was apparent by the look on his face how he felt about her.

It wasn't as if Roxy thought for a minute she'd have a chance with David, age difference and all, and she certainly would never deny her mother an ounce of happiness after the marriage she'd endured. Still, she found herself strangely attracted to this remarkable man, despite every impulse arguing otherwise.

"Good afternoon, David. I hope I didn't keep you waiting," Rose said, her voice breathless as she negotiated the final steps, reluctant to release her shaky grip from the rail.

"You can keep me waiting anytime, Rose, when you look this amazing," he said, his eyes piercing hers.

Rose possessed a natural beauty, though she was oblivious to its effect on the jealous women whose looks could kill and the amorous men looking to score. Eugene had kept her under wraps, hidden from the power of her beauty, unaware of the men willing to be puppets on a string wrapped around her pretty finger, stumbling over themselves to open her doors, lavish her with gifts and treat her to expensive dinners. Little did she know of her power to control the strings that snapped men to attention, but she was about to find out.

"May I have the honor?" David asked, offering an arm to mother and daughter alike.

Confused about her feelings, not knowing whether to laugh or cry, Roxy gritted her teeth and forced a smile as they headed for the door like a sultan with his harem.

"What a lucky man I am to accompany two such beautiful women," David preened. And though his smile was charming, his words were too little too late to spare Roxy her crushed feelings—her bubble already burst.

Still, she couldn't help but draw herself in closer to him as all three stepped out onto the veranda.

Rustling wind chimes and sweet-scented petunias greeted them on the warm, afternoon breeze. Smiling, David drew in the scent. "Fortunately for us the weather's cooperating, perfect for the top down. So," he paused, casting his gaze from one beautiful woman to the other, "who wants to ride first?"

Considering the sleek, black Corvette parked alongside the curb, Rose ran the scenario over in her head—room enough for only two passengers, bucket seats in close proximity, no escape from a moving vehicle—and with a panicked look at Roxy said, "Darling, you go first."

***

Wind-whipped clothing caressed her tingling skin. Wanton fingers clung deep into the soft, leather seat. Throbbing sensations riffed through her body. Roxy felt like a woman, a ravenous woman, alongside her leading man in a close-up scene, cameras rolling, their desire palpable and consuming one another, electrifying the screen.

David's right arm found itself draped nonchalant over the back of Roxy's seat, its closeness to her neck playing havoc with her hormones. Masterfully, he maneuvered between cars, accelerating to break free, his playful laughter escaping with the wind. The speed, his daring, those eyes—all enraptured her; she felt aroused, out of control, wanting to scream. Instead, she clung deeper into the leather.

***

You can do this, Rose kept repeating to herself as David shifted into high gear, her heart racing along at the dizzying speed. She closed her eyes to the passing blur, trying to visualize herself home on her veranda, serene in her rocking chair. David leaned in and touched her arm. "Let the wind in your hair," he shouted over the highway din, using pantomime to indicate the removal of her head wrap. "It's liberating," he yelled, smiling from ear to ear.

Rose wasn't so sure she wanted to set her hair free. She felt secure wrapped up in her shawl. Besides, the decision was hers to make, not his. She was the one in control, after all. But then Roxy's words came flooding back. "Live a little," she had said, "enjoy life." Rose had always chosen caution over imprudence, her husband having stifled any chance for her to 'let her hair down' and relish life. Today's ride was a giant step in the right direction. How difficult could one more small gesture be? Loosening its grip from her head she dropped the shawl to her shoulders, releasing her hair and herself from their self-imposed prisons. Captured by the wind, her auburn locks surrendered to their new master, while Rose smiled with abandon as they raced down the highway.

5

THE AWAKENING

Monday, August 18, 1997

ROSE WANTED TO CAPTURE her Victorian home on canvas ever since the day she moved in, as if the mere act of painting it would signify the end of an old life and the beginning of a new. Now with the morning sun bathing the veranda, its colorful hanging baskets of sweet petunias and white wicker furniture on full display, she was certain that the setting was not only perfect for the still life she was about to paint, but for the new life she was about to live.

Next door, within his kitchen, Nick stood back from the window in the shadows, watching. He watched Rose set up her easel and carefully secure a canvas under the shade of an old oak tree. He observed her deliberate placement of a wooden stool on sturdy ground and her cautious decent onto its seat. He witnessed her judicious spreading of oil paints onto a palate, while noting the dapples of morning light settling like snowflakes upon the apron of her white artist's smock and the deeply shaded lawn below. All this he viewed with detached curiosity, unsuspecting of what was to come. But as Rose lifted her maestro arm to air and led her brush rhythmically across the canvas, something stirred deep within him, touching him at his very core.

At first it was barely perceptible, like the low hum of a bumble bee, but with each of her flowing brushstrokes a familiar yearning began to resonate. Long dormant, he was surprised by the awakening of this uninvited guest and his melancholic reaction to it, like having found a treasured piece long thought lost.

Unconsciously, Nick drew nearer the window and, as if Rose could feel his eyes upon her, she looked up. He stood there … smiling. She returned his smile, thinking it was meant for her, and waved for him to come join her.

The air was warm and still, his approach soft, silent almost, as he passed behind her, their breathing in sync to the swish of her brush, like ballet dancers in air. Reverently, he observed her artwork taking form, her passion conspiring with light and color upon the canvas.

Nick's paintings once spoke to such passion, years ago during happier times. Now as he sat watching Rose paint, his back against the mighty oak and the cool, green grass a blanket beneath him, a spark was re-kindling. The symphony, once stilled, began to play again upon the canvas of his heart.

"When did you first learn to paint?" he asked, surprised by his own enthusiasm.

Rose heard the voice in her head reply, *When my husband started beating me,* but she dared not speak the truth, shocking even to her as her mind voiced it. Painting had been a necessary escape, a release valve of sorts for her threatened sanity, but how does one explain the correlation of physical abuse with learning to paint? Instead, she simply replied, "When I got married."

Nick considered her youthful appearance and the fact that she had an eighteen-year-old daughter. "You must have married young," he said, the personal nature of his insensitive comment not fully contemplated until too late, the words winging from his lips like an escaped bird from its cage, impossible to retrieve. He cringed.

"Yes," Rose said softly, "too young."

Rose had always prided her good judgement of character, but she had been no match for her husband's cunning. Instead of heeding the warning bells in her head she followed her heart, allowing Eugene to seduce her with the prospect of marriage. But then what choice did she have? The day Rose walked down the aisle and vowed eternal love she was already three months pregnant.

"I couldn't help noticing your wonderful paintings the other day," Rose said, changing venue. "Have you ever thought about exhibiting them?"

"Why, no … I mean … you are very kind, but," Nick stammered, his discomfort obvious.

"Food for thought," she said quickly, lengthening the unintentional lasso she had thrown around him. "But should you be interested, I'd be happy to help. I have connections."

Nick wanted to say more but, afraid of opening Pandora's Box, chose instead to say nothing.

"Tell me," Rose continued, undaunted, her brush working the canvas, "do you have plans to attend college this fall?"

Her back to Nick, she bore no witness to the sudden morphing of his sun-kissed skin turning a pasty white, nor to his shoulders slumping or eyes welling. Only his voice hinted of something amiss.

"I was accepted into Harvard," he said with attempted pride, his vocal cords aquiver. "I planned on attending up until last week, only," his voice cracked as the dreaded words spilt from his lips, "my cancer came back."

Rose froze mid-stroke, turning to face him.

"I won't be able to handle school … at least not right away … the treatments will exhaust me," he explained.

"I'm so sorry, Nick," she said, their eyes briefly touching before a wall of silence arose. She studied the ambiguity of his face, the alternating traces of fear and helplessness taking turns at ownership, feelings she knew well. But there was something more struggling for expression—the same fragmented feelings she'd glimpsed the first time she saw him—shards of something imprisoned deep inside … as if banging the cell bars begging for release.

She forged on.

"Perhaps between treatments, when you feel up to it, you'd like to join me in my studio."

"Your studio?" he asked, his moist eyes peering up at hers.

"Yes," she said, wiping paint from her brush, "Roxy is helping me set up a studio in the sunroom so I can paint year-round in the comfort of home. I'd enjoy your company."

His gaze held fast to hers like a tether to a sinking ship. "I'd like that Rose … very much," he said.

Rose swore that somewhere up from the depths of his ocean blue eyes a glimmer of hope surfaced, only to submerge again into their watery abyss.

"Mother!" Roxy yelled as she pushed through the screen door, leaving it to bang shut behind her as she bounded down the veranda steps.

"Mother," she repeated, her voice elevated, "you'll never guess who just called me!"

Roxy came to an abrupt stop in front of Rose, out of breath and too excited to wait for her mother's response. "Megan O'Malley! My roommate!" she declared, as if it should have been obvious.

"Why isn't that nice, dear," Rose managed to slip in before Megan commandeered the conversation again.

"She's coming down from Maine with her father to visit Boston before college starts and thought it would be nice to meet before our move-in day. I agreed, so I invited them both to dinner tomorrow night. I hope you don't mind."

"Of course I don't mind. It's a wonderful idea," Rose said, and then glancing over at Nick, his eyes studying the ground, added, "Perhaps Nick and David would like to join us for dinner as well?"

Nick looked up, his mouth open, waiting for his brain to catch up with the words.

"Of course they'll come. And we won't take no for an answer," Roxy interjected, not waiting for Nick's response. "It's all settled then," she said, leaving no room for further discussion. "How exciting!" she squealed, giddy with anticipation. She turned to go and then, stopping mid-stride, spun back around. "Nick, I could really use some help with planning the menu," she said, her words at once both a request and command. Either way, it mattered not to Nick; he was already caught up in her euphoria. Roxy had a way of creating a whirlwind about her that sucked people in like a spinning top, directing their attentions to her center of gravity. She was a force with which you were compelled to comply. Nick did not resist. He found himself rising from his seated position and drawn, like attracting magnets, to her side.

"Great!" she beamed, "Let's get moving … so much to do and so little time!" She grabbed his arm and yanked him along, all the while offering up possible dishes for tomorrow night's feast.

Rose marveled at her daughter's resilience and smiled as she watched her conscript Nick into her own personal army. She knew that Roxy battled her demons every night and in the light of day valiantly fought for normalcy. Roxy would always be the inveterate soldier. And now Nick had joined her ranks in the fight for survival.

6

THE DINNER PARTY

Tuesday, August 19, 1997

ROSE WOKE UP GRATEFUL this morning, not only for God's apparent blessings of late, but for the dinner party this evening. She was adamant in her belief that divine intervention was responsible for tonight's gathering; after all, who else but God would have arranged such a diversion for Roxy on the sixth anniversary of her father's death.

Roxy woke up grateful as well. For the first time in six years her demons had been outmaneuvered at their own game—Lady Luck had wrested away their playing cards and dealt Roxy a full house of dinner guests to occupy her mind.

Feeling not in the least bit silly wearing a white ruffled apron, Nick stood at the kitchen sink taking orders from Roxy. It didn't require much coaxing on her part to enlist his help; Nick was more than a willing servant, grateful to be kept busy. Besides, he liked how she made him laugh and, in some inexplicable way, understood him without his having to speak. Spending time with Roxy today, of all days, meant a lot to Nick. He wanted to tell her, but just didn't know how. Instead, he stood quietly by, peeling potatoes, no thoughts to the future or memories of the past invading his space, living only in the moment—the textured potato weighting his hand, the metal blade slicing its skin, the earthy odor oozing out and the brown shavings dropping to the sink. In the here and now there were no regrets. Potatoes assigned no blame. They just existed. And that was all Nick wanted to do.

Who exactly is Nick Bennett? Roxy thought, standing next to him at the kitchen counter chopping onions, tears spilling down her cheeks from her stinging eyes. She realized she knew very little about him. One thing she did know—he suffered demons. They needed no introduction that day in Nick's kitchen, staring out at her from behind his weary eyes. It was like looking at herself in the mirror. At the time this realization disturbed her, but now she found it strangely comforting knowing she wasn't alone, that Nick was like her. Roxy wanted to ask him about a lot of things: his paintings, his parents, the fire, and now his cancer—she had learned of it last night from her mother, and it had frightened her. This was a demon she knew very little about, but she would wait for Nick to speak first of such things. Instead, she stood quietly by, chopping onions.

Rose kept the assembly line moving, supervising the teens as they prepared each course, slicing and dicing their way through the menu. She was proud of the way Roxy had taken Nick under her wing, like a protective mama bird looking out for her chick. And as Rose watched the two quietly working side by side, she felt positive there was a greater purpose to their meeting.

With the last pot scrubbed and tucked away, the threesome let out a collective sigh. In the foyer, the grandfather clock chimed five times—one hour to go before guests would arrive. Roxy stood back and smiled, proud of what she'd accomplished. The time for worrying was past. If Megan didn't like her, she realized now, it didn't matter. For the first time in six years, she felt good about herself. And that was enough.

***

The 'welcome committee' gathered in the front parlor to await the arrival of the guests from Maine. Complete strangers just three days ago, the Pendleton women were now engaged in small talk with the Bennett brothers, interspersed with nervous laughter and sips of punch.

Standing within arm's length of David, Rose watched his mouth moving in conversation, but she was half listening—her thoughts drifting.

Who exactly is David Bennett? she thought, considering the handsome man standing before her. It had been the question on her mind ever since they first met. Their conversations had been purely perfunctory since then. Even their 'first date' had failed to provide any details of substance by way of his background. *I should have gotten to know him better first,* she thought, second guessing their ride together in his Corvette and regretting her loss of control, David literally taking over the driver's seat. As he talked on about the weather, her eyes slowly inched upward, briefly touching upon his like a stone skipping water before tugging her gaze back down to the drink in her hand, the ice cubes shaking. *Yes, I did enjoy the ride,* she conceded to herself, but now she also recognized the need to step back, take time to get to know him and slow the dizzying pace. If her marriage to Eugene had taught her anything, it was that trust shouldn't be given away lightly, nor was it earned overnight. Rose drew a deep breath and leveled her gaze.

"So, David," she said through a trembling smile, "tell me about yourself."

Her directness surprised him. David's whole persona brightened, pleased with the shift from small talk to more familiar grounds.

"Well," he began with his disarming smile, "I grew up on my parents' dairy farm in New Hampshire ... honestly, the happiest time of my life with nature right outside the back door. What more could a kid want?" he said with childlike wonderment. "Only ... poor Mom," he shook his head, "I'm afraid I was quite a handful ... full of the devil and curiosity. But she kept me in line and out of trouble cleaning out the barn, changing the feed and milking the cows—all before school started!" David's deep-throated laughter filled the room.

Rose laughed, too.

Encouraged, David continued, clearly enjoying the spotlight she now cast upon him.

"I got quite an education on the farm from Dad ... always looking to improve the strain of his Holsteins," he said. "He taught me about selective breeding—breeding for desirable traits—like good udders for increased milk production. I was totally fascinated. It's what started me on the road to my current profession ... "

David paused to swig his punch, while Rose stood by, spellbound like a child focused on a magician's kerchief waiting for the big reveal.

"Genetics," he finally said, pulling the rabbit out from his hat. "I lead a small research lab here in Cambridge. It's my hope that one day the work we do will contribute to the betterment of mankind."

Rose felt like she had walked into a room, and everyone yelled, "Surprise!" She never saw it coming, his newly exposed altruism—it spoke to her heart. Suddenly, this charming man became even more attractive.

"Your work sounds fascinating, David," she said, her eyes now locked on his.

Enchanted by this beautiful woman standing before him, and emboldened by their new direction in conversation, David threw the question right back at her.

"Your turn now," he said like a little boy playing a game, "tell me all about your wonderful self."

"I'm afraid my life pales by comparison," she demurred.

"Au contraire, dear Rose, nothing holds a candle to you."

Rose lowered her gaze, a wave of red washing over her.

"Well," she began, the good and bad memories stumbling over each other for attention, "I grew up on a farm, too, except it was a horse farm in Connecticut. My father raised thoroughbreds and raced them as well, still does," she sighed, "always chasing the illusive Triple Crown, the demands of which left precious little time for family. So my dear departed mother filled the void by devoting much of her time to charitable work with our church … and dragging me along with her kicking and screaming." Rose laughed. "But before long, I found myself actually looking forward to those outings … helping people just made me feel good." Her smile lit up the room. "My mother always said, 'To give is to receive,' and now my paintings allow me to follow in her charitable footsteps. It's remarkable, a blessing really, that so many worthy causes are funded through the sale of my art." Her eyes floated over to the still-life portrait of her home, now framed and hung above the settee.

David followed her gaze.

"It seems you and Nick share a common interest," he said, his eyes wandering from the painting down to his brother, now seated beside Roxy on the settee. "You know," he said, his voice lowered as he leaned in closer to Rose, "it's been years since he's talked about painting. I can't tell you how surprised I was when he told me about his time spent watching you yesterday. I want you to know, Rose, I appreciate your thoughtfulness … inviting Nick to visit your studio. It's been tough on him, his diagnosis and all," David said, worry lines creasing his forehead.

"Tough on both of you," Rose corrected, touching his arm.

"Yes," he sighed, "on the both of us."

Roxy kept an eye on the grandfather clock and an ear on the conversation as she ran to and from the kitchen checking on dinner. As she re-entered the parlor from her latest foray, a parade of aromas followed her out the kitchen door. David's stomach rumbled in response.

"Roxy," he called out, his eyes coming to rest on her, catching her immediate attention. "Nick tells me you're quite the cook."

The sound of his voice invoking her name sent shivers up her spine.

"Actually," she said, sashaying on over to his side, "I learned everything I know from mother." Managing to peel her eyes away from his, Roxy exchanged a knowing smile with Rose. "Starting when I was little," she said, "mother and I would prepare family dinners together… "

Family dinners, Roxy thought, her mind wandering back in time. There were no servants in the Pendleton household, although they could well afford them. Eugene had insisted early on that a woman's place was in the home, and that she and her mother were to take on all household tasks, including the cooking. Meals were to be served the moment he stepped in the door—and heaven help you if you overcooked the roast.

"Desserts are my specialty," she said, shaking off the memory.

"Well then, I had better save room," David said, patting his stomach, "but it won't be easy—everything smells delicious."

You smell delicious, she thought, their bodies queued up so close she couldn't help but drink in his cologne.

"I'll just have to run a few extra miles on the tread mill," he laughed.

Roxy laughed, too, though not because of David's comment, but because of her nerves—and the absurdity of her crush.

The minutes slowly ticked by on the grandfather clock.

Roxy looked over at Nick on the settee, his knee bouncing and eyes glassy. *First a mysterious fire and now cancer,* she thought. The demons were having a field day with him, but damn if she was going to let them continue their cruel game of taunts. She made her way over and sat next to him.

"So, are you ready for Megan's five-minute reckoning?" she asked.

"I beg your pardon?" he said, casually rubbing his red eyes and feigning a yawn.

Roxy knew tiredness wasn't Nick's ailment as she craned her neck to peer out through the stain glass window.

"You can tell a lot about people within the first five minutes of meeting them," she ventured on. "My grandfather calls it the five-minute reckoning, but he applies it to horses. He can look at a foal and within five minutes size up its worth as a thoroughbred. But I believe people are like racehorses; they're either winners or losers, and five minutes is all you need to know."

"Well, I never gave it much thought; but I have to admit, when we first met, I knew the minute you grabbed that grocery bag from my arms that I liked you," he said with a sheepish grin.

"And I knew I liked you when you laughed at my Fred Flintstone impression of your brother," Roxy said, the two of them giggling now in recollection.

"So," Roxy continued, attempting seriousness again, "when Megan arrives, we can begin her five-minute reckoning."

"We?" He sniffled.

"Yes. You must help, too," she said. "I'm counting on your expert opinion."

Nick grinned from ear to ear.

When the doorbell rang, Roxy jumped up. The one moment she had allowed her attention to drift, she had been caught off-guard. She froze while her mother answered the door.

"Welcome!" she heard her mother say. "I'm Rose Pendleton. Won't you please come in?"

Megan O'Malley cleared the threshold first. Right away she scored points with Roxy—she was tall! Not quite six feet like Roxy, but tall enough. And just as Roxy had pictured, her shoulder-length hair was strawberry-blond, its curls wrapping her fair, freckled face like ribbons on a present.

The girls flashed a nervous smile at one another.

Following on Megan's heels was her father, Sean O'Malley, a ruddy-faced, scarlet-haired behemoth of a man who grasped everyone's hand as if landing a fish and then proceeded to shake the living daylights out of them.

"Glad ter meet yer, young lady," he boomed upon introduction to Roxy, his brogue thick and blue eyes twinkling. "You're a beauty, yer are."

Roxy blushed.

"I'm Megan," his daughter said, stepping forward and taking hold of Roxy's hand. Their connection was immediate, like identical twins in the womb, the same life force flowing through them. "It's really nice to finally meet you, Roxanne," she said, her voice warm and emerald eyes soft. "Thank you so much for your dinner invitation on such short notice."

"Please … call me Roxy. And not at all," Roxy said, "Mother and I are thrilled you both could come. And I'm so glad we could meet sooner than later."

Roxy and Megan stood there, hands joined, suspended in time, like two old souls meeting again after lifetimes apart. And when the spell broke with the release of their hands, Roxy glanced over at Nick. He was smiling—his two thumbs up.

★★★

The guests and their hosts convened to the dining room, taking up seats around the newly purchased mahogany table, two flickering candelabras reflected in its polished finish. It was a grand piece, an elegant addition to the room complimenting the Victorian's finely crafted woodwork; but more than that, it was meant to relinquish the bad memories its Connecticut counterpart had represented, to embody happier scenes now of welcomed guests in better times. Tonight, seated at the table's inaugural dinner, mother and daughter held out great expectations; but things did not go exactly as planned.

Conversation started slowly with innocuous exchanges about weather and traffic but was instantly catapulted to an extraordinary level of interest when it was revealed that the O'Malley's home was on an island with a lighthouse off the coast of Maine. Totally absorbed in their rapid-fire questioning about island life, the dinner guests paid little notice to Roxy's feverish sprints to and from the kitchen delivering up first course, her not wanting to miss out on a single word. But what finally drew Roxy in and glued her to her seat was when David posed the question, "Were you ever in danger during a storm?"

A hush fell over the room as all eyes flitted between father and daughter. Sean O'Malley hesitated. The look on his face gave Roxy chills. When he finally spoke, his words cut through the silence like a glacier cracking.

"Me bonny bride Kathleen, Megan's ma, lost 'er life six years ago the day, Lord kip 'er soul, swept oyt ter sea by a mighty 'urricane dat struk de islan'."

A collective gasp filled the room followed by stunned silence, as if all had just fallen through thin ice—bodies frozen, senses numbed and lungs void of air—and only when the shocking reality of his words fully registered in their brains did their aggrieved voices break free, resurfacing all at once in remorseful solidarity.

"Please, please … everyone," Sean pleaded, leaning forward in his seat, his chest tightening from their distressed voices. "Such 'eartfelt condolences are appreciated, but oi apologize for upsettin' yer al' so, 'twas not me intent," he said, dabbing his forehead with his napkin as he settled back into his chair. The words he spoke next were slow and measured. "We 'ad many gran' an' wonderful years together, an' dohs are de memories Kathleen wud want us ter mind," he said. "Grievous things 'appen … but we can only move forward."

We can only move forward, Rose repeated to herself, and unbeknown to her, so did everyone else at the table.

The coincidence of such unspeakable horror befalling their two families from the same hurricane rattled Roxy. She shifted uncomfortably in her seat and noticed Nick fidgeting with his dinner napkin, twisting it around his finger, head down. When she glanced across the table, Megan met her eyes—a look of shared sorrow passing between them.

In his gut, David felt a familiar knot growing, the uncomfortable feeling of helplessness once again rearing its ugly head. All his life he had been master of his universe, every aspect of it answering to his command. But nature's fury is master to none, holding us hostage to her will and humbling us often. David understood this now better than most. He had been admired for his intellect, sought after for his counsel, and always, always in control—until he was brought down to his knees and put in his place by a hurricane six years ago. Now, when he looked at Sean, he knew how helpless he, too, must have felt.

"Everyone … please forgive me for what I am about to say," David said, his eyes slowly taking in each person seated around the table, "but I feel compelled by the enormity of the coincidence to share with you Nick's and my own personal sorrow. You see," he said, hesitating, "a lightning storm, spurned from the very same hurricane you speak of, sparked a barn fire on my parents' farm—killing them both."

Nick's head remained down, eyes closed, a single tear staining his cheek. Megan covered her mouth with her hand. Roxy stared wide-eyed at David, the words he spoke still reverberating in her head when she heard her mother speak.

"There's no such thing as a coincidence," Rose said.

All heads turned in one motion to face her.

"God's ways are not always known to us, but there is meaning in all that happens," she said. "And I believe our paths were meant to cross this evening, perhaps even to help one other in some way … you see," she said, "that hurricane killed my husband as well."

★★★

Journal Entry, August 19, 1997:

Three families united by the same hurricane –

If it was the hand of God at work, as Mother believes, then how do you explain the evil of it all? Surely a loving God wouldn't permit such affliction on beings created in his so-called image. But Mother has unquestioning faith; and it is easy for her to believe in the mysterious works of God because she doesn't see evil, only the good in all things.

But I'm not like mother. I have questioning doubts. I see no higher hand at work, only demons—drooling over our heartfelt sorrows and lapping up our hurtful wounds. They are the orchestrators of our pain—hiding behind the curtain, directing the chaos … laughing at us.

7

— · —

DOC'S CALL

Wednesday, August 20, 1997

DAVID TOOK BLUE INK to white parchment and carefully scrolled her name. "Rose," he breathed, the written word made manifest upon his breath. How was it possible it had been only days since their first meeting when it felt as if he'd known her a lifetime. Yet, the feeling in his heart concurred completely with his head—he was smitten. She was ever in his thoughts, tantalizing his dreams and tormenting his waking hours until they met again. In his rosy days of youth, he had secretly longed for a love at first sight; but now with his age pushing forty, was it still too much to hope for? But how else to explain it, the constant paralysis he felt in a world that only spun because she breathed?

David placed pen and paper aside and sat back in his chair. Outside his study window the sky was threatening rain. He considered heading into work at the lab but decided against it; his mind as clouded as the darkening skies, he'd be of little use to anyone anyway. Instead, he closed his eyes and resolved to contemplate Rose; but as he did so, the phone rang. Slow to register the intrusion, it took five incessant rings before he answered with a catatonic, "Hello."

"David … how the hell are you?" the cantankerous, old voice asked on the other end of the line.

Though his reverie interrupted, a smile bloomed on David's face. "Just fine, Doc, just fine," he answered. "It's been a while."

"Yeah, I know, too long … but you know me, an unapologetic workaholic. Listen …," Doc said into his satellite phone, "why don't I just cut to the chase?"

Here it comes, David thought, still smiling into the receiver. He only heard from his long-time friend and mentor, Doctor Benjamin Shaw, when he was in over his head with something; and David wasn't so sure he wanted to know what he was up to now.

"How'd you like to join me for some R&R in the jungle?" Doc asked.

David laughed. Doc never relaxed. He had been in the rain forest of Brazil for the past five years researching plants for medicinal use and building an herbal farm business with the help of local natives. The last time David saw him was a year ago, the two of them up to their eyeballs in brush fulfilling Doc's sudden request to build a lab in the jungle.

"I need your help David," he said, his voice at once serious and strained, "but I can't go into details over the phone. Ramon's in Manaus getting supplies. If you fly in tomorrow night, I'll have him meet you in the morning with the boat. We can discuss everything when you get here."

Rose … her essence tugging once again at the sleeve of his thoughts. How could he possibly leave her; the very idea was anathema to him. But then Doc never asked for help if it wasn't important, and there was something in his voice that didn't sit well. Besides, as timing would have it, David had a favor to ask of his old friend.

"Okay Doc," he said, "tell Ramon to stock up on bug spray." Doc laughed and then the line went dead.

David hung up the phone and, pushing back in his chair, kicked his feet up onto the desk. Hands behind his head staring through the rain-splattered glass, he mulled Doc's call—until his thoughts were highjacked again by the woman of his dreams suddenly appearing outside, umbrella up, running toward her car. David came to at the sight of her and bolted from his chair.

***

"Rose!" he yelled, flying out the front door and descending the steps, raindrops slicking his hair and imprinting his shirt.

Rose stood by the door of her sedan fumbling with her keys.

"Rose … have dinner with me tonight," David pleaded as he neared her.

His outburst startled her, although a smile was already forming on her lips when he came under the canopy of her umbrella.

"Please," he begged, his winded breath warm on her face. "Tomorrow I'm heading to Brazil, and I can't bear leaving without seeing you again."

Rose, more than pleasantly surprised by his invitation after last night's disastrous dinner party, was amazed at how easily the words sprang from her lips. "Why, I'd be most pleased to dine with you, David."

"Wonderful!" he said looking down into her eyes. "I'll pick you up at seven."

Their gaze lingered longer than Rose usually found comfortable, but this time she did not flinch.

"I'll be ready," she said.

★★★

The lighting was low, the room a mellow glow of candlelit tables covered in white linen. Her perfume transcended his senses, rendering him hopelessly lost in the cloud of her existence. Her eyes, so soft and yet so powerful, drew in every inch of him, every breath and beat of his heart. Oh, many a beautiful woman had been escorted on his arm before, but Rose was different; she had not only tamed the tiger in him but had him chasing his tail. David's world was spinning. He reached across the table and took hold of her hand.

"Thank you, Rose," he said, an all-encompassing thank you—for dining with him tonight, for being so beautiful, for coming into his life. He held up his wine glass, she raised hers, a high note crystalized into the air at their confluence. Outside of their table-for-two David's world blurred. Faint piano chords lingered in the distance, while shadowy figures swirled past with silver trays floating as if on air. If time existed, it didn't now … not for David.

And when they left the restaurant, walking arm in arm under the moon and the stars, David felt as if the night sky had been painted just for them. It was an evening like no other—one that he would remember to his dying day.

"Rose," he said, feeling young in his heart and light in his step as they strolled through the Boston Public Garden.

"Yes, David," she replied.

"R o s e … R o s e … R o s e," he sang out suddenly into the warm night air, his body spinning round and round, arms and eyes raised seeking the heavens. "Your name is like a song!" he exclaimed, coming to a wobbly stop, reaching out for her and clinging on. "Only I don't do it justice," he said breathlessly into her hair. "It deserves better … angels perhaps … yes, the voices of angels."

"Come," Rose said, trying not to encourage him as she took his arm and led him to a bench alongside the flowered walkway. "You know what I'd like, David," she said, the two sitting down, Rose resisting the urge to rest her head against his shoulder.

"Name it Rose and it's yours."

"I'd like to come back here in daylight and paint this lovely place."

"Done. When I get back from Brazil, I promise to take you."

"Promise?"

"Promise."

In the light of the moon, David's hand gently touched her chin and lifted her beautiful face to his. Her resolve melted as their lips met, softly at first and then with intensity. David's world spun again, and if it never stopped, he didn't care. He was happier than he'd ever been.

"I love you, Rose."

The words just came as natural as breath, exhaled out onto the ethers of time. And if it took an eternity for Rose to echo them back, David would wait—he would wait forever.

8

— · —

BRANDY

Friday, August 22, 1997

DAVID THREW OPEN THE hotel curtains to a sunny morning in Manaus—six o'clock and already the Brazilian city was bustling with businessmen and street peddlers alike, the latter setting up their wares for the early shoppers looking to beat the day's inevitable heat. He checked his watch. Ramon would be meeting him dockside in an hour.

David looked in the mirror and ran his fingers over the stubble of his chin and then back through the thick of his hair. Traces of darkness appeared beneath his eyes, a tell-tale sign of his late-night arrival from Boston.

David thought back to last year when he first made this trip—helping Doc set up a lab in the jungle—it had been just like the old days at Harvard, working side by side with his mentor. He missed the camaraderie and the challenge Doc always brought to the table. Sure, he could be a crotchety old geezer, but when Doc's softer side broke surface, David couldn't help but love the guy. He wondered what Doc had up his sleeve now.

He ran the water in the shower and unzipped his backpack on the unmade bed. Out in the hallway, Portuguese-speaking voices came and went. He made a mental note to review his English-to-Portuguese dictionary. If there was one thing David hated, it was being vulnerable; and after an inflated cab fare from the airport last night, he was determined to stem any future exposure.

If speaking Portuguese wasn't his strong suit, packing the essentials was. David's eyes perused the contents of his backpack spread out on the unmade bed: Lightweight cotton clothing; hooded waterproof jacket; wide-brimmed hat; comfortable hiking boots; insect repellent and sunscreen; sunglasses; binoculars; compass; Swiss army knife; headlamp and matches; a self-sealed plastic bag with documents; water canteen; first aid kit and a waterproof day pack. In his youth David had been an Eagle Scout and the White Mountains of New Hampshire his training ground. He took to heart the scouts' motto, 'Be Prepared,' carrying it into adulthood. It wasn't a fool-proof guarantee of a positive outcome by any means, but better than the alternative.

Freshly showered and belly fed, he could already feel beads of perspiration forming under his shirt as he stood on the dock overlooking the dark waters of the Rio Negro. The port was bursting with activity as the hodgepodge of river boats prepared to transport cargo and passengers alike up and downstream. David adjusted the backpack on his shoulders and scanned the crowds for Ramon.

"Senhor David!"

David's head turned in the direction of the familiar voice.

"Ramon!"

"Good see you again, Senhor David!"

Ramon approached David with an outstretched hand and a cratered smile. The young man—early twenties, dark skinned and muscularly lean—spoke with a slight lisp.

"Thanks, Ramon. It's great to be back," David said, accepting a firm handshake. "How's Doc these days?"

"Still cranky, old man," Ramon laughed. "This way, Senhor David."

Ramon pointed to where a long, wooden motorboat stood bobbing at the pier, the word "Brandy" painted on its sides—David smiled at the obvious nod to Doc's favorite drink. Inside the boat a young man stood, readying himself to assist David on board. He resembled Ramon.

"Senhor David, Cousin Bruno," Ramon said, by way of introduction.

The two smiled a quick hello while the young man gripped David's arm as he stepped into the boat.

"Thank you, Bruno," David said, regaining his footing and safely taking a seat.

"De nada, Senhor," Bruno replied.

Ramon stepped deftly into the point seat.

"Bruno good river man, but speak little English," he said, as the two cousins worked in tandem slipping the boat's moorings. "Season dry now, Senhor David; water low, travel slow." And then he gestured to a cooler tucked under the seat. "Help you self."

With Bruno at the tiller, Brandy's motor roared to life. Slowly, she edged out onto the waterway, her small wake barely noticed by the larger river boats now taking on paying customers. David watched longingly as the tourists and natives alike settled into colorful hammocks strung like flags on a banner across their covered decks. Suddenly the wooden bench upon which he sat felt all the harder. *It's going to be a long ride,* he thought.

Following curving riverbanks along the outskirts of the city, Brandy motored past shanty towns built high on stilts for rainy season. *Man's futile attempt at thwarting nature,* David thought as he swatted at the intrepid mosquitoes. The irony was lost on him as he reached into his bag for insect repellent and sprayed a halo of mist all around him. Ramon looked on, amused.

"Look, Senhor David," Ramon said, pointing ahead as Brandy approached the confluence of the Rio Negro's cold black waters with the warm sandy-colored Solimoes—two rivers running side by side, separated for three and a half miles like oil and vinegar, until blending to form the mighty Amazon. This seemed to David a fitting metaphor for his personal journey into the rain forest—a forced melding of the civil with the wild. The only question remained, what was the product of such a union?

As Brandy traversed the confluence he thought, *If Rose could only see this.* He missed her terribly and wished she were here by his side; but David knew that a trip like this was fraught with hardships, both those you prepared for and those you didn't. Before he left, he had promised Rose he'd be careful, but the jungle is held to no such agreement. And just as with Rose, the jungle drew him in—the mystery of both mistresses leaving him at a loss to resist.

Ramon thoroughly enjoyed his role as guide. Having grown up an indigenous member of the Amazon basin, he greatly impressed David with his factual repertoire of the wildlife both seen and hidden after only an hour's ride out from Manaus; but what impressed David more so was his speech.

"Tell me, Ramon," he said, "how did you learn to speak English?"

"Ramon teach Senhor Doc plants, Senhor Doc teach Ramon English—everybody win!" he said, his checkered grin stretching as wide as the Amazon. "Ramon teach Senhor David plants, too?" he asked, eager to please.

"Senhor David would rather learn Portuguese," he said, half in jest.

"No problem," Ramon said, barely able to contain his enthusiasm in his new-found teacher's status. "Class begin now."

In short order, David had mastered basic phrases as well as words relevant to survival. He was under no illusion mere words could save his life, but that didn't stop him from pulling out a small notebook and writing them down anyway. Ramon looked on approvingly, preening over his star pupil.

Rounding the river bend Brandy approached a wooden structure on the water buoyed up on log pontoons and secured with ropes to inland trees, allowing for its rise and fall with the rains. *Never underestimate man's ability to do business anywhere,* David thought as they drew nearer the floating convenience shop. Inside, the proprietors sold everything from chewing gum to shotguns, while outside, their industrious children waved and called out to potential customers, urging their patronage. "No sale today—boat full up," Ramon yelled back, his hand gesturing to the ample supplies filling Brandy's belly. Bruno directed the tiller away, but the children remained undaunted. With long-armed sloths dangling like fur collars about their necks and colorful parrots perched like hats on their heads, they continued to plead. David shook his head at the ludicrous sight, laughing and returning their waves as Brandy veered past.

The hours on the long, lazy river passed slowly, the day stretching its arms and legs as if just awakening. With the sun climaxing and the heat intensifying, sitting in the boat proved taxing on David. Ramon obliged his long-legged passenger and had Bruno divert the craft onto a sandy tract, allowing David to disembark, stretch and relieve himself. Bruno stood guard nearby, machete in hand. Looking over his shoulder as he stood pissing into the brush, David laughed out loud at the surreal scene. Bruno studied his charge; he wasn't laughing.

Back in the boat, David pushed his sunglasses back up the sweaty bridge of his nose and lowered the brim of his hat under the pulsating sun. Soon, the heat and hypnotic calls of the rain forest were wrestling with his consciousness, seducing him like a mistress beckoning her lover. The deeper their boat penetrated the jungle the more David gave himself over to her. Intoxicated, he had just about given up the struggle when Ramon shouted.

"Senhor David!"

David's head bolted upright. His hand, idly skimming the waters, cannon shot skyward as the hungry visitor swam by, all fifteen feet of him.

Ramon lowered his shot gun, the crocodile no longer interested. "No sleep, Senhor David! Please … no safe!" he admonished.

David suddenly felt like a schoolboy chastised by his teacher. "Don't worry, Ramon, it won't happen again," he assured him, his trembling hand reaching into the cooler for a bottle of cola—as close to caffeine as he could get.

By early afternoon, Brandy parted ways with the mighty Amazon and angled onto a smaller tributary. The diminished rains had noticeably altered its depth, a problem for the larger riverboats but not yet for Brandy. Bruno maneuvered the craft upstream with the agility of a fish in water. Life in the surrounding jungle erupted into a shrilled cacophony from the boat's intrusive drone. Several minutes in, Bruno cut the motor. In the surrounding trees the screeching of playful capuchins called attention to themselves like children on swings. In the air squawking macaws, feather-dressed in vivid scarlet and blue, swooped overhead. Cupping his hands to lips, Bruno's bird calls sent them winging back for a closer look. But when at last he fired up the motor, all along the lush riverbanks tortoises withdrew into their shells while lizards froze to blend in with the foliage, camouflaged once again in the dissonant jungle. Brandy navigated the snake-like current deeper and deeper into the rain forest, oblivious to it all. David, however, could feel the eyes of the jungle upon him the entire time.

When the tributary deposited Brandy onto one of its smaller branches, it came as no surprise to the seasoned crew to find this once-flowing passageway a mere shadow of its former self; indeed, dry season now stunted river transport throughout the entire basin. But the locals took it all in stride—literally walking the extra distance. And so, when movement on the river finally grounded to a halt, the three men disembarked Brandy, abandoning her for the slow, overland haul.

The transition from open river to canopied forest assailed David's senses. Blinded by the sudden darkness, he stood still in the shadowy flora and removed his sunglasses, waiting until mellow shafts of light piercing the interlocking treetops filtered down around him, restoring his vision. Despite little rain the humidity remained high, the air damp on his skin and pungent with the smell of vegetation. His ears filled with the serenade of insects—an incessant whine that made his flesh crawl. David rolled down his shirt cuffs and buttoned up his collar.

"Senhor David fear bugs," Ramon observed.

"Only those I can't see. And you, Ramon," David rounded, "what do you fear?"

The young guide cracked a smile and said, "Ramon fear Senhor Doc if late."

David's hearty laughter added to the jungle's cacophony as the trio headed out.

There was no such thing as a path in this magical and menacing place. "Stay close," Ramon instructed David. The two guides formed bookends around him, machete in their hands and shot gun over their shoulders, prepared for brush and foe alike as they began the final leg of their journey. With luck Ramon said they'd make it by sundown. David didn't have much faith in luck; his faith was in the cousins—he trusted them with his life. He had no choice, really—he'd done the math. The skills he obviously lacked, they more than provided. Without them, he was vulnerable—and David hated being vulnerable.

9

CIVICS 101

Girl Flashback

*T*HE DAY GOT OFF *to a horrible start. It was early and it was hot. All nine-year-old Girl wanted was a cold shower and breakfast. Her father wanted otherwise. He had awoken her at the crack of dawn with an urgency—today he would teach her a civics lesson. After all, how was she to follow in his footsteps if she wasn't introduced to the facts—the hard, cold facts of governing. The idea that she may not want to enter politics never once entered his mind because what she wanted was irrelevant. So Girl sat down at the kitchen table, her stomach growling and perspiration percolating, as Eugene pushed aside her empty bowl and served up a breakfast of Civics 101.*

Girl knew as much about politics as she cared to know. She had long ago decided that anything her father liked, she wouldn't. In no way did she want to be like him. Even his choice of cereal was off limits, though now she might have considered it had he offered her a bowl, her hunger growing.

"Listen up, Girl," he said, taking a chair opposite her, "I am about to school you in the ways of our republic. You would be wise to pay attention, as not all appears to be what it seems," he said, pushing pad and pen across the table. "But first, think carefully and tell me exactly what you know about the operation of our government."

Girl took her time to formulate a cohesive answer, not wanting to anger her father and prove an unsatisfactory student before the lesson had even begun. "There are three branches," she said, the drilling voice of her father echoing in her head, "Executive, Legislative and Judicial."

"Correct. Now tell me which is more important," he said, an expectant look in his eyes.

God, if you're there, help me, *Girl thought. And then, as if the inspiration for her answer had come from the lips of the Creator himself, she thought,* Of course, a trick question, *and sputtered:* "All three."

Obviously, from the look on Eugene's face, it was not the answer he wanted. "That is the textbook answer, the one taught in classrooms, but not in this classroom. Pick up your pen and write this down," he demanded. "The United States Legislature is the most essential branch of government." He paused to watch her write it. "Good. Now I suppose you would ask why?" Girl stared back like a deer in headlights. "Because," he said with exasperation, "the legislature is responsible for writing the laws that run this country. Think of it," he said, "the thousands upon thousands of laws that have made this country the living, breathing organism of democracy that is the envy of the world! That is no easy task—and accomplished no thanks to the 'purported' checks and balances of a three-branch system," he huffed, leaning back in his chair. "But there are halfwits out there who wouldn't recognize the hard, cold facts if they tripped over them—who would blindly swallow the spoon-fed drivel of an equally-scaled government, accepting the executive and judicial branches uniformly as vital as the legislative. Vital my ass," Eugene thundered, rising from his seat and pacing the kitchen floor. "Unless you consider as vital the futile presidential veto of well-crafted legislation amounting to nothing more than an executive save-face measure destined to be overridden by a simple majority vote of congress. Or," he bloviated on, "you consider as vital nine justices wasting their days interpreting the constitutionality of legislation which previously the Legislature took great pains upon writing to assure such constitutionality. No. Make no mistake, Girl," he said, his fist pounding the table, causing both it and Girl to jump, "the United States Legislature is the workhorse that runs this country—what makes this United States of America great!"

Eugene strode to the refrigerator and swung open its door, retrieving a jug of milk along with a box of cereal from the cupboard shelf. "As long as I live and breathe, may the ill-conceived notion of equality within our three-branch government kiss my ass," he said, filling Girl's bowl to the brim and then his own, slurping over his with his spoon.

Girl looked down at her bowl and decided then and there that the world her father lived in was a delusional democracy—and hers a dictatorship. She picked up her spoon, filled her mouth with cereal, and swallowed the hard, cold facts.

10

COLLEGE BOUND

Friday, August 22, 1997

NO SOONER MOVED IN, one week later Roxy was packing up again. She closed her overstuffed suitcase upon the bed and promptly sat on it, tugging the zipper around its bulging circumference.

The mood enveloping her this evening wasn't melancholic about leaving her new home, as there hadn't been time enough to form attachment to it let alone feel sad about leaving it. No, the familiar, restive feeling she'd attempted to ignore all day was through with being snubbed—now, with her imminent departure for college come morning, anxiety's furtive fingers blatantly lunged for her throat. Suddenly short of breath, she slid from her suitcase onto the floor, heart hammering her rib cage and the room reeling. She cradled her head between her knees and clenched her eyes shut.

For her entire young life, Roxy has waged war against her demons by means of temporary exorcisms—medication, journaling, role-play—though nothing prescribed by therapists or her mother or her own imagination could eliminate her pain. And though her father's death had seemingly surrendered back control of her life, a guilty conscience preying upon her was a constant struggle. And now, to worsen matters, come morning she'll be moving away from her sole support when all else failed—her mother.

Her body huddled at the side of her bed, Roxy waited. When her temples ceased to throb and her world to spin she looked up, and there in the open doorway stood her mother, smiling with outstretched arms. Roxy ran to her warm embrace.

Rose enfolded her daughter and, speaking softly into her ear, said, "College is only twenty minutes away, dear; it's not like you're going to the moon."

"I know, mother, but …"

"You'll be fine," Rose consoled. "Come now," she said, holding Roxy at arm's length, "let's bring your luggage downstairs."

★★★

Journal Entry, August 22, 1997:

Tomorrow, my life begins a new chapter. So I make this promise to you, Father, and to me: No one will ever again control my life. Now destiny is mine alone to determine; and in the process of getting there, I intend to have fun. Fun, Father, a concept you disdained as wasteful—a childhood right you denied me. You denied me so much, Father. But not anymore. Now it's my turn to make the choices. Now—I'm the boss.

11

DOC

"WELL, IT'S ABOUT TIME you got here!" Doc said, embracing David like a long-lost son. "I was beginning to get worried."

"No need. I was in good hands," David said, acknowledging his two young guides with a nod before bending to bear-hug his old friend.

"Well, you look like shit," Doc said, stepping back for a better look. "Ramon … show David where to wash up before dinner."

David smiled, grateful that some things never change, as he dutifully followed Ramon toward a row of wooden cabins. The old man, stooped and truncated by his seventy years, shouted after him, "No ass-dragging, son. We've got a lot of catching up to do."

★★★

The tropical night air echoed with millions of trilling insects vibrating as one. Amid the blackness, a sentinel of flaming torches surrounded an open-air pavilion. Beneath its thatched roof, Doc sat alone at a long wooden table, pensive.

"Evening Doc," David said as he emerged from the shadows.

"David, come join me," Doc said, his thoughts scattering. "You must be hungry," he said, pushing a plate of meat across the table. "I hope you like monkey." David's face blanched. Doc laughed. "Not to worry, my friend—although Carlos has been known to whip up quite a delicacy of it—tonight, in honor of your visit, he's prepared wild boar. Brandy?" he asked, not waiting for an answer before filling two sniffers.

"To health," he toasted, clinking David's raised glass. "When you reach my age, practicality precludes youthful dreams of fame and fortune," he said, swirling his drink below his nose and then gulping. "Speaking of youth … how's that kid brother or yours doing?"

David looked down at his drink, his face somber.

"Not so well, Doc," he said. "Nick's chemo failed … his leukemia's back."

"I'm sorry to hear that, son. What a rotten piece of luck. Has he started treatment yet?"

David pushed the food around his plate with his fork. "His doctors are considering experimental therapy when I get back," he said.

Doc remained silent. They'd had this same discussion a year ago.

"Doc," David said, looking up into the old man's discerning eyes, "I know I wasn't ready to accept your help before … but I'm ready now … if the offer still stands."

Doc knew how difficult it was for his young, conventional friend to acquiesce to unconventional measures. He reached out across the table and gripped David's arm. "Of course," he said with a tender smile, but we can talk about this later. Eat up. Your dinner's getting cold."

David picked up his fork and stabbed his meat. "So," he said, chowing down a mouthful, "what's so important you couldn't tell me over the phone?"

Doc swirled his brandy and stared at the liquid coating the glass. "It's a long story," he said.

David observed his weary mentor, appearing older now than he'd remembered. "Got all night," he smiled.

Doc swigged his brandy and began. "About a year ago, out of the blue, I get a visit from an old army buddy of mine, literally standing here outside my cabin door. Probably forty years since I last heard from him. We served together in the Korean War, 24th Infantry Division … I was a medic, and he was a second lieutenant. Our paths crossed when a stray bullet found his head—he credits me with saving his life. After the war we met for drinks a few times, then lost touch. Turns out he stayed on with the army and made general. Now he's with the U.S. Department of

Defense … a big wig in their Defense Intelligence Agency. His name's General Arthur Rand."

Doc paused, downing his brandy and licking his lips.

David looked on, confused.

"I'm getting there, son … stay with me," he said, clearing his throat. "It seems that my research on the medicinal use of rain forest plants spurred an idea within the U.S. Government for a world-wide clandestine operation … crazy, I know," Doc said, answering David's raised eyebrow. "So I'm sitting there thinking Rand's joking, but he's completely serious," Doc continued. "So I ask him the operation's objective. Are you ready for this? He says: eliminate aggression. So I ask why the hell the Government would want to do that. His answer: remove aggression from the world's troublemakers and you eliminate global hot spots. So I ask how, exactly, is that supposed to work. He says like a contagious airborne disease. Now Rand's got my attention, I admit. So I ask the all-important question, why me? Because, he says, if anyone can find a plant that can do this, I'm the guy … and better yet … the Food and Drug Administration won't be breathing down my neck here in the jungle; I can use my business as a front—work under the radar. So now I'm thinking either this guy is legit or a lunatic, so I cut to the chase … I ask him what's in it for me. His answer: money for a laboratory and the privilege of serving my country."

David studied Doc. He was waiting for the punch line, but it never came. "You're serious, aren't you?" he asked.

"Dead serious," Doc said, pouring himself another drink.

"Well," David said, rubbing the stubble on his chin, "I guess that explains last year's trip to set up a laboratory."

"You'd be correct about that," Doc said.

"And so, am I to presume that my presence here now means you've found such a plant?"

"You'd be correct about that, too"

"Shit."

***

As the clear light of dawn filtered down through the canopy showcasing the lush flora in brilliant shades of green, the erupting chatter of hungry wildlife roused David from his sleep. Suspended in his hammock from the cabin's rafters, mosquito netting splayed about him, David breathed in the humid, heavily oxygenated air now laden with the unmistakable scent of coffee. Flinging netting aside, matador style, he stood and stretched and then walked outside.

"Morning," Doc said, ascending the porch steps with a mug of steaming Joe in his outstretched hand.

David accepted the brew, his body in dire need of lubricant before his engine could rev. "Thanks Doc," he said, carefully sipping from the cup. "Great day."

"Sure is—with no time to waste," Doc said. "Grab some breakfast from Carlos. I already ate. Ramon will come by for you shortly. We'll catch up at the farm."

★★★

Beyond the wooden cabins that bunked the workers, Ramon led David over a narrow footbridge across a shallow river and out through the jungle's fringe onto a clearing. There, nestled within a ring of forest, grew Doc's herbal farm. The natives were busy working the harvest and shouted greetings as the two passed by. Hearing the commotion Doc, down on his knees in the thick of the plantings, used his arm like a tripod to help him stand and then brushed the dirt from his hands. Although erect, his slight figure remained bent as he walked out to meet them.

Five years ago, in a race against his aging clock, Doc had left Harvard and his illustrious career as a biologist behind, landing in Brazil on a personal mission: to identify and catalogue as many medicinal rain forest plants as possible. A practical thinker with an eye to the future, Doc knew that the valuable and irreplaceable knowledge of the plants would one day die along with the indigenous people. With that in mind, he convinced the local tribesmen that an herbal farm was a win-win deal for everyone. The tribe would reap sustainable crops for cash year-round and preserve their land from the rape of clear-cutters intent on lining their pockets. And, in return, Doc would not only get to pick the brains of the elders of their immeasurable knowledge on healing plants but, as a bonus, he would occasionally discover an herb possessing anticancer properties.

"So, what do you think?" Doc asked.

"Remarkable," David replied, his eyes surveying the lush site. "Everything's so well established. You must feel proud of your efforts."

"The benefits these plants offer is my reward. My only concern now is the damn irrigation; the river's lower than ever this year. Maybe I should do a rain dance," Doc said, a mischievous grin deepening the creases around his eyes. He then placed one hand on David's back and indicated with the other the way forward. "Come," he said, "let's visit the lab."

It was hardly a 'walk in the park', as Doc had claimed. With the whoop-whoop sound of machete strikes clearing the underbrush, Ramon led the men through the once familiar passage, practically hidden now in their absence. There was no taming the jungle, Ramon knew, its shorn branches bowing in submission today only to make their tangled return tomorrow. The young guide, fully aware that a jungle finds order in chaos, accepted his foolhardy mission as all in a day's work.

"So how long did you say it's been since you were last here?" David asked.

"Only a week," Doc replied, "but bear in mind, the lab's supposed to be hidden."

"Well, there's no problem with that," David said, taking in the encroaching brush, his eyes and ears alert to every movement as the three moved cautiously forward.

The trio could have walked right past the lab had they not known its location, its walls completely masked in flora. Ramon chopped away the plaited vines tethered to the metal door. Then Doc punched in a code and stood back, beckoning David to enter. When he crossed the threshold, it was like falling down a rabbit hole into Wonderland—the lights kicked on, illuminating a white and sterile world of glass and steel before him. A year later it still amazed him, the incongruity of it all—a modern science lab tucked amid an ancient forest. And so did something else.

"Where did that come from?" he asked. In the middle of the room stood a large and costly, state-of-the art microscope.

A year ago, David had accepted Doc's explanation on the merits of a homespun lab where the processing of medicinal plants could be kept under his tight control. He also accepted his explanation that the funding of the lab was through Doc's personal savings, money enough to build and outfit the lab with the bare essentials. Now, however, the expensive piece of equipment staring him in the face warranted further explanation.

"Uncle Sam," Doc replied. "Delivered after you departed last year. A necessary precaution for the operation's secrecy until the Feds vetted you—which, by the way, you passed with flying colors." Doc grinned. "Come," he said before David could respond, "take a look."

Doc sat down at the microscope, head bent over the eyepiece, adjusting a slide. When he finished, he had David take his seat.

"It's DNA from the blood of a native belonging to the Moksha tribe," Doc said, taking an opposite stool while David studied it.

"The tribe's pretty much isolated from outsiders," he continued. "When I first arrived in Brazil, Ramon led me to them. They have no social hierarchy—no chieftain or shaman—everyone's placed on an equal footing. Theirs is an inclusive, non-competitive, sharing society—especially when it comes to food. As for their daily sustenance, I have observed a steady diet of nuts and berries and an all-important grain from a plant they call Pran. Now, to hear the Moksha tell it, Pran is not just any plant in the Amazon … it's the holy grail of plants—reproducing itself both from seeds and spores—an unheard-of wonder in the plant kingdom."

Doc handed David a slide with a sample from the extracted plant. "As Moksha folklore goes," he continued while David replaced the slide, "they believe this plant was manifested by Diva—their Creator—and bestowed upon their ancestors, giving all who partook of it mystical insight. It's completely integrated into their existence—they eat it, drink it, venerate it," he said. "After Rand's visit, I got to thinking about the tribe and this plant, and how in my five years of observing these indigenous people, never once have I witnessed an aggressive tendency."

David looked up from the microscope, conferring a hairy-eyeball upon Doc over the lens. Doc ignored him.

"I decided to follow my hunch and collected blood samples from all one hundred twenty-seven tribal members, children included—though it took some doing before they consented to being stuck with a needle." Doc laughed. "Funny thing though … no one was scared, just curious … and then they all smiled like lunatics the whole time I drew blood. And crazier still," he said, shaking his head, "to the person, each DNA analysis indicated the same mutated gene."

David sat upright on his stool, his focus now on Doc. "A wild guess," he said, not bothering to hide his sarcasm, "their aggression genes."

"Precisely," Doc concurred.

"Let me get this straight," David quipped. "You think this plant is responsible for their lack of aggression?"

"It's a theory," Doc said. "Look, I tested the plant's nutrients and found high levels of magnesium—a possible influence on their non-aggressive tendencies—but what part it played, if any, in altering their genes is the million-dollar question."

"I assume that's where I come in," David said.

"Quite so my friend," Doc said. "And one other thing—they never get sick."

"Excuse me?"

"In my five years of observing the Moksha, I've never once witnessed a snotty kid."

"Doc," David said, his face screaming skepticism, "have you been mixing juju juice in with your brandy?"

"There's a connection, I tell you," Doc declared, his hand slamming the metal table to make his point, rattling a rack of glass vials resting there. "Look," he said, exhaling, "I know it sounds crazy, but humor me, will you?"

"Finding a common denominator is a tall order, Doc," David said, not bothering to hide his lack of conviction.

"I have faith in you," Doc said, pushing off his stool and heading for the door. "Come on."

"Where to?"

"A trip back in time."

12

— · —

SUNRISE

Sunday, August 24, 1997

Pre-occupying her mind on painting was the natural response whenever Rose felt angst, and so it was not unusual in the pre-dawn hours to find her bathrobe clad and poised behind a canvas.

It had been nearly four days, but to Rose it had seemed a lifetime since she last saw David. Secretly, she welcomed the mandatory slow track their relationship was now forced to travel, because no matter how hard she had tried, her resolve always seemed to melt in his presence. Things were escalating beyond her control, and that simply would not do.

Rose knew, of course, that David wasn't the sole source of her anxiety. Yesterday, her only child had left for college, signaling the start of a new chapter in both of their lives. So much upheaval to her existence all at one time had played on her nerves. It was no surprise then, as she mixed her paints on her palette, that a knocking against the outside window quickened her heart.

***

It had been bad enough since the fire, what with Nick's demons trolling his dreams, but now with David gone, sleep had proven virtually impossible. Lying awake, staring out of his bedroom window into the pre-dawn darkness, a sudden burst of light emanating from Rose's Victorian lit up the yard. Glowing bright in a shroud of mist, it attracted Nick like a moth to flame. He quickly donned his robe and slippers and exited his house. Traipsing softly between properties across cool, dew-covered lawns, inhaling the sweet, heady scent of lavender skirting Rose's garden, Nick encroached slowly upon the windowed enclosure of her well-lit sunroom. Spying her within like a fish in a glass bowl, he stopped dead in his tracks. Observing her so felt wrong, but his urge for companionship pushed aside his momentary hesitation. He moved in closer, his knuckles rapping the glass.

***

Her breath sucked in at the unexpected sound, but then their eyes met through the glass. Rose exhaled.

"Come around to the side," she said, her heart still pounding as she pointed to the door. "You half scared me to death," she said, letting Nick in.

"I'm really sorry, Rose. I should have rung the bell."

"Oh, never mind. I would have jumped at that, too, the state I'm in," she said, shutting the door behind him and locking it. "I'm not used to living alone in such a big house. It'll take some getting used to, I suppose."

"I know what you mean," Nick said, "all those creaky sounds coming out of the woodwork at night … like the house is haunted."

"Yes, well … how about some coffee?" she said, not wanting to entertain thoughts of ghosts ambling about her rickety floorboards. "I've got a pot going in the kitchen. Be an angel and fetch us some, would you?" she said, picking up a tube of paint and squeezing a dollop onto her palate.

"Sure thing," Nick said shuffling off, damp slippers flopping against exposed heels.

"Sugar bowl's on the counter and cream's in the fridge. I take mine black, thank you. And if you're hungry," she shouted after him, "there's a jar of homemade sugar cookies on the table."

After some rummaging about in the kitchen, Nick re-entered the sunroom, carefully orchestrating a loaded serving tray onto an overstuffed ottoman.

"These cookies are really great," he said between mouthfuls.

"Roxy's favorite—made her a batch for college—comfort food, you know." The moment she said it, Rose wished she hadn't. It felt insensitive of her, Nick not being able to attend college now and all. But if it bothered him, he didn't let on, at least not outwardly.

"She's lucky to have a mom like you, Rose. Especially one who bakes this good," he said, licking the sugary bits clinging to his fingers.

Rose smiled. "I swear that girl would live on sweets if I let her," she said.

"You miss her a lot, don't you?"

"Terribly."

"Well at least Boston's close by, near enough for her to come home on weekends."

"True. But I hope she doesn't make a habit of it. I'd rather she stay on campus and partake in activities … make new friends."

"Oh, you don't have to worry about Roxy making friends. They'll be drawn to her like bees to honey."

"Yes, she does have that quality about her, doesn't she?" Rose laughed. "A real queen bee, at that."

His stomach appeased by the cookies, Nick pulled up a chair nearer her blank canvas, his artistic appetite now whetted. "What are you planning to paint?" he asked.

"I thought I'd catch the sunrise coming up behind that majestic oak," she said pointing eastward, out into the darkness of her property, a far-away look in her eyes. "When I was a young girl," she said, "I'd wake up before dawn and saddle up my filly, Star. We'd ride down to the meadow and plant ourselves under a grand old oak—nothing but Star and me melding with the blackness and morning dew, waiting for the sun. It's a magical time … sunrise," she said settling down onto her wooden stool and returning her china cup to its saucer and her mind to the present.

"Well, when I was a kid on my parent's farm, there wasn't much magic in daybreak," Nick countered, "just the rooster calling us to work."

Rose laughed. "Yes, David mentioned having to do chores before school. Tell me," she said, her curiosity getting the better of her, "how was it between the two of you growing up?"

"Despite the obvious age difference—best friends—still are," he said.

"You're lucky," Rose said. "I always wanted a sibling, but I was an only child."

"Nothing wrong with that. Bet you were spoiled by all the attention you got."

"You would think so," Rose said, sighing at the thought of her father rendering a horse more attention than his own flesh and blood. But her sigh passed unnoticed as Nick continued speaking.

"But there are advantages to having an older brother," he said.

"Oh?"

"Yeah, growing up gay has its drawbacks," Nick said, forcing a smile. "But David had my back. He helped me find the courage to face the school bullies."

Rose set down her palate. "I imagine your parents supported you."

"About the bullies?

"No … about being gay."

Nick's eyes lowered. "I never got the chance to tell them."

"I see," Rose said.

"I had plans to, only … everything turned out wrong," he said, his expression suddenly distant and his voice agitated. And then, like the fizz of uncorked champagne, suppressed memories bubbled up and exploded in a violent release. "FIRE," he cried, jumping to his feet, suddenly twelve years old again. "FIRE EVERYWHERE … TIMBERS BLAZING, CRASHING DOWN … BLACK SMOKE … I CAN'T SEE … CAN'T BREATHE," he gasped, hands covering his ashen face and tear-gushing eyes.

Though caught by surprise, straight away Rose wrapped Nick's trembling body into her protective arms. Sobbing onto her shoulder, the two rocked as one in a dance of despair until, finally, when his hysteria subsided and his sobs hushed, a faint whisper escaped his lips.

"Magical," Nick said.

"Magical?" Rose repeated.

"Sunrise."

Rose turned her head toward the glow coming over the horizon and smiled.

"Yes," she said, "it's magical."

13

—·—

BUCK

Girl Flashback

GIRL USUALLY ENJOYED VISITING *her grandfather's ranch, its smells of hay and horses—even the manure—offering her a comforting reprieve from her house of horrors. She delighted in watching the thoroughbreds run and listening to Grandpa Max talk about the tricks of his trade. But not so today.*

She was frightened by the horse, its legs taller than she as she stood there waiting to mount. She preferred ponies, much lower to the ground and less threatening. But she was tall for her age of six, and her father had insisted that she was ready for proper riding lessons, though the horse he chose for her, a stallion, had unnerved even veteran riders with its excitable temperament. There was no one to stop him from this lunacy—his sharp glance silencing her mother in her tracks, her grandmother now four years dead and buried, and her grandfather off to another horse race. Even the ranch hands were reluctant to speak up, shying away from a confrontation they assuredly would lose.

"There's nothing to it," Eugene said, the ranch hands looking on in quiet horror as he lifted her high onto the saddle. "Be strong. Show him who's boss. He can sense fear and fear spooks a horse."

Girl wished she could be strong, wished she could calm her clamoring heart and thoughts of dread. But she was only six, after all, barely able to ride a bicycle, much less a high-strung stallion.

Holding the reins and with an air of authority, Eugene led them once around the pen. "His name is Buck. Talk to him," he commanded.

Girl leaned forward toward Buck's ears and, hoping he didn't live up to his name, whispered, "Good Buck."

"Louder Girl. Be forceful," Eugene admonished. "Remember who's in charge."

Stroking his thick, black mane with a tentative hand, she repeated her mantra. "Good Buck," she said with more muster.

"Better. Now take the reins," he said, holding them out to her.

As Girl looked at him with pleading eyes, and the ranch hands stood slack-jawed at his madness, Rose grabbed the reins from his hands.

"Surely another time around the pen wouldn't hurt," she said, avoiding her husband's eyes as she smiled up at her terrified daughter. "Now let's show father what a big girl you are, shall we?" she said, tugging on the reins and bringing Buck around to a walk.

Eugene didn't say a word. Didn't have to. Rose knew what awaited her. But that was of no concern to her now. Her daughter was all that mattered. But knowing the man she was dealing with, perhaps Rose should have reconsidered, because she had been highly mistaken to think Eugene would postpone punishment for her indiscretion. Challenge to his authority was not suffered lightly. And, after all, a woman must know her place.

"Why don't you join her, Rose? Double up," he offered as they circled back around. "Show her there's nothing to fear."

Something was rotten. Rose could smell it. Magnanimity was never his strong suit, and his words reeked of deceit. But if the stakes had just been raised, the thought of riding on that horse with her daughter was more palatable than her daughter riding alone.

The ranch hands were more than happy to help her up. Rose settled in behind Girl, encircling her within her arms as she leaned forward and took hold of the reins. Buck back-stepped and snorted, protesting the additional weight. "Whoa, easy boy," Rose intoned, tightening the reins. Buck shook his head and whinnied in defiance before begrudgingly settling down. Rose rendered a gentle nudge, and they began retracing his steps.

Eugene waited patiently for them to circle the pen, his fingers twitching at the riding crop tucked beneath his arm. Timing was everything, in horse racing and in life, and he was not about to miss his moment.

Perhaps, at first, Buck sensed fear in his riders; but in the end it was Eugene's sudden movement that spooked him, and the lashing of his hindquarter that made him rear.

Rose had barely time to grab hold of her daughter before Buck bolted, jumping the post and beam fencing; and it was all she could do to keep Girl from slipping off the frightened animal, let alone rein him in. Galloping full speed, hoofs thrashing across open fields and trampling grassy meadows, Buck's nostrils flared, and his eyes bulged in their sockets.

Rose cried out silently to God to save them. Then, in the distance she saw it—her childhood retreat. It called to her … the old oak under which she and Star found solace. She pulled hard on the reigns, aligning Buck's nose with the tree. And then, somehow, it was as if Rose was back on Star, a young girl again, riding the wind and overtaken by the pure joy of freedom. Her fear began to fade. Buck must have felt it, too. He slowed to a cantor, and then a trot.

When he came to a halt beneath the oak's massive canopy, Girl raised her head. Her fingers still entwined in Buck's mane, she stared wide-eyed at the old, senescent giant, its gnarly branches seemingly outstretched in embrace.

Rose, her heart racing, swung a leg over Buck's backside and dismounted. Unsteady on her landing she clung fast to the stirrup, her face thrusted upward against the stallion's coat in perfect alignment to observe her daughter. And what she witnessed then was a moment of pride she would never forget: perched high atop this massive beast, tenderly stroking his mane, her brave little girl leaned forward toward his open ear and whispered … "Good Buck."

14

— · —

LIVINGSTON

Sunday, August 24, 1997

BENEATH THE LUSH, GREEN canopy of interlocking treetops, hidden within the recesses of the rain forest, an ancient civilization was about to make itself known to David. He felt at once terror stricken with each step taken in the dense and treacherous jungle and lightheaded at the prospect of coming face to face with a primitive tribe. His heart racing at maximum speed, adrenaline pumping through his veins, David was barely able to contain himself with the adventure of a lifetime playing out before his eyes.

They had set up camp in the middle of God knows where last night—a long and steamy day of trail blazing behind them. David's body ached, every muscle tensed from fear and exhaustion; but it was a good ache, his cramps acknowledging a momentous task completed, like crossing the finish line of a marathon. And though the revelry of surviving day one was sweet, it was short-lived. Come the break of dawn, David once again found himself shadowing the footsteps of Ramon, with Doc and Bruno bringing up the rear.

"River ahead," Ramon yelled back, its odor and murmur thick on the still air. Indeed, a wide tributary blocked their path. Its muddied current was slow enough for crossing; but Doc wasn't about to wade through, unsure of what lurked below, and backtracking was out of the question, never one to waste time.

"Raft time boys," he called out in a matter-of-fact manner. Without question, the cousins went to work. Splinters flew as Bruno's axe separated limb from tree while Ramon hacked at a nest of dangling vines. It became clear to David they had done this before as he watched the young guides deftly plait limb with vine into a makeshift raft—a craft he'd hoped sturdy enough to safely navigate the current and cross downstream to the other side.

With two solid limbs masquerading as oars anchored deep within the river's murky bed, Ramon and Bruno held the raft firm against the slogging current. *Not exactly seaworthy,* David thought as he took a deep breath and stepped part and parcel onto the bobbing craft. When it was Doc's turn, he wasted no time climbing aboard with the others, more put out by the inconvenience of it all. Castoff swept up a warm breeze onto their sweaty faces as they floated downstream, focused on spotting a landing site on the opposite side.

Within minutes, Doc stretched out his arm and pointed. "There!" he yelled. Protruding from the forest's edge, a strip of sand was fast-approaching. Ramon and Bruno diverted the craft toward the embankment; but as land drew imminent, movement within the brush caught David's eye.

"Shit!" he yelled, losing his footing as the raft skidded aground in a fit of tremors and bumps. Landing on his knees, he heard the growl first. Looking up, two green eyes met his through the brush.

WHOOSH.

Something whizzed past him.

From its hidden perch on a low-lying branch, the jaguar fell hard, parting the vegetation where it lay.

"Livingston, my good man, what took you so long?" Doc bellowed as the nearby foliage divided, revealing a short, brown man wearing a big smile and little else.

Baffled and shaken at what had just transpired, David found his footing and slowly stood, watching the two men greet one another. It took a few seconds, but the light finally dawned—this was the moment David had been waiting for.

"Livingston," Doc said smiling, "I'd like you to meet my good friend, David."

It wasn't a dream but sure felt like one when David stepped forward to greet a man who lived much as his ancestors did hundreds of years ago, primitive and much preserved from the outside world—a man of the Moksha tribe. He stared into the young native's eyes, imagining what wonder of wonders they've witnessed; and though David judged himself to be more than twice this man's age, he was certain his own life experiences were nothing by comparison.

Livingston grasped David's forearms, acknowledging him with a nod and his trademark crescent smile, and then, lean and light-footed, took his leave to kneel before his felled prey. With one skillful tug, he dislodged the dart from the big cat's throat, then stood. "Come," the sinewy native said, and taking the lead, slipped back through the undergrowth to quickly disappear. One by one his new-found entourage followed suit, each swallowed up by the brush.

"Livingston?" David questioned Doc, his voice lowered as they pecked their way through the vegetation, "as in Dr. Livingston?"

"You presume correctly," Doc answered with an impish smile.

Though nothing Doc did surprised him anymore, David regarded his old friend with an incredulous look.

"What? An old man's not allowed some indulgences. Besides, he likes it," Doc said.

"It's a good thing you never had kids Doc, or Lord knows what names they'd answer to … Livingston," he repeated a little too loudly shaking his head with a laugh. At the mention of his name, the wiry tribesman turned toward David and smiled. David, feeling awkward, rendered the native a cursory wave and a weak smile back. Doc was smiling, too, though David knew his mentor's shit-eating grin was meant for him.

They followed the sun's movement in and out of branches and leaves, lightening and darkening the forest as they went. David pinched himself. As impossible as it seemed, a man of ancient tribal origins was leading them through the Amazon. Oddly, he found it comforting. After all, Livingston had just proven his worth protecting them from a jaguar, and who's to say what awaited them still. In fact, David took relief in the jungle-book education of all his travel companions which, when stacked against the fleeting memory of his Harvard degree, left him concluding intelligence was all relative.

As the sun climbed to its apex, David employed every bit of energy to keep going, even as every pore in his body wept from the oppressive heat. But he had greater concerns than fatigue and drenched clothing. Tangled footsteps among clawing creepers could easily break an ankle, and tree trunks covered in three-inch spikes could impale more than one's apparel. For David, it was a laborious effort to remain aware of all that was above and below with each footstep forward—but seemingly not so for Livingston, who left the impression that navigating the jungle was mere child's play.

"How does he do it?" David asked.

"Do what?" Doc said.

"Find his way. There's no clear-cut path here and everything looks the same."

"Even an Indian has a method to his madness … watch," Doc said, as he snapped a small branch between thumb and forefinger into a boomerang shape. "These bent twigs are his road map home," he explained. "Livingston makes them as he walks to find his way back—like Hansel and Gretel's breadcrumbs, so to speak."

As a young scout, David had learned of such markings used by Native Americans, but his trusty compass was more often employed than not whenever a question of direction came up. It seemed cleverness was better left to the Indians if you wanted to make it back to camp in time for dinner. David observed the bent twig and frowned. As far as he was concerned, it was like reading braille. There was no way he could ever discern this dangling, man-made sign among the dense growth, not even if his life depended on it. His admiration for the wiry, little man weaving his way through giant ferns was ever-growing.

"What's he like?" David asked.

"A decent fellow, really," Doc said, "very generous. He'd have given me the shirt off his back if he had one, but I settled instead for his blood."

David laughed. "Spoken like a true scientist."

"Wait till you meet the missus and kids," Doc added. "Quite the family tree. Clearly, heredity has influenced their DNA. But then genetics is your expertise." Doc smiled.

Livingston held up his hand and stopped at the front of the column. Ahead was the unmistakable sound of yet another river crossing. A mammoth tree trunk spanned its murky waters—thirty feet below. It was obvious that someone had shorn the branches and notched its bark for traction; and as they all stood there silently contemplating this fact, David's stomach turned. Not that he wasn't up to the task, his body still fit despite the years; but with age comes wisdom, and the thought of a single misstep dumping him three stories into unsure depths and unknown realms made him want to vomit.

"Senhor David. It easy. Watch," Ramon said, acknowledging the stricken face of his star pupil. His back laden with supplies, Ramon hopped up onto the weathered trunk and, never looking down, focused entirely on placing one foot in front of the other until he reached the opposite side. "See," he yelled jumping onto solid ground, his arms outstretched in triumph. "Easy."

David wasn't so sure.

Not one to pussyfoot around Doc volunteered to go next, rebuffing all offers of help, stating he may be old, but he wasn't feeble. A smooth and steady start, he negotiated half the distance before a patch of damp moss launched his footing. His body wavered from side to side, arms extended like a tight-rope walker as he struggled for balance. It would have been comical had he not been thirty feet high in elevation. Cursing, he managed to reclaim his footing and, embarrassed more than frightened, pressed on, dogged to the end. Climbing down from the trunk, his pride restored, Doc's smile flashed victorious.

Livingston urged David to go next. His stomach protested with a mouthful of bile, but he knew there was no going back. Bearing the weight of his companions' stares, David stepped up to the challenge and onto the trunk. Glancing down into the muddy waters, a wave of nausea rushed over him. *Don't look …* he told himself, as he focused on his feet. Although the trunk's breadth was rotund, the actual walkway was a mere foot wide, its surface littered with odd-shaped stubs like obstacles on a racetrack. But David's steps found purchase on the notched bark, like rough strips underfoot in a bathtub. *One step at a time,* he kept telling himself, hovering at the three-quarters mark with victory so close he could taste it. Only … a loud squawking erupted overhead. David looked up, and the moment he did he knew it was a mistake. A toucan roosting nearby had taken flight, soon followed by another, and then another, until an entire flock was flapping furiously past him, their mournful cries echoing beneath the canopy. Any hope he may have had of maintaining balance was dashed the moment he panicked. Before he knew what had happened, his body was dangling midair—his backpack's strap snagged on a stub. Terrified, David held his breath in a motionless suspension. Then a shadow settled over him—*the shadow of death,* he thought as his life passed before his eyes. But when he looked up, an outstretched arm appeared. With his heartbeat reverberating in his ears, aware that the slightest movement could unhinge him, he inched his hand upward to meet it. The grasp was firm with the locking of arms, but so was the snap—a sickening sound unleashing the tree stub and freeing his pack's strap with it. David dangled like an aerialist, arm locked in arm, as the stub fell into the hungry waters below, never more to be seen. Palm sweating and grasp slipping, he made a decision—he wasn't going to die today, not like this. With a burst of adrenaline, he swung his dangling legs upside the trunk, his feet fighting to take root while his free hand clawed at the bark. It was then he felt his belt tugging at his middle and the rough bark tearing at his clothes—he was being hauled up. His body, drenched in sweat and drained of energy, lay draped over the trunk, shaking. After what seemed a lifetime, he looked up, found his breath—and the smiling face of Livingston.

15

— • —

TAKE-YOUR-SON-TO-WORK DAY

Girl Flashback

*H*E SAT GIRL IN *the far corner of his spacious office like one more object in the room—a book on the shelf or paperweight on his desk—and handed her pen and paper. "Take notes on the master at work," he said, and then returned to his ornate desk and pressed the button on his intercom. "Send him in," he said. Eugene Pendleton, the Senior Senator from Connecticut and Republican Majority Leader, sank back into his supple leather chair readying to take full measure of the man now coming through the door. "Stanley, have a seat," he said, dispensing with cordialities.*

The slender young man, polished in a blue silk suit and coiffed blond hair, stood eyeing Girl in the corner. Eugene responded to his gaze. "Take-Your-Son-to-Work Day," he said, making no attempt at introductions. Stanley, assuming the awkward matter closed, took a seat opposite the senator.

Girl hated coming to her father's office, especially on this day—Take-Your-Son-to-Work Day. Her father's delusion of her as his son was ever present; even on this day of the year he couldn't admit she was a girl. She was ten now and used to the ritual, but it never got any easier.

"Stanley, time's getting short," Eugene said, his steely eyes penetrating his youthful colleague. "The first congressional session begins in less than a week and Senator McCord's encroaching on my lead. Damn it, I need those three votes to tip the scales, or I can kiss my eight-year run as Majority Leader goodbye," Eugene railed. "What have you learned?"

Boy-faced Stanley Greene, Republican Junior Senator from Connecticut, bounced his knees against his cupped hands. "The news isn't good, sir. The esteemed senators are holding out, waiting to see which way the wind blows before committing."

"Sons of bitches," Eugene barked. "I need commitments, and I need them now."

Stanley knew Senator Pendleton was not to be crossed. He had a healthy respect for the senior senator's position, but also a sound fear of the man himself. But Stanley was a realist. He understood that loyalty to Senator Pendleton went well-rewarded, and that any opposition must be trod with care, lest he'd find his coveted office banished into the Capitol's bowels and any hope of advancement within the ranks dashed.

"All right, then, Stanley, it's time to show our three fence-sitting colleagues which way the wind blows," Eugene said, his formidable tone declaring commencement of backroom politics. "Tell the senators if they back me, they can each expect an additional chairmanship. If not, they can kiss the ones they have goodbye." He rose and walked around his desk. "Tell them," he said with added emphasis to drive his message home, 'they have nothing to lose and everything to gain with a vote for Senator Eugene Pendleton."

"Yes, sir. I'll take care of it right away, sir," Stanley said, rising.

"Good," Eugene said, his arm wrapped about the Junior Senator's shoulders as they walked to the door. "I know I can count on you, Stanley. Play your cards right, and there just might be a chairmanship in it for you."

"Thank you, sir. I won't let you down, sir."

"I know you won't, Stanley. I know you won't."

Girl watched her father close the door on the compliant young senator, and when he turned and met her eyes, she dropped her gaze.

"Someone is always wanting for something, Girl," he said, walking back to his desk. "And when you are in a position to satisfy such wants, you have power." He sank back into his chair and kicked up his feet. "Remember this: If you want control of your destiny, you must make yourself indispensable." And, liking the sound of his words, he ordered, "Write that down."

Girl studied the sheet of paper in front of her, the page covered in doodles. She picked up her pen ... and drew one more.

16

—·—

ORIENTATION

Monday, August 25, 1997

WITH OVERSTUFFED BAGGAGE AND goodies from home, Roxy arrived on campus along with her freshman class for orientation. It didn't take her long to fall into a rhythm of eating, attending sessions, sleeping and, of course, meeting the opposite sex. The same could not be said for her roommate.

Megan sat legs crossed, head down, taking notes while the Performing Arts instructor spoke. Sitting next to her, Roxy donned a studious look; however, her note taking had taken a back seat to the boy ogling her from across the aisle. She loved this game boys played, and stringing the bait was a sport in which she excelled—especially when the catch was worth reeling in. Roxy made little attempt to hide her awareness of his gaze, concentrated on her from the moment she sat down. This one was a catch by anyone's standards—clearly affirmed by his doting female fan club perched nearby. But Roxy wasn't interested in group membership. For her, it was all about control. Her father taught her well the power in possessing what someone else wanted, and if this boy wanted her on his list of conquests, well … he had another thing coming.

Two can play at this game, she thought, casting him a smile.

Encouraged, he scribbled a note and lifted the pad for her to read: "Buy you lunch?"

Bait taken, she thought, nodding her acceptance, *hook, line and sinker.* The young man, completely unaware of the predatory waters into which he was plunging, flashed a grin.

The bell rang and the session ended, everyone bee-lining it for the door.

"Who's that cute boy you were flirting with?" Megan whispered as they fell in line up the aisle.

"No idea, but I'm about to find out. He's buying me lunch," Roxy said, as they stepped outside into the fresh air. "Come along … bet he's got a friend."

"No thanks … not interested."

Roxy's jaw dropped; her face chiseled in disbelief. "Not interested?" She was all about having fun now, hell-bent on making up the lost time of her youth and found it impossible to believe that her shy roommate couldn't benefit as well by a little mingling with the opposite sex.

"In case you haven't noticed, dear girl, the college scene is a breeding ground of testosterone-laden boys all looking for a good time. Mind you, you don't have to do it to have a good time," she said, defending Megan's honor.

"You go on ahead," Megan urged. "I'm not hungry. I'll catch up with you later at the dorm."

The fact that Roxy seemed so self-assured, so easily adjusted to the new environment, magnified even more Megan's own lack of confidence and awkward acclimation to college life. Of course, she knew nothing of Roxy's demons or her ability to re-invent herself at whim; all she knew was that she, alone, was responsible for her current situation and her conscious decision to remain a wallflower. Megan turned and began her retreat up the brick pathway.

"Okay, but you're missing out," Roxy lamented in her most con-vincing voice, and in a last-ditch effort added, "You'll be sorry." Megan just kept walking, turning only to wave at Roxy, never breaking stride.

★★★

"Hi," he said, looking up as she approached. He was waiting for her on the Student Union steps.

"Hi," she echoed.

God he's hot, Roxy thought, a corona of sunlight brandishing his golden hair. This was going to be harder than she imagined. *Stay focused,* she berated herself.

He stood tall and tempting, his hand outstretched.

"My name's Zach … Zach Tanner," he said, his crystal-blue eyes piercing hers.

Roxy clasped his hand.

"Nice to meet you, Zach Tanner. I'm Roxy … Roxy Pendleton," she said, following his lead.

"A pleasure … Roxy Pendleton. I believe I promised you lunch. Allow me," he said, opening the door.

"Thank you," she said, aware of his scrutinizing gaze as she sashayed past and entered the building.

The lunch line at the buffet was already growing long. And everywhere was the busy-bee movement of students with trays darting here and there, getting on with the business of eating—some gathered at tables abuzz with talk, others a quiet hum.

"Trust me to select your lunch while you grab a table?" Zach asked as they watched the lunch line flexing into curves.

"Brilliant minds think alike," she said.

Zach took off, zigzagging through the crowd like a Grand Prix driver, while Roxy chose a small corner table tucked by a window where, studying her reflection, she tended to her stray hairs before sitting.

From afar, as if watching a silent film, she observed with studied interest her female counterparts in line next to Zach. Though their words inaudible, their body language was crystal clear as they moved in closer like purring felines in heat. He certainly seemed to enjoy the attention, and who didn't like attention, she had to admit. Besides, how could any guy with good looks like his possibly swear off adoring advances, even if he wanted to? She suspected it was a question over which Zach lost little sleep.

Looking over her way, he waved. Roxy's breath caught in her throat. Had he caught her staring? She had thought her eyes discrete. But the idea of Zach misinterpreting her gaze, giving him reason to carve one more notch in his mental belt of conquests, irritated her. She swallowed hard and waved back, her face five shades of red.

"Hope you like grilled cheese," he said ten minutes later, sliding the tray between them. "Figure it's pretty innocuous."

"Thanks," she said with forced cheeriness, disguising her disappointment in a menu selection as bland as the food.

"So what are you majoring in, Roxy?" Zach asked, pulling in his chair.

"Writing," she said, opening her napkin and placing it onto her lap.

Zach popped open a bag of chips, a few escapees scattered across the tabletop.

"Cool," he said. "What got you interested?"

"My journal," she said, the words slipping out before she could stop them, her stomach suddenly churning from the indigestion of her past.

"Really? I could never keep a journal—not with my uninteresting life—unless writing about an average kid growing up in an average family in an average American town is considered interesting," he said.

Average, she thought, how foreign and yet comforting a word. Nothing in her past had ever been average. She had lived in a world of extremes, blacks and whites with no middle ground. As a child she had longed for the momentary warmth and security dispensed by a blanket of average, but it would have been her undoing. Better to remain hardened to the cold if one was expected to survive. Comfort had no place in her world.

"And what's your major, Zach?" she said, shifting the conversation's direction.

"Acting, actually."

Roxy was intrigued. She could envision Zach on stage commanding the audience with his powerful presence. "Recite some lines for me," she demanded like a director, putting him on the spot.

Zach's eyebrows arched and then knitted together. Slowly, his features transformed so that his face seemed no longer his own:

"'Did my heart love till now? forswear it, sight! For I ne'er saw true beauty till this night.'" Zach's eyes fell upon Roxy's and, in the ensuing silence, hers tarried in his gaze.

Awkward in the moment she clapped suddenly. "Bravo!" she said. "You'd make Shakespeare proud." Zach smiled from across the table and attempted a waist-up bow, while she chided herself for dropping her guard. Ignoring her burning cheeks, she aimed the spotlight back. "Are you from the New England area?" she asked.

"California … Santa Cruz, actually. Great surfing there. You surf?" he asked.

"No," she said, "What's it like?"

"Incredible," he said. "Just you and the wave—one trying to outlast the other. I can't wait to surf the Atlantic."

"Won't it be cold?" Roxy asked.

"Sure, but I've got a wet suit. Nothing holds back a dedicated surfer," he said, "not even hurricanes—best waves ever."

Roxy cringed, her brain seizing upon an image of Megan's mother undulating out to sea on the swells.

"What about you, Roxy … you from here?"

"Connecticut, originally," she said, letting go the image, watching it ebb out onto the horizon of her mind and disappear. "We recently moved up to Cambridge. According to Mother, it's just far enough from college for my autonomy and still near enough for me to get home …" *in case of a mental meltdown,* she thought.

"A practical woman, your mother, and I'll bet beautiful, too … like her daughter."

"Zach!" a lanky, bespectacled young man called out from the crowd, his approach to their table impeccably timed to assuage Roxy further embarrassment.

"Paul, what's happening," Zach replied, a high five passing between them.

"Been looking everywhere for you, man, but I can see now why you're in hiding," Paul said, eyeing Roxy with an approving once-over.

"Paul, this is Roxy Pendleton. Roxy, my friend Paul Revere."

"The name was my dad's idea … he's a revolutionary buff," Paul interjected per his usual introductory addendum, cutting off any chance for a snide remark. He shook her hand.

"Well, I'm glad to meet you, Paul" Roxy said. "And I like your name. It has character."

Paul smiled. "I like this girl!" he said. "You wouldn't happen to have a sister, would you?"

Roxy grinned with delight. "A sister of sorts," she teased.

"Well, if this sister of sorts is as pretty as you," he said with a wide, goofy grin, "maybe we could double date sometime." But before Roxy could reply, his eye caught the cafeteria clock. "Crap," he stammered,

"I'm late for class. Gotta fly." Performing one more obligatory high five with Zach he bolted for the door. "Looking forward to our double date," he shouted over his shoulder as the crowd ate him up.

Turning back in his seat to face Roxy, Zach said, "Childhood friends," by way of explanation. "We grew up together in grade school, best pals until his family up and moved to Florida. It's weird … all those years without contact and then on our first day of orientation I hear this familiar voice behind me talking about growing up in Santa Cruz." Zach laughed. "Who'd have guessed? Maybe it's fate. Anyhow, we've got four years now to catch up with each other. Oh, and best thing yet? He's studying film production. We've got big plans to make a movie together after graduation. Hey …" Zach paused, a light bulb going off, "maybe you'd be interested in writing the script?"

Roxy's brain scrambled for the words. She opened her mouth, but nothing came out.

Zach persisted. "You can choose the genre, Roxy, just as long as I play leading man," he said, sitting up straight to strut his imaginary feathers. "No rush for an answer, just think about it … you've got four years," he said with a magnanimous smile.

Her nod was barely perceptible but enough to satisfy Zach. The two returned to the business of eating, silent as they caught up with their own thoughts.

When their meals were finished, Roxy spoke. "Thanks for lunch, Zach. It was so nice meeting you," she said, standing to go.

"How about a movie this week?" Zach asked, rising to meet her.

Roxy hesitated. The moment of truth had arrived.

"We could do that double date thing with Paul?" he said, unflagging in his pursuit.

Roxy wasn't surprised that he'd asked her out; indeed, she rather expected it. Earlier, she was perfectly prepared to send him packing, but now she considered accepting his invitation. The very idea that he valued her creative mind was an outright aphrodisiac—a thrill that he would trust her ability to write a script without ever having read one iota of her work—it sent chills up her spine. Of course, the possibility did cross her mind that perhaps she was the only writer Zach knew to ask. Yet, she couldn't help but think that perhaps this Romeo had more to offer than good looks. Five-minute reckoning be damned, she was going to give him the benefit of the doubt, only not right away. First, he'd have to prove his worthiness—if he truly wanted her, he'd have to chase her. Better he courts her like a treasure worth hunting rather than a cheap trinket discarded when boredom set in.

"I appreciate the offer, Zach," she said, "but I'm really busy this week."

"Well, how about dinner … everyone has to eat," he said, hopeful.

"I'll have to check my schedule, but I can't promise you anything."

"Well then, at least let me walk you back to your dorm," he begged.

The line cast … and bait taken.

"By all means," she said, reeling him in.

***

All eyes seemed to stare down at Megan from the posters plastered above Roxy's bed—not a spare inch of wall space to be had among the overlapping tributes to her favorite alternative rock bands. Megan's walls were relatively bare by comparison, adorned with only a few family photos shot on Rocky Point Island. Roxy had offered to share her prized poster collection; and although Megan didn't say it, she wasn't interested in a wall paying homage to sexy young men. She had a clear image of the life she wanted to build for herself, and the road she was on didn't allow for such temptations. It was bad enough she'd have to contend with all those sultry eyes above Roxy's bed leering down at her day and night.

"Hi," Roxy said, breathless, the dorm room door slamming shut behind her as she dropped her backpack to the floor. "You should have come," she said, exultant, her chest heaving from the trek up three flights of stairs. "I told you he'd have a friend—really cute—he wants to meet you," she teased, crumpling onto her bed, bolstering her head with pillows.

Megan's body stiffened under her quilted comforter. But how could she be upset with Roxy; she was only being nice. She had no way of knowing Megan held no interest in encouraging suitors, although the lovely Irish lass turned plenty of heads.

"Boys are so predictable," Roxy continued, kicking off her shoes and cuddling her knees to her chest. "I had Zach eating out of my hand in no time."

"Zach?"

"Zach Tanner. He's actually not so bad … has potential. Just needs proper guidance, that's all."

Proper guidance … Megan pondered the possibility. Could she manage a young man just enough to gain his passing interest and yet keep him from wanting to stick around?

"He asked me … actually us … out to dinner with his friend, Paul Revere," Roxy said. "Can you imagine a parent saddling a child with a name like that? Anyway, I didn't commit—not yet. Let them drool over us first," she said laughing, enjoying her competitive one-upmanship. And then it was as if noticing Megan for the first time, pajama clad and pale-faced squirreled beneath her bedcovers. "Is everything okay?" she asked, alarmed, "you look ill."

Since their first day of orientation together Megan had stood in her roommate's shadow, intentionally allowing Roxy the limelight. Only now, listening to Roxy, she realized with dread that her life was condemned to the shadows forever. But it was her fate—no, her punishment—and there was no going back.

"Nothing's wrong," she said, brushing off Roxy's concern. "I'm just tired, that's all."

Roxy knew a ruse when she smelled one.

"Looks like you could use a nap," she said, playing along. "Tell you what … I'll take notes at afternoon session for the both of us and grab some pizza on the way back. We can dine in tonight in our pajamas—it'll be fun! Deal?"

Megan looked up at Roxy, relief spreading through her veins like morphine. "Deal," she said, closing her eyes, the burden of her sentence granted a temporary reprieve.

17

THE OUTBURST

Monday, August 25, 1997

Dark, rolling waves grew higher and higher tousled by the gale winds and spewing cold sprays of white against her shivering body. There were no stars or moon by which to see but seeing wasn't necessary to discern the hurricane's clear presence, adamantly announced in its fury. Megan clung hopelessly to the rocks. "Mama!" she wailed, but the roar of blackness echoing from every crevice of the rocky shoreline overwhelmed her cry, mocking her frail attempt to be heard. "I'm sorry, Mama … I'm sorry," she sobbed, her hold weakening despite her resolve. Another black wall of wet washed over her, its salty waters filling her throat and convulsing her lungs. Beneath her slipping grip the rocks endured the pummeling, submissive to nature's wrath after years of abuse; but the girl who often played upon these rocks found no allegiance in their familiarity, the rocks just as easily giving her up to the ocean's wanton fingers as not. "Mama!" she screamed with her last breath as the wet blackness tore her loose and wrapped its cold arms about her.

"Megan, wake up!" Roxy yelled, shaking her roommate's shoulders. "You're having a bad dream!"

Megan's eyelids popped opened to a wild, wide-eyed stare, her chest heaving and runaway tears glistening her cheeks.

"Are you okay?" Roxy asked, gently brushing away the droplets with her fingers. "Can I get you some water?"

"Yes," Megan rasped, still caught between worlds, "thank you."

Roxy strode to the mini fridge, swung the door open and grabbed hold of a bottle. "Here you go," she said, unscrewing the cap and handing it off to her roommate. Megan sat upright and took several sips, while Roxy eased herself down onto the edge of the bed—and waited.

Whatever was troubling Megan, Roxy was hell bent to find out, but all in due course. She knew from experience that patience was the thing. You can't rush someone into spilling their guts. You must give them space and time, and more important than that—you must build trust. It's a slow process, this trust-building business; but she had learned that anything worth having was worth the wait.

"Was I talking in my sleep?" Megan asked timidly.

"There was a lot of mumbling, but I did hear you shout, Mama."

Megan lowered her eyes, fighting back embarrassment and more tears.

Over the past several days of rooming together, Roxy had sensed she and Megan shared a whole lot more than a love of writing. Now, with Megan's outburst, she knew without a doubt her roommate fought demons, too. But Roxy also knew it would only be a matter of time before the tables turned and she would find herself on the receiving end of an explosive bad dream. Still, Roxy couldn't help but feel relief, grateful that her outburst hadn't happened first.

"I picked us up some pizza. You hungry? I'm starved," Roxy said getting up, recognizing the cue for a scene change. "But first, a pajama party requires pajamas," she said, and rifling through her drawer, she dug out an ensemble and quickly changed clothes as well as persona, casting herself as a supermodel strutting a runway walk down the center of their dorm room. "This year's latest in sleepwear: hot pink baby dolls complete with complementary fuchsia slippers," she said, pirouetting to tickle Megan's nose with her fluffy raised foot. Megan giggled, and with it the spell was broken. "Come on, let's eat," Roxy said, whipping the comforter off her bed and spreading it out onto the dorm room floor, the two plunking themselves down onto its softness—a hot box of pizza between them.

"Hope you like Hawaiian," she said, opening the lid and separating the pieces, pulling loose a long string of dangling cheese from her slice and depositing it into her mouth. "I just love pineapple." She plucked a juicy chunk out from the topping and admired it briefly before devouring it. "I hear Hawaii has plantations full of them—a regular pineapple paradise."

"My parents met in Hawaii," Megan offered softly. "They were training there for the Peace Corp."

Roxy stopped chewing. "Really?"

"Their first assignment was in Africa."

"Wow, that's crazy," Roxy said. "What'd they do there?"

"Helped the villagers dig a well for drinking water. Here, let me show you." Megan got up and, from her nightstand, removed one of many stacked photo albums. She sat back down next to Roxy and flipped through a few pages, finally pointing to a picture. "Here's my parents standing next to the well," she said.

Roxy leaned in for a closer look.

"It made a huge difference for the women of the village, not having to lug huge jugs on their heads to and from the river—especially with lions making their way to the same watering hole."

"Geez," Roxy said, shivering at the thought, her eyes taking in the younger version of Megan's father sporting the same fiery red hair. Then she inspected the image of Megan's mother—a tall, slender figure clad all in white, her porcelain face peeking out from under a wide-brimmed hat no doubt intended as protection from a brutal African sun. Unlike Roxy, there was scant resemblance between Megan and her parents. *Probably a good thing,* Roxy thought. Better to not inherit impossible standards to live up to or those that you despise. "Your mother was stunning," was all she said.

"Yes," Megan replied, and without further commentary, took the album from Roxy and closed it, returning it to the nightstand.

Roxy was disappointed that her window into Megan's world had been cut short, but she understood her roommate's life was her private story and considered herself privileged to have shared a glimpse of one chapter.

"I've been thinking about our double date," Roxy said, switching gears. Megan's shudder didn't escape her this time. Pretending not to have noticed, she licked the tomato sauce clinging to her fingers and reached up onto her desk, grabbing her Magic 8 Ball—a gift from Mother for her seventh birthday for a kid in need of easy answers ... though her need for easy answers somehow never stopped. Toying with it, she said, "There's a posting at the Student Union Center for a rock band competition Friday night at a club in Cambridge." Roxy paused, rotating the black and white ball in her hands, watching the prescribed answers pop up. "Zach wants us to double date." She looked over at Megan, hoping for a positive response, but all she got was silence. "Tell you what," she said, "let's ask the Magic 8 Ball if we should go." She tipped it purposefully down and then up, a smile landing on her face with the answer. "Signs point to yes!" she read. And then added with haste, "Great, I'll let Zach know," quickly negating any opportunity for Megan to back out. She dropped the Magic 8 ball along with the subject and reached for a second slice of pizza.

★★★

Journal Entry, August 25, 1997:

First mother and now Megan. For the life of me, I can't understand their hang-ups about dating. It's not like you're making a long-term commitment or anything. You get taken out—and it doesn't even cost you a dime!

18

LANYA

Tuesday, August 26, 1997

THE CHILDREN POPPED IN and out of the foliage grinning and giggling at the column of weary men soldiering by. It was a welcome sight after three long, unnerving days of trailblazing. David played along in their surreal jungle game of now you see me, now you don't. Donned in nature's birthday suits, the children frolicked through the forest content in their play; and only when their thatched huts poked their rounded roofs through the flora did the children scatter and run on ahead to the village.

Livingston called out through the brush, his announcement eliciting excited commotion among the tribal members who gathered like flies to fruit around the visitors. Bold in their display of curiosity, the children swarmed David who stood as Goliath in their midst; and although uncomfortable in his newly acquired rock-star status, he soon warmed to their inquisitiveness, even as his own curiosity consumed him.

"David," he said, poking his index finger to his chest attempting introductions. Doc suddenly charged their inner circle like a bull in a china shop, the young ones disseminating in all directions laughing with delight. "Better run if you know what's good for you," he yelled after them with a devilish grin, but the children only kept coming back for more.

David noticed how easily the old man's shenanigans endeared the children to him, but then it was understandable, considering how David was enamored of his mentor as well.

"And here comes the happy couple now," Doc wheezed, doubled over and catching his breath as a beautiful young woman approached hand in hand with Livingston. She stood small in David's shadow, barely five feet tall, alluring in her smile and obsidian eyes dark as the night. A single white flower adorned her long, raven hair while a ringlet of the blooms veiled her round, firm breasts.

"Lanya," she said, speaking her name softly, the palm of her hand resting over her heart as she looked up at David, her eyes piercing his.

Dumbfounded, David stood stuck in her gaze and a prolonged silence.

"Cat got your tongue," Doc teased.

"David," he sputtered, coming to, "my name is David."

Lanya smiled.

"And these fine, young rug rats are the happy couples brood." Doc's sweeping arm encompassed the children running circles around them. Reaching out, he captured the youngest member within his embrace and struggled to keep hold. "This squirming, little imp I call Viper," he said, "slippery as a snake, and fast." And as if to prove the worthiness of his nickname, the boy wriggled from Doc's grip, taking refuge behind David's tall legs before slithering away to hide among the tribe.

The children's folly whipped up a concoction of laughter and encouragement from the villagers, everyone willing participants in the game. And amid their antics, David felt Lanya take hold of his hand. Come, her eyes said. He went willingly, following her through a dark, winding passage of well-trodden undergrowth, her presence oddly trumping any concern for his safety.

Their path opened onto a tranquil pool of water, the sun's rays diffused and dancing upon its surface. Above the pool a gentle stream cascaded over an outcropping of rocks, plunging fifteen feet into the deep-blue oasis, concentric rings bubbling up and rippling outward. The two stood side by side at water's edge, their odd-couple reflection staring back at them. Wading in, Lanya shattered the image, her naked body a chameleon of darkness and light as she swam in and out of the shadows. Treading water, her hands beckoned David to enter. Without thinking, he found himself stripped of clothing and submerged, his body tingling, re-invigorated by the coolness as he propelled himself upward several strokes. When he broke surface, Lanya was under the waterfall, laughing. David swam to her. Overhead, the streaming waters struck his flesh with a sharpness, as if a slap from nature awakening him. And as the waters flowed off his shoulders, Lanya removed her floral necklace and placed it over his head, her eyes never leaving his. Once again, David languished in a motionless suspension, although this time not by a strap adhering to a stub but by Lanya's eyes. He was drowning in her gaze, unable to breathe or blink while her eyes searched his, reaching deep, as if tugging for his soul. And yet he felt no compulsion for struggle, no desire for release. He was in a place that, had he a choice, he would never leave—but then her gaze broke, and she was gone. Slipping beneath the cool waters, she swam for shore. David followed in reflexive pursuit and, reaching dry soil, stood before her dazed and dripping like a fish out of water—like a heavenly soul forced to return from the dead.

When the two returned to the village, a large fire had been built, its glowing cinders spitting high and sputtering out, like fireflies in twilight.

"I see you've been introduced to the baptismal waters," Doc grinned, David's wet hair and partially clad body a dead giveaway. "Come … sit with me by the fire," he said, patting the ground beside him.

David obeyed, saying nothing as he sat and stared into the flames, orange-red tongues of warmth reaching out to lap at his damp skin.

"She's a remarkable woman, Lanya," Doc said, his eyes following her retreat from the fire. "She has a sixth sense—all the Moksha do—but none like her." He paused, throwing a twig into the flames.

David shifted uncomfortably but said nothing, his gaze transfixed on the fire.

"There's a strong connection between you two. She saw it in your eyes the instant you met," Doc said, pausing momentarily to consider what next to say, hardly expecting David to accept his explanation any more than he had. Not knowing how else to put it, he just spat it out—incredulous words that sent a tremor rippling up David's spine: "Lanya believes you once walked with the Moksha—in another lifetime. And today, through her eyes, you pierced the waterfall of illusion and glimpsed a deeper reality—the source of all you are."

David fingered the flowers about his neck, inhaling their sweet scent, and then broke his silence but not his gaze. "How do you know all this?"

"Five years ago, I took the obligatory dunking as well," Doc answered, his smile empathetic; but David wasn't smiling, his face a portrait of etched confusion.

"And you believe this?" he said.

"Who's to say what's possible in the realms of the unknown."

David closed his eyes and, as if trying to convince himself, said, "It can't be possible, what happened … how I felt," desperation creeping into his voice, the truth in his soul bearing down on him with as much certainty as his need to breathe.

"Go on," Doc urged, "tell me."

His eyes still closed, David sighed deeply, then spoke. "In the pool I was surrounded by water, its coolness touching my skin; then, looking into her eyes, all separation left me—I was the water." Fighting the feeling, refusing to accept what transpired as real, the scientist in him demanding concrete data, he opened his eyes and shook his head. "I must be crazy," he said.

"All things become clearer with time, son," Doc said, as the still night air suddenly took wing with surreal song. He stood, offering an extended hand to his young, bewildered protege.

Under the cloak of darkness, ethereal notes escaping wooden flutes undulated beneath the hidden canopy. One by one, ghostly figures encircled the firelight, dark bodies illuminated with white painted patterns, chanting and swaying in rhythmic dance.

"What are they doing?" David asked, unhinged.

"Invoking Diva, their Creator … giving thanks for your return to this world."

David's face was troubled. "I didn't know I left," he said.

Doc turned toward the new initiate to explain the unexplainable. "The Moksha believe that after death a spirit travels to other worlds, seeking knowledge and wisdom, and if it should choose an Earthly return, it is to help those still here on life's journey. It would seem you have returned for a greater purpose, my friend," he said, patting David's back reassuringly.

David wasn't so reassured.

"And what's with the body paint?" he asked, nodding towards the ghostly figures.

"A sign of respect—like putting on your Sunday best when attending church," Doc said, his mischievous grin evocative of a gum-chewing-altar boy.

David appreciated Doc's attempt at levity, but what he needed most now was some distance from it all. It wasn't that he felt threatened, but he was more than a bit uneasy with the undefined role he was now expected to play. His salvation presented itself on the outskirts where firelight melded into shadow. There the familiar duo, Ramon and Bruno, stood feet spread and arms crossed, as David excused himself and made his approach. Taking comfort in the safety of numbers, he eased himself between them.

"Where have you two been?" he asked Ramon.

"Collect medicine plants for Senhor Doc," he answered.

David's body language didn't escape Ramon. "No need worry," he said, having travelled this road with Doc before. "Dance end soon. Everybody eat."

David could only hope. He cast a cautious glance back at the fire where, oblivious to ritual formalities, the children cawed and hopped, casting bird-like shadows into the firelight. Their innocent play made him smile, loosening his tension-rod shoulders.

Viper spied David watching. Breaking from his friends, he ran up to the tall man and took hold of his hand. Within David's large palm he placed a small crystal, wrapping David's long fingers around it. David didn't know what to make of it. He opened his hand to examine the gift, smooth and clear, but when he looked up, the dance had ended—and Viper was gone.

The nuts and berries David popped into his mouth did little to appease his hunger; it was the wafers made from Pran that quelled his aching belly and calmed his busy brain. Satisfied, he reclined next to the fire. His head felt clearer now. The jungle's mysterious grasp over his attentions had finally relented to its competition … *Rose,* he thought. Strange how she had deserted his mind, quietly slipping out its back door when only days earlier she had consumed it. There was a sense of guilt in this acknowledgment. David loved Rose, and he could feel his body arouse now just thinking of her. But he had been haunted by Lanya—it was different with her; and although he couldn't put to words his feelings, he would later understand she had aroused his soul.

David yawned and surrendered his eyelids under the weight of sleep. He was tired and looking forward to getting home, although he knew there would be no rest for him there. Nick's cancer was yet another mountain to climb. And though Doc had promised his help, David wasn't counting on a miracle. He thought about Pran and his mentor's ludicrous theory linking it to the tribe's good health. *Doc seems so certain,* he thought. Perhaps five years in the rain forest does something to a man—the scientist who once demanded empirical proof now freely acknowledging a sixth sense.

"David." He heard his name as in a dream and opened his eyes. Doc loomed over him. "Come," the old man said, "it's time."

"Time for what?" he asked wearily and, taking Doc's extended hand, arose.

A smile, wide like a ravine, cracked Doc's face. "A rendezvous with Nirvana," he said.

19

DEMON COUNTRY

Wednesday, August 27, 1997

ROXY CAPPED HER PEN and closed her journal, yet another day's entry recorded—her life spelled out in Ouija board fashion, hand moving as though possessed across the page. Rose had encouraged her daughter's nightly routine believing that writing, like painting, speaks to truth—and truth is liberating. Well, the light of day may hold Roxy's daytime demons at bay, but a stronger shield than words is needed in her darkest hours of night.

She peered over at Megan, her still body basking in the glow of a lamp perpetually lit between their beds. Seemingly in peaceful slumber, Roxy studied her roommate's face—brow smooth and facial muscles relaxed. She wished the same for herself and rolled over, her back to Megan and her poster boys grinning down at her. She envied those for whom sleep came without thought. Roxy, however, gave much thought to sleep and, in her case, deemed it an opportunistic window for demons to invade her dreams. And though her battle to stave off slumber would eventually give way to heavy eyelids, she refused to yield outright. Restless, she rolled over to face Megan again and considered tomorrow's double date. The last several days had proven unsuccessful in her tedious attempts at convincing Megan to attend sessions; and she knew that it wouldn't be unlike her roommate to bow out again come tomorrow night. A backup plan was needed.

Roxy wasn't above coercion if it came to that. Nothing heavy-handed, just a gentle reminder of the growing debt Megan owed her: for the absence excuses she made up to the professors; for the class notes she took and shared; and for the daily food runs she made to avert starvation because her roommate refused to leave their room. But after some thought she opted for a less confrontational approach. Megan once spoke of owning a horse, a gift from her parents as a companion for a child on an isolated island. Perhaps dangling the carrot of a visit to her grandfather's horse ranch might convince her if she conceded to the double date. Content with her plan and beyond weary, Roxy's lids slammed shut, along with any further thoughts on tomorrow. She was in demon country now.

★★★

Roxy moaned and woke with a start, rubbing her father's tormenting image from her eyes. She quickly looked over at Megan and breathed a sigh of relief not to have awakened her roommate, her tranquil face still aglow in the lamplight. It was a small miracle, if such things exist. Roxy doubted it but thanked the heavens just the same, because she wasn't ready to explain her nocturnal behavior just yet.

The clock read 1 a.m. She sat upright, exhausted from fighting sleep like a toddler afraid of the dark. But toddlers eventually grow up and put their childish fears aside; Roxy's boogeyman, however, matured right along with her. Quietly, she got up and dressed, plumping her pillows under the bedcovers to simulate her body, and then tiptoed to the door, closing it softly behind her.

Roxy stepped out from the dorm into the darkness of a moonless sky, a cool breeze tousling her hair and clearing her mind. She tucked her flyaway tresses behind her ears and shoved her hands into her jacket pockets, casting furtive glances as she navigated the shadowy, tree-lined walkway. Ahead in the darkness, the library's dimly lit interior cast it aglow like a candle-lit pumpkin. As she neared its entrance Roxy stopped short, eyes wide, and watched as a dark shadow rose up from its steps.

"Roxy," her name sang out on the breeze. "Didn't know you were a night owl," the shadowy image said, taking a final drag of cigarette before squelching the glowing stub with his foot on the ground.

"Zach," she said, relieved, "it's you."

"Last time I checked," he laughed, descending the steps to meet her. "What are you doing out at this hour?"

"Insomnia," she lied.

"Me too. A drag, isn't it? And even worse, I have early morning classes. Sucks being a freshman." He reached into his jacket pocket, retrieved a pack of cigarettes and tapped the open end against his palm. Two poked out. "Like one," he offered.

"My mother calls them cancer sticks," she said.

"Mine calls them coffin nails." He smiled. "Doesn't stop me."

Roxy smiled back, hesitant. Then took one.

Zach flicked his lighter near her face. "First time?" he said, his smile sexy. "Don't worry, I'll be gentle."

Roxy lightly punched his shoulder and, with a nervous giggle, tucked the cigarette between her lips.

Zach bent over her, cupping his hands around the lighter in the breeze, her face glowing. He could have kissed her just then, cigarette and all, wanted to, but lit the cigarette instead.

Roxy took her first drag, envisioning herself a latter-day Rita Hayworth with her long-handled smoke. But it went nothing like on the gilded screen—her lungs convulsing into a coughing fit.

Zach couldn't help bursting with laughter. And though it was at her expense, Roxy didn't mind, laughing through her hacking, too.

"Don't feel like you have to," he said at last, his voice under control.

Roxy, turning serious, looked him straight in the eye and put the cigarette back between her lips. This time round she got the hang of it, blowing smoke in his face.

"Glad your first time was with me," he teased, grinning.

Roxy punched his shoulder again and grinned back.

"I'm looking forward to our double date tomorrow night," he said.

"And Paul?" Roxy asked between puffs.

"Are you kidding? It's all he's been talking about. But who, exactly, is this "sister-of-sorts" date you hooked him up with, anyway?" he said, lighting up a smoke of his own.

"My roommate, Megan O'Malley."

Exhaling, Zach watched the smoke wending on the breeze. "You mean the girl who hasn't answered roll call since the start of orientation?"

"She's the one."

"Something wrong with her?"

"No," Roxy said defensively, "she's just a little shy."

"Shy is she? Well then, she has nothing to worry about. Talking's Paul's forte … especially about himself," Zach laughed.

A strong wind kicked up. Roxy shivered. Zach moved in and put his arm around her shoulders.

"I should be getting back," she said, taking a step forward and undraping herself.

"I'll walk you," he said, undaunted.

As they headed back up the walkway, the whirring wind rustled the leaves. "What's the battle of the bands like," Roxy asked, flipping her jacket collar up.

"Really cool," Zach enthused. "Five bands battle for the audience's top pick. Competition can be fierce. But if you like rock, you're in for a good time," he said. "Oh, and don't worry about IDs to get in—I've got it covered."

Roxy looked at him, her eyebrow a questioning arch.

"The venue serves alcohol—need to be 21," he explained.

She was okay with that but thought it best not to make mention to Megan, lord knows how she'd react. "No problem," she said, exhaling her cigarette like a pro. "Sounds like fun."

"Great!" Zach said, as they arrived at her dorm. "Paul and I will swing by at seven."

Roxy inhaled one last drag, flicked the cigarette to the ground and stomped it out as if second nature. "Perfect," she said, exhaling. Then, leaning in, she pecked Zach's cheek, scurrying up the steps and into the building before he knew what hit him.

★★★

Journal Entry, Wednesday, August 27, 1997:

Zach … what to do about you? My heart skips whenever you're near— but I can't allow that to happen. Ever. I made a promise.

20

NIRVANA

Wednesday, August 27, 1997

A WHOLE DAY ... gone, although it had seemed like an eternity when David finally came to. His head was heavy and his brain foggy, his stare straight ahead, fixated on the coiled fibers of mosquito netting splayed about him. His consciousness registered a background of chattering wildlife and the heavily saturated scent of vegetation mixed with humidity. He could sense a parallel world pulling him back, familiar and yet separate from the one his memory now clung to. He resisted parting from a place that permeated his being with such ferocity of belonging. But alas, fight as he might, his return was certain.

"Welcome back," came the familiar voice.

David's blurred vision locked onto Doc's hovering face.

"You've been on quite a trip, son. Take it slow," Doc said.

"Doc," David croaked, his mouth dry and tongue numb.

"Don't try to talk just yet. Here," he said, propping David's head up and tipping a cup of water to his lips. "Sip slowly," he urged. "The effects will wear off in a few hours. Don't fight it—just enjoy the ride while it lasts."

David tried moving but his legs held firm, the weight of reality trapping him once again. Thoughts swarmed in his head, flashing images of two worlds competing with one another for possession of his mind. It was out of his control. Resigned, David gave himself over to the struggle. *Let the best man win,* he thought, sinking back into his hammock.

***

The darkness seemed a balm between David's two worlds as he made his way toward the glow of the fire.

"What's for dinner? I'm starved," he said, stepping one wobbly foot in front of the other.

"Other-worldly travel seems to do that," Doc said. "Come. Sit."

"If my legs let me," David said, carefully lowering himself, crossing one shaky leg under the other, Indian style. He pocketed a few nuts into his mouth and, chewing, accepted Doc's flask. He took one swig and with surprised indignation, said, "What's this?" not expecting water.

Doc cracked a wry smile. "It's not good to mix your drinks," he said, alluding to Livingston's Pran potion, of which David had ingested twenty-four hours earlier.

David's appetite was voracious. Doc waited, enduring his counterpart's fete, watching him eat as if it were his last meal, only with more gusto, until Doc could hold his patience no longer. "So what did you think of the potion?" he finally blurted out.

David wiped his mouth with the back of his hand. "Beyond imagination, Doc—far beyond," he said, his voice trailing off into silence, embarrassed to give further utterance to the lunacy of his thoughts.

A self-satisfied look alighted Doc's face. He knew the only way David would understand was to experience the potion himself. "Go on," he prodded.

David closed his eyes, hoping against hope that when he opened them all would be gone. But it was not to be. Doc wasn't going anywhere, and neither was the memory of what had happened. He caved.

"It was like with Lanya in the pool under the falls," he said, "only more intense—a feeling of complete and utter belonging … at one with my surroundings, yet separate. Sounds crazy, I know. It is crazy. Forget it," he said, feeling foolish.

"It's not crazy," Doc said. "You experienced a sixth sense—what the Moksha call the invisible thread."

"The what?" David said.

"The invisible thread … the interconnectedness of all things. It's their belief that an invisible thread connects all of creation—each individual part linked together to form the whole," Doc said. "At first I considered this myth pure bunk until, like you, I experienced the waterfall with Lanya and then Livingston's potion. Since then, I've been doing a lot of thinking about interconnectedness, and here's the thing. In each of these cases, both of us experienced a temporary, altered state of mind. But the Moksha … they live permanently in an altered state of mind—day in, day out. They don't need potions to go there—they are there. How is this possible? My theory: their ingestion of Pran over the centuries not only spawned the removal of aggression from their gene pool but also heightened their sixth-sense abilities and their resultant level of interconnectedness. But," Doc paused, "the big bonus of this mutation? … Fear no longer exists."

David's face read skepticism.

"Hear me out," Doc said, holding up both hands. "Since the dawn of man, what keeps us alive? Fear. It gets our adrenaline pumping in response to predators, prepares our bodies for fight or flight. But if fear can spur an aggressive response in our bodies, it only makes sense that the reverse should hold true … remove aggression from the mix, and you short circuit fear. And when individuals no longer fear for self-preservation, a shared spirit of cooperation can then take hold … people can concentrate on doing what is best for all, which translates into a more connected society."

David mulled over Doc's words. "Your theory has a huge hole in it," he declared.

Doc raised his eyebrows. "Go on."

"You said it yourself … fear has kept us alive. How, then, is it possible to live in a jungle and exist without fear?"

"It's all in how you look at it," Doc said. "It's not that the Moksha are desensitized to danger, they just view it differently. Without fear, their interconnectedness has given rise to a heightened awareness. They live in the now with a view toward the positive. All life is treated with great respect—no life is ever taken, not even if it means their own."

David opened his mouth to protest, but Doc cut him off.

"Think back to our first encounter with Livingston, his felling of the jaguar with a poisonous dart—a seemingly aggressive act you'd say?

You remember how he removed the dart from the stricken animal and then stood and simply walked away. Did you ever wonder why he left the jaguar behind? It's because the animal wasn't dead—just sedated. Understand something. The Moksha exist on nuts and berries and grains of Pran; they have no need to kill animals. This poisonous shoot served one purpose only—to protect and preserve both lives."

"But surely there are times when the animal prevails," David argued.

"Absolutely, a badly aimed or ill-timed dart could conceivably miss its mark—unfortunately, that's what helps to keep the Moksha population down."

"Yeh, I guess that would be so, considering they never get sick," David said, his sarcasm intended.

Doc let out a long sigh. "Look, David," he said, "I know you think my theory's a stretch, but when you think about it, it makes perfect sense: When you eliminate aggression you eliminate fear; when you eliminate fear you eliminate negativity; and when you eliminate negativity you eliminate disease. In other words, when fear can no longer pollute mind and body with negativity, people don't get sick. The Moksha are living proof; we just need to connect the dots."

David considered his dear friend and mentor who now asked the impossible of him. But asking the impossible, he knew, was Doc's forte.

"Okay, Doc, I'll humor you," he said, "but on one condition."

"Name it."

"No more theories."

Doc cracked a shit-eating grin.

21

THE PAINTING

Wednesday, August 27, 1997

IT WAS WITH A fury that his brush moved, right up to the final stroke. Breathless, he took a step back, and then another, and even then, it was not far enough. He strode to the back of the room. And when he turned and faced his work, the ceiling-to-floor canvas overwhelmed him—and so did his tears.

He had given his all, every ounce, to the painting—and now nothing was left in him. He just stood there, empty, eyes riveted to the canvas—his essence glaring back at him entrapped in the oils … rage and fury in oranges and reds.

Nick closed his eyes. He wanted to forget, but that would never be possible. He could still hear their screams.

Her hand rested gently on his shoulder. "It needs a name," Rose said. "Label it and then let it go."

If only it were that easy, he thought. Life had never been that easy and letting go of the past futile, but the resoluteness in her voice urged him on.

"Injustice," he said, the word spewing forth indignant from his lips. It had all been so unfair, after all, what had happened in his life.

"Yes. Injustice," Rose repeated, her grasp of his shoulder firm now, the two of them staring down the painting as if mere eyes could will the transfer of pain. After a long moment of silence Rose spoke. "Come," she said. "There is someone I want you to meet."

Too weary to question her motives, Nick did as told, trailing her out from the sunroom.

The two rode silently in her car through the back roads of Cambridge into Harvard Square. Down a narrow street Rose pulled up curbside along a brick-fronted building with three glass windows—a natural frame for the oil paintings displayed within. Above, the building's signage read: Art is Life. She turned off the engine and looked over at Nick. "Come into the gallery with me," she said, smiling. The two exited her car, Rose taking hold of his arm as they entered the building together.

First-time visitors always found the foyer startling—a cantilevered balcony vaulting a brightly lit space two stories down. But even more startling today was the added commotion soaring up from the building's belly, immediately drawing Nick and Rose's attention over the railing. Below, a row of twelve abandoned easels had been knocked helter-skelter, their attached canvases thrown askew, while a cluster of riotous young men shot belligerent profanities and punches at one another.

Though Rose wasn't green to the roughneck behavior now on display having witnessed it before, she still cringed at the vulgarity and brutality and hoped that it wouldn't negatively color Nick's first impression of Michael's boys. But then, he'd have to know what he'd be up against if all went according to her plan.

"Boys, boys, break it up," a man's baritone voice soared over the din. "Come now … let's be civil," he continued, stepping between two ruffians and pulling them apart. "Everyone knows the drill—shake hands and then get this place cleaned up." More cusses followed, and then everyone did as told. A minute later, the belittling banter would resume.

From above, Rose recognized the man behind the baritone voice and felt a tingle course her body. Just then, he looked up.

"Rose!" he shouted. The robust man with a sun-bleached goatee and bandana-wrapped hair flew past the hooligans and on up the open staircase, his smile and arms ever-widening as he neared her. "Is it really you?" he asked, his embrace lifting her off of her feet and spinning her around before planting her softly back down. "Let me look at you," he said stepping back, his hands sliding down her arms to cup her fingers. "Why, you're more beautiful than ever!"

Rose allowed her gaze to rest in the soft, gray sanctuary of his eyes and her hands to linger in the warmth of his touch. "It's wonderful to see you again, Michael," she said, her cheeks aglow.

Feeling like a third wheel, Nick shifted uncomfortably and dug his hands deep inside his pant pockets.

"Michael," Rose said, regaining her focus, "this is the young man I spoke to you about … Nick Bennett."

Caught off-guard by her statement, Nick stared at Rose.

"Nick, I'd like you to meet Michael Campo," she said, "a very dear friend of mine."

"I've been looking forward to our meeting, Nick," Michael said, his extended hand clasping the teen's with a firm grip. "Sorry for the brouhaha," he said, his groomed goatee nodding along with his chin toward the renewed mayhem below. "Please, come into my office where we can hear ourselves talk," he said, steering them away from the ruckus.

Boxes of art supplies overflowed the room. Michael cleared the clutter from two chairs and transplanted it onto his desktop. "Sorry for the mess, but I haven't had time to breathe, let alone organize. Please … have a seat."

The two guests sat down.

Nick's stomach was tied up in knots. Even as a kid he never liked surprises, and now the uncertainty of this visit was killing him, his legs bouncing in a ceaseless tic.

Michael headed for the cooler. "I'm afraid water is the only sanctioned beverage on the premises. Although," he said, "as you probably noticed, my boys aren't for want of stimulant." He laughed, filling a paper cup and extending it to Nick.

My boys? Nick thought as he gratefully accepted the water, his throat gone dry.

"None for me, thank you," Rose said, graciously waving hers off.

Michael gulped her drink.

"Okay now," he said, crumpling his cup and pitching it into the wastebasket, "let's get down to business." He propped himself onto the edge of his desktop, careful not to topple the clutter, and directed his gaze at the young man seated across from him. "Nick, I suppose you're wondering why Rose brought you here," he said. "Well, to answer that question, let me first tell you the story of how I came to be here." He cleared his throat.

"It all began five years ago when a friend of mine, a probation officer working within the Connecticut Juvenile Court System, walked into my art studio with a very intriguing proposition. He told me about the troubled kids he dealt with, and how not long into the job it became clear to him that placing kids in detention did little to change behavior. He was convinced that, as an alternative, community service was the road to rehabilitation. It took some time for his idea to garner traction, but eventually Juvenile Court sanctioned a trial project: painting murals onto city walls. The experiment was twofold: to use art as a means for these kids to make restitution to their community and, more importantly, for them to be seen in a positive light by their community. The hope was, over time, community service would instill a positive self-image and in turn forge good behavior that would affect entire communities for the better. But," he said, taking a breath, "all of this starts with inspiration … and I was asked to be that inspiration.

"Now I assure you, mentoring was never an aspiration of mine, but life turns on a dime and here I am five years later spreading our program to Boston. And that's where Rose comes in." Michael glanced over and caught her smile.

'We first met three years ago at a charitable event in Connecti-cut. I call it a coincidence, but Rose calls it divine intervention." He laughed. "Anyhow, we started talking and realized how much we had in common—both of us artists and philanthropists involved in charitable pursuits. Over time, our friendship grew. But when Rose moved to Massachusetts … well, I was devastated to say the least; but then here we are coincidentally in the same neighborhood again," he said, beaming. "When I arrived, I called to let her know I was working here on a new project. And that's when she mentioned you, Nick. Rose seems to think you have much to offer the cause."

Nick was dumb struck, but Michael plowed on, not waiting for any response.

"On your way in you observed the programs first initiates—a thick-skinned bunch of kids … have to be to survive what life's thrown at them. On day one of the program each kid receives rudimentary instructions along with supplies. For most of them it's their first time in front of a canvas but, by the end of the program, it's remarkable what comes of it. You can see the transformation in their faces, the empowerment, because to create something is a powerful thing—it speaks to who you are. These kids come here labeled as troublemakers or worse. Most are lost. I believe opportunity is the difference between becoming good or bad. Here, they get the opportunity to believe in themselves, to build self-worth through pride in their work. They get a second chance at life—through art."

"Art is Life," Nick mumbled.

"Yes … I see you noticed our signage," Michael said grinning. "It's hardly original but true in sentiment. Some kids get it, some don't. But if only one kid turns his life around because of this program, it's worth it. That's what keeps me going. But enough about me," Michael said, his unnerving gaze now barreling down on Nick.

"Rose tells me you're a skilled artist, Nick, but more importantly, a passionate one. Passion gives rise to purpose. Unfortunately for the boys here, their passion for violence and guns has led to destructive rather than constructive purposes. That's where you come in. Nick, I hope you don't mind that Rose has told me of the challenges life has thrown at you, but she was convinced that because of them, you would be perfect for a mentorship position here. It would involve setting up shop alongside the boys, getting to know them and allowing them to know you—to observe your passion … your fearlessness of expression in putting it all out there on the canvas. And just maybe in the process something rubs off … maybe art helps them to overcome their hurdles in life, too. You see, it's easy to show bravado when a gun's in your hand, but you can show them an alternative, Nick—that it's possible, through art, to stand strong against adversity without having to reach for a weapon." Michael shifted his gaze to Rose, who nodded her approval, and then back to Nick.

"And any organizational skills you could lend wouldn't hurt either," he said, scanning the room's disarray with a self-deprecating grin.

Nick bit his lower lip and remained silent, his tongue tied and his legs still bouncing. He never saw this low branch coming. He knew Rose meant well, and he appreciated Michael's offer; but the thought of opening himself up to complete strangers sent him into a panic—being gay had always closeted such ideas. No, he just couldn't handle Michael's boys, along with everything else.

"Tell you what," Michael said, noting Nick's tongue-tying anxiety, "why don't you come back for a day or two next week and try things out. Give each of us a chance to get to know one another better and see if this mentorship position would be a good fit." Then Michael stood and shook the young man's hand. "It's been a pleasure meeting you, Nick."

Nick left with Rose, his knees still bouncing on the quiet ride home.

22

—·—

SPHATIKA

Thursday, August 28, 1997

TIME WAS GROWING SHORT, and David was getting antsy. He had already lost a day thanks to Livingston's potion, and now he was anxious to experience Moksha life firsthand.

"I've got some business to tend to with Ramon and Bruno, but Viper can show you around," Doc said, his arm draped about the youngster's slim shoulders. He winked at the eager boy, who returned his gesture with a look of adoration.

"Well then," David said, noticing the exchange, "whenever you're ready Viper, I'm all yours." The youngster bounded to the lead. David combed back his hair with his fingers and covered his head with his hat, winking at Doc as he followed.

Small in stature, David figured the boy's age for around eight, his lean body graceful and sure-footed on the tangled ground—a bit of his father, Livingston, in him for sure; but his eyes were his mother's, dark and disquieting like Lanya's. He was a confident youth, quite comfortable in occupying a latitude and longitude most adults would shudder to consider their home.

Shafts of morning light stretched fingerlike throughout the vegetation, enhancing the jungle's myriad shades of green to higher levels of vibrancy and, by extension, to David's spirit as well. He felt invigorated, up for just about anything, or so he thought, until the two came to a halt outside the community hut and Viper stood aside, bidding David enter. All his new-found energy drained in an instant as he considered who awaited within. But he had no choice—the young boy patiently standing by, bidding him to enter—he could not disappoint. David ducked his head clear of the thatched roofline and crossed the threshold. On the dirt floor before him, the women of the tribe sat about tending to the business of weaving. A gaggle of young, giggling girls stared up at the interloper, sprays of dried palm fronds piled high beside them. Some of the girls were separating the fronds into strips of fiber, twisting out fine threads with their fingers. Others dipped those strands into colorful dyes, laying them out to dry. Lanya sat among the women on the far side of the hut, handing down the art of pattern intricacies to her elder daughter, the two engaged in weaving a hammock. David was afraid to meet her eyes, still unsettled by the unexplained 'sights' she had led him to see, but her eyes lured his like a bad car wreck, his wanting to look away, but unable. Steeling himself, he made his approach.

"Beautiful," he said of the hammock's fine workmanship, stammering the word like a nervous schoolboy. Lanya smiled and stood, passing off the ball of string to her daughter who continued weaving where she had left off. With graceful stealth Lanya moved to retrieve one of several amulets dangling from a bamboo wall, and presented the small woven pouch to David, draping it about his neck.

Viper was quick to point out he wore one, too, and loosening the strings of his own, plucked from its innards a shiny object. "Sphatika," he said, cradling it in his palm. David recognized it at once.

"Ahh … quartz," he said, and reached deep into his trouser pocket for Viper's gift. "Sphatika?" he repeated, receiving an affirmative nod from the boy as he withdrew the small crystal and held it up like a communion wafer for all to see.

"Deva … here," Viper said, tapping the space between his own eyes with his crystal, his mother nodding agreement—their dark eyes probing his.

David had no idea how to respond, his words lost in limbo. *Where were Doc or Ramon when you needed them,* he thought, doing his best to fend off their magnetic stares. Viper intervened. "We go," he said suddenly, dropping his crystal back within his amulet and securing the strings. Grateful, David followed suit. Within seconds Viper was outside, David fast on the boy's heels, ready to follow him into a snake pit if it meant escaping Lanya's eyes.

The two nearly collided when Viper stopped short before a circle of children gathered around Livingston. The sinewy native was refining a newly made blowgun, the three-foot long weapon perched at a forty-five-degree angle between the notches of two wooden stakes. The little man's dark skin glistened as his arm muscles flexed with each forward thrust of a wooden ream down its bore. He kept ramming the rod down the hole, stopping every so often to fill his mouth with water and spitting it into the opening. Each time he added ever finer granules of sand before once again resuming the rhythm, the byproducts spilling out the lower end, polishing the bore.

"How long to make," David asked Viper, aware that the blowgun's manifestation didn't just happen overnight. "Moons," the boy said, holding up two fingers. *Two months,* he thought with incredulity as his curious, boyhood self longed to have witnessed the masterful work in the making—to have watched Livingston cut and plane two identical halves of palm wood with a stone ax, chisel a groove exactly down the center of each, glue the two halves together with beeswax and then wrap the entire length with a long strip of bark—but alas, David had not been present. Still, it amazed him—and even more so considering that, after all his effort, Livingston's blowgun would never be used to kill.

Wiping his brow with the back of his hand, Livingston paused to converse with his son. When done speaking, Viper nodded and stooped to retrieve one of several newly shaved darts from a pile. Nearby, erected over a wooden bowl, a large-funneled leaf filled with vine shavings and water oozed a dark liquid out the narrower end. "Liptaka," the boy said to David, pointing to the drippings before dipping the dart into the bowl.

"Poison," David muttered, taking a step back and immediately feeling embarrassed, though better embarrassed than dead. He was not unfamiliar with curare, a jungle poison-turned-drug employed during modern-day surgery as a muscle relaxant; but here in the jungle there were no regulations or oversight, and concentrated curare became deadly if it entered the bloodstream.

"Ahh, I found you," Doc said, sneaking up from behind, Ramon and Bruno shadowing him. "And from the look of things, not a moment too soon," he said nodding towards the poisonous dart, his face at first stern and then breaking into a grin as he watched David ebbing further back like a wave from shore. "Just kidding!" the old trickster laughed, patting

David's back. "Trust me; your life is in good hands. Livingston dilutes his poison—remember the jaguar?" he encouraged. Then he held out his arm to the boy. "Come," he said. "We must show David your favorite place." Viper returned the dart to its pile and led the way.

The strong smell of urine announced the primates well before their sighting. Lifting his chin and cupping his lips, Viper howled and then waited. The reply came within seconds, followed by another, and then another, until a barrage of monkeys clamored out from within the leafy canopy to investigate the intrusion of their sanctuary. Looking up, Viper laughed at the frenzied trapeze act of swinging vines brandishing the howling, hairy creatures. The boy teased the monkeys, mimicking their facial expressions and swaying arm movements, bantering back and forth as if carrying on a real conversation. By all accounts, it seemed the monkeys enjoyed his company as well, giving in to their showing off for his amusement. And it would seem to the casual observer no more than sheer antics on both their parts, but there was always more than meets the eye when it came to the boy—with Viper, things were never as they seemed.

The morning light gilded the canopy as the howlers carried on with their spectacle. Doc rested his mottled hands upon the boy's slender shoulders, a robust laugh escaping his lips. Looking up, David's grin was ear to ear. Even the normally stoic faces of Ramon and Bruno shared a look of amusement. But Viper paid no mind to the men, the vibrations of his thoughts now finding equilibrium with those of the monkeys. Cupping his lips one last time, he let out a blood-curdling howl. And like a curtain falling on their final act, the monkeys fell silent. Stunned, David's eyes met the boy's. *Impossible,* he thought. Viper just laughed and, as children do, bounded off to his next adventure. David stood there, speechless, the hairs down his neck standing at attention.

"Viper has a flair for theatrics," Doc said, placing a hand on David's shoulder. "No matter how many times I've witnessed it, the kid still gives me goose bumps."

David remained quiet, his face a distress beacon signaling S.O.S.

Doc resisted the call, saying only, "I can see you have questions, son, but anything I could say right now would fall short. The answers will come when you're ready to receive them." And offering no further explanation, walked off.

David called after him, "What the hell does that mean, Doc?" But his old friend just smiled and kept walking, trailing in the boy's footsteps back to the village.

Ramon sidled up to his charge. "Find answers with Sphatika," he said, pointing to David's amulet. Then placing his own finger onto David's middle brow said, "Open third eye."

If Ramon's advice was meant to help David, it didn't. "What are you talking about?" he said, gawking at Ramon like he was from another planet.

"Ramon no explain … Ramon show," he said. "Must go to cave."

The cousins bookended David as the trio veered back into the brush. The three amigos had come a long way together and David felt secure in their presence, though not so naive as to feel invincible. Caution had become his mantra on this journey, his sensory perception on perpetual high alert. It was an exhausting existence, though his one consolation at the end of the day was a guaranteed good night's sleep. Only, that would not be the case tonight.

The steep, downward grade wound the men about the base of a wooded hill. There, partly covered in brush and seemingly out of nowhere, a small cavity presented itself. Bruno unleashed his machete and chopped a clearing through to the cave's entry. Inside, several grass torches reclined against the earthen walls. Ramon flicked his lighter and lit the resin-coated brush of one and then, using that torch, lit two others, handing them off to each of his companions. With heads bent and bodies stooped, the three amigos entered the blackness as one unit of light, edging downward along the curving, dirt passage. The deeper their descent, the more the scent of dampened earth filled their nostrils as the moistened walls shimmered in the torchlight. Perhaps it was his imagination or just the darkness playing tricks with his eyes, but David swore something slithered over his foot. He held no fondness for snakes, but any apprehension on his part had little to do with reptiles and more to do with what awaited him at the bottom. Problem was, the cousins refused to reveal their destination, leaving him literally and figuratively in the dark, not to mention feeling vulnerable. And, of course, David hated feeling vulnerable.

The few intersections of tunneled passageways caused no panic for Ramon—seemingly familiar with each turn, he didn't hesitate in his choice of direction. David trusted Ramon. But even as a boy scout he had never been a huge a fan of caves, and now, he would have given anything for a spool of Lanya's twine to mark their way. Still, he was a trooper. Even when forced to crouch on his bottom through the tunnel's cramped confines, mud saturating his last pair of clean boxer shorts, he endeavored to remain positive … until a sobering thought sabotaged his outlook—he'd have to make it out of the cave alive for the state of his underwear to even matter. But as David struggled with his contrary mind and the never-ending descent of twists and turns, the bottom finally came up to meet him.

Single file, they followed Ramon as he illuminated torch after fiery torch planted along their pathway, like a sidewalk of glowing lampposts. It wasn't long before David saw them—for as far as their torchlight could carry—prisms sparkling in the darkness. "Quartz," he murmured to himself, amazed.

They meandered through the winding minefields of dripping growths protruding from ceiling and floor, some coming together in the middle, until ahead in the chamber's vastness, a giant pool of water reflected their torchlight like thousands of tiny mirrors on its surface. And as he drew nearer the water's edge, David's eyes widened. There, three crystal structures sat uniquely formed—in the shape of bowls.

Ramon stood over the middle bowl, the largest of the three, and turned to face David. "Have question? See answer," he said, tapping David's middle brow. And then lowering his hand over the drum-sized basin, he ran his fingers around its moist rim. Once. Twice. Half-way around the third revolution a vibratory note of incredible beauty emerged. He kept going, each revolution increasing in pitch, louder and louder, carried across the still waters and reverberating off the cavernous walls. Using both hands, he reached for the two outer bowls and did the same, alternating back and forth, playing all three basins like a musician in a band. And then the impossible seemed to happen. One by one, each of the cave's crystalized formations responded in kind, the entire cavern a synthesized symphony, energy transmitted and received, vibrating in perfect equilibrium.

David could feel a growing tremor on his chest. Instinctively, he reached for his amulet and removed the small crystal within. Ramon seized David's hand, raising the crystal to touch his charge's brow. When the crystal's smooth surface touched David's skin, his entire body shuddered, and then he fell back into Bruno's arms.

***

As twilight's shadow hovered over flora and fauna, millions of cicadas convened conversation; but the trio of weary spelunkers walked silently back to the village.

"Senhor David no talk," Bruno announced, the normally quiet cousin voicing concern for his charge and pretty much summing it up for Doc.

Over Bruno's shoulder Doc watched the palms sway and then splay apart, revealing his young counterpart leaning on Ramon for support.

"You set me up, Doc," David spat out at him as he emerged from the brush, his annoyance finally voiced.

"I admit it," Doc said, holding up his arms in surrender. "I arranged it with the boys."

"And then you saw fit to abandon me!"

"You were never alone, David … and you can't expect an old man like me to crawl through tunnels now, can you? Besides, you survived."

"I blacked out!"

"Perhaps I overestimated your readiness," Doc countered.

"My readiness?!"

"Tell me," Doc said, ignoring David's exasperation as he leaned in closer, his voice softening, "did you experience anything?"

"What? You mean like a ball of fire hurtling up my spine!" David barked, his face turning red.

"And?"

"And what? And nothing! I blacked out!"

Disappointed, Doc stepped back, muttering.

"What did you say?" David seethed.

Doc cleared his throat. "I said … perhaps your energy portals need flushing out."

"Flush out your own damn portals, Doc!" David erupted. "I'm not your guinea pig! And I'm tired of all this voodoo crap. That whole damn cave could have blown … and us in it!"

David was beside himself—frustrated at losing control over the situation, angry at Doc for his secretiveness, and desperate over his beloved mentor's threatened conversion to psychic persuasion.

"Trust me, David. Have I ever steered you wrong?" Doc asked, his voice conciliatory.

"You really don't want me to answer that," David said, exhausted, all his bluster sucked clean.

"Go rest," Doc said, not willing to push further. "We'll talk later."

★★★

David lay in his hammock not feeling in the least bit guilty for withholding information from Doc. He had, in fact, experienced something more before fainting—a vision—only, he didn't understand it. Too tired to think, he closed his eyes, his hands resting over his amulet. He could feel a small tremor within, like a cat purring on his chest, comforting as his mind drifted off to sleep.

Visions spun like film clips in his head—Ramon's fingers circling the bowls, shimmering waters, vibrating crystals—all the while hearing Ramon's words repeating over and over like some surreal scene in a horror flick: "Have question? … Have question?" David shifted uncomfortably in his sleep, the projector of his mind suddenly freezing on the final frame as its image burned up on the screen—the dream so real he could feel tongues of fire shooting up his spine. He cried out. And then a burst of brilliance reached the crown of his head and, once again, he saw it—a man clothed in a shimmering white robe—his last vision lingering just long enough to recall before bolting upright, awake in a sweat, with Ramon's words repeating over and over in his head: "See answer … See answer."

23

RIGHT ANSWER

Girl Flashback

"*S*HOW SOME STRENGTH, GIRL," *her father taunted with all of his menacing, shameless self-importance like the bully that he was. "Will you always be a weakling? Look me in the face, Girl! If you don't want to go, then tell me to piss off! Go on … do it!"*

What was an innocent nine-year-old child to do? Eugene was almost three times her size, a formidable foe, not ever likely to show leniency. She knew she was doomed with the wrong answer. This was just another of his petty confrontations around which her life revolved to make him feel significant. Didn't he have more important things to do than pick on a child? Of course he did, but this was so much more entertaining.

Girl had rubbed her father the wrong way, yet again, with her lack-luster enthusiasm for his suggestion, which really wasn't a suggestion but rather an order, to forego her plans with her mother to help with a church fundraiser and, instead, to accompany him to the library. This was not a venture with the intent of fun, heavens forbid. No, forget the Nancy Drew mysteries, Girl would be lugging home a satchel of boring textbooks on the democratic system of governing. Evidently, one was never too young to begin priming for a future office within the Republican Party.

But Girl was no longer herself, her mind already transposed to that of a teacher in high school, someone for whom the answers flowed with assured ease. She looked her father straight in the face and with a strong and fearless voice, said, "There's a time and a place for everything, Father. I can go with Mother another day."

Eugene didn't get the fight he was looking for. Grunting, he looked at his watch begrudgingly. "Never mind, Girl. We'll go another time," he said, having never intended to go in the first place. And just when she thought she was off the hook, Eugene said, "Instead, we can read from one of my volumes in my study." Still toying with her emotions, he enjoyed watching her shoulders slump. But then she straightened and held her head high. "Yes, Father," she said, another version of herself forming as an animal tamer in a circus, unafraid of the mounted deer heads on his study walls.

"Right answer," Eugene said.

24

DOUBLE DATE

Friday, August 29, 1997

T HE FOUR TEENS SQUEEZED through the boisterous crowd to a small table near the stage. The first band of the night was busy setting up, testing speakers and tuning instruments. A waitress hoisting a tray of sloshing beers zipped past, unyielding to Zach's call as she melded in again with the growing throng. The surrounding walls were black, the lighting low, and the floors sticky. It was by no means a club for the aesthetically inclined, but perfect for the indiscriminate college student.

Roxy looked over at Paul and Megan seated across the table. Paul was completely taken with Megan, leaning into her ear, consuming her attention. Megan remained polite, though her face looked strained. Thankfully, Paul had kept her a captive audience at the club's entrance, distracted from the bouncer manning the door and his seeming blindness to the Asian girls pictured on the fake id's Roxy had presented him. Now she could only hope that the loud music, rowdy crowd and flowing beer would supplant her roommate's inhibitions.

The waitress, finally corralled, bent near Zach's face, her voice raised over the din. "What can I get you?"

"Four drafts and some chips," he responded in kind.

She nodded and vanished back into the throng.

Zach removed a cigarette pack from his shirt pocket and leaned into Roxy. "Like one?"

Why not, she thought, and nodded.

He lit hers first, placing it between her lips, and then lit his own.

Megan observed from across the table. If Roxy's behavior surprised her, she didn't show it. Roxy thought about offering one to Megan, but in the short time she had known her roommate there was little doubt of her strait-laced character; and now, with Megan teetering on the edge of jumping ship, it was probably best not to rock the boat.

The waitress made a speedy return to their table, the overflow from four pilsners christening her tray and their unsuspecting bowl of chips. Zach instructed her to run a tab and then he and his underaged cohorts indulged in their first round of illegal brews.

The lights suddenly dimmed, and the room quieted as the emcee took to the stage, his open microphone humming. "I want to thank all of you for coming out tonight," he enthused, the spotlight directed on him. "We have a great show in store for you—a talented lineup eager to please—so don't be shy about showing your appreciation and support. And now, without further ado, everyone put your hands together and give it up for the night's first contender: The Mavericks!" Applause rang out, eclipsed immediately by the boom of drums and the shrill of electric guitars.

Megan winced at the sudden rise in decibels, though grateful for a reprieve from Paul's attentions. *It was a mistake to have come,* she thought. *How could I have been so stupid.* Her mind reeled in panic for a plausible excuse to leave. She had agreed to her date with Paul, a one-time fling she could later forget, to appease Roxy. Only, he had taken an interest in her; and worse, she liked him. The situation was impossible. She could never infer interest. She'd made a pledge. So now she needed to walk away before things went too far. Megan grabbed her purse and stood.

Roxy took one look at her roommate's face and knew Megan wasn't heading for the powder room. Roxy stood, too, casually making her way around the table with a calculated smile cast towards the boys, before latching Megan by the arm and guiding her from the room.

Roxy pushed open the ladies' room door and directed Megan in. A sickly-sweet floral freshener assailed their airways as Roxy scanned the stalls. All empty. She pulled Megan over to the far corner and said, "I'm not looking to hear an excuse." Lord knows she'd heard an earful since orientation. "Just answer me this," she said, her voice softening. "If you could choose anywhere in the world to live, where would it be?"

"Pardon me?" Megan said, confused.

"Come on. There must be some place you'd rather be than here, some place that speaks to your heart."

Megan didn't have to think twice. "Hawaii," she said.

"Hawaii, where your parents met?"

Megan nodded.

"Well, here's what I want you to do. It's a game I play when I'm anxious and afraid. I imagine I'm someone else living in a better place, and in my mind, I escape this awful moment and go there. And though fear surrounds me in the present, I don't flinch—because I'm no longer here." Roxy took Megan by the shoulders. "You think you can do that? Sit out there at that table and be someone else tonight, someone else at a club in Hawaii?"

The idea intrigued Megan. If she didn't have to be herself, if she could be someone else on a date with Paul, there'd be no pledge to honor. She could break free of her chains and let go of her guilt, if only for one night. "But I'd be a fraud," she lamented.

"Fraud's a harsh word," Roxy said, and leaned in closer. "Sometimes, in order to survive, one must refashion the truth. Trust me, Megan. Play the game."

The two held each other's gaze.

Lord knows I have the rest of my life to pay my debt … to be Megan O'Malley, the Irish lass thought, considering the proposition. *Why not play the game … just this once. Besides, I'll never see Paul again. What harm can it do.*

"Deal?" Roxy said.

"Deal."

"That's my girl. Now come on." Roxy grabbed Megan's arm and led her back out to the table.

The crowd was applauding the first band's performance as the girls retook their seats. Zach leaned into Roxy holding up four fingers. "Four out of ten," he shouted over the clamor. Evidently, she hadn't missed much. Roxy reached for her beer and took a gulp. She glanced at Megan across the table. Paul was breathing down her neck again, only this time she was smiling. Roxy smiled too and held up her beer. "To Hawaii," she toasted her roommate, and though her voice was muffled by the din, Megan read her lips and raised her glass. The boys caught the tail end of what was happening and, coming late to the party, hastily raised their glasses. The girls burst out laughing.

"What?" Paul said, flummoxed. "What's so funny?"

The girls laughed all the harder.

★★★

Journal Entry, Friday, August 29, 1997:

We all have monsters under our beds. Megan is paralyzed by hers. I can empathize. But tonight, she showed progress—baby steps really. She just needs time. I can give her that.

25

RAMATI

Friday, August 29, 1997

Morning broke to the pitter patter of rain drops splattering on leaves and the exuberant chirping of parakeets shaking their fine feathered bodies of the unexpected wetness showering them. David welcomed the concerto of sounds and wasted no time extricating himself from the confines of sleep to lift his face unto the soft drizzle. His sleep had been fitful, reliving his ordeal in the cave, and now it felt good just to stand with eyes closed and arms spread, embracing the rain and the resurrected life it breathed into the parched forest and, by extension, into him. It was an anointing of sorts, this watering of soil and soul—life once again trumping death, germination besting decay in the rain forest continuum.

"If you stand like that much longer, I'll have to take an oil can to you," Doc joked as he approached, Ramon and Bruno in lockstep.

David lingered a moment, a willing hostage to the inner stillness and surprise cleansing that nature had bestowed upon him, before opening his eyes and smiling.

"A passing shower … just a tease," Doc acknowledged with indifference, handing David his morning brew. "Grab some breakfast and finish up packing. We head out within the hour," he directed, before rushing off, never one to waste time.

The two cousins tarried. Ramon could tell his star pupil had had little rest. "In day, Senhor David chase dream; in night, dream chase Senhor David," he said knowingly. "Sphatika powerful. No wear when sleep …

no want busy mind." And then before departing he and Bruno clapped David on the shoulder, a well-earned declaration of camaraderie after yesterday's ordeal. David smiled as his friends walked away, knowing he owed them both big time.

In the rain-slicked forest, gathering droplets rolled off the canopy's umbrella and broke like water balloons below, splattering the column of marching men. Viper had been present for their early morning send off, receiving a bear hug from Doc and a mussing of his hair from David. But when it had come time for David to take his leave of Lanya, he struggled, completely unprepared for their final meeting of eyes—a flickering of unexplainable recognition caught somewhere between space and time, knowing that their paths would cross again. Perhaps goodbyes were folly, then. Unsure and confused, he simply smiled and then dared not look back.

Livingston took the lead through the forest mist. Trailing him, Doc brushed aside the wet, clinging fingers of fern as he glanced over his shoulder at David. Noticing his companion's knitted brow, Doc said, "A penny for your thoughts."

"I've been thinking about when we first ran into Livingston … how lucky we were he appeared when he did," David said, the jaguar's image still chiseled in his mind.

"Luck had nothing to do with it. He knew we were coming," Doc said, the truth of his statement as firm as his step. "Each of my past visits to the Moksha has been met by Livingston's mysterious arrival, always coming to my aid with precision timing."

"You make him sound like Superman … minus the cape," David said, half joking, half serious, with a touch of sarcasm thrown in for good measure—unsure what to believe anymore.

"I told you … the Moksha have a sixth sense about things. I have a theory …"

"Doc, stop … you promised," David reprimanded, all joking aside now. He was struggling enough already to process all that had happened—not to mention questioning his sanity—he didn't need to add to his confusion.

"I have a theory," Doc continued, ignoring the rebuke. "Although not yet discovered, I believe we're all born with a psychic gene, only for most of us our abilities are either limited or completely hidden in the pathways of our brains. But with the Moksha, their psychic pathways are open and fully activated. Perhaps the more connected one is, the more one's psychic abilities are developed. In any case, Livingston knew where to find us."

"So you're telling me Livingston's clairvoyant … next I expect you'll claim he's a mind reader."

Doc flashed David a wicked grin.

"Just forget I mentioned it," David said, rolling his eyes. Three days with the Moksha had besieged David's analytical mind with all kinds of questions and doubts. And it didn't help, either, that his partner in crime seemed to be defecting to the other side. But his inner turmoil, if anything, made him more determined to find a rational reason for all he had experienced. David knew things would be different once he got back home, back to the normalcy of his life and the regiment of his work where he could think more clearly and sort things out, make sense of it all. He would find the answers and, if not … he would at least find Rose.

God knows he missed her. He wondered what she was doing this very moment and was kicking himself for leaving her so long. How he yearned to hold her in his arms, gaze into those beautiful eyes and kiss those tender lips. Only a fool would have given that up; only a fool would have chanced someone else stepping in to take his place. David's heart raced at the thought, and all at once it crystalized—he had to get home. Now, weary of the jungle more than ever, he wanted out.

Suddenly the wet and ancient forest filled with sunlight, and David's gloom dissipated along with the mist. He stopped dead in his tracks, evicted from his thoughts by the spectacle before him—a sea of tall, white blooms stretching skyward, the air awash with their sweet perfume. He knew the scent, his hand reaching for the string of blossoms now absent from his neck.

"The Moksha call this garden Ramati … Paradise," Doc said, his outstretched arm encircling the sacred plants. "Legend has it that Deva first appeared here bearing the gift of Pran and its promise of mystical insight," he explained.

David watched Livingston wade into the tall white mass, the plants as high as the man. *Paradise?* he thought. Nothing came close to paradise anywhere he'd ever been. And as beautiful as this garden was, he felt it lacking. Perhaps paradise was more than a place … more than these plants.

Livingston ran his fingers through the blooms of these unorthodox plants, culling their seeds into his palm and pocketing them within a rolled leaf, and then repeating the procedure, except this time brushing under the leaves and culling their spores. It was a practice of generations past, handed down from the adult to child—a vital link to their existence and Creator. He tucked the bundles under his arm and, reappearing, presented his gifts to David with a silent and respectful nod. Then, steering clear of the garden called Paradise, Livingston took up the march once again, his entourage in close pursuit.

David's days with the Moksha were coming to an end, and he was leaving with more questions than answers. Though his Sphatika had provided a vision in the cave—an image of a man in a shimmering white robe—it had made no sense. Not that much had made sense lately, including his feelings about Livingston. Perhaps it was a false security, one he would never admit to Doc, but David liked having this fearless leader around. And the idea that in a few short hours Livingston would take his leave, well, the very thought made him cringe—the wiry, little man had saved his life twice, after all, not some trivial fact. And it was also fact that David felt beholden, though Livingston required nothing of David save his friendship.

And so their arrival at the river crossing where Livingston had first appeared was greeted with mixed emotions as David bid his new-found friend goodbye. Livingston grasped the tall man's arms. "David walk with Moksha," he said. Rather than debate opinion, David acquiesced with a nod. What response could he give to a statement like that, anyway? But as he watched Livingston's backside disappearing through the foliage, the little man's words rattled in his bones.

26

DEPRESSION

Saturday, August 30, 1997

NICK HADN'T COME OUT of his house in days, the shades drawn from morning to night, and no signs of life. Rose had ventured to communicate numerous times—the front doorbell always ignored and phone calls gone unanswered. She had been so certain he was ready to move on with his life when she took him to meet Michael Campo, though in hindsight now she realized that her timing had been off. How could Nick possibly help others when he wasn't yet ready to help himself. She had pushed him too soon. Now she felt responsible and deeply worried. He was obviously depressed. *What if he tried to hurt himself?* she thought. David was in Brazil and of no help. Maybe she should break in? Call the police? *Calm yourself,* she thought. *Wait for Roxy.* Her daughter was expected home for the weekend. Maybe, somehow, she could reach out to the young man. Rose prayed so.

***

Roxy rang the bell of the stately colonial. She tried peering through the door's sidelight windows, but it was dark within, and she saw nothing. She banged the knocker and shouted Nick's name. Still no response. Not about to give up, she descended the front steps and made her way around to the back of the house. She was curious. From her property, the Bennett's back yard was shielded by fencing. Now she would finally get to see their secret garden. She traversed a stepping-stone path to an arbored gate climbing with white roses and buzzing with bees collecting sweet nectar. She pushed it open with purpose and passed through, only to halt in her step at a sight so compelling it begged to be admired: colorful flower beds wrapped by lush, manicured lawns; hideaway nooks nestled with bayberries and rod iron seating; Japanese maples strung with hand-painted bird houses and lanterns; and tucked in the far corner of the lot—a surprising, miniature greenhouse. Roxy walked towards it, her image reflected in its glass and growing larger as she approached. All was quiet, save for the tinkling of wind chimes dangling on delicate dogwoods. And then within the greenhouse a shadow moved. She paused, waiting to see if her eyes had deceived her, but it moved again. Without thinking Roxy proceeded to its glass door, propped open by a pot of forget-me-nots, and stepped inside. It was hot and stifling, a paltry flow of air whirring from a portable fan. The back of her neck dampened, and a smell of moistened earth filled her nostrils as if after a spring shower. All along the glass walls, rows of metal shelving displayed colorful plantings of all shapes and sizes, with the center of the room anchored by a hefty wooden table. But it was the figure adjacent to it that caught her attention. There, Nick stood bent over a clay pot, filling it with soil.

As if the hot air could sense a disturbance, or the plants had murmured to him of her presence, he turned his head slowly towards her. Roxy smiled. He smiled back. She walked to his side. Nick gently took her hand, his damp fingers transferring clinging brown fragments of dirt with a seedling to within her palm, then gave her the pot. She planted the seedling, covering it with soil. Then, side by side in the sunbaked, glass house, they moved on to the next.

27

— · —

THE WAITING GAME

Saturday, August 30, 1997

AFTER PARTING WAYS WITH Livingston, the troop advanced much in silence, the day hot and the mosquitoes biting. But David had made peace with the dichotomy that surrounded him—the bugs and butterflies that equally annoy and dazzle. He had even come so far as to accept his blistered feet and overtaxed muscles as the necessary cost of breaching these wondrous and ancient woods.

It was an hour before sunset when the men descended upon a rock-strewn river. Dinner on their minds, Ramon and Bruno each fashioned spears from bamboo and took up their positions—standing like Colossus with legs apart and feet planted onto rocks, the river running between, as they prepared to skewer piranha. And while the cousins bantered back and forth with good-natured sparring over each other's prowess, Doc wandered downstream alone. David watched him go. The two hadn't spoken much since their break with Livingston. Perhaps David felt the need for concentration over conversation now that the weight of survival rested more heavily on his shoulders; or possibly he couldn't bear the scrutiny of Doc's inquiring eyes for answers he did not have; or maybe he blamed Doc for his fogginess in judgment where once clarity stood. Perhaps it was all three.

"Got one!" Ramon yelled, lifting his spear high in triumph, the impaled creature unmoving. But Bruno was not to be outdone, staking two consecutive piranhas onto his spear within seconds. David looked on, amused; and when he peered back over his shoulder for Doc, he was nowhere to be seen. That's when they all heard it—a gunshot. The three bolted toward the sound.

"Doc," David yelled, the blood rushing loud in his head as he lumbered from rock to rock downstream, the encroaching brush blocking the possibility of any overland passage. Outpaced and outmaneuvered, the youthful Ramon and Bruno leap-frogged down river on past him, disappearing around the bend.

"Senhor David," came Ramon's shout seconds later, "over here!"

Twenty feet into a clearing they found Doc's body slumped against the trunk of a palm tree, his rifle clasped within his hands and the colorful fragments of a coral snake scattered about his feet.

Catching up, David surveyed the scene. It didn't look good.

"It was hidden under the leaves. Apparently didn't like being stepped on," Doc said, his concern masked with attempted sarcasm. "The damn bugger latched onto my leg like Fido on a bone—only released after I shot it."

Ramon knelt to examine Doc's leg. He was familiar with coral snakes, whose small mouths and short fangs take longer to deliver venom, latching on to their prey with a chewing motion while biding their time. Observing the puncture marks above Doc's boot and aware that half the time coral snakes strike but deliver no venom, attacking only to scare predators away, he said with some encouragement, "Sometime dry bite but no take chance. Ramon get anti-venom from backpack."

"Ramon, wait," Doc said, looking pale. "You won't find it there," he said, somewhat embarrassed. "I forgot it back at the lab."

"You did what?" David exploded. "Why didn't you say something? We could have gone back for it!"

"We were already two days in when I realized it, and I wasn't about to turn around. Besides, I've been in this jungle for five years and never had a need for it," Doc said.

"Well, you have a need for it now!" David admonished, anger masking his fear for his beloved friend and mentor.

"Senhor Doc, no move," Ramon ordered, though they all knew that was futile advice because if the poison was indeed in him, any movement would merely hasten his certain death.

Doc closed his eyes for a few moments of anguished contemplation, failing to stifle the grimace on his face with each breath taken. "David," he said, finally opening his eyes, his face serious, "there are some things we need to discuss … in case I don't make it."

"We can talk later," David objected, rejecting the possibility. But Doc would hear none of it.

"Just listen," he said. "When you get back, start that kid brother of yours on low doses of Livingston's potion, slowly working up to full-strength. Administer it at night so he can function during the day. Observe his mood. If my theory's correct, his depression will diminish as his aggression gene mutates and his white blood cell count improves. From that point on, my friend," Doc smiled, "Nick's days of living with cancer are numbered. But, whatever you do," he warned, "don't breathe a word of this to anyone—not to his doctors, and certainly not to General Rand."

David's eyes widened.

"Oh yes, if I die, he'll most certainly come calling," Doc said. "You can count on it. But he mustn't catch wind of Nick's treatments. Better to keep the kid out of it."

David wasn't about to argue, not with a seventy-year-old man possibly on his death bed. But he knew that if push came to shove with Rand, without question his little brother took precedence over Big Brother. "Okay Doc, mums the word," he said, hoping against hope that the old boy would pull through.

"Look in my backpack," Doc instructed. "You'll find a satellite phone … compliments of Rand. Call him. Let him know the situation. And one more thing," he said, as David turned to go. "I want you to promise me you'll look after the farm. I haven't spent five years of sweat in this mosquito-laden factory to have my work go for not. Promise me!"

David promised, though he hadn't the slightest idea how the business ran, let alone the medicinal knowledge of the farm's herbal plants. But if Doc could cling to breath, he could cling to the hope that he wouldn't need to know.

Satisfied, Doc rested his head back against the tree, closed his eyes and exhaled a long, slow breath. The waiting game was on.

David returned to the open river, grateful for a clearing in the canopy and hopeful not only for a strong signal to reach Rand but that there was something the general could do. He located Doc's backpack and retrieved the phone inside. Two numbers in permanent ink appeared on the handset, his and Rand's. He dialed Rand's number and mentally crossed his fingers. A voice answered, "Agent Jenks here."

"Agent Jenks …" David stammered, startled it wasn't Rand but relieved for the connection, "this is David Bennett."

"Well fuck me if you aren't just the man I came to see," Jenks said.

"Pardon me?" David said, his train of thought broken.

"I've traveled all the way to this God-forsaken jungle to meet you, Bennett. Where the hell are you?"

Exactly who this stranger was and why he would have traveled here to meet him, David had no idea. His mind reeling, he said, "Agent Jenks, I'm with Doctor Benjamin Shaw. He's been bitten by a coral snake and the anti-venom was left back at the farm."

"Well, if that isn't the old geezer's bad-fucking luck," Jenks scoffed. Dead silence followed.

"Is there anything you can do?" David angrily beseeched, put off by the man's rude indifference. "We're a day out at best."

"Realistically? If the venom's in him," Jenks said, his voice detached, "it's not likely he'll survive. Good luck, Bennett." And with that, the line went dead.

David was speechless. He stared at the phone in disbelief, not even sure this conversation happened. And then his anger turned to rage—rage at Jenks … rage at life. But it was, after all, just the nature of things—the fire that killed his parents, the cancer killing his brother, and now the snake bite that could kill Doc—but David was tiring of nature and tiring of helplessness. And though fear gnawed at his gut and made him want to vomit, he refused to bend the knee. He made his way back to where Doc lay and, gazing down upon his stricken friend, was sickened by the prospect of life without him. David had known Doc since his early days at Harvard, conducting cancer research in his mentor's lab. It had been a thrill for David to work alongside the renowned Doctor Benjamin Shaw as his main assistant, rewarded with the position for no other reason than for his penchant to play devil's advocate—Doc found their verbal jousting, often loud and always contentious, energizing. And despite their coming from two different angles at times, Doc always had a way of meeting David in the middle. David admired that. But even more, he admired Doc's fearlessness. This was Doc's driving force, what made him tick—what brought him to the Amazon. And it was the underlying reason David followed him here, not just because the old man had asked a favor of him, or that David needed one in return, but because Doc challenged him to step out of the box, to go against convention and look beyond—to see what others could not.

With the sun in decent and night fast approaching, the men began setting up camp. The cousins cleared the surrounding brush with their machetes and built a fire. Then David helped them move Doc into his hammock, careful to keep his chest high and his bitten leg low to stall any venom traveling throughout his body. After covering him with a blanket and splaying his hammock in netting to ward off both the chilly night air and the barrage of insects, the trio sat in silence, transfixed by the flames as they picked at their dinner of roasted piranha. They knew poisonous venom could take hours to manifest symptoms, but little more could be done until morning. So, with a long day ahead still awaiting, the weary companheiros acquiesced to tiredness and settled in for the night—all except for David.

His hand reached down and found the amulet strung from his neck, the quartz crystal within purring. He remembered Ramon's warning to remove it for a peaceful night's sleep, but David had first watch and little hope of sleep anyway. It was pitch dark, save for the campfire's glow silhouetting his companions. He sat in his hammock watching the fire, adrenaline pumping and senses alert. The nocturnal jungle was boisterous, its creatures wide awake and changing shifts like workers in a factory. But David didn't mind the clamor—the whirring of nature freed his mind to think. And he had much to think about.

28

BRIBERY

Sunday, August 31, 1997

Doc awoke to worried faces surrounding him, his brain drowsy and body weak. "I'm fine," he said, his slurred speech unconvincing as he eyed, with some trepidation, his companions and then the makeshift stretcher beside him.

David reached down and pulled back Doc's pant leg. Unmistakable edema was setting in. "You're traveling by litter," he decreed.

For five years in this uncertain jungle Doc had faced danger. The man didn't scare easily. But now, as he studied his leg and then each man's face, the confidence in his eyes wavered. "Three against one," he said, "no point in arguing." And just like that, the normally headstrong adversary rolled over without a fight. That, more than this uncertain jungle, scared David half to death.

The road ahead had just become longer. David knew his old friend would be lucky to survive the journey back to the farm. And as ludicrous as it seemed, for a split second he thought of turning back to seek out Livingston but then shook off the notion as quickly as it came, abashed at the thought. David needed clarity. He needed direction. Ramon provided.

"We go now," the young guide said.

Gingerly, the cousins transferred Doc onto a makeshift stretcher of bamboo. David said a silent prayer to a God he hadn't spoken to in years and headed out with the troop.

It had been a day since leaving the Moksha, and under normal circumstances they would reach the farm before sunset; but traveling with a litter slowed them considerably. David took turns in rotation with Ramon and Bruno—muscles burning and hands blistering—but physical hardships paled to his worry over Doc. He kicked himself for what had happened, believing that had he engaged his old friend in conversation, he wouldn't have wandered—wouldn't have been bitten. But it was too late now for guilty would-have-beens; there was nothing he could do to change the past. But if he wanted a future with Doc in it, he knew with absolute certainty he had to overcome the critical present.

For the sake of the others, Doc struck a tough veneer; but he wasn't kidding himself—he knew his chances. For the second time in his life, history had unwittingly repeated itself. Back when he was a ten-year old kid on vacation with his family in Arizona, they visited the sequoia-filled Sonora Desert. His ever-inquisitive little brother wandered ahead to explore. A shadowy movement caught the attention of the precocious six-year-old and before anyone could stop him, he overturned a loose rock and was summarily bitten. The venom from the coral snake proved fatal to such a small boy. It was a traumatic memory though one Doc never spoke of, not even with David. Still, the idea of living in the Amazon among deadly creatures never once deterred Doc from his work. He just never fathomed lightning striking twice.

Hot and exhausted from hours of little progress, the troop stopped to rest. Doc had fallen asleep along the way, the fight in him replaced by growing weariness. But David wasn't about to surrender to the helplessness and fear consuming him. Deep in thought, he feverishly paced back and forth, retracing his steps and wearing down the undergrowth. "We need a change of strategy," he ruminated out loud. "At this rate, we've got no chance of making it back to the farm in time."

His young guide spoke up. "Ramon go to farm … get anti-venom … return."

The boy's loyalty to Doc made David smile. "Ramon, there's no doubt you're fast on your feet," he said, "but not fast enough to return by sunset. What we could use is a God-damn air express," he said in frustration, kicking Doc's backpack in passing. And that's when it hit him. He stopped pacing and grabbed the pack, fishing around inside until he found what he was after. David pulled out the satellite phone and dialed.

"Agent Jenks," the voice answered, the connection breaking up with static under the jungle's canopy.

"Jenks, Bennett here. I need your help," David said. "I want an air drop."

"A what?"

"An air drop," David repeated, "of anti-venom. Our satellite phone has GPS capabilities. Triangulate our position and make a drop—today."

"Now hold on a minute," Jenks objected, his voice fading in and out with the connection.

"No, there isn't time to hold on. You do this for me, Jenks, and I'll deliver your anti-aggression contagion. Otherwise … deal's off."

Static followed. And then Jenks spoke. "You realize what you're asking takes time …"

"We don't have time, Jenks," David interrupted. "Today … or no deal."

The airways crackled, then Jenks spoke. "Stay on the line."

More static.

David's hands were shaking. He had no idea if, in fact, he could create an anti-aggression contagion. But it was the only tool in his box, and he used it. And he felt certain his request was well within the means of Rand's covert operation, their having spared no expense in outfitting Doc's lab. In fact, his gut feeling from the start was that this shadow operation had powerful backing—but just how powerful he was yet to learn.

Ten minutes later Jenks was back.

"You're on, Bennett," he said, and then cut to the chase. "There's a clearing two miles due north of your current location. ETA for the drop is thirteen hundred hours. Any questions?"

"None. Thanks Jenks."

"You owe me, Bennett."

Dead air.

David's hands couldn't stop shaking but he managed a grin. He looked down at his sleeping mentor and could just imagine the old boy's reaction to his bribing an undercover agent of the US Government.

***

"You did what?!!" Doc spat through slurred speech, a vestige of his cantankerous old self awakening.

"Ramon's on his way to the drop as we speak. Figures he'll make it back well before sundown. You should be feeling better by morning." David beamed.

"Don't put the cart before the horse," Doc mumbled. "Lots can go wrong."

David's elation fizzled from his face. "Don't worry, Doc. Everything will be fine," he said, wanting to truly believe it.

With Ramon gone the trio waited, wilting in the static heat under the dense jungle canopy. David kept his eyes on Doc like a trusty dog unwilling to wander far from his master. Bruno, however strayed out of sight in search of their next meal and, in his absence, David's anxious imagination ran wild. First with negative thoughts: *What if a jaguar attacked; what if both cousins didn't come back; what if Doc died?* Then positive: *Bruno will come back with dinner, Ramon will return with the anti-venom, and everyone will make it back to the farm, alive.* And that's how it went, bad to good to bad thoughts again, a merry-go-round of emotions from which he couldn't disembark—until the leaves rustled. David's heart leapt to his throat and his hand to his axe. Without the cousins acting as shields, every sound and movement spooked him. Nine times out of ten nothing materialized, as most jungle creatures want not to be seen. But this time when the greenery swished and the leaves splayed, a brown-skinned man appeared with two ruddy quail doves dangling from his hands.

"Bruno," David exhaled, his grip on the axe relaxing, "thank God it's you." The quiet cousin grinned wide and, settling onto a stump near Doc, employed his knife to the nasty business of gutting.

David checked his watch—thirteen hundred hours. *Ramon should be at the drop site by now,* he thought. The two had figured it would take a maximum of two hours to cover ground, there and back. Ramon was confident, as usual. David had his doubts, his nervous insistence overruling Ramon's protests to take along his trusty scout compass, even though he knew Ramon was unlikely to use it. He looked over at Doc, the old man's breath laboring and his body seeming to stiffen before his eyes, and then he looked back at his watch. Time was their enemy. *Hurry, Ramon,* he thought. *Hurry.*

While Bruno prepared the birds, David, axe in hand, gathered nearby kindling for fire, collecting bark and branches and bits of dry grass—his boyhood scouting days coming back. Never in a million years would he have imagined then this wilderness road he was on now, or how it would change the course of his life. But if, as a boy, he had had a crystal ball, it may have made little difference.

As the birds crackled on a spit above the fire, David settled down next to Bruno, awaiting dinner. But the flames were transfixing, transporting his mind back to the Moksha village—the painted bodies chanting and dancing around the bonfire, welcoming his spirit back. He touched the amulet strung from his neck and removed the quartz crystal within. Bandying it on his palm, he watched its prisms catch and reflect the firelight—a product of nature, a thing of beauty. It had brought him unexplained visions and angst, as had Lanya's eyes and Livingston's potion. Yet these same things brought the Moksha truth and peace. It was a paradox. But then everything about the Moksha was a paradox, haunting him, and returning to haunt time and again over the years, unrelenting—until it would change him forever.

"Sphatika," Bruno said, nodding with admiration.

"Yes, Sphatika," David agreed, and dropped the crystal back into its pouch.

His stomach satisfied and body exhausted, David must have dozed off. He awoke with a start to the rhythmic scraping of metal on stone. In a sleepy state, his eyes followed the sound to where Bruno sat on a stump, sharpening the blade of his knife with quick, short strokes against a stone. Yawning, David sat up and cast his eyes over at Doc who, surprisingly, was staring back.

"Who's Rose?" Doc asked, his breathing strained.

"What?" David said, taken off guard. He had never mentioned Rose to Doc. Not that he was hiding anything—and though he had high hopes for a fruitful relationship, they had only just met, after all—but at the mention of her name, heat crept up his neck. Embarrassed, he pulled up his collar.

"You talk in your sleep," Doc said, his words slipping together.

"She's my neighbor," David said with swift recovery.

"Neighbors kiss?" Doc asked, winking.

"Enough talk," David said, flustered, shooting a furtive glance at Bruno and wondering how much he understood; but the young native just kept on sharpening his knife. "You're supposed to be resting," he admonished.

Doc closed his eyes with a smug smile. David wasn't about to begrudge the old man that; he was glad to have a fleeting remnant of his feisty friend back.

Rose, he thought, giving life to her name. Would he ever make it back to her, to once again touch the shore of civilization and her soft lips. Before he left, he spoke in vague generalities about this uncertain place, not wanting to cause her alarm. But he knew then as now, the jungle finds order in chaos—and survival isn't discretionary.

He checked his watch: one-half hour to go. It was as if the sun was anchored in place, forcing the minutes to linger. He could bear the heat and mosquitoes, the long days of bush whacking and diligence to danger, but what he couldn't bear was the waiting. Waiting ceded control to time, and he had little patience for that. So now, having done all that he could for Doc and forced to twiddle his thumbs, you might as well have pulled out his fingernails, it pained him as much.

Restless, he retrieved his backpack and pulled out his notebook. Flipping through pages of Portuguese words and phrases recorded from Ramon's lessons, he began an audible review. Bruno listened in silence as David repeated words and phrases of cordiality mixed in with words of warning. After several rounds and getting bored, David about to abandon his notebook, Bruno spoke.

"Faca," he said, brandishing his sharpened blade in the air.

Surprised, it took David a few seconds before he caught on. "Knife," he said, "faca is knife in English."

"Knife," Bruno mimicked, pleased with himself when David nodded his validation.

Encouraged, Bruno continued the game, each taking turns sharing words and a camaraderie as they passed the interminable day—until Doc moaned.

David put the notebook down and stood. He looked at his old friend, fitful in slumber. Not since the morning had he checked his wound, afraid of what he'd find. So now, apprehension spilling from his pores like sweat, he approached the litter and pulled up the leg of Doc's pant. The impact was immediate. David swooned. His legs gave out. All went black.

Visions came and went. Surreal and yet so real. So real he could smell the blossoms, feel her breath, see her eyes. Her eyes. They captured his and he saw what she saw. Became what she saw. Boundaries faded. Shapes merged. A lightness. A knowing. A calm … and then someone touched his arm.

David opened his eyes expecting to see Lanya. Instead, his fuzzy vision settled on the gapping smile of a man … holding a syringe of anti-venom.

29

LABOR DAY

Monday, September 1, 1997

Roxy had decided to make good on her deal with Megan. She had, after all, held up her end of the bargain and went on their double date. So the two made plans to visit her grandfather's horse ranch on Labor Day. Rose, of course, was more than happy to drive. But what to do about Nick. They couldn't simply up and leave him in good conscience; it just wouldn't be right. So Roxy just told him he was coming, and Nick didn't put up a fight.

Rose had looked forward to the two-hour-ride to her father's ranch, hoping to learn more about her daughter's friends along the way. But it was like pulling teeth to get Nick to talk—he seemed someplace else—and Megan wasn't much better, sharing little about her life and clamming up at the mentioned of her mother. So Rose spent the entire trip conversing with Roxy catching up on their new lives, until her car turned down the familiar dirt road and passed beneath the post and beam arbor with its curlicue wrought-iron signage reading: Triple Crown Ranch. *Dad's big dream,* she thought, sighing, *and still chasing it.*

Rose honked the horn, announcing their arrival. Maximilian Maxwell strode out from the stables, lean and as fit as his horses. Outfitted with cowboy hat and snake-skinned boots, the trim sixty-year-old appeared more like a young Texas wrangler than that of a grandfather. Everyone piled out of the car, happy to stretch and meet Roxy's grandpa.

"Welcome to the ranch," Max greeted them, all smiles. Roxy luxuriated in his embrace, his Old Spice aftershave and soft flannel shirt invoking a familiar comfort. Both Megan and Nick were on the receiving end of a firm handshake. Rose, however, received the perfunctory peck on the cheek and tentative embrace, at least that was how she perceived it.

"Who's hungry? I can rustle us up some burgers," he said, rubbing his hands together with anticipation.

"Actually, Father, we stopped along the way," Rose said, her voice polite but stiff. "I think the kids are anxious to see the horses."

"Well, alright then, let's see the horses," he said, happy to oblige and directed them toward the stables.

Memories are strange things and the triggers that elicit them. For Rose, her first footsteps into the stable conjured a long-ago image of Star in the first stall to her right, the sound of his whinnying, the smell of his coat, and the feel of his powerful body beneath her. She was transported back to a time that now seemed non-existent. A time of innocence. A time when all that mattered was riding Star and the assurance of her parents' love. She missed Star, long put down from a shattered leg; and she missed her mother, dead sixteen years now, killed in an automobile accident when Roxy was only two. Had her mother lived perhaps Rose could have summoned the courage to leave Eugene. Her mother would have stood up for her, defended her—instead she was left with a father too busy with his horses to protect her or even care.

All ten stalls were occupied, though none of the horses were familiar to Rose now—her trips home few and far between. She watched as the teenagers walked the length of the stable, each drawn to a different horse. That didn't surprise her. She believed, if given the opportunity, people and horses naturally aligned—a sort of recognition in each other of similar innate qualities. To recognize them, you simply had to experience them; and with this group of humans and equines alike, vulnerability and fear were common experiences.

Max came and stood alongside Nick, dangling a carrot into the stall. The gelding made his way over. "You'd have never guessed Dancer once feared the starting gate to watch him take off from it now. Took a lot of patient prodding to get him to enter and round the stall, offering plenty of praise and more than a few treats in the process," Max laughed. "But we eventually got him to relax and trust us. Now when he's in the stall, instead of rearing and backing up, he can't wait to break out in a gallop." Dancer clenched his carrot and chomped.

Nick stood in awe and with some unease as this magnificent creature moved in closer to him.

"Go ahead," Max said, "pat him."

The teen reached out a tentative hand and stroked the gelding's broad face. Dancer didn't flinch.

Rose sidled up alongside Nick. "I see you've made a friend," she said. And after allowing several minutes of silent bonding to pass between the young man and beast, she posed her question: "Nick, have you ever ridden before?"

He shook his head no.

"Would you like to?"

He hesitated.

His indecision was enough for Rose. She looked to her father for his approval.

"Well today's your lucky day, son," Max said, grinning.

Worry painted the young man's face.

"Nothing to it," Max assured. "We'll take it one step at a time."

The horse whinnied and nudged Nick's hand resting on the rail, looking for attention. Everyone laughed.

"Seems Dancer's taken a real shine to you, son," Max said. "Safe to say you've passed introductions. Time to move on to step two." He lifted the gelding's hefty saddle off its hook and passed it to his new riding student. "Let's saddle up."

★★★

The girls sat perched on the corral fencing shouting encouragements to Nick as he placed one foot in the stirrup while Max ten-fingered the other up and over Dancer's backside. Sitting in the saddle he looked like a kid put on the bus for his first day of school—excited but scared, not sure what to expect.

"Now comes the easy part," Max said, looking up at the fidgeting young man, "balance in the saddle."

As Max instructed Nick about shoulder, hip and heel alignment, Rose mounted her horse, a comely mare named Chestnut, so called for her dark, rich color—a stark contrast to Dancer's snow-white coat. She waited for her father to finish schooling Nick and then moved in closer. The teenager was doing his best to relax and remember his instructions when Max handed the reins off to his daughter and announced: "Rose will take it from here, son. Good luck." He tipped his hat to them both and then headed for the girls still perched on the fencing.

Rose looked at Nick. "You ready to learn walking and halting?" she asked.

"As ready as I'll ever be," he said, trying to sound confident.

"Don't worry. I'll be right beside you."

Max approached the girls, his blue eyes sparkling in the sunlight as he lifted the brim of his hat to scratch his silver hair. "I hear tell you know how to ride, Megan," he said.

"Well, fair enough to keep to the saddle," she laughed.

"Okay then, let's get the two of you saddled up. Can't let Nick have all the fun," he said with a wink. The girls jumped off the fencing, beaming at one another as they trailed Max back inside the stable.

★★★

They rode three abreast, heading for the open fields under a late summer sun.

Growing up, every chance Roxy got to escape her house of horrors, she would spend riding at her grandfather's ranch. She was never happier than astride a horse. As a kid she used to fantasize about becoming a jockey until a growth spurt ended her dream. But even so, riding was in her blood—a descendant in a long line of Maxwell ranchers, breeders and racers. And now, back in the saddle after a long absence, she was that kid again fantasizing her dream.

Megan felt as in a dream. Not since the hurricane had she felt such freedom. She knew she had Roxy to thank, first for the double date and now a day at the ranch; but she also knew this was just a reprieve. Tomorrow she'd be back at college and back into hiding. Still, she planned on making the most of today.

The smile on his lips kept growing broader. Max was pleased as pie to be escorting the two young women. It made him feel like a young buck again, the wind at his back and his dreams within grasp. He looked over to his granddaughter—she was so beautiful, just like her mother. And then a shudder of guilt passed through him. *Let the past stay in the past,* he thought. Anyway, there was little now he could do about it. He shook off the uncomfortable feeling and, instead, allowed himself to feel young again. "Come on, girls, let's kick it up a notch," he shouted, bolting to a gallop, the warm summer sun on his back and the girls in hot pursuit.

★★★

"You're getting the hang of it," Rose said. "One more time around the corral and then we'll move out to the pasture."

Nick looked at her, astonished, his confidence boosted by hers in him. "If you're sure, okay then," he said, and nudged Dancer to a walk.

The meadow was picture perfect, its tall grasses bowing with the breeze against a backdrop of puffy, white clouds in a powder-blue sky. Rose felt the day heaven made. She was exhilarated to be riding again, and drawing Nick out of his shell would be the cherry on top. For the most part, though, he remained quiet. Whether he was concentrating or brooding, she couldn't tell. Maybe he existed in both realms at the same time. But she wasn't about to upset the apple cart like she had before, pushing him before he was ready. No, her focus would remain strictly on riding lessons, leaving Nick to decide his own terms on when and if he wanted to initiate personal dialogue. And then it happened.

"Rose," he said, gaining her immediate attention, "did you teach Roxy to ride?"

"Yes I did, and her Grandfather Max did too," she said.

"What about her father?"

Rose felt a chill. "No," she said. "He had no patience."

They rode some minutes more in silence. Then Nick said, "Roxy never speaks of him … her father."

Where was this coming from, she wondered and struggled for an answer. "He died when she was young," she said.

"Oh," Nick said, "I see." And then, as if he could perceive her daughter's horror, said, "Some things are best left in the grave."

Rose was thunderstruck, his words echoing in her head as they continued in silence.

***

The three dismounted beside a bubbling creek, the perfect watering hole for their horses. The girls, faces flush and hair windswept, smiled from ear to ear. Max himself was glowing like a schoolboy charmed by two ardent admirers.

"What a rush," Megan said, barely able to contain herself. "I could never gallop like that on Rocky Point."

"Rocky Point?" Max said.

"The island I grew up on in Maine," she said. "Papa cleared a loop to open a riding path for me, but there's no comparison to this," she said, her eyes scanning the vast, open expanse.

"That's pretty unusual," Max said, "a horse on an island."

"There were no other children to play with," Megan explained, "so my parents gave me Princess as a companion."

"Well, you show great command of your horse," Max said. "You must have had a good teacher."

"Thank you, I did," she said, and then, providing no further comment, fell silent.

Roxy recognized the cue and changed topic. "Grandpa," she said, "is the grand oak still standing?"

"I believe so," he said, "though I haven't ridden out that way in some time."

"Let's show Megan."

"All right," Max agreed, though if he'd had his druthers, he'd rather not. They mounted up and, this time, Roxy led the way, her internal compass on auto drive like it was yesterday.

***

"I wish my dad raised horses instead of cows," Nick said, breaking the tension of their silence. He and Rose had been riding side by side for ten minutes without speaking so much as a word.

"Well," Rose laughed, seizing the opportunity to lighten up the mood, "at least you got free milk from the deal!" A sliver of a smile escaped Nick's lips. "But don't be fooled by the glamor of it all," Rose went on. "Horses are a lot of work. And my father was a stickler. If you wanted to ride, you had to earn the privilege—though I didn't mind the grooming and feeding if it meant I could ride Star," she said, her voice wistful.

"Yeah, but you can't ride a cow," Nick countered.

"No, you can't," Rose agreed, "but then neither can you milk a horse!"

They both laughed, and Rose felt hopeful. Maybe, even if just for a day, she might break Nick of his gloomy facade. But then his facial expression stiffened, and his bleakness returned.

***

When she saw it, Roxy broke into a gallop. Her mother's favorite retreat as a young girl and, later, their haven from a depraved husband and father, the grand oak beckoned her heart as she drew nearer.

She thought of that day years ago, the two clinging for dear life to the back of Buck, her mother subduing brute force with gentle strength. It was what Rose had practiced throughout her entire marriage to that monster. But it was God to whom she gave all credit. As for Roxy, all she knew was that somehow under that tree she, too, had found her strength.

For Max, on the other hand, the tree was a stark reminder of his failings. He had avoided it all these years rather than torture himself with the memory of that infamous day—the day he was needed by his daughter and grandchild and was absent from their lives yet again, the day he could have lost them both to a demented son-in-law. Returning now to this spot bled his heart. He let Roxy and Megan race on ahead while he followed at a slow trot, his mind rewinding the past.

Years back, early on in his daughter's marriage, Max had sensed something awry. He had noticed the less than warm affection between the young couple and the frequent bruising on his daughter's pale skin, always attributed to accident. Once, when he inferred abuse, his daughter's denial was adamant, followed by nervous laughter and averted eyes. Only when he confronted Eugene did he get the truth. "Yes, and what of it?" Eugene had brazenly responded. "You can't do anything about it." Filled with outrage, Max thundered, "I most certainly can. I can take Rose and Roxanne away from you!"

"You won't," Eugene said.

"Don't be ridiculous, man. I can and I will!"

"You won't, and I'll tell you why you won't. You see, Max, I know you better than you know yourself. I know what means the most to you, and it's not your family. No, Max, you live and breathe for your horses. Now, I'm a powerful man. I know people. People responsible for licensing horse farms throughout Connecticut. All I'd have to do is say the word and your training operation will be shut down, out of business, just like that," he said, snapping his fingers. "So go home, Max, and be a good father-in-law. Stay out of my marriage."

Dumbfounded, Max went home.

Now, years later, guilt still churned his insides out. He had failed as a father and grandfather. And though he tried his best to make up for it after Eugene's death, some hurts are never forgotten, even if forgiven. He was certain Rose thought him uncaring, but better that than to know the truth—to know him a coward. She would never forgive him that.

Max stopped his horse fifty yards short of the tree. He couldn't bear to ride closer. "Come on, girls," he called out. "Last one back cleans the stalls!" And turning his horse on its hoofs, he hightailed it back to the ranch.

★★★

As sunset fell around the campfire, Rose felt her father's eyes upon her. She stared back at him through the fire's blaze, his expression a real-life rendition of a tortured soul in a Michelangelo painting. It sent a shiver through her. She realized she never really knew the man. They never grew close, never comfortable in the presence of one other. Now, any conversation between them more than likely concerned horses. But it was something to cling to, at least, something that still brought them together, making their interaction tolerable—at least for Roxanne's sake.

"Okay kids," Rose said, suddenly standing, breaking from his stare, "we need to think about getting back."

Reluctant moans followed with obedience, and soon the teen-filled car awaited Rose for its departure. She and Max stood some yards away. He spoke a few words and embraced her. On the car ride home, those departing words lingered, tugging on her mind and heart: "I know I haven't always been there for you, but you've done well by Roxanne. I'm proud of you." It was the first time he'd given her a compliment … and perhaps the closest he'd ever come to saying I'm sorry.

★★★

Journal Entry, Monday, September 1, 1997:

Today was a great day at Triple Crown, though Megan and Nick needed more prodding than horses to open up about their lives. And Grandpa and mother were no better, putting on a false front with one another. None of them fooled me. They all have painful, guilty secrets. Everyone does. But what if one day we woke up and found all pain from guilt gone? Maybe then I'd believe as Mother does in a higher hand at work. But that miracle will never happen … so I won't hold my breath.

30

A HERO

Tuesday, September 2, 1997

"YOU KNOW YOU'RE A lucky son-of-a-bitch," David said. "Your limbs were stiffening, you barely had a pulse, and you talked like a drunk. If not for Ramon, you wouldn't be here right now giving us shit."

Doc laughed. And then his face drew serious. "You all saved my life, and I am forever grateful, my friends."

"Well, if you're so damn grateful, stop giving us grief and let us help you," David said, slipping his arm under Doc's for support.

After receiving a shot of anti-venom Doc had rested a full day and now, feeling more like his crusty old self, was anxious to get back to the farm. But he was done with stretchers, and though still weak, insisted on walking.

"You know, a shot of Brandy could help with my circulation," he said, eyes twinkling.

"The only thing helping your circulation right now is the anti-venom, and a swift kick in the ass if you don't stop complaining."

Doc laughed and wrapped his arm about David's tall back, the two mismatches forging ahead like Mutt and Jeff through the brush.

David was flying high. Yes, there was still the stress of getting Doc back to the farm in one piece. But Doc was alive. He had beaten the odds and was on the road to recovery. Nothing could deflate David now ... or so he thought.

The farm was drawing near but, yet again, Doc needed to rest. Ramon helped settle him onto the trunk of a fallen tree—its exterior smelling of fresh creeping moss, its interior reeking of rot—and drew his canteen to Doc's lips for a swig. Bruno leaned against an opposite tree and removed his bandana, wringing out the sweat. David fiddled with his compass, returned from Ramon no worse for the wear, and then checked his watch. It was nearing sunset and though he knew Doc needed a break, David didn't want to lose daylight. Already, shadows were forming. When he looked up from his watch contemplating this fact, he froze. With great calm he said, "Bruno, não se mexa (don't move)." Ramon's knife flew within seconds, landing with a thud above Bruno's head. Bruno looked up. Coiled on a low-hanging limb he saw ten feet of emerald-green scales.

"Sweet Jesus," Doc exclaimed.

Bruno embraced his cousin with gusto, and then hugged David with equal enthusiasm, saying in halting English, "Thank you, Mister David."

"De nada, Bruno," David replied, smiling.

Ramon looked at them both in amazement. "See," he beamed at his two star pupils, "practice make perfect," and reaching up, pulled his knife out from the boa constrictor's head.

At first, David felt good about himself. Ramon called him a hero. Told him he had saved Bruno, and Doc before him, with his intelligence, which was just as important as a man's skill or muscle. David no longer felt his presence as dead weight dragging the others down. Finally, a contributor, he'd earned the respect of his companions and could hold his head high. And yet, when he looked over at the scaly corpse slung on the branch, his heart tugged. He thought of Livingston and the gentle tribesman's reaction to the killing of this magnificent creature.

Guilt soon overshadowed glory, and David's euphoria died. So much confusion inside him, so much tumult of emotion. Could he ever again embrace the surety of his old self. For the rest of the journey he remained unsettled, and as the troop drew nearer the farm, rather than feel celebratory, he grew ever more anxious.

He knew little about General Rand and even less about Agent Jenks. He didn't like him; of that he was certain. And now Jenks had traveled to the farm intent on their meeting. Why? He didn't have a good feeling about it.

David had never questioned his mentor's speedy acquiescence to participate in Rand's covert operation. He didn't have to. He understood Doc was still a patriot at heart—willing to follow orders, willing to sacrifice all for country. But he did, however, have reservations about the secrecy of it all. He didn't like the idea of getting caught in a web not of his spinning, only to find himself eaten by the spider if the job went awry. After all, who would defend him then—not an agency that didn't exist. And now his bribe gave their emerging relationship a black eye. But he sensed, bribery or not, Jenks and Rand were not their friends, and that he and Doc were merely the means to an end—and on their own.

★★★

As the sun dipped below the horizon, they arrived at the farm. Exhausted and ravished, all David desired was meat to fill his belly and a hammock to rest his bones. But then there was the matter of Agent Jenks. Not wanting to burden Doc with more worry, he hadn't told him of Jenks' arrival. So now David was obliged to meet the man, remain cordial for Doc's sake, and glean the true motive behind his visit. He aimed to keep Doc out of it; but before he could slip the recovering patient off to bed, Carlos ran out from the kitchen with news of their visitor. Though David argued for rest, Doc would hear none of it. Suddenly energized by his surprise guest, he freed himself of David's support and walked on his own toward the pavilion. David followed, vulnerability creeping over him with the growing darkness.

The surrounding torchlights relegated their dilated pupils temporarily blind and cast the pavilion beyond into shadows, including the long wooden table beneath its thatched roof and the squat man now seated there. "Federal Agent Jenks, I'm Doctor Benjamin Shaw," Doc said, his eyes adjusted and hand extended as he and David entered the pavilion. "An honor to have you here, sir."

Jenks stood, his short body built like a spark plug. "Wasn't sure I'd get to meet you, Doc," he said, his handshake strong, a Cuban cigar jutting from his mouth. "You're one tough son-of-a-bitch." Then he turned to the tall man. "And you're David Bennett. I know all about you," he said and, not bothering to turn aside, exhaled a stream of smoke into David's face while the two shook hands. David was annoyed, not because his eyes stung or his lungs gasped, or even because of this stranger's rudeness, but because of the man's sheer presumptuousness—Jenks knew nothing of who David was.

Doc called out to Carlos. The cook appeared in an instant. "My good man. Some brandy before dinner, if you would." Carlos nodded and set off. "Nothing like a civilized drink in an uncivilized setting," he said. *Uncivilized setting indeed,* David thought, though it wasn't the jungle he was referencing, but rather the presence of this obnoxious man.

"So, Agent Jenks," Doc said, as he and David drew up seats opposite the undercover agent, "what brings you all the way to the Amazon?"

Jenks steeled his gaze on David, another puff of smoke exiting his mouth and floating between them. He'd already investigated the geneticist's research, delved into his residency records while at Harvard, even scoured his family history. He knew all about David, but what he didn't know was the man's mind, how his brain ticked, and its gears turned. He needed to know if David would toe the line, fall in with the rank and file and follow orders, not entertain rogue ideas—ideas like triangulated coordinates and drop-shipments. *Perhaps it was a one-time anomaly,* Jenks thought, *or maybe just the tip of the iceberg.* He had to know. So now he searched David's face, scrutinized his tone of voice, observed his body language for any small infraction to hang his hat on as proof of his suspicion—that David was a rebel.

"You might say I'm here to bless this mission," Jenks answered. "But before any spraying of holy water, let's be clear on the ground rules. First, I run the show, gentlemen. Any problems go through me to General Rand. Second," he said, glowering at David, "we stick to the script: Deviation from the mission is prohibited; discussion of your work outside our circle is prohibited; and compromising our cover is prohibited." He let his words hang on the air along with his smoke, his eyes evaluating David.

For David's part, he knew that the words Jenks spoke were directed at him, but even more than his words, what was left unspoken—the consequences of nonconformity. But he knew better than to confront Jenks. After their initial interaction via satellite phone David knew involvement with the man, even remotely, was bad news. And it was far too late to pull out now; he had committed to Doc and wouldn't leave his old friend vulnerable. Even so, being thrown under the bus if something went wrong wasn't an option. Jenks was a bully and liked playing the part, but David knew even a bully has an Achilles heel. He swore he would find the man's weakness, and if Jenks ever left the two of them out to dry—he would take the bastard down.

"And third," Jenks said, concluding his rant, "from this point forward all communications for this operation will reference its code name: Octane."

"Octane?" Doc queried.

"Our secret weapon, gentlemen," Jenks said with a conspiratorial smile, "the anti-aggression contagion that will halt global fanaticism. Simply put, we intend to pump up the troublemakers with octane and remove the knocks from their engines." And, as if pleased with his ingenious analogy, Jenks smiled again, his cigar gritted between his teeth.

Out from the darkness Carlos appeared in his white apron like a ghost shuttling in chains, three shot glasses and a bottle of brandy rattling on his metal tray. All eyes followed his trail to the table where he deposited his wares and then retreated forthwith back into the void. Doc picked up the bottle, measured out three equal portions and handed each man his share.

"To Operation Octane," he said, raising his glass.

As all three glasses converged, David observed Jenks, a small man who thought himself important; but David would maintain the man's delusion for now because the undercover agent had, in so many words, threatened him—veiled threats, but threats no less.

31

THE CANDIDATE

Girl Flashback

"*IF I TOLD YOU once I told you twice, Girl. Stand up straight. Project a man of action—a doer. Only the lazy slouch.*"

Girl arched her shoulders back and thrust her chest forward. Slouching to appear shorter had become a habit. She hated towering over the twelve-year-old boys and having to put up with their cruel japes. But she hated her father more, blaming him for her misfortune; though to hear him tell it, misfortune befalls short people who are doomed to follow, whereas those who lead are tall.

Girl had been dreading this day like no other, having to appear as one big happy family in front of the cameras when her father announced his bid for the republican nomination to the 1992 presidential election. She tried pretending she was some other politician's child, imagining the pride they felt on such a momentous occasion. But the only pride Girl could muster was in the lustrous polish she'd given the sterling tea set now serving the media in their drawing room.

Girl and her mother flanked the senator as the cameras began to roll. She could have given his speech herself, having heard him rehearse it a hundred times over while pacing his study floor. His announcement—replete with hubris, especially his rational for a 180-degree change in mindset to run for an office he had much maligned—ended with a peppering of questions from the press. And just when Girl thought it was over and she was in the clear, she heard a reporter call out her name. Startled, she looked up from her feet. All eyes were on her. And worse—the cameras. Her heart thrummed, the blood rushing so loud in her head she barely heard the question he asked: "What's it like being the senator's daughter?"She could sense his person stiffen as he stood next to her. A lump rose in Girl's throat. Answer with the truth and she'd have to answer to her father later; answer with a lie and it would eat her alive. Temples pulsing and throat dry, she swallowed hard and said, "Different every day." Silence filled the room ... and then a burst of laughter. "You schooled her well, Senator," she heard the reporter say. And with that, the news and camera men splintered, the senator joining them in off-the-record discourse. Girl was still standing there when she felt her mother's hand take hers, leading her from the room. When she looked back over her shoulder toward the crowd of press, her father met her eyes. What she saw there startled her. You could almost call it pride—though she was certain it was not the usual sort parents bestowed upon their child. No, this was different. And then it hit her. She had just passed the litmus test as a true politician's offspring—answering a reporter's question without truly answering. And as her heart sank at the prospect of any resemblance to this monstrous man, for the first and only time Girl could recall, he smiled at her.

32

CLASS PRESIDENT

Tuesday, September 2, 1997

ALL AROUND CAMPUS POSTERS went up for student government elections. Plastered over walls everywhere, Roxy couldn't avoid them. She held little interest in the process, her father's life in politics having tainted her outlook. When he died, three months after announcing his bid for the Republican presidential nomination, it had been a huge relief to rid herself of the political yoke that expected she follow in his footsteps. Now, six years later, the sour taste of politics still remained in her mouth, to the point where she couldn't care less if she ever voted.

"What's wrong?" Zach asked, approaching Roxy inside the student union center, a pile of flyers in his hands. "You look like you just ate a lemon."

"I don't like politics, that's all," she said, the hopeful faces of candidates on the posters leering over her shoulder.

"Why not? It's a noble calling."

"Power can corrupt even the noble minded."

"Whoa! Such depth of thought so early in the morning."

Roxy ignored him, asking, "What are those?"

"A friend in theatre is running for class president. I told him I'd help spread the word. Want to lend a hand," Zach said, holding up a stack of flyers, "that is, if it's not too political a gesture for you." He smirked.

Roxy fist-bumped his shoulder.

"I'll take that to mean yes," he said, handing her half the pile. "You distribute here, and I'll cover the library. When you're done meet me in the cafeteria. We can discuss your political discontent over some coffee." Zach grinned and sprinted off.

Roxy sighed and looked down at the flyers—a young man's smiling face staring back. She considered the attributes that made a quintessential politician and thought of her father: Certainly a gift for gab and a boat load of charm—and definitely ambition. But ambition courts power, and therein lies the rub—to achieve political success on the straight and narrow or via power's slippery slope? She knew how her father did it. *As for this young man,* she thought, *time will tell.*

Her flyers dumped forthwith into a nearby trash bin, Roxy arrived at the cafeteria well before Zach. She bought three coffees—one each for her and Zach and a third promised for Megan—then found a seat with a view to the door. She sat sipping her brew in a futile attempt to dispel her mounting anxiety from the surrounding political hoopla. But her thoughts landed on her father's presidential bid, and therein they stewed.

At the time of his run, she'd had mixed emotions about the prospect of his winning. Had he become Commander-in-Chief, life in the White House might not have been so bad, what with Secret Service protection for her and her mother 24/7 ... no way he could have hurt them then. But his untimely death had brought an end to such speculation. Her mother had said it wasn't in God's plan for her father to become president. Whether you believed that or not, Roxy thought the country was done a great favor.

Fifteen minutes later Zach breezed through the door. Roxy grabbed his attention with a wave. She pushed his coffee toward him as he slid into his chair.

"Thanks," he said. "How'd you know I like it black?"

"You strike me as a simple kind of guy."

"I'm not sure how I should take that."

"In a good way."

"Meaning?"

"Complexity requires much energy and time. Living life simply is freeing. And you seem ... unburdened."

"Well, I do like my toast plain," he grinned. "Now you, on the other hand, strike me as someone who coats hers in butter and jam."

Roxy looked down at her coffee, suppressing a smile. She caught his drift. Her life was certainly complicated, but she provided neither confirmation nor denial to his assumption.

"Soooo," Zach said, moving on, "you don't like politics. Care to elaborate?"

Her brain tried to formulate an explanation, but there was no simple answer. "It's complicated," she sighed, and realizing what she'd said, they laughed.

"Well then, we'll just keep it simple," Zach offered. "I'll ask you a question, and you provide a one-word answer. Ready?"

She nodded.

"How long have you felt this way?"

For as long as Roxy could remember, her father's political rants echoed in her head. It was as if she came out of the womb spieling his legislative drool. She looked up at Zach and answered: "Forever."

"Did someone make you feel this way?"

"Yes."

"Who?"

His name was there on the tip of her tongue. She wanted to spit it out as she would a mouthful of spoiled milk. But instead, the lump of sourness sat festering, forcing her either to swallow or choke on it. She swallowed. "I have to go," she said, pushing back her chair, "Megan's waiting for her coffee." She grabbed the styrofoam-filled cup from the table and bolted for the door.

Slack jawed, Zach just sat there watching her go. "So much for simplicity," he muttered.

33

CALL 911

Friday, September 5, 1997

DAVID WAITED TWO WHOLE days before leaving Doc's farm, allowing Agent Jenks plenty of leeway between their departures. The last thing he wanted was to run into the little bully on his way home. Besides, he needed the extra time to talk with Doc and gather specimens to bring back with him to the States. He'd tried convincing Doc to return with him for a medical check-up. He was, after all, a seventy-year-old recovering from a poisonous snake bite. But Doc would hear none of it, his usual obstinate self professing too much work to be done at the farm.

When it did come time to leave, David hugged Doc, telling his stubborn mentor to take it easy and that he'd be back once Nick's situation was in hand. Then, once again, Ramon and Bruno served as guides on his return trip, first retracing their steps overland through the jungle to their abandoned boat, then motoring through the connecting tributaries back to the mighty Amazon, and finally disembarking where their journey had begun, in Manaus, where David's flight home awaited. With heartfelt embraces and few words spoken, the three amigos parted ways with the understanding that this wasn't goodbye, just back to business as usual until they met again.

***

Gone two weeks, David arrived home on a Friday night to a cloistered house, its shades drawn and interior dark. It didn't feel right. When his taxi pulled into the driveway, he glanced over to Rose's Victorian. It glowed. He paid the cabby, grabbed hold of his backpack and exited the vehicle, closing its door with a purposeful bang, thereby giving notice he was home. Still no obvious movement from within. His heart quickened. He climbed the front steps and slid his key into the door lock, a cold fear gripping him. His hand on the knob, he stood paralyzed, afraid to enter. Then came the light brush of fingers along his shoulder. He jumped.

"I'm sorry," a soft voice came from behind.

"Rose," David exhaled.

"I'm so glad you're home," she said, breathless from her run at the sound of the car door. "I've been so worried about Nick."

The look on her face told him all he needed to know. His heartbeat pounding in his ears, David quickly turned the knob, and they entered the house. Darkness. He fumbled for the light switch and flicked it on. "Nick," he called out. "It's David. I'm home." Silence. He rushed through the cavernous foyer, opening doors to adjoining rooms, turning on lights, to no avail. "He must be upstairs," he said to Rose, panic in his voice.

Close on his heels, she followed him up the curved staircase and down the hall, their footsteps muffled by thick carpeting. Nick's door was ajar, his room dark. Rose stood back, half in fear, and waited. David entered. When the light flicked on, she heard him cry out, "Oh God!" Trembling, she stepped inside. David rushed to Nick's bedside, the gaunt and ghostly young man lying there, eyes closed.

"Nick," he said, shaking his brother's shoulders, "Nick, wake up."

A whimper slid past the boy's unmoving lips.

"Call 911," David yelled.

Rose ran for the phone on Nick's nightstand … next to the spilt bottle of sleeping pills.

34

— • —

THAT HORRID THING

Girl Flashback

THAT HORRID THING … what was it? Eleven-year-old Girl's groggy mind strained to remember a thread. She looked up to the ceiling, down to her bed covers and over to her nightstand and the little plastic bottles sitting there—sleeping, depression and anxiety pills. How many had she taken? Enough to temporarily escape the present, though never enough to escape the past. Each morning it rolled back in with the dawn, inching up with the sun until fully exposed and glaring at her, its intensity overwhelming. Girl drew the covers up over her eyes, the realization upon her—she must face another day … and that horrid thing of last night.

She was used to her father's verbal abuse and sudden backhanded whacks. And though his discipline of her had been abusive and harsh, his wrath rarely rested upon her because, up to this point in her young life, she had assumed the role of a 'son' in her father's twisted mind. No, it was Rose who took the brunt. But last night that dynamic changed forever.

★★★

They had just finished dinner and Girl stood to clear the table. A sudden cramping overtook her, which she summarily dismissed as indigestion. But her discomfort lingered and soon proved to be none other than the time-worn passage to womanhood that all young girls must travel, and one for which she was totally unprepared. Then it happened—a red stain bloodying the backside of her white skirt and spreading outward through linen fibers.

Her father stood, eyes glaring and finger pointing, declaring her not only a sinful woman but mankind's scourge. She had crossed the line—the 'son' Eugene was breeding had become a woman. The blood sealed the deal. From now on when he looked at her there could be no distinction. The scales once tipped in deference to Girl had just been leveled, his anger free now to swing out equally at wife or daughter, whoever was in his way.

And Girl couldn't get out of his way fast enough. Eugene was on her like a starved animal, his fury an eruption of epic proportions—she had betrayed him! And it hadn't helped matters that half a bottle of bourbon was already coursing his veins.

Poor Rose. She tried to intercede, but Eugene shoved her aside like an annoying pup, her head hitting the wall hard and knocking her out.

Girl ran. But she wasn't fast enough. And when Eugene caught her, she wasn't strong enough. He pinned her arms back with one hand and struck her face with the other. Disgusted and deranged, he cursed and insulted her with blow after blow. The poor child screamed and kicked, struggling until her world went black. Then, like a tiger tired of toying with his prey, he dropped her limp body and moved on.

***

Girl rose from her bed and approached the dresser mirror—Mother, she thought, staring at the reflection gawking back. But this bruised and battered image wasn't mother. Girl's trembling fingers alighted the bandaged bridge of her nose and traced the swollen bruises around her eyes. It was then that the stifled memories of the prior night's melee surfaced—escaping her lips in a primal scream.

Asleep in a nearby chair, Rose jumped to. She had spent the entire night comforting her child. And when Girl had finally given in to slumber, Rose wept, the realization upon her that a new cycle of violence had begun. Now, rushing to her daughter's aid, she cradled her broken child within her arms, praying to God all the while for divine intervention, because who else could she turn to?

Girl clung tight to Rose, her voice unrecognizable as her own as she screamed over her mother's shoulder, her eyes fixed on the end table beside her bed—and the prescription pills on it.

35

— · —

SLEEPING PILLS

Saturday, September 6, 1997

ROSE SAT CURLED UP like a cat on her sunroom couch. And though the warm morning sun felt good on her skin, she felt shaken to the core by what had happened to Nick. She hadn't slept a wink last night and, looking down at the steaming cup of coffee nestled in her hands, realized she probably wasn't doing herself any favors by drinking the caffeinated brew.

How could I have ignored the signs? she thought, overwhelmed by guilt. She knew what severe depression looked like—Roxy, unfortunately, having been her educator. But when they had returned home from visiting her father's ranch and Nick went back into seclusion, she fought her own best instincts, worrying instead about pushing him too hard too fast. She didn't want to make that mistake again. Now they were both paying the price.

"I thought I'd find you here." Still in her baby doll pajamas at ten o'clock in the morning, Roxy entered the room and cozied up beside her mother, resting her head on her shoulder—the dark shadows beneath Roxy's eyes tell-tale signs the sandman had passed over her, too. "Megan's finally asleep," she said. "It was a rough night."

After the call from Rose the teens had grabbed a cab for the hospital, but upon arrival Rose sent them home, having insisted there was nothing they could do there. They both understood, but Roxy was never good at waiting—especially now, with guilt pointing its ugly finger at her for not having done more. She, of all people, should have known Nick's fragile state. *I should have been there for him,* she had lamented all night.

Roxy looked up at her mother. "He'll be home soon?"

"Yes," Rose said, "any time now. But we must give him space."

"Of course," Roxy said, despite a terrible urge to run to him the moment David's car pulled in. She thought of the sleeping pills he took—his attempt to end it all; but then had he really wanted to, she reasoned, he would have taken the entire bottle. *Poor boy,* she thought, *waking up to the same old life in the same old world.* She knew what that was like … and pitied him.

Outside, the familiar revving of an approaching sports car brought both women to their feet. Rose grasped Roxy's hand with purposeful restraint, though her smile made it appear altruistic. The two stood peering out the sunroom window as the Corvette pulled into the Bennett's driveway and stopped. Their eyes were glued to David as he exited and came round to the passenger side. They watched him open the door and lean in, maneuvering to help his brother out and then, practically holding the frail young man up, began the long, arduous walk into the house.

Roxy gasped. Haggard and scarcely able to walk, the robust teen who had sat astride a horse a mere week ago was now barely recognizable. Tears welled as she fought to deny the truth before her eyes. *I'll make it up to you, Nick,* she thought, though her promise was as much for her own guilt-ridden sake as it was for him.

A wave of nausea seized Rose. *Look at him,* she thought. *Look at what I've done. Oh God, why did I wait?*

Mother and daughter stood clutching one another in their own silent hells as they watched the men make their slow and steady tread along Nick's flowered walkway, up the brick portico steps and into the grand colonial—its massive wooden door closing behind them with a resounding thud.

36

— · —

CARETAKER

Sunday, September 7, 1997

ROSE JOLTED AWAKE AT the doorbell's ring. She had fallen asleep on the sunroom couch where she had chosen to bed the last two nights, her gnawing conscience preventing any reasonable rest. She hurried into the front parlor, tightening the sash of her robe and combing her hair with her fingers as she went. *Too early for visitors,* she thought, glancing at the grandfather clock standing sentry by the door, its pointy hour-hand nearing six. She peered out the stained-glass window … and then swept open the door.

"David … come in," she said, endeavoring to stifle her self-consciousness.

"I'm sorry," he said, seeing her in her robe and realizing his mistake, "I'll come back later."

"You'll do no such thing." She took him by the arm and led him in.

As he stood there feeling awkward and tired, he couldn't help marvel at her beauty, even in her bathrobe.

"Come," she said, "I'll make us some coffee."

He followed her into the kitchen where she pulled out a chair from the round wooden table and directed him to sit. David sat without comment, his weary eyes following her graceful movements as she went about the kitchen. Not until this very moment did he realize just how much he had missed her, only now, unfortunately, his joy at their reunion was tempered by his brother's suffering.

When the coffee maker finished brewing, Rose poured two steaming cups and set them on the table. "Would you like something to eat?" she asked.

He waved her off. "No thanks. Come sit."

Rose acquiesced, and picking up her cup took a sip, indulging in the only pleasure she'd allowed herself these past two days.

From across the table David met her eyes, and for a moment held her gaze, saying nothing. Then he took a deep breath and spat it all out before his emotions got the better of him. "I want to thank you Rose. I don't know how I would have managed if you hadn't been with me," he said, his voice cracking.

Her hands shaking, Rose put down her cup. "Oh David, if only I had done more … helped Nick sooner. If only I hadn't waited …"

"Stop, Rose. Stop right now," David said, taking a firm hold of her hands. "You're not to blame in this. If it hadn't been for your concern—checking in on him while I was gone and taking him to your father's ranch—his deteriorating condition would have driven him to act much sooner, I'm convinced of it. Instead of coming home to a half-comatose brother, I'd be coming home to make funeral arrangements," he said, lowering his gaze to his cup, unable to meet her eyes. Then, his gaze still lowered, he made a confession. "At first, when I couldn't reach Nick through Doc's satellite phone, I wasn't alarmed. I just figured my timing was off and I'd try again later. But the dense canopy hindered our connection for days … and then Doc got bit," he said, weariness in his voice. "When we finally made it back to the farm and my attempt to reach him again failed … well, I couldn't allow myself to think the worst. I'm ashamed to admit it now, but the ordeal with Doc drained me, and I just didn't have the stamina to entertain one more emergency. So I relegated calling Nick to the back burner of my mind until I reached Manaus. Of course, he didn't answer then, either, and by the time I got to Boston …" David looked up at Rose. He needn't explain any further—she knew the rest of the story. "I never should have left him alone, Rose" he said, struggling for composure. "It's all my fault."

Rose cupped his face with her hand, studying his ocean blue eyes and the guilt treading water there, refusing to sink.

He turned his cheek and kissed her palm, then, swallowing the lump in his throat, said, "Nick's asking to see you, Rose. Roxy and Megan, too."

"Not too soon for visitors?" she questioned.

"Some company will do him well … help him get his mind off things."

"The girls will be heartened to hear it," she said, feeling her own spirits lift, too. "When should we come by?"

"Today, after lunch," he said. And then, pausing, added, "You should know, I've arranged for a caregiver to be with him … for a while. At least until he is stable again." David didn't know when that would be but refused to consider the alternative. All he knew was he would do everything in his power to help his brother. Whatever it took—he would have his back.

***

She opened the door immediately after the first ring, as if she'd been standing there waiting. The middle-aged woman of solid build, blond hair pulled tightly back into a bun, occupied much of the space within the door frame, her scrutinizing baby-blue eyes sizing up the three visitors. "I'm Nurse Annika," she said, a Scandinavian accent lilting from her tongue. "Come in please" she said, her smile tight through weathered skin as she stepped back to brace the door.

The three women edged past her sizable figure and into the foyer. Rose extended her hand. "It's nice to meet you, Nurse Annika. I'm Rose," she said, expecting a firm handshake, but Annika's grip was surprisingly gentle. The girls stepped forward in turn, each doing likewise. An awkward silence followed. Feeling like an intruder instead of invited guest, Rose cleared her throat and took the lead. "Would it be alright if we visited with Nick?" she asked meekly.

"Ja, certainly … go on up. He is expecting you," Annika said. And then promptly added, "A few minutes only. He tires easily. Ja?"

"Yes. Of course. Thank you," Rose said, and as she climbed the curved staircase, she could feel the weight of Annika's examining eyes upon her. The girls followed in single file behind her to the top landing and down the hall, all coming to a stop outside of Nick's closed bedroom door. Rose stood there for a moment fighting back the disturbing image ingrained on her retinas from two nights prior, then tapped the door.

"Come in," the weak voice responded.

Nick was sitting up in his bed, freshly shaven, hair combed. He cleaned up well, but Rose noticed that beneath the pajamas a frail frame was evident, and that the skin surrounding his eyes had darkened like a raccoon's. He smiled, but it was fleeting, as if it hurt to do so.

The women flanked his bed in silence, all at a loss for words.

"You met Nurse Annika," Nick said at last, breaking the ice.

"Yes, she seems … nice," Roxy said, settling for an innocuous adjective.

"I guess so," Nick said, looking down at his hands and twisting the bed sheet around his finger, "only, she feels like the Gestapo."

Rose smiled. "And here I thought it was just me," she said.

Nick looked up at her with a half grin, though it came off as a grimace.

"Well, you're looking better," Megan lied, "and before you know it, you won't be needing her."

"Right," Roxy added, "before you know it, you'll be back riding horses."

Everyone wanted to believe that, especially Nick. But he knew better. "What are you painting now, Rose?" he asked, shifting topics.

"Actually," she said, welcoming a chance for meaningful dialogue, not to mention a divergence for this sick boy, "I'm working on several paintings for a charitable cause, based on an idea that came to me in a dream."

Nick sat forward, his interest peaked. "Really?" he said. "What was the dream about?"

"Armageddon," she said, pausing, all eyes now on her. "In my dream, wars raged and natural disasters ravaged," she explained. "In the end, all was lost—all but for the little children … and the look I saw on their faces. When I woke, I knew I had to paint them."

"What look did you see, Rose," Nick asked. "Fear?"

She closed her eyes as if reliving the dream. "No," she smiled, "not fear … love." The word hung a moment on the air, and then she opened her eyes, asserting, "It was clear to me that this was a message from God." Rose studied their faces. Smelled their skepticism. "Think about it," she said, undeterred. "Little children are pure, honest. They have yet to be corrupted. Who better than innocents to show the world the only lasting truth." No one argued, though Rose caught Roxy rolling her eyes. But Nick seemed to be chewing on it, his brow furrowed.

"Do you think all dreams have meaning?" he asked.

"I'm not sure," Rose said. "But I think dreams that speak to you shouldn't be dismissed outright. Interpretation is personal, of course, and a lot of it is intuitive, but it's also how it makes you feel. My mother used to say: Be still, listen to the voice within, and then trust your gut."

David stuck his head in through the open doorway. He had been standing outside of Nick's room, listening, intrigued by the conversation. He, too, had experienced a dream that spoke to him—a recurring dream. It had revisited him every night since receiving the quartz crystal from Viper, each time lasting longer than before, though he was no closer to discerning its meaning. And though he cursed the crystal every day, he still bore it close to his chest each night in hope of a revelation. It was exhausting, his tormented sleep, but he had to know. "Forgive my intrusion," he said, "but Nurse Annika says Nick should rest now."

Nick was about to protest, but Rose cut him off. "It's quite all right, dear," she said, patting his hand, "We'll be back soon." Then she bent to his forehead and planted a kiss. And when Megan and Roxy followed suit, the mortified young man rolled over and drew up his covers as if to sleep.

The girls went on ahead down the stairs while David hung back with Rose.

"So, Nurse Annika's got you doing her dirty work," Rose teased, slipping her arm into his as they walked down the hallway.

"Actually, I volunteered to come up," he said. "I wanted to see you."

Arm and arm they descended the curved staircase to the grand foyer, the girls already outside. David walked her to the door. "Thank you for coming, Rose" he said. "It meant the world to Nick … and to me, too." He tilted her chin up with his fingers and stole a kiss.

Such unexpected ardor stirred Rose, her body tingling from head to toe.

"How about dinner tomorrow night?" he ventured.

"Oh David, I'm sorry," she said, "but I'm afraid that's not possible. I've made a previous commitment." It was a struggle not to give in to this man, the attraction and all; but Rose truly had prior plans. Although truth be told, the feeling of control, of pulling the strings that make men jump, felt strangely seductive. "Another time?" she proposed, her voice consolatory.

"Of course," David said, flustered at her rebuff. He opened the door.

"Get some sleep," she said, cupping his tired face in her hand before stepping out onto the portico. And with one last look before turning to join the girls, she wished him sweet dreams.

"Only if they're of you," he replied, his longing eyes following her down the flowered walkway.

***

David fell into a restless sleep. Despite Annika's round-the-clock vigil of his brother, his sleep came in fits and starts due to his guilt-induced paranoia that something bad would happen if he, too, failed to stand guard. And his agitated state was compounded by his refusal to follow Ramon's advice for a peaceful night's rest by removing his quartz crystal at bedtime. But his dream had become like a drug, and he was addicted to learning the mystery of its meaning. And so, unable to let it go, he tossed and turned, and dreamed …

He knew it was Lanya, her presence somehow familiar in the brilliant white light. He felt weightless—free of borders, free of time. There was only patience. It was the lesson he must learn. But David was an impatient man. He demanded answers. The problem was, he was not yet ready to receive them. Before such forbidden fruit should dangle within his reach, he must learn to wait … and prepare … because the answers he sought to pluck from the Tree of Knowledge would harvest profound consequences.

37

—·—

OLD SOULS

Monday, September 8, 1997

"LANYA." DAVID AWOKE FROM his dream calling her name. She had a hold on him—mind, body and soul—and yet he knew so little about her. And worse, while at the Moksha village, he had found Doc's explanation about her utterly inconceivable when he had asked the question: "Where are all the old people?"

"Think," Doc replied. "Without sickness, the aging process is slowed … many here are old souls."

"How old?" David pressed.

"Lanya's the oldest—by her account she has lived over 200 years."

"But that's impossible," David protested. "She has young children!"

"So she has," Doc smiled. "So she has."

"Lanya," he sighed again, now frustrated and fully awake. There was so much he didn't understand. But today, he vowed, would be the start to finding the answers. He threw on his clothes and, after a final check on Nick, headed out to the lab.

***

It was dark, an hour before sunrise, when he pulled his Corvette into the deserted parking lot and entered the small, concrete building. At first, the scent of chemicals was disconcerting after two weeks of breathing unadulterated rain forest air; but once the fluorescent lighting buzzed on and its reflective glow off of metal and glass brought the lab to life, David, at last, felt at home.

His office was as he'd left it—clear of clutter and well-organized—like his old mentor had once described his protege's mind. He smiled now at the memory as he sat behind his tidy desk and peered out through the sleek floor-to-ceiling glass wall separating his office from the lab. His eyes swept the sterile vista. Assured he was alone, he placed his leather briefcase onto his desktop and rotated the lock's cylinders to the opening combination. Flipping the dual latches, he lifted the lid and, from within, removed a key with which he used to open the bottom right drawer of his desk. Carefully, he withdrew the contents from his briefcase, placed them into the drawer, closed it, and once again secured its lock. The key was then returned to his briefcase, latches fastened, and cylinders rotated. Satisfied, he exhaled and headed for the coffee machine.

David leaned against the wall of the break room watching the brew drip into his mug as he mulled his plan of action. He had decided his approach to Pran would be to benefit his brother first and foremost. To hell with Rand and Jenks. They could wait. But David's confidence in Pran's ability to heal Nick's cancer bordered on the impossible, despite Doc's credence in its healing properties. Still, what choice did he have? He'd already given the established medical profession a shot, and they'd failed miserably. And though he understood that this fishing expedition could end in failure, too, the difference this time was that the one person David trusted most in the world had faith. So, despite his skepticism, he clung to that fine thread like a lifeline. Maybe, just maybe, the old boy was on to something. Just then, from within the amulet worn beneath his shirt, he felt the quartz crystal 'purr'. *Coincidence?* he thought. Before he had met Rose ... before he had met Lanya ... he would have said so. Now ... he wasn't so sure. David retrieved his steaming mug of joe and took a long, satisfying sip.

"Welcome back, boss," came a voice from behind.

David gagged mid-swallow.

Brad Parks—an overachieving, self-proclaimed lab geek—always arrived early. David had been 99 percent certain, however, that he'd arrived before his young research assistant—before Brad could have eyed him placing the contents of his briefcase within his desk drawer—but still ...

"Thanks," David croaked, clearing his throat. "I didn't see your car in the lot. Just arriving?" he asked, breath held as he considered the handsome twenty-eight old standing before him, his jawline strong and dark eyes penetrating. He reminded David of himself at that age—conscientious to a fault and full of promise. Maybe that was why he liked him.

"Yeh, car trouble. I took a cab, or I'd have beat you in," Brad answered, competitiveness in his voice as he nestled his mug beneath the coffee maker's spout and pressed the start button.

David exhaled. "Well, thanks for holding down the fort while I was gone. It seemed like forever … I couldn't wait to get back."

"Really? I'd have traded places in a heartbeat," Brad said. "I mean—we're talking the Amazon!"

David grinned. "Play your cards right and you'll get there," he said, patting his young assistant' shoulder before walking away.

"Oh, you can count on it, boss!" Brad called out after him, the coffee maker spitting its last steaming drip into his mug.

What to do about Brad, David thought. Out of the half-dozen employees who worked at the lab, he was the most concerning, what with his insatiable curiosity that often found his nose poking into other peoples' business. Normally, in this line of work, David would consider that a positive trait, as collaborating ideas and data often led to discovery. But now, however, a more cautious approach was needed to his research on Pran, not knowing where his work would lead and how closely he'd be watched—yes, watched—for he was under no illusion that Agent Jenks wouldn't keep tabs, maybe even bug his office for all he knew. No, the last thing David needed was Brad getting involved. Best to keep his inquisitive young assistant well beyond arm's length of his research. The question was, how?

Sipping from his mug, his eyes following David's retreat to his office, Brad contemplated his boss—and the mysterious contents locked in his bottom desk drawer.

38

JEALOUSY

Tuesday, September 9, 1997

V OICES WOKE HIM—NOT THOSE in his dream or from the confines of his home—voices from outside his bedroom window. David arose from his bed feeling vulnerable in the darkness, his feet obeying his brain to follow the laughter—hers familiar and light, his strange and hardy—a harmonious blend that unexpectedly nauseated his gut. He sank to the floor, forearms coming to rest upon the windowsill, eyes fixated on the veranda next door and the shadowy image of a couple embracing.

It was midnight, or so read the dimly lit clock on his nightstand. David felt the hour much later. He'd arrived home beat from his first full day back at the lab, barely able to ingest the dinner Annika had left for him before crawling off to bed. What with his body still travel weary and mind yet on high alert—though now his fear of snakes was replaced by his fear of Nick's cancer—plus his annoying crystal adding to the mix, was it any wonder the exhausted state he was in. But the root cause of his sudden nausea was hardly exhaustion. No, it was an emotion as old as time itself and as debilitating as fear—jealousy. For the sweet voice that had once laughed with his on the ethers of time was now laughing with someone else's.

David was a rational man, or so he thought. And though his left brain argued for logic, his right brain continued to cast doubt, his status with Rose now in question as he watched her embracing her 'previous commitment.' The voice in his head continued its taunt: Was he or was he not the Alpha male willing to defend his territory from predatory attack in the dark of night? His adrenaline responded. David threw on his robe and bolted down the stairs, casting open the front door just as the stranger's car pulled away from the curb, its headlights washing over him as it swung past. He felt robbed at first, so wanting to have marched over there and taken a swing at the guy. But as the seconds passed and a cooler head could prevail, he stepped back and closed the door, thankful he hadn't made a fool of himself.

★★★

Dawn broke and David awoke, aroused not by his alarm clock but by his brother's cry. When he reached Nick, Annika was already by his side.

Though Nick's eyes were wide open, the teen was caught in a dream—lost in another time and gripped with fear. David had witnessed this before. "Nick," he said, sitting beside his brother on the bed and gently shaking his shoulders. "Nick, wake up."

The young man, struggling with reality, blinked several times before his big brother came into focus.

"Good morning, Nick," David said, smiling as usual to mask his worry.

"And a fine one it is," Annika chimed in, drawing the drapes to fill the room's dreary crevices with sunshine. "I'll leave it to the two of you while I whip up breakfast—delicious blueberry pancakes with real maple syrup—none of that imitation stuff, mind you," she said as she exited the room, closing the door behind her.

David observed his brother twisting the sheet around his finger. "Another bad dream?" he asked.

Nick nodded.

"Want to talk about it?"

The teen stared out the window. It was always the same response.

"Nick," he said, gently taking his brother's face between his hands and directing it toward him, "do you trust me?"

The stricken teen met his eyes. "Of course," he answered, his voice hurt at any suggestion otherwise.

"Good, because what I am about to propose will require not only your trust, but your secrecy."

Nick was silent, his eyes still locked on David's. For him, as far as his big brother was concerned, there was never any question. "I'm listening."

39

THE MOVIES

Tuesday, September 9, 1997

IT WAS LATE AFTERNOON; classes had ended, and Megan was in her bed napping. The very act of attending sessions had seemingly worn her out, but to Roxy's relief, at least she was finally going.

Roxy, sitting at her desk, tore yet another yellow-lined sheet of paper from its pad and, crumpling it, dropped it into her wastebasket, the pile mounting. Ever since her visit with Nick, she had found it hard to concentrate on schoolwork. Her guilt over what had befallen him, however misplaced, was eating her alive. So now, with Megan asleep and their room quiet, the time seemed ripe for a much-needed distraction—a stab at her first draft of Zach's screenplay.

Her mind had been mulling the subject for some time now, waiting for a spark of inspiration. Today she had one—the same one she had been tossing aside for weeks—only now the insistence of her gut overpowered her brain and pushed her off this never-ending merry-go-round. If she ever expected to become a writer, she had to acknowledge it was now or never to shit or get off the pot. Yes, the battle her ghosts would wage with her emotions when the whole horrid truth rose to the light of day would prove difficult, possibly debilitating—yet, she felt compelled to write what she knew best. So, trepidation mixed with defiance, one bad start after another, she persevered until she landed upon the critical opening scene. She picked up her pen and wrote: The hurricane's gale-force winds howled throughout the 40-acre backwoods—obliterating her screams.

***

Zach came by for Roxy at quarter to seven. He was excited. She had agreed to accompany him to a viewing of The Marx Brothers comedy *Duck Soup* at the Student Union Center, a first date of sorts without Paul and Megan in tow. The last couple of days she had seemed distant, so when he asked her out, he had prepared himself for disappointment. Her positive response more than surprised him—it gave him hope. Little did he know her decision to go was based on the turn of her Magic 8 Ball.

She opened her dorm room door within seconds of his knocking and quickly stepped outside. Roxy was certain her roommate, if left to her own devices, would sleep through an earthquake, but she still made the effort to be quiet.

"Hi," she said, coming within inches of Zach, his body leaning against her doorpost.

"Hi," he said. "You look great."

She didn't feel great. The written reprisal of a chapter in her former life had resurrected her father's tormenting control of a terror-stricken child. But now that Zach was here, she felt things would be different. *Now, I'm in control,* she thought.

"Thanks," she said and, stepping away, took the lead down the stairwell. Zach followed in her downdraft.

Exiting the building, the September sun was on the cusp of setting, low in the sky and blinding.

"Let's walk backwards," Zach said, quickly turning an about face away from the brightness. Roxy followed suit.

"The first one to trip has to buy the other popcorn," she said, looking over her shoulder.

"Deal," Zach said and then promptly tripped. "No fairs," he whined, "you saw that tree root coming."

"You said deal," she taunted, and then took off, sprinting down the walkway to the Student Union Center.

"Hey, wait up!" Zach yelled, bolting after her.

At the building's entrance, Zach caught up and held open the door. "You know, I have a policy of not rewarding cheaters with popcorn."

"That's too bad. I guess you'll just have to watch me enjoy mine," Roxy deadpanned and headed for the concession stand.

Zach came up behind her in line. "Butter or plain?" he said, conceding. "No wait, don't answer that. Let me guess." And after faking contemplation, said, "Butter, of course."

"What makes you so sure?" she asked, rounding on him.

"Why, I'd expect nothing less from 'Little Miss Complicated,'" he zinged.

Roxy jabbed his shoulder playfully with her fist. "Make it a large," she ordered. "I'm willing to share my reward."

The couple settled into their end seats in the back row, popcorn between them, Zach's legs stretching out into the aisle. And as the lights dimmed and the projector rolled, the audience fell silent watching the credits scroll up the screen. In the darkness Roxy thought back to when she was a kid, how venturing off to the movies was out of the question whenever her father was around. The mother-daughter duo would have to wait until he was at work in D.C. before they could feel safe about going, what with his disdain for all things fun. But now she was free to do as she pleased whenever and however much she liked. So tonight, with Zach, that was her sole intention.

Roxy laughed until her stomach hurt at the comedic antics transpiring on the screen. She was totally immersed in the zany Marx Brothers' film, detached from the cares of the world—until Zach kissed her lips. There is nothing like the human touch to center a person. Roxy came round. Zach kissed her again. And when he pulled away, she leaned in and met his lips once more, lingering there, her fingers running through his corona curls, grasping the back of his neck and drawing him in closer, a sudden hunger overtaking her. Zach seized her hand and yanked her from her seat, the couple running from the room to a roar of audience laughter booming in their wake, then fading into muffled silence as the door shut behind them.

The chilly night air slapped their faces as they exited the building, running down the steps and up the walkway like star-struck lovers, hands still clasped. They stopped midway, out of breath and leaning on one another for support—Roxy's wanton mouth hard on Zach's, his libido in overdrive.

"Come on," he said, the two renewing their hastened stride until they reached Zach's dorm room door. "My roomy's still at the movies—the place is ours," he proclaimed as they entered the darkness. Zach stumbled over to a desk lamp and pulled the chain. "Mood lighting," he said, and held out his hand. Roxy moved toward him, locked and loaded like a gun about to go off. He pulled her close, their hands roaming, fingers fumbling, the two landing on Zach's bed at fever pitch.

In the here and now, there was no reasoning, no sensibilities, just a physical need to fulfill. In the here and now this is what she told herself. But tomorrows are full of regrets. Tomorrow, she might regret the next level to which she'd propelled their relationship, with Zach laying claim to her heart—and hers struggling against the chains. Tomorrow she might regret forgetting her own warning: If I surrender my heart, my mind will follow ... and then I'll lose myself.

40

THE PROMISE

Wednesday, September 10, 1997

T HE DAY COULDN'T HAVE been more perfect for playing hooky and fulfilling his promise. The morning sun poked in and out of cumulous clouds floating on a lazy breeze, while black-capped chickadees vied for a perch on Rose's white picket fence. David had forced himself to wait until a decent hour to call on her. It had been torture watching the clock drag its hands, but he didn't want to appear any more anxious than he already felt, visions of her shadowy embrace of another man still taunting. Only when the clock struck eight did he climb her veranda steps and ring the bell. Within seconds the door opened. He stepped back.

"Hello, David," she said, feather duster in hand and looking ravishing even with a ponytail, loose auburn sprigs escaping at her temples. "What a pleasant surprise. Please ... come in."

"Actually," he said, remaining where he was standing, "I just wanted to ask you something. Spur of the moment, I know, but if you are free today, I wonder ... would you like to accompany me into Boston? A beautiful day to paint at the Public Garden," he said, his dazzling smile masking his nerves as his offer dangled before her.

Her face lit. "Why yes, David" she said, without a second thought. "Yes, I would!"

***

Rose set up shop on a verdant patch of lawn, her easel and canvas aligned with the pond view, its waters reflective of the passing swan boat full of happy faces. She had seen pictures of this lovely place, but it wasn't until being here now, in person, in the sunlight, among the flowered walkways and weeping willows, that the Garden's true beauty eclipsed those photographs.

David spread a nearby blanket and watched her painting take form from his prone position, clouds passing overhead. This was one of those moments that froze in the memory of time. One you lived fully in the now, but later, recalled with deja vu precision. He took in every moment of it, every detail, down to the curve of her back and the way the light danced in her eyes. *If I died now,* David thought, *I'd die a happy man.*

Rose marveled at this handsome man sequestered on the blanket. He had managed to surprise her, and even more so, had the patience to just sit and watch her paint and seem happy to do so. *Who is David Bennett?* she thought, certainly not for the first time. The more she was getting to know him, the more she was finding to like.

The informal setting unleashed a relaxed rhythm of give-and-take conversation. David spoke of his work at the lab and his quest of a cure for cancer, as well as regaled her with his Amazonian tales—some tall, some not. Rose spoke of her charitable work and her love of painting, providing an enthusiastic if somewhat abbreviated version of Oil Painting 101 in response to David's queries. The two intuitively steered clear of unpleasantries. There would be time enough for that kind of talk later. For now, they just wanted to enjoy one another. There was one topic, unpleasant though it was, that David did wish to know more about—the man on the veranda. But unwilling to admit to spying, he wasn't about to bring it up.

After three hours, Rose's plein air painting was finished. David, surprising her once again, withdrew from a wicker basket a checkered tablecloth along with china plates and crystal wine glasses, accompanied by a spread of smoke-salmon canopies and Chardonnay. But it was the Red Velvet cake that won Rose over.

"You sure know the way to a woman's heart," Rose quipped, wiping chocolate frosting from the corner of her mouth with a linen napkin.

David smiled and took her hand into his. "So, what will you do with your painting?" he asked.

"I'll be donating it for a charitable cause," she said. And then a light dawned. "Would you be interested in attending my exhibition?" she asked, turning to look at him in earnest. "Bear in mind, you're not required to buy my paintings," she laughed, her hopeful eyes locked on his.

"Yes of course. Anything to help a worthy cause," David said.

"Wonderful! You'll like Michael."

"Michael?"

"Michael Campo—he owns the gallery. We discussed my paintings last evening. Isn't it all so exciting!"

"Yes … exciting," David said, his voice straining for enthusiasm while the shadowy vision crawled back into his head and their haunting laughter once again knotted his gut.

41

—·—

SHEILA DARLING

Girl Flashback

SIX-YEAR-OLD GIRL WAS EAVESDROPPING *outside of her father's study, drawn to its open door by the jovial nature of his voice on the phone, an unusual occurrence in the Pendleton household. Holding her breath, she bent her ear closer, careful her footing steered clear of squeaky floorboards. She was captivated by this stranger with her father's voice, and the longer she listened, the sprightlier his voice became, even filled with bouts of laughter.*

Girl couldn't tell who he was talking to, but she knew one thing—it wasn't a man. With men, she knew her father to be gruff, demanding, controlling. This call was anything but. Yet, to her recollection, there wasn't a lady he'd ever spoke to in such a manner, not even her mother. But she did clearly hear mention of her mother's name in passing, her father's harsh change in tone hardly subtle.

Girl reckoned that this lady on the phone must be someone special to change her father so. She liked hearing him this way and wondered what the lady's secret was … what magical power perhaps she, too, could learn.

It was just the two of them in the manor, Girl and her father, with her mother out on an errand. Girl wished her mother was home to ask her about this mysterious lady on the phone, as she would never dare to ask her father. And then she heard him say her name, 'Sheila Darling,' just before her father hung up the phone.

The call over she went to move, her foot snagging the squeaky corner of parquet.

"Girl," he called out. "Come in here."

"Yes Father," she answered, and entered the windowless room, her tail between her trembling legs.

"It's not good manners to listen to private conversations. You understand?"

"Yes Father," she said, wincing at what would come next.

"Now run along … and not a word of what you heard to your mother. You hear, Girl?" he said, without a hint of menace in his voice.

"Yes Father," she said, and scurried from the study, relieved, confused and totally amazed. In her mind, Girl thanked 'Sheila Darling' for the spell she had put her father under—how else to explain her escape without a spanking, and more so, his allowing her to do so … happily.

42

NO STRINGS

Thursday, September 11, 1997

Roxy slept like a baby—wrapped in Zach's arms. The morning sunlight escaped the crack along the room's drawn shade and found her eyes. Awakening in someone else's bed was a bit of a surprise, but not unsettling. Lying still, she assessed the situation—Zach's arm lapping her stomach, clothes strewn across the floor, a dark-haired roommate asleep in the opposite bed, and the clock on the wall indicating she had twenty minutes before her first morning session. *Shit,* she thought, now unsettled, not because she was afraid of being late for class, but because she had to rouse Megan.

Carefully, she moved Zach's arm aside and quietly slipped from beneath the covers, throwing on her blouse first and then balancing heron-like on each leg as she slid into her pants. Quickly, she gathered up the rest of her belongings and, glancing over her shoulder at a comatose Zach, sprinted from the room.

★★★

Roxy slowly opened her dorm room door and peeked around the corner.

"How was the movie?" Megan said, already up and dressed and sitting on her made bed. Before Roxy could respond she added, "You look … disheveled."

"Movie—what I saw of it—was hilarious," Roxy answered, startled her roommate was up, but pleased. "As for my looks," she said, glancing into the wall mirror, "I agree." Watching herself tuck in her blouse she thought, *Who am I?,* and struggled for an answer. Was she her own girl … or Zach's. Done taming her wild bed hair with her fingers, she sighed, "That'll have to do. Let's go."

★★★

The two girls slid into seats at the back of the classroom, their English professor's eyes noting their late arrival but not breaking pace with his lecture on William Strunk's 'Elementary Principles of Composition.'

Roxy looked over at Megan—stylishly groomed and fully alert, a pleasant departure from the depressed rag-a-muffin under the covers—and was grateful that her roommate had finally stepped up and taken responsibility for her life. Timing couldn't have been better because now Roxy needed to contemplate her own, the enormity of last evening coming home to roost. *What was I thinking?* she worried, so sure that Zach had totally fallen for her. But it wasn't all his fault; she had allowed her heart to conspire with desire—a deadly combination and clearly not her intent—and in that moment of weakness, lost control. Now she needed to change the narrative and set the record straight.

"Today we will study a principle Strunk encouraged every good writer to heed," her professor said, stressing the phrase he had written on the chalkboard: "Omit needless words."

Roxy's head jerked up. Something about his exhortation clicked, providing an answer to her dilemma—*just keep it short and simple,* she thought.

Resolute, she picked up her pen and wrote Zach a straightforward note—she owed him as much.

★★★

In the middle of a deep dream the sound of something scratching along the floor seemed real to Zach, so real it woke him. He sat up in bed, his ears trained in the direction of the sound, eyes landing on an envelope that had been slipped under his door. He stood and stretched, aware now that his roomy was already up and gone, and Roxy too—strewn clothes and all. He smiled at the thought of her as he walked to the door and bent to retrieve the envelope, his name scrolled across its face. He tore it open and read the enclosed note:

Dear Zach,

Last night was fun. Let's keep it that way. No strings.

Roxy

***

Journal Entry, Wednesday, September 10, 1997:

To quote one of Mother's favorite expressions, guess it's 'wait and see' now with Zach. Will he be amenable to a casual relationship … or want to call it quits? The way of the heart is the determining factor—are his feelings too strong and his heartbreak too painful to see me in any other light? Or can he get past his emotions long enough to enjoy my company and expect nothing more? Tomorrow will tell.

43

TINY SEEDS

Friday, September 12, 1997

Nick found solace these days in his greenhouse nurturing his plants. He could pass the hours in a quasi-meditative state, the warm rays of light through the sunbaked glass relaxing his muscles like hot stones. Here, no distractions sidelined his focus. Tomorrow may be on the horizon, but today … the plants needed him, and he needed the plants.

The watering can full, Nick positioned its spout over the first of a dozen clay pots lining the metal shelving—their soil newly planted with the seeds of Pran—and poured. His life had taken on a strange interconnectedness with these tiny seeds ever since David had revealed his secret plan for Nick's cancer treatment. Now it seemed to Nick that his survival and that of his plants quite possibly depended on each other.

"Thought I'd find you here," David said, stepping inside the greenhouse. "How's it going?"

"Fine. The seedlings should appear in about a week, give or take," Nick said, not bothering to look up from his watering.

"Great," David said. "And how are you feeling? I mean, are you noticing any side effects from the potion?" Nick had been ingesting a concoction of Pran at bedtime for the last several nights, just as Doc had ordered, and David was monitoring his brother for any positive or negative reactions.

"Nothing … just a crazy dream," Nick said.

"How do you mean?" David asked.

"It's the same dream … every night."

"Every night since you've started Pran?"

"Yes."

David felt his heart race. "Tell me about it."

"Nothing to tell really. I just see eyes."

"Eyes?"

"Yes, a woman's eyes."

"How do you know they're a woman's?

"They're beautiful. They draw me in … like I'm hypnotized."

David sucked in his breath. "And then what?" he asked.

"Nothing."

"Nothing?"

"That's all I remember until I wake up."

David studied his brother's face. "And how does this dream make you feel?" he asked.

"Relaxed," Nick said. "I've been sleeping like a baby."

"I see," David said, disappointed more of the dream hadn't been revealed, but thankful his brother hadn't suffered the anxiety-induced aftermath the likes of which his own Sphatika-driven dreams had spawned. "Well, I guess that's a good thing," he said, though still unsettled about the eyes … the eyes of a woman.

"Rose said we shouldn't dismiss dreams that speak to us," Nick said. "I'm not sure what mine means, but I feel like it's trying to tell me something."

"All things become clearer with time," David spouted before he could stop himself, the very words Doc had said to him the night of the Moksha bonfire celebrating his soul's return. He didn't know why he said it, let alone if he even believed it. But there it was. Regardless, for the moment, it seemed to help appease his brother.

"Nick, I was wondering," David said, "I'm attending an exhibition of Rose's paintings tomorrow night and thought maybe you'd like to join me. She'd be thrilled if you came." David knew that his brother, who tended now to go nowhere and see no one—happy to spend his days in this greenhouse from dawn to dusk—would benefit from the much-needed distraction.

Nick looked up at his brother. "Will they include her paintings of the little children … the ones from her dream about Armageddon?"

"I'm not sure, perhaps," David said, recalling the overheard conversation Rose had with Nick as he stood outside the bedroom door.

"Yes, I'll go," Nick said, surprising David, who was so sure his depressed brother would put up his usual fight.

"Great! That's great!" David said. "I'll let her know."

"And let Roxy and Megan know, too," Nick added, his eyes focused back on his watering. "It'd be nice to see them."

44

— • —

THE EXHIBITION

Saturday, September 13, 1997

HER NERVES ON EDGE, Rose arrived early at the gallery, hoping Michael Campo could talk her down the tree before the guests started arriving. This wasn't her first rodeo, but like every artist, she had reservations about her work's worthiness, despite Michael's accolades, or maybe because of them, fearing his feelings for her may have rendered his judgment less than impartial.

"My dear Rose," he said, patting her hand, "there is nothing to worry about. It will be a successful night. You'll see I'm not the only one who admires your work."

"I hope you're right, Michael," she said. "I'd hate to disappoint the charities who stand to benefit."

"Disappoint? Why Rose, if your past accomplishments are any measure—the causes you have taken on, the money you have raised, the lives you've changed for the better—you could never disappoint."

"Thank you, Michael. That's so kind of you to say."

"I simply speak the truth. Come now," he said, his hand outstretched, "let's greet our guests."

Outside of the gallery, a crowd had begun to swell. When Michael opened the door, David and Nick, having arrived early, stood first in line. Upon their entering Rose pecked David affectionately on the cheek, though for his younger brother she bestowed a long, smothering hug. "Nick, I am so happy you came!" she effused. Of course, the unexpected and very public display of affection embarrassed the young man. But

Rose paid no mind and, after quickly introducing them to Michael, she returned her attention to Nick. "Come with me," she said and, taking him by the arm, led him from the cantilevered balcony and down the open staircase into the belly of the gallery.

David, left alone with his rival, knew this sudden opportunity to extract the truth—to find out exactly what Michael meant to Rose—would be fleeting. So, staring Michael down with his ocean-blue eyes, and with a now-or-never, no-nonsense mindset, he asked him outright. "Tell me, Michael, what's your history with Rose?"

★★★

Patiently, Rose waited while Nick stood silently before each of the child portraits she had rendered from her dream, hung now against the backdrop of plain, white walls. She knew better than to interrupt the intellect's absorption of art. Her only hope was that her intuitive interpretation spoke to his heart.

When Nick did finally speak, his voice choked up. "They're beautiful, Rose," he said. "Thank you."

"Why are you thanking me?" she asked, truly bewildered.

"For painting what you felt."

"I agree," came an unfamiliar voice from behind, its distinctive accent Creole. A very tall woman wrapped from head to foot in a bedazzling array of colorful fabrics hovered over them, her emerald eyes riveting from portrait to portrait to portrait, to finally resting upon Rose. "Your paintings of 'The Innocents' are remarkable," she gushed, extending her hand as she introduced herself.

"My name is Lori West. May I take a minute of your time, Mrs. Pendleton," she asked rhetorically, before diving headlong into her spiel. "I'm chief executive of The Artistic Collaborative of New York. Perhaps you've heard of us?" Again, she didn't wait for Rose to answer. "Our annual mission is to seek out extraordinary, original works of art by American artists, awarding each year's top contender with a feature in the critically acclaimed and nationally syndicated magazine, *Art Today*. Mrs. Pendleton," she said, her enthused voice rising, "I invite you to enter your incredible paintings into this year's competition. What do you say?"

Rose could hardly think. She took a deep breath and glanced down at her hands, which had begun to shake. "Ms. West," she said, exhaling as she looked back up, "I am truly stunned by such a gracious and unexpected offer but, as enticing as it may be, I cannot possibly withdraw my art from tonight's exhibition as I am obligated to sell my pieces for the benefit of the charities we are sponsoring."

"You misunderstand, Mrs. Pendleton," Lori said. "Your charities shall certainly benefit from the sale of your work, as I have every intention of purchasing your amazing paintings … if you agree to my invitation." Lori smiled coyly.

For the first time this evening, Rose felt the weight of the world lift from her shoulders. Without hesitation, she reached out her hand. "Deal," she said.

"Wonderful," Lori beamed, shaking her hand with fervor. "Now if you will excuse me, I have a purchase to make." And, turning on her heels, she scurried off up the open staircase.

Rose, in a completely dumbfounded moment, stood speechless.

"Wow," Nick said, aptly expressing her thoughts.

"Have I missed anything?" David asked, finally catching up, delayed after a rather informative discussion with Michael Campo, who was now engaged in conversation with an animated, flamboyantly dressed tall woman.

But before Rose could answer, Roxy and Megan, who had just arrived at the gallery, waved to her from the balcony and were hurrying down the staircase.

Nick, foregoing the social courtesy of greetings, was unable to contain his excitement and immediately blurted out, "You'll never guess what just happened."

David gaped at his brother, startled to hear him sounding so upbeat.

"What happened?" Roxy asked.

"Tell them, Rose," Nick demurred, his voice dramatic.

"Well," she said, pausing for her own theatrics, "I just sold my paintings of "The Innocents!"

"What?" "So soon?" "To whom?" they all asked, the questions flying.

"Congratulations!" Michael Campo interjected as he joined the tumult. "I just completed the sale. I'm so proud of you, Rose!" he said, embracing her.

David's adrenaline flowed.

"This calls for a celebration," Michael said, raising his hand to wave down the wait staff who, summarily, delivered a glass-filled tray of champagne.

Rose didn't bat an eye when all three teens scooped a fluted stemware of alcohol.

"To Rose, a generous and talented woman," Michael toasted. Cries of "Here, here!" abounded as all clinked glasses.

Roxy downed her drink. "Now tell us everything, Mother," she implored, giddy from the news and perhaps the bubbly.

As Rose complied, David steamed under his collar watching Michael wrap his arm around her shoulders. Actually, he hadn't stopped steaming since his earlier conversation with the man. David had had little idea of the devoted relationship bonding the two artists, a relationship he was beginning to envy, a relationship he felt ill-equipped with which to compete. They had a history together, after all. The kind of history that would always exclude him from their laughter at past references, or from the familiar comfort of just being together, with no words needed. David wanted in to this closeness with Rose, but so long as Michael was in the picture, he would always be third person out.

When Rose finished the retelling of her good fortune, which still hadn't sunk in, she excused herself from the group to mingle with the other guests. She had, after all, other paintings of hers to promote this evening, other paintings near and dear to her heart that would hopefully sell. She had entered this evening's exhibition feeling uncertain, unworthy even, but now she embraced high hopes. And somewhere in the back of her mind she heard the whisper of her beloved, deceased mother, "To give is to receive."

Rose smiled.

PART THREE

Four Years Later – 2001

TreesTales Publishing

45

—·—

MICHAEL'S BOYS

Tuesday, May 1, 2001

NICK STIRRED AWAKE TO the sound of knocking on his bedroom door. "Come in," he said, groggily.

Nurse Annika entered the room like a strong wind gusting. "Rise and shine," her lilted voice sang as she placed a breakfast tray bedside and moved briskly to draw open the drapes.

Nick stretched, and through a yawn announced, "Another sunny day."

"That it is, dear boy," Annika agreed, the morning rays blinding, "that it is."

In truth, every day Nick's awoken for the last four years could be deemed 'sunny'. Ever since he nourished Pran's seeds into healthy plants, and they in turn nourished him, his life has changed for the better—his depression a thing of the past, his cancer in remission, and his demeanor and outlook on life calm and positive.

David had asked Annika to stay on despite Nick's remarkable recovery because her presence brought him peace of mind whenever he was away. Though if he were honest, David would confess to sleeping lightly even when home, one ear always trained on his brother down the hall. But Annika, it seems, had turned out to be not only a fine nurse but a good cook and a suitable companion for Nick in his absence, the two entertained with occasional games of scrabble to pass the time. But time for games these days was rather in short supply, ever since Nick committed to helping Michael Campo with his troubled teens.

Gulping down a heaping breakfast of Annika's famous blueberry pancakes soaked in authentic Vermont maple syrup, Nick finished in time to catch the bus traveling into Harvard Square.

***

Upon entering Michael's gallery, the sudden cacophony of voices rising up from its belly no longer filled him with dread. Instead, the sound of life asserting itself felt like a refreshing splash of cold water, awakening him. In fact, any inclination to run from the discomfort of interacting with Michael's boys was gone, along with his old negative self. Now his darkest days of four years ago seemed like a distant dream. Nick had put his trust in his brother, and that had made all the difference. And so, he aimed to pay it forward—helping Michael's boys—though not in quite the manner that Michael had envisioned.

Nick ran down the open staircase to shouts of, "Morning bro" and "It's 'bout time you got your lazy ass in here." These 'good-natured' greetings had been slow in coming, Michael's boys initially neither hospitable nor respectful of their new mentor, nor of one another for that matter. Constantly at each other's throats, often more barroom-brawlers than potential artists, suspicious and untrusting of anyone or anything offering help, it had not been an easy task for Nick to enmesh himself with these self-styled hoodlums. The old Nick of four years ago ran from them; the new Nick embraced them. Over time, he and Michael's boys had become a loose band of brothers. And for Nick, this was a first. Guy friends had always eluded him in high school. He'd blame it on shyness, or not being a jock, but deep in his heart he knew the buried truth. But it wasn't until after the fire killed his parents that he'd found the courage to come out to his brother—though his being gay hadn't been news to David. Now, Nick finally felt comfortable in his skin. And Michael's boys, despite knowing this about him, accepted him. That meant the world to Nick.

"So who died and made ya king?" Santiago asked, his short, muscular body awash in tattoos.

Dwayne, a tall and lanky kid whose Afro haircut made him taller still, responded, "Just stand back and look, bro, is all I'm saying."

"Ya can't tell your ass from your elbow, and I'm s'pose to listen to you?" Santiago declared.

"Don't take it from me, bro. Ask the pro," Dwayne said, nodding toward Nick, who was bounding off of the bottom stair.

"Ask me what?" Nick said, delivering high fives all around.

"His painting lacks perspective, man. You can't tell if the seascape is up close or far off. Either it needs a boat beached on shore or cruisin' on distant waves. That's all," Dwayne explained.

Nick took a step back, his ocean blue eyes taking full stock of Santiago's painting. "Perspective can be a useful tool," he said, rubbing his chin, "but remember, the view an artist paints represents how he sees the world. And it doesn't always need to pay homage to convention. Maybe there shouldn't be a boat at all. Maybe a lack of perspective invites imagination, makes the painting more interesting ... more mysterious. There's no right or wrong answer, guys. It's all in how the artist sees it."

"See," Santiago said, "it's all in how I see it."

"Yeh, well I still say ya need a boat," Dwayne huffed.

"Nick, can you lend me a hand," Michael called down from the balcony above.

"Sure thing," Nick replied, and bounded back up the staircase two steps at a time.

"Our water delivery just arrived," Michael said. "Can you see to it the boys' cooler gets a refill, and the rest gets put into storage."

"You got it, boss," Nick said, eyeing the jugs grouped by the entry door, per usual. Grabbing a nearby dolly he proceeded to transport the jugs into a storage room, setting all the jugs onto a shelf, but one. Then, after spying over his shoulder and determining the coast clear, he quickly uncapped the remaining jug. From his pant pocket he retrieved a syringe and injected a clear, odorless liquid into the water. Once done, he tucked the empty syringe back into his pant pocket and recapped the jug. The procedure took less than a minute, one he'd performed multiple times for multiple weeks without a hitch. Today was no different.

Down in the belly of the gallery, he replaced the empty jug from the boys' water cooler with the enhanced refill ... and then he offered each of the boys a cupful.

46

SURPRISES

Monday, May 7, 2001

DAVID SAT AT HIS office desk and checked his watch. He had a luncheon date with Rose and didn't want to be late. Things had been hectic at the lab over these past four years, what with David's frequent trips to Brazil resulting in numerous plant samples constantly under evaluation at his lab for use in the fight against cancer. Despite Pran's success with his brother, David couldn't go there. He was obliged to keep mum on the top-secret plant knowing that if knowledge leaked of Nick's breakthrough cure it would put their lives at risk. He had no misgivings about his nemesis, Agent Jenks. The man meant business. Curing the ill was not of his concern; wiping out the fanatical youth of the world was. And after four years David was feeling the pressure, though he was no closer to delivering a contagious airborne disease.

Staring through his floor-to-ceiling glass wall David observed Brad, his young protege, working across from him. Extremely bright and eager, his inquisitive research assistant had proven his value a hundred times over. He easily stepped in to fill David's shoes at the lab whenever travel called, giving his boss peace of mind to concentrate on the task at hand. But David was not without some reservation in abandoning the ship to his understudy. He had an ever-present concern that Brad's overactive curiosity might lead him down the rabbit hole to his undercover work on Octane, despite always being careful to cover his tracks. And as much as David tried to relegate his research on Pran primarily to Doc's lab in Brazil, there were occasions when the constraints of time prevented him from doing so. It was such times as those that Brad would find himself sent on wild goose chases for research supplies, donut runs—whatever it took to get him out of the lab and provide David some privacy. Checking his watch again, David stood and quickly left the room.

Brad looked up from his microscope and watched his boss leave. The moment the door closed on David's backside he stood and walked to the window, observing the black Corvette pull out of the parking lot. He checked his watch. One hour for lunch. *Time enough to snoop,* he thought, though always on guard for an earlier-than-expected return. Brad didn't relish being taken by surprise.

***

David spotted Rose the moment he entered the restaurant. He swore she looked more beautiful each time he saw her. He was still in the battle of his life for her love—his competition, Michael Campo, refusing to exit the picture. And worse, Rose had turned down David's proposal of marriage twice over the past four years, always with the claim she wasn't ready. But he wasn't giving up hope, not so long as Rose enjoyed being in his company.

Her head down studying the menu, he snuck up and whispered into her ear, "Hello gorgeous."

"Why, hello David," she said, startled but pleased.

"Have you been waiting long?" he asked. "Traffic was horrendous."

"Not long," she said, "I went ahead and ordered our favorite."

David pulled his chair kitty-corner to hers at their small, square table and sat. "Perfect," he said, "I'm starving." Then leaning in close to Rose he asked, "So … what's the big surprise?"

Rose smiled and said, "You're just like a little kid who can't stand not knowing what's inside the wrapped box."

"Well, you can't blame a man who's been kept dangling a whole day," he said. "Is it my fault you refused telling me over the phone?"

"Some things are best told in person," she said, as the waiter delivered their luncheon plates of crusted salmon to the table.

David's stomach rumbled. "Mmmm … smells delicious," he said, placing his napkin onto his lap.

As Rose watched him take his first bite, a feeling of deja vu took hold.

"What? Do I have food on my face?" he asked, misreading her facial expression and quickly dabbing his mouth with his napkin.

"No," she laughed. "I was just recalling our first dinner date … and our wonderful stroll afterwards through the Boston Public Garden. Seems like yesterday," she said.

"Yes," David agreed, "hard to believe four years have passed. So much has happened since then."

"Yes, the most wonderful of which is Nick's recovery," Rose enthused. "A miracle, pure and simple, his cancer disappearing like that. Even his doctors were left without explanation … totally astonished."

David swallowed his mouthful hard. It pained him not to have been truthful with Rose, but he had to protect her. Any slip of her tongue could prove dangerous. As far as he was concerned, it was far better having Rose believe in God's mysterious ways than handing Agent Jenks a new target.

"And so, that brings me to my big surprise," she said.

David put down his fork and smiled. "I'm all ears," he said.

"Yesterday, I received a phone call from Lori West informing me that The Artistic Collaborative of New York would like to offer Nick the opportunity to enter his paintings into this year's contest of original works by American artists. Isn't it wonderful, David!"

"That's incredible news, Rose! First you, now Nick!"

"This was meant to be, David. And I have no doubt Nick will win top prize," she said, her voice full of pride.

David smiled at her faith, though privately acknowledging it didn't hurt having someone with connections, a previous winner herself, pulling for his brother.

"Does Nick know?" he asked.

"Lori's dropping into Michael's gallery as we speak. He's going to be so surprised!"

***

Dwayne stood back, drop-jawed, as he peered at Santiago's painting.

"Hey bro. Am I seeing things? Or is that a beached boat on the shore?"

"I decided to give it perspective after all, mi amigo, like ya said."

"Well fuck me, there's hope for ya yet, bro," Dwayne declared, high-fiving his pal.

"Hey Nick," Dwayne yelled up to his mentor on the balcony, "you gotta come take a look at this, man."

Nick beelined it down into the cluster of young men crowding Santiago's painting. Moving aside for Nick, they awaited his reaction.

He paused, eyes pensive, studying his student's work. "Santiago," he said finally, "you're just full of surprises."

"I think you mean full of shit," Dwayne countered.

"That too," Nick agreed to roaring laughter.

"Hey Nick, would you mind coming up, please," Michael shouted over the balcony. "You've got a visitor."

"Be right there," Nick yelled back.

***

David pulled his Corvette between the lines of his personal parking space and turned off the engine. He sat in his leather bucket seat feeling lightheaded between the glass of wine and the good news about Nick, not to mention just being with Rose. He felt like playing hooky, but there was no getting around the work awaiting him—or rather, the self-imposed pressure from the demands of Agent Jenks. He sighed and opened the car door.

When his boss re-entered the building, Brad was in the lab frantically attempting to make sense of his findings. His suspicions had begun innocently enough four years prior with his wondering about David's hidden stash in his desk drawer, though nothing concrete ever came of it, just an increase in David's odd and secretive behavior in the years since. But it wasn't until David's brother, Nick, mysteriously kicked his cancer that Brad's beagle nose fully kicked into high gear. Then today, while poking around the extracts of plants derived from Doc's Brazilian farm, extracts that had been deemed unworthy of a cancer cure and set aside, his beagle nose discovered there, among the discards, an extract that was left uncatalogued in the lab's register—an odd occurrence, given David's meticulous standards. Of course, human error could logically explain the lapse, but … what if the extract was purposely stashed in with the discards—a place less likely to be scrutinized by human eyes, and the last place one would look to find a viable cure for cancer. Not sure exactly what he had on his hands, and wary of jumping to conclusions about any nefarious actions on the part of his boss, Brad decided to keep mum until he could delve deeper into his surprise discovery.

47

— · —

ROMANCE NOVELS

Girl Flashback

GIRL LIKED READING ROMANCE novels whenever her father was away, a treat her mother readily allowed her maturing, twelve-year-old daughter. She imagined a handsome beau of her own one day who would treasure her above all else—the antithesis of her father, who made her feel like loose change in his pocket, weighing him down, her value uncounted and questionable. Was it too much to hope for? Not in the imagination of a wishful twelve-year old.

The very first time she saw Billy at the start of the school year she felt this way about him. Some call it puppy love at such a young age—but be that as it may, Girl felt her heart stir. The two schoolmates had never actually met, having been assigned to different sixth grade classrooms but, just like in one of her romance novels, fate worked its wonders.

With her father out of town, mother and daughter secretly planned an outing to the county fair. Rose, afraid of heights, refused at the last minute to ride the Ferris wheel, leaving Girl in line determined to go it alone. But when the operator of the ride brought the next seat to the load zone and its current occupants departed, he turned to the waiting line and said, "Next two." Thrown off guard by his comment, she turned to look behind her. There, in the flesh, with his soft brown eyes and chestnut hair, stood her sixth-grade heartthrob.

Billy smiled … and she melted.

"I'm game if you are," he said.

Right then, no greater words had ever been spoken to her. "Sure," she smiled back.

"I'm Billy, by the way," he said, climbing into the dangling seat. "You're Roxy, right?"

Oh my gosh, *she thought,* He knows my name. *She nodded.*

The safety bar down and locked in place, and the two settled onto their cushioned seat, the Ferris wheel slowly moved up, notch by notch, allowing further passengers on.

"What a view from up here," Billy said, as they inched closer the top, their seat swaying with the slightest of movement.

"Amazing," Girl agreed, hardly able to breathe.

Billy suddenly leaned forward and yelled to a friend he spotted in the crowd below. "Sammy ... hey Sammy!" Evidently Sammy couldn't hear him over the fairground's clamor, so Billy turned his attention back to Girl.

"Here we go," he said with anticipation as they reached the very top and then kept going, sweeping round and round, rotation after rotation, their seat rocking and their hair billowing.

Girl was in another world, like in one of her romance novels and, just then, thought of a favorite line, "There is no time where passion exists." She liked that, because it was how she felt right now, suspended in time, happy in the moment. But, alas, the ride was soon over and so, too, her bliss.

When their seat came to a halt at the bottom, and the safety bar raised, the two exited.

"Thanks for riding with me," Billy said. And before Girl could respond, someone called his name. He turned, and with a huge grin, yelled, "Sammy!"

Sammy was a girl.

She ran up and pecked his cheek, then grabbed his hand and tugged. "Come on," she said, "let's try the ring toss." And the two were off.

So it wasn't a storybook ending for Girl, standing there stunned and stranded like a fish out of water, but the sea was a big place, and there would be other fish to catch—though some would inevitably slip back in.

48

THE BIG DAY

Saturday, May 19, 2001

I t was finally the big day for Roxy and Megan—college graduation. Four years gone in a flash, and now the real world awaited
them.

Roxy sat silently at her bedroom desk, a large brown envelope
perched on its top. She ran her fingers tenderly over the hand-printed
name on its face, her gaze fixed on the writing but her mind far off.

"Are you ready dear?" the familiar voice interrupted, drifting up the
stairs.

"Yes, mother, I'm ready," Roxy answered, picking up her package
along with her graduation cap, its silk tassel swaying while her gown
swished as she walked out of the room.

***

Their ride to the ceremony was driven much in silence, not that Rose
wasn't up for talk, but she had sensed Roxy's mood this morning as
rather introspective at the breakfast table—answers being short but
polite to any inquiries, adding nothing of her own to the conversation
—and Rose knew from experience better to give her daughter quiet
space than to crowd her thoughts during anxious times.

But as soon as they pulled into the parking lot and Roxy spotted Megan,
she expelled a massive sigh. "Megan!" she cried, waving wildly out the

window. The two girls ran to each other, hugging and laughing, while Rose and Megan's dad, Sean, looked on, amused.

"Mother, we have to join our classmates in the lineup," Roxy said, a smile on her face. "We'll catch up with you both after the ceremony."

"I'll be applauding from the stands when you receive your diploma," Rose said, and kissed her daughter's cheek.

"Aye," Sean said, "I'll be singin' and dancin' a jig!"

Everyone laughed and the girls darted off.

"Shall we find seats before the good ones are taken?" Rose asked Sean.

"Wouldn't want dat ter 'appen, wud we," he replied, and the two proud parents made their way into the auditorium.

★★★

"Can you believe it! I thought this day would never come," Roxy enthused, as the two best friends took their place in the procession line right next to each other—O'Malley alphabetically followed by Pendleton—an unbelievable coincidence, but Roxy knew her mother would say otherwise.

"Yeh, me too. I'm ready to move on … only I still can't make up my mind what I want to do," Megan said. "My dad suggested I take the summer off … think about it … not make any hasty decisions. Though I think he's really a bit melancholy over the possibility of my taking a job away from home and this is his way of forestalling the inevitable."

"I know what you mean. I'm having a hard time deciding as well," Roxy agreed, though, in truth, she would have no trouble living at home the rest of her life, her mother there as her comfort blanket.

"Rox, I've been thinking. How would you feel about the two of us visiting one another over the summer."

"Absolutely! Yes! That would be so much fun!" Roxy said, squeezing Megan tight, so glad to have something to look forward to, a welcome distraction from decision-making about her future and the anxiety it brought.

***

David and Nick arrived late, delayed by an emergency at the lab. A power outage had shut down ongoing research, and worse, the backup generator had failed to kick on. He wasn't in a good mood. And, as if that wasn't enough, when they finally found Rose, Sean and Michael Campo had bookended her. Oh, Michael was cool and cordial per usual, a gentleman always. And oh, how David wanted to wipe that smug smile from his face. But he was a gentleman, too, so he and Nick graciously took the two seats next to Sean.

David spent the entire ceremony eavesdropping on Rose and Michael's conversation, all the while still trying to maintain small talk with Megan's dad. He was a nice enough fellow, and David had felt a bond with Sean over the loss of his wife and that of his own parents during the same storm ten years ago. But David never liked being the underdog in any situation, and least of all playing second fiddle where Rose was concerned. There was, however, a silver lining in his fiasco of a day—and that was that his brother, Nick, was here with him, healthy and happy.

It didn't bother Nick that he had personally missed out on graduating from college. He had resigned himself to having cancer four years ago and then, even when his body took a turn for the better, he had decided to bypass college to paint—his true passion. With Rose's encouragement, somehow doors kept opening for him. His paintings began to sell. His name became known locally and now the offer from Lori West to enter his work in a national contest would bring him further renown, even if he didn't win. The young man was on a roll. But the thing that brought him the most satisfaction was working with Michael's boys. Rose had been right to introduce him to these needy teens, though he'd felt he gotten the better deal, the job giving him a moral compass and a meaningful direction upon which to set his life's path. Rose, of course, relished it all, having taken him under her wing. Yet, she gave him room to fly. And it seemed to her the more that he spread his wings, the more the world would benefit.

***

The pomp and circumstance went as expected, the two best friends crossing the wooden stage and walking off one after the other, diplomas in hand and faces radiant. After the ceremony, they made their way out to the parking lot along with the rest of their graduating class to await their parents.

Still overjoyed, the two young women embraced each other, rocking back and forth with glee next to Rose's car.

Suddenly Megan stopped rocking. "Don't look now," she whispered calmly into Roxy's ear.

Roxy turned, and then her heart leapt in her chest. Zach Tanner was making his way toward them, his buddy Paul Revere on his tail.

"Hey Rox! Megan! How's it going? Well, we finally made it!" he said, looking more handsome than ever, his corona hair glistening in the sun. He and Roxy had signed onto keeping theirs a casual, no-strings-attached relationship throughout the remainder of college, as per Roxy's request. Though, if it had been up to Zach, Roxy would have been wearing his ring.

"Yeh, miracles do happen," Paul said with a nervous chuckle, eying Megan.

She, for her part, had held to her promise and didn't see Paul again after their one double date, nor did she date anyone else for that matter. After four years, Roxy gave up trying to convince her roommate otherwise.

"You and Paul heading west after graduation?" Roxy asked, cutting to the chase.

As much as she craved control over her life, telling herself Zach's influence would impinge on her freedom and that she'd be better off without him, she couldn't deny her feelings every time she saw him.

"Yep, going straight to LA. Might as well aim big. Take Hollywood by storm!" Zach said.

"Speaking of Hollywood, I've got something for you." Roxy opened the car door and retrieved the large brown envelope. "I hope you like it," she said, handing it to Zach. "If not, you can always use it as fire fodder."

"Is this what I think it is?" Zach said, disbelief in his voice.

Roxy nodded.

"Wow! You actually wrote a movie script! I can't believe it! I mean … after freshman orientation you never mentioned it again … so naturally I thought …

"Well … good luck," Roxy said, a lump rising in her throat with the reality of his imminent departure from her life. "Let me know when the movie premieres."

"You bet," Zach said. "You'll be my guest of honor."

"I'd better be," Roxy said, struggling to maintain composure.

"Thanks, Roxy. For this … and for everything," Zach said, then he leaned in and kissed her lips.

Her world spun.

Megan backed up a step, not waiting for Paul to get any similar ideas.

"Well, guess we'll be going," Zach said. "See you some time in the future."

"Yeh, see you," Roxy said.

Zach and Paul walked away, the two turning once to wave before blending in with the crowd.

Roxy ran for the bathroom, her tears flowing.

★★★

Journal Entry, Saturday May 19, 2001:

I felt anxious today—everyone's eyes on me walking across the stage for my diploma. But worse than that, seeing Zach for the last time. It was hard to say goodbye. Everyone says, 'out of sight, out of mind.' I suppose it will get easier with time. But I made my decision, and now I need to get on with my life … whatever that turns out to be.

49

BOWLS OF FOOD

Thursday, May 24, 2001

DAVID MOANED IN HIS sleep, his heart racing and breath gasping, caught in a dream—its reality overtaking him. His moaning drifted down the hallway into Nick's room, who promptly threw his bedding aside and ran to his brother's aid.

"David," Nick said, shaking his brother's shoulders. "David, wake up."

Coming to, it took David a moment to focus.

"You were moaning. Are you alright?" Nick asked, his brow furrowed.

David thought for a second, his fingers still caressing the quartz crystal strung from his neck and the dream still vivid in his mind. A smile came to his face.

"What?" Nick asked, confused.

David had returned to his recurring dream with Lanya, the two totally immersed in their alternate world. It was ecstasy beyond description … beyond comprehension … for which, even now, David failed to find the words.

"What?" Nick asked again.

"I just had an unbelievable wet dream, dear brother," David said, winking at Nick, trying to make light of it, not wanting to tell him about Lanya.

Nick laughed. "I thought you were having a heart attack!"

"On the brink of one had I gone any longer," David joked. "Sorry I woke you. Go back to bed."

"You didn't wake me," he said. "One of 'those dreams' woke me earlier."

"Oh?" David said, knowing that his brother had been experiencing his own otherworldly dreams ever since he began ingesting nightly Pran potions, and he wondered if this one provided any further pieces to the puzzle. "Tell me about it."

When his dreams first began four years ago, Nick saw eyes—beautiful eyes of a woman—that seemed to look through him and beyond. Since then, those same eyes have revealed bits and pieces of visions—recurring visions, each one building upon the last.

"Okay," Nick said, obliging, "but it makes no sense."

He began, "It's like before … a group of men are sitting at a table—a large, round table—with bowls of food on it. And, again, the men are in conversation—their discussion serious, like the weight of the world is resting on them. Now the new part—the bowls of food are passed around, and someone calls the food … Octane?" Nick shook his head. "I have no idea what that even means."

David sucked in his breath, hardly able to believe what he just heard … Octane. His mind raced to come to terms with the danger this may pose for his brother—his possession of what exactly? Information? Knowledge he was not supposed to have? Whatever you'd call it, David knew it would prove fatal for them both if leaked.

"Listen, Nick," he said, trying to remain calm. "It's important to never mention your dreams to anyone but me. Okay? Please trust me on this. Do I have your word?"

Nick was baffled. Who'd be interested in his crazy dreams anyways. But if David wanted him to keep mum, he'd keep mum, no question. He trusted his brother with his life.

"Sure thing, David. No problem," he said, his fingers performing a pretend zip of his lips.

"Good. Now let's try and get some sleep. Shall we?"

"See you in the morning, bro," Nick said, and made his way back to his room.

David sat awake the rest of the night, trying to make sense of it all. But he, a scientist, knew trying to make sense of the paranormal was a constant uphill battle with his intellect. And damned if ever the two shall meet.

50

—·—

THE ROSE

Friday, June 1, 2001

ROSE HAD BEEN WANTING to open her own gallery for a long time, and now, with her daughter's graduation under her belt, she'd have more time to concentrate on making her dream come true. With Michael Campo's help, she found a perfect spot not far from his own gallery in Harvard Square. He wasn't averse to the competition, quite the opposite. He was excited that the two could resume their philanthropic ventures together, just like the old days. But there was no denying Michael was even more excited at the prospect of upping the ante on courting Rose.

David wasn't thrilled, of course, though he'd never let on, outwardly. But this new curve in his plans to win over Rose called for some adjustment on his part. Now it seemed his only course of action required enmeshing himself even more into her life. And the road to doing that involved him giving more time to her and less to his work. This wasn't going to be easy nor, he feared, acceptable to Agent Jenks. But that was fallout he would just have to deal with when it came. David's priority now was Rose.

★★★

"Where would you like this one?" David asked.

"Over there, on that wall," Rose said, pointing.

David mounted a large contemporary piece of art, quite good but, as far as he was concerned, never on par with those of his brother's.

"Perfect," Rose said, straightening the canvas slightly to the left.

Rose had been glad for David's help these past several weeks and, more so, found she liked having him around. She had been afraid of letting him into her life more completely, convincing herself that she liked the life she had built just the way it was. But now, having David around, she was growing less inclined to think so.

"Oh, it looks so beautiful, mother!" Roxy said, coming out of the back storage room and stopping to admire the painting. She was thrilled to be helping out since graduation. It was like winning a double lottery—spending long, summer days with her mother while, at the same time, avoiding decisions about her future. All in all, she couldn't complain.

"Thank you, my two darlings, for all your help. I couldn't have done this myself," Rose said embracing them both.

"The gallery needs a name, mother," Roxy said.

"Yes, it does. Any suggestions?"

"How about The Rose Gallery, but more informally we can just call it The Rose?"

"I like the sound of that," David agreed.

"It's not too pretentious, is it, using my name?"

"Mother, you are forgetting The Isabella Stewart Gardner Museum—now that sounds pretentious."

Everyone laughed.

"Well," Rose said, "if it's the consensus, then The Rose it is."

The gallery's door suddenly flew open.

"I won, I won," Nick shouted, storming in. "I won the contest!"

Roxy rushed Nick and, bear-hugging him, gushed, "That's fantastic!"

"I'm proud of you, brother!" David effused, getting in on the act.

Rose beamed from the sidelines and, once Nick had freed himself from their clutches, she said, "I am so very pleased, Nick. You deserve it."

He walked over and embraced her. "I owe it all to you," he said, his voice cracking.

"No, Nick," she said. "It was all you."

"Well, I think this calls for a celebration," David said. "Dinner's on me!"

51

NATURAL BORN SNOOP

Monday, June18, 2001

IT WAS PERFECT TIMING for Brad. With David spending so much time outside of the lab helping Rose, it gave him more time to delve into his secret discovery. He felt like a kid again performing at-home science experiments in search of nature's secrets. The thrill of discovery never left him and now, at the age of twenty-eight, he was still a science geek on a mission ... and a natural born snoop. Enticed by the 'hidden' plant extract, Brad was driven to learn more about it, first through analysis of its elements and then through its DNA. He was going to cross every T and dot every I in his evaluation, determined to either justify its unworthy status as a discard, or to find credible evidence that this extract, in fact, offered potential in the fight against cancer. If the latter proved true, either a mistake will have been corrected, or a coverup will have been exposed. But that was putting the cart before the horse. One step at a time, Brad had to keep telling himself, as he checked over his shoulder for unwanted company.

★★★

It was the end of the day when David decided to show up at the laboratory.

He had just left Rose at the gallery feeling more optimistic than ever about their relationship now that they had been sharing more time together. His hopes were flying high and, once again, his thoughts were entertaining wedding bells. He knew timing was everything and opportunity fleeting, and if he waited too long to propose again, he might lose Rose to Michael. But he was also aware that pushing her too hard when she wasn't ready could leave him spurned a third time. Proposing was tricky business; but David had made up his mind. He was willing to wager his pride and the possibility of another stab to his heart, because he could never consider the alternative—life without her. His mind simply refused to give credence to that thought. No, if she rebuffed him again, he would simply persevere.

When David entered the lab, he wasn't surprised to find Brad working late; still, it gave him pause, as it did each time upon his return, expecting to be outed for his undercover work at any moment.

The young research assistant looked up at the sound of the door and smiled. "Hey, boss," he said. "How's it going?"

"Great. Wonderful in fact," David said, his thoughts returning to Rose. "Any issues come up in my absence?"

"Nah, ship's holding tight," Brad said, his matter-of-fact demeanor belying the adrenaline rush in his veins from a day of digging for treasure.

"Good. Keep me posted," David said, "and go home, for God's sake. The lab will be here in the morning."

"Sure thing, boss. You have a good night," Brad said, while thinking, *Just leave already.*

He waited for David's Corvette to pull out of the lot and then dove eagerly back into his research.

52

— · —

MAGIC 8 BALL

Girl Flashback

"*O*H, MOTHER, THANK YOU!"

There was only one thing Girl wanted for her seventh birthday—a Magic 8 Ball. A classmate had brought one in for Show and Tell and, ever since then, it was all she could think about. And now her mother had acquiesced to her daughter's wish, about which her father knew nothing.

"Ask it a question, Mother!" Girl said, wanting to test it out.

"Is it a good time to divide my daylilies?"

Girl tipped the ball. "It says, 'It is decidedly so.'"

"Well then, I guess I will decidedly do so!" Rose laughed.

Even after her mother left the room she kept the questions coming, intrigued by the quick-fire responses popping up each time—a lot more fun than coming up with the answers herself. It went on like this for weeks, just a game to fill in times of boredom. And then, somehow, it happened ... the Magic 8 Ball took on a life of its own—and play turned into reality.

It started small at first, with her angst over insignificant decisions like should she buy ice cream with her allowance but then accelerated to more concerning issues like should she fess up to scraping her Sunday best shoes. Soon she found making hard decisions was much easier having quick and easy answers at her fingertips. And so, her Magic 8 Ball became a habit-forming crutch.

"Darling, why don't you give your Magic 8 Ball a rest and come help me outside with the garden," Rose said. "It's much too nice a day to be in."

If not for the fact that her mother was standing right in front of her, Girl would have been tempted to first consult her 8 Ball. Instead, she threw it onto her bed and, with a longing look over her shoulder, left with her mother for the garden.

With gardening gloves on and pruning shears in hand, the two knelt in the morning sunshine onto the rich-smelling soil and began the slow process of deadheading the marigolds.

"Mother, how did you choose which flowers to plant in your garden?" Girl asked, discarding the spent blooms into a bucket.

"Your grandmother taught me to first determine whether my garden would be in the sun or shade," Rose said. "So this being a sunny location, that narrowed my choices."

Girl kept snipping off the brown, shriveled-up blooms. Then, her forehead furrowed, she said, "But there are so many flowers that grow well in the sun. How did you decide?"

"Well, first I had to consider did I want an annual or perennial garden … or a mix of both. And then the size of the plants when fully matured—back row blooms the tallest, front row the smallest. Also, color scheme—did I want blooms with harmonizing hues or all one color. After that …"

"Mother … didn't all those decisions make your head hurt?"

Rose laughed. "No, darling. It was exciting, creating my own unique garden."

Girl sighed. "Well, Mother," she said, "if I ever grow a garden of my own, all the flowers will be one kind, one height, one color and perennials … so that I don't ever have to replant them again."

And, *she thought to herself,* my Magic 8 Ball will have the final say on everything.

53

—·—

A JOURNALIST

Friday, July 6, 2001

IT WAS A HOT summer morning. The old Victorian had many virtues—air-conditioning not one of them. Roxy opened all her bedroom windows wide and turned on a fan. Lying back on her bed with her trusty Magic 8 Ball rotating in her sweaty palms she thought, *Who am I?* as she considered her future calling while awaiting the doorbell's ring. Today, Megan was coming to visit! The last time the two had seen one another was on graduation day. Since then, Roxy still hadn't chosen a profession to make good on her college degree and now, with Rose anxious for her daughter to focus on making a career choice, Roxy wondered if Megan had made hers. One thing she knew for certain—whatever she chose to become, it would have nothing to do with politics.

While the fan whirred, Roxy stared at her Magic 8 Ball and contemplated her first question. Finally, she asked out loud, "Should I become a copywriter?" and then flipped the ball. The answer popped up: "Very doubtful." *Whew,* she thought, grateful to have eliminated her least favorite possibility from the list. She moved on, "How about a screenwriter?" Completing the script for Zach had imbued confidence in her writing skills, but its too-close-to-home subject matter had worn her down and soured her perspective. She turned the ball: "Don't count on it." *Okay,* she thought with relief, *moving on.* "What do you say to working as a journalist?" She rotated the ball and stared at the answer: "Outlook good." "A journalist," she said into the air, liking the sound of it. And then the idea dawned, "I could freelance!" She threw the ball onto her bed and ran down the stairs.

"Mother," she exclaimed, storming into the sunroom, "I know what I want to be."

Rose, busy at her easel, turned around in surprise.

"I'm going to be a journalist!"

"Why, that's wonderful, darling," Rose said, hardly able to believe her ears.

"But best of all … I can freelance!" Roxy gushed. "Which means I decide what I write, when I write and—the cherry on top— where I write! I can literally work from home, Mother! Isn't that fantastic!"

"Yes, darling, it is," Rose said with enthusiasm in her voice but worry clouding her mind. Of course, she was quite pleased her daughter had settled on a vocation, but she had hoped Roxy would spread her wings and finally fly from the nest. But rather than dampen the moment with a wet blanket of worry, Rose put her trust in the Almighty. *God will provide,* she thought.

"I can't wait to tell Megan," Roxy said. And as fast as she came, she disappeared from the sunroom, leaving Rose in the aftermath of her whirlwind.

Roxy plunked herself down on the settee in the front parlor and peered out through the stain glass window. A weight seemed to have lifted from her, and she felt like she was floating on air. When she spotted Mr. O'Malley's car pulling up to the curb, Roxy raced to open the door before anyone could ring the bell.

"I'm so glad you made it!" she said stepping out onto the veranda, her heart pumping with excitement as she greeted her former roommate and best friend.

"Me too!" Megan said, climbing the steps and embracing her.

Then, noticing she was alone, Roxy asked, "Where's your father?"

"Oh, I drove down by myself. Dad lent me his car," Megan said, beaming with pride.

Rose poked her head outside. "I thought I heard voices," she said, stepping onto the veranda and bestowing Megan with a big hug. "Well done on your driving, dear," she said. "I've been trying to get Roxanne behind the wheel ever since high school."

"Some people aren't meant to drive, Mother."

"Only those with chauffeurs, darling," Rose said with a Mona Lisa smile. "Well, off with you both. I'm sure you have a lot of catching up to do."

★★★

The two plopped onto Roxy's bed, heads sinking into plumped pillows. Being together again felt so comfortable. Roxy hadn't realized how much she missed spending time with Megan until this very moment.

Sitting up suddenly, she said, "I can't wait any longer to tell you, Meg."

"Tell me what?" Megan said, pushing up onto her elbows.

"I've made a decision about what I want to do with my life," Roxy said. "I'm going to become a journalist!"

"A journalist," Megan repeated thoughtfully, "that's such a perfect fit, Rox! You're an amazing writer. How did you decide?"

"My Magic 8 Ball," Roxy said, picking it up from the bed.

Megan stared at her best friend and smirked, unsurprised by her rationale. "I should have guessed," she said, knowing ten times out of ten Roxy consulted her Magic 8 Ball for counsel.

"Well, it does feel like a perfect fit. And you know Mother always says there's no such thing as coincidence so ..."

"Since when have you ever held to your mother's belief?" Megan interrupted.

"Well, it doesn't hurt to cover all the bases, just in case she's right."

"Yah, especially when her belief conveniently aligns with yours," Megan said, dishing it right back.

Roxy looked at her best friend and smiled. "You haven't changed."

"Well, neither have you!" Megan retorted.

The two burst into laughter.

"Okay, then," Roxy said, getting serious again. "So what about you? Any career decisions?"

"I'm almost afraid to say after this whole coincidence speech ..."

"What? ... Are you're kidding ... a journalist, too?"

Megan nodded her head."

"That's fantastic! We could co-author an article now and then! It'll be so much fun! Come on," Roxy said, clasping Megan's hand, "let's go tell mother!"

★★★

Journal Entry, Friday, July 6, 2001:

I can just picture it, a shared byline with Meg in The New Yorker, or some other major publication! It will be so much fun working together! Though I still want to work from home. After all, I need to get my feet wet in the business first before contemplating what comes next. And I'm sure Mother will love having me here with her. My leaving would just break her heart.

54

—·—

PEOPLE WERE NOTICING

Tuesday, July 31, 2001

Nick was out back in his greenhouse tending to the plants. It was where he liked to spend his free time, being at one with nature. The burdens of life had taken on new meaning since Pran—no longer weighing him down but, instead, lifting him up—each negative moment an opportunity to do good. Like helping Michael's boys. Only now … people were noticing. Michael, of course, contributed the behavioral metamorphosis of his students to their participation in the art program. Rose naturally saw it as a message from God that love conquers all. But when she spoke of the troubled youths' incredible transformation to David, the first he had learned of it, a chill ran up his spine. He decided to confront his brother.

"How's it going, little bro," David said, lowering his head to gain entry, the greenhouse like a sauna on this steamy, summer afternoon.

"Couldn't be better," Nick said, his disposition cheerful, especially when surrounded by an abundance of healthy plants.

David was elated his brother's good health had remained steady these past four years though, truth be told, he was always waiting for the other shoe to drop, mindful of the old adage that good things don't last forever. He wished he could have faith like Rose, but he just wasn't made like her.

"Rose tells me things are going really well at Michael's with the boys," he said, watching his brother closely for a reaction.

Without flinching, Nick replied with a smile, "Yes, we've made friends."

"Good … good," David said. Still fishing, he continued, "She says they've calmed down a great deal—no more outbursts to speak of."

"That's right," Nick said, his response short as his eyes focused on his work.

David wanted to hear more, a nagging suspicion grabbing fierce hold.

"Look at me Nick," David said, beads of sweat forming on his brow, and not entirely from the heat. "Tell me the truth. What's going on?"

Nick had promised his brother never to tell a soul about Pran, and he kept that promise. But when it came to helping others, he couldn't see the harm so long as no one knew. Now, as his brother's ocean blue eyes stared him down, he knew he had to confess.

Nick spilled the beans.

At first, the tale seemed fantastical—like something out of a science fiction novel. Though really, had David thought about it, what he was being asked to do for General Rand wasn't far off the mark either. And though his emotions wavered from incredulity to fear, David couldn't suppress the pride he felt in his brother's altruism. And then it hit him. If Michael's boys did, in fact, benefit from Pran in their water … their DNA would show proof.

"I'm going to ask something of you, Nick … something important," David said. "I need you to collect the boys' used drinking cups for analysis. Can you do that?"

Nick was so thrilled his brother wasn't upset; he would have agreed to jump off a bridge had David asked. "Easy peasy," he said smiling, his two thumbs up. "Michael's got me on trash duty."

"Good … and one more thing," David added. "Keep serving up the water."

★★★

The moment David reached his car in the driveway, he could smell it in the air—cigar smoke. He pirouetted, his eyes like a hawk's, taking in his surroundings.

He had carried Federal Agent Jenks like a monkey on his back for the past four years, the arrogant, little bully often appearing out of nowhere like a ship in fog stalking him. It has been a lesson in endurance for David, coming to terms with this prick's preferred method of getting results—intimidation. Despite his force-feeding the man crumbs for placation, he knew this Hansel and Gretel trail was reaching the end of the road. Jenks was losing patience. But now, thanks to Nick, David felt he might be on to something.

He opened his car door and jumped in, his eyes making a final sweep of the neighborhood before he turned the key in the ignition. Had Jenks overheard his conversation with his brother? It was always a possibility; but for Nick's sake, he hoped not. And then, tired of the cat and mouse game and the constant pressure of Operation Octane, he thought, *Just let the little bastard confront me now,* before shifting into reverse and backing up, feeling, for the first time since his brother had kicked cancer, hopeful.

55

ROCKY POINT ISLAND

Sunday, August 19, 2001

A S SHAFTS OF MORNING light refracted off the ocean's rolling waves and a warm, salty breeze tousled her hair, Megan paced the dock, an impatient host awaiting her weekend guest and former roommate, traveling up by bus. But when her father pulled up his motorboat alongside the jetty, she was caught unawares to find not only her father and Roxy on board, but also Nick. "Welcome to Rocky Point Island," she said, her cheerful greeting delivered without a hint of question.

Sean O'Malley stepped off first and lent a strong hand to Roxy, helping her disembark. "I couldn't just leave him in that greenhouse all alone," she said to Megan beneath her breath while Sean tended to Nick. Still bearing responsibility for Nick's past breakdown, Roxy felt obligated to keep an eye on him, even though he seemed to have made a miraculous recovery. But Megan knew it wasn't just Roxy's undue concern for Nick's welfare that had brought him to Rocky Point Island. She was well aware of what today was—the tenth anniversary of the hurricane that tore all three of their lives apart. But no mention needed be made; one could feel it like static in the air.

Stepping onto the dock, his land legs unsteady but back under him, Nick smiled, saying, "Roxy insisted I come, Megan. Hope that's okay."

Megan loved him like a brother and could bear no complaint with his joining them, especially on this day. "It's so wonderful to have my two dearest friends here with me," she said, wrapping her arms around them both and squeezing. "Come on," she said, leading them forward, "we have so much to talk about, and I have so much to show you both."

★★★

As to where Roxy and Nick wanted first to explore, it was a no-brainer. With its imposing height and majestic setting on a bluff, the two couldn't wait to step foot inside of the lighthouse. Megan surprised them all by her fleet-footed assent up the 90-foot tower's spiral staircase, leaving the less agile Roxy and Nick in her wake. Wobbly-legged and huffing the two arrived at the top, their efforts rewarded with a breath-taking view.

"Wow, this is incredible," Roxy said, circling the glass windows of the lantern room, a massive beacon at its core.

"Such a force of nature," Nick said before going silent, allowing his senses to absorb it all—the thunderous, rock-battering waves and plumes of salty, sea mist.

Megan knew that truth all too well. She offered no response—just stood there trancelike staring out at the horizon's edge.

Roxy cast a glance at Megan, mesmerized by the undulating blue, and knew she was thinking of her mother. She couldn't help wondering what, exactly, had happened that day ten years ago. Because whatever had occurred, Roxy was certain its aftermath had induced Megan to self-cloister.

And Nick? The poor boy had certainly had his share of suffering between his parents' deaths and his cancer, but there was more to it than that, Roxy had no doubt. She had seen the demons in his eyes the first time they had met.

Enough is enough, she thought, considering the hurricane that changed their lives and their ensuing ten years of sacrificial offerings on the altar of guilt. The moment of truth had come for honesty with one another, to stop hiding in self-imposed prisons and to share the true horrors of their pasts. So, for the first time in her life, Roxy was ready to bear her soul. She inhaled a deep breath and then spat out the words she had never uttered:

"I tried to kill my father."

And like a dam breached, the horrific story of her childhood rushed out.

***

The tragic story was of another place and time and Roxy, the storyteller, held her audience captive with her tale. And then, with the telling complete, she set them free, but not without consequences. For the storyteller had planted the seeds of her heartache within each of them, and her horrors were now theirs—forever.

***

It was a lot to take in, the realization that the Roxy they knew was so much more complicated. But then, really, how well do we know one another? Everyone has skeletons in their closets, weaknesses and fears never exposed should they be turned against us. There is only so much stamina in a person facing shame ... or worse, guilt. Humans are imperfect beings whose imperfect natures are the root cause of all pain. So how does one move past the pain? Rose would say forgiveness. But if it were that easy, psychiatrists would be out of business and depression drugs non-existent. Roxy knew her decision to tell all would never erase her pain, but sharing her burden helped to alleviate her carrying it alone—and that, she hoped, would make all the difference.

***

Sitting on the floor of the lantern room with Roxy cradled in her arms, Megan could feel relief washing over her best friend. And then something unexpected happened. Roxy looked up into her eyes and, just as occurred when they first met, a knowing passed between them. Megan's eyes suddenly filled with remorseful tears and, from somewhere deep within, she summoned the courage to free the long-held skeleton in her closet:

"I should have been the one who died."

56

— · —

MEGAN'S STORY

Sunday, August 19, 2001

ROXY UNWRAPPED HER BODY from within Megan's embrace and sat up; now it was her turn to support her friend. She took Megan's hand into hers, and Megan closed her teary eyes. Within seconds, the memories repossessed her mind, the words falling softly from her lips.

"It was a sultry, summer morning—white puffy clouds floating on a brilliant blue sky," she began, reliving the image in her mind before reopening her eyes, only to stare straight ahead. "The ocean appeared docile. You couldn't tell then that a storm was coming.

"Mom made us a quick breakfast on the griddle; she was in a hurry for an early doctor's appointment on the mainland. When we finished, Dad brought her over on the motorboat, and I went out to the stable to tend to Princess, my filly. I fed her and brushed her beautiful white coat, and when I finished cleaning the stall, we headed out on our daily jaunt.

"We followed the usual path around the island, resting halfway at our favorite stop overlooking the ocean—a steep outcropping of rocks called Rocky Ridge. We spent our morning there … I skipped stones off the waves and searched the crags for periwinkles, and when I got bored told Princess stories I'd made up.

"As the morning wore on the temperature grew hotter and my stomach hungrier. So I climbed back up onto Princess and we headed home. By then, Mom had returned from her doctor appointment and was making us lunch.

"We all ate and then Dad returned to his never-ending job of maintaining the lighthouse. I helped Mom with the dishes. When we finished, she asked me to sit down—she had something to tell me. But first she made me promise not to say a word to Dad. It was going to be a surprise.

"Turns out her doctor appointment found that she was pregnant. She had no idea—a complete shock. But she wanted to tell me first because she wanted me to know that this changed nothing between us … that she loved me more than life itself," Megan said, choking up. "You see," she said, composing herself, "my parents had been trying for years to have a baby … before they decided to adopt me."

Roxy was taken aback. At first, she was hurt that Megan had felt the need to hide this knowledge from her. Adoption was nothing to be ashamed of. But then, she couldn't be upset with her best friend—everyone is due their privacy and has their reasons.

"I told Mom I was thrilled … and I was." Megan continued, visibly overcome with excitement. "I couldn't wait to be the big sister, teach my sibling all about the island, how to ride Princess, share stories. And Mom was so happy she cried. Together, we started planning the baby's room—paint colors and where the crib would go. It was all so exciting," she said, and then her voice trailed off, "… only now it seems like a dream."

Roxy watched her best friend's expression go to a dark place—she squeezed Megan's hand.

"By early evening, everything changed," Megan said, her words shaky. "There was little warning—the skies darkened, the winds grew stronger and the waves swelled. Then the heaven's opened up and the rains fell. The celebratory dinner we had planned with Dad never happened; we were all too busy scurrying around like mice securing the property—Dad to the lighthouse, Mom to bolt the cottage shutters, and me to the stable.

"Princess didn't like thunder, and lightening not much better. She was spooked, snorting and pacing in her stall. I tried calming her, talking softly, reassuring her, but she was too worked up. So I went into the stall with her, running my hands slowly over her coat, still reassuring her as I stroked her mane, and just as she began to submit to calm, the sky lit up with a bolt of lightning. She reared … and then a thunderous boom of thunder shook the stable—she bolted.

"It was my fault she escaped. In my haste to calm her, I was careless—I'd left the stable door wide open and then failed to secure the latch on her stall after I'd entered. She was gone in a flash. I ran out after her but, in the downpour, lost sight of her. But it didn't matter—I knew where she was headed.

"The gales knocked me down more times than I could count, but I kept to the path, which was washing out before my eyes and littered with downed branches. It was harrowing and dangerous, and I thought I'd seen the worst of it, until I got to Rocky Ridge … terrifying." Megan paused, her heart racing with the memory. "I couldn't see in front of me, not with the sea spray and torrents of thrashing rain. But there was no mistaking that sea-monster roar pounding the ridge just beyond me. My gut screamed, turn back. But I had come this far to find Princess; I couldn't abandon her now, not without trying. So I strained to see through the deluge, searching out the ridge for any sign of her, but it was hopeless. In desperation, I hollered her name—but only the tempest roared back. I was despondent, not sure what to do. And then, for a fleeting instant, the storm slackened, and in that moment of clarity … I heard her. Elated and terrified at the same time I got down on my belly, scrabbling for handholds on the slippery rocks, inching forward towards her cry. But as I neared the ridge, conditions escalated. First, giant sea sprays enveloped me. And then the surf blindsided me, wave after towering cold wave wrenching at my body and filling my lungs. I was scared out of my mind. I froze … sure I was a goner.

"Every rational impulse inside me cried to flee, but my love for Princess ensnared me. She was close—I could feel her. How could I forsake her now? But then, before I could think, the storm fell on me like an avalanche and made my decision for me. At that point, whether I retreated or advanced, it didn't matter—the reality was that at any moment I could die. So I decided then if I was going to die, I wanted to die next to Princess. 'Move,' I told myself. 'Find her.'

"I crept forward, my body shivering and growing rigid, my grip slipping. Wave after raging wave pounced, determined to pull me in. I was struggling to keep hold, inching slowly through the murk, my fingers groping, groping, until they touched something … soft. My breath stopped, hardly able to believe my senses. There in the blackness, lying frightened and hurt, I found Princess. I nuzzled into her massive body, stroked her beautiful white coat, consoled her—and in that moment of inner calm, resigned myself to facing our fate together. And so, in that hellish place, thinking of my parents and happy they'd have another child should I die, I clung to Princess—and waited.

"I can't say how long it took for Princess to expire, leaving me to wait at death's door alone. And I have no idea how what I am about to say is even possible. But somehow, defying the watery grave reaching out for me, like an angel in the darkness … my mother appeared. She signaled for me to come. I was so scared I couldn't breathe, but despite my fear, despite having to leave Princess, she gave me the courage to move.

"Our retreat on the rocks was treacherous as we picked our way back from the ridge, struggling against the overpowering grip of the tempest. And then, without warning—death came knocking. A monstrous wave wrapped its icy, cold fingers around my mother and pulled her in. No goodbyes. No embrace. Only my wails on the wind—until death came back for me.

"Into the dark, cold torrent it tossed my wretched body and left me to die. But the beacon, that ceaseless light of hope, found my ragged soul tangled in the rocky shore where another angel … my dad … pulled me out."

Megan went silent, but she wasn't done yet. As tears streamed down her cheeks, she rose to her feet and looked out beyond the rhythmic waves to the horizon's edge … and there her gaze stalled.

"After that day, my life on the island changed," she said. "I was lost without my mom and Princess. Dad said he didn't blame me for what happened, but I did. And it grew harder and harder to face him, knowing my mom's secret—the secret I've kept from him for the last ten years. But how could I tell him he not only lost his beloved wife … but a baby as well? How could I compound his sorrow? No. It was all my fault, and I alone should bear the burden. I alone should face the consequences. He should have lived to grow old with my mom, enjoyed raising a family. I robbed them of that. Now it was my turn to be denied—to pay a penance."

Roxy looked at Megan and suddenly understood her best friend. "You mean to tell me your refusal to date is because you think you don't deserve to have a relationship, a marriage, a family?"

"I am not worthy," Megan answered.

57

NICK'S STORY

Sunday, August 19, 2001

"I AM NOT WORTHY, either," Nick said, his slender frame huddled on the cool concrete floor, knees drawn in. Megan and Roxy turned in unison, staring at him, but then, understanding what was happening, silently pulled up floor space beside him—and waited.

"It was my twelfth birthday," Nick said, pausing to recall the memory. "I woke up with an uncomfortable feeling in my stomach, a mix of happiness and apprehension, because this was the day I had decided to reveal to my family the most important secret of my life—that I was gay." He inhaled and then proceeded full speed, needing to spill it all.

"The morning began as usual, rising before dawn to help dad tend the Holsteins on our small farm in New Hampshire. Annabelle was my favorite. She knew her name and came when I called her. I stroked her smooth patchwork hide and, as usual, fed her a treat. Then I brushed and hosed her down before setting to work, pulling up a stool and leaning into her wonderful body heat to stave off the morning chill. Annabelle's first milk was the best—warm, creamy and sweet. I savored that first cupful." He smiled. "But, in truth, what I savored even more than her milk was her companionship. When I was with Annabelle, I never felt hurt ... never felt alone." Nick stood suddenly and peered out through the glass windows of the lantern room.

"That morning," he continued, "my mom was in the farmhouse preparing all of my favorite dishes for my birthday. She spoiled me rotten, caving to my every whim, probably because I was a surprise baby. She said I was a blessing to her and Dad, bringing new meaning into their lives after David had left for college fourteen years prior, leaving them empty nesters. She'd noticed I wasn't feeling quite myself lately and drove me to the clinic. Blood work was ordered and sent to the lab. We'd been waiting for the results when the call came smack in the middle of her preparations. I happened to be sitting on the stoop, just outside the screen door, when she answered the phone. The call didn't last long and, just as it ended, my dad strode into the kitchen to find mom bent over the ladder-back chair, her face drained of color and the phone dangling from its cord. She stared through him like a ghost when he asked what was wrong. I can still hear the pain in her voice with her answer: 'Nick has cancer.' Outside, I bellied over, unable to hold back my vomit. Annabelle was in the pasture, so I leapt the fence and ran to her, clinging to her neck and sobbing into her ear: 'Annabelle, I'm dying.'"

Roxy and Megan noticed that, even as Nick spoke these words, he displayed no emotion. An odd disconnect they thought strange, but Nick continued as if normal. But this was, in fact, the new normal for Nick. Pran had altered his DNA. Negative emotions were now a thing of the past. Yes, he could remember those experiences, but he could no longer feel them, be tortured by them—his depression now obsolete.

"My parents managed to pry me loose and helped me to my room," he continued. "I rested there, waiting for my brother to arrive. David hadn't learned yet of my diagnosis. He was coming up from Massachusetts as planned for my birthday celebration, only I doubted there'd be much celebrating after he heard the news. But I was glad he was coming. David always had my back—like when he helped me stand up to the schoolyard bullies by enrolling me in karate lessons. I still got beat up, but the important thing was I learned to stand my ground and not run like a scaredy cat anymore. In the end, I took some good lickings, but I gave a few, too. I survived school with as few scars as possible because David helped me to learn courage. So his coming on my birthday, at the most crucial time of my life, meant the world to me." Nick's footsteps slowly circled the beacon, his eyes on the ocean but his mind on the past.

"When my parents learned about the hurricane heading our way they were upset and tried calling David to stop his coming, but he'd already left Cambridge, presumably racing north on the interstate trying to beat out the storm, bucking not only the traffic but the high winds. It was bad enough his having to deal with all that on the road without throwing my cancer diagnosis in his face when he arrived—he didn't deserve that. But bad news usually travels in threes, and this wouldn't be the last of it before the day was over," Nick said, his foreshadowing sending chills up the girls' spines.

"In fact, it was mid-afternoon when the devil came calling," he said point blank. "That's when I awakened from a nap to my mother's screams. I bolted upright on the bed. Then I heard the front door bang and my dad yelling after her. I flew to my bedroom window and, through the downpour, caught a glimpse of him chasing her towards the barn. And that's when I saw it—the barn's roof … ablaze.

"Without thinking, I raced out into the storm. The sound hit me first—unlike anything I'd ever heard—such a mighty force. Straight away, I was soaked and tossed about by the gales, taking two steps back for every one forward. As I struggled nearer the barn, mom and two Holsteins appeared as apparitions exiting through the smoke. Dad followed her out with two more. I rushed to meet them. I yelled, 'Where's Annabelle!' My dad grabbed my arm, warning me it wasn't safe to go in. But I broke free of his hold and raced into the fire.

"When I entered the barn the acrid smoke was roiling, burning my eyes and throat. I pulled my shirt up over my nose and mouth and let my eyes water as I searched through the haze for Annabelle. I knew where she should be, but in her fright, she'd fled her stall. The flames were lapping the roof's structural beams and spreading like a lit fuse down the side walls, but I kept moving, yelling out her name. Then, from further back, I heard a faint moo. As I headed toward the sound, the fire was consuming the roof, exposing a growing hole and feeding fresh oxygen to the flames. Before I knew it, the blaze intensified, and my world closed in. With a horrifying roar, the roof timbers collapsed behind me, blocking my exit. I was fighting to breathe and searching in panic for another way out. I thought I was going to die. Then the entire back wall of the barn buckled under the stress, collapsing, but I saw a path out through the burning rubble and took it. Outside, the hurricane raging, I crumpled into the mud and watched the inferno glowing bright against blackened skies, unaware that I, alone, had survived." Nick sat back down, dry eyed, and then calmly picked up his story.

"David found me on the ground in shock and carried me into the house, and then, come morning when I awoke, he carried the burden of breaking the bad news—that both my parents had perished in the fire … Annabelle, too. It was unfathomable. Even as I stared at the charred remains where the barn had stood, it didn't seem real. I was bewildered, grief stricken, angry—demanding answers. And angrier still when they came.

"First, David told me that our barn was hit by a lightning strike which sparked the fire. Hearing that was bad enough, but when he told me that lightning in a hurricane was an unusual occurrence but can, in fact, happen during powerful ones, I blamed everything—nature, fate, God—questioning why it had to happen at this time, with this hurricane … to us? Of course, it wasn't just the fire, but my own guilt, that laid at the crux of my anger. I had refused to heed my father's warning, choosing to satisfy my own selfish needs instead. If only I had listened, my parents would be alive. But I didn't—so they followed me in." Nick stared at the floor and then, like a robot reciting a passage aloud from a book, he finished his story.

"By day's end my birthday had passed without celebration, my secret still remained a secret, and life as I knew it was forever changed. This wasn't how things were supposed to have happened." Done, he closed his eyes as if weary and in need of a nap, speaking no more.

Roxy and Megan stared at one another.

Later that evening, in private, the two young women discussed Nick's unemotional telling of his story—no tears, no struggle for composure, no sign whatsoever of distress. It was as if he was a discarnate spirit reviewing his life after death with detachment. They considered his maleness as a factor in keeping his emotions in check but soon discarded that premise, as many a man has wept openly at the loss of a loved one. They themselves had witnessed a tear spill from Nick's eye four years prior at Roxy's dinner party when the gathering first learned of their shared sorrows in a hurricane. And now, not knowing where to ascribe his placidity in his telling of such horrendous loss, they chalked it up to trauma and let the matter drop. After all, they reasoned, we all suffer differently.

***

Journal Entry, Sunday, August 19, 2001:

Who hasn't suffered for mistakes? Life is defined by such things. But it is those shared experiences that bind us and make life livable. After all, misery loves company, no? Nick, Megan and I are a testament to that. But even human beings, with all our human frailties, can't be denied a hope of deliverance from suffering, can we? Or maybe it's just too much to ask.

58

BREAKTHROUGH

Wednesday, August 22, 2001

"Incredible," David breathed. Each one of the DNA samples obtained from the cache of disposed paper cups Nick had gathered from Michael's gallery had evidenced a mutated aggression gene. It shouldn't have been a surprise to David. After all, his brother was living proof of the powers of Pran. Still, the scientist in him wasn't ready to yield. But now, with these findings of DNA testing, he had empirical proof. And better yet, the results in Michael's boys were achieved by ingesting a simple, water-based solution rather than the more potent and complex potion he had fed nightly to Nick. His mind was reeling with the possibilities.

David had to get Federal Agent Jenks off his back, and until he could come up with a contagious airborne disease, as General Rand requested, perhaps he could pacify them both with one that was waterborne—a test case, if you will—one that, perhaps, could target a specific watering hole of a terrorist enclave. If successful, the power of Pran would be validated and, better yet, provide David the time he needed to produce their airborne weapon-of-choice against aggression—Octane.

Of course, even if David could successfully create a waterborne disease, there was the matter of delivery. But he wasn't concerned with the tactical aspects of the operation; on the contrary, he was certain that the backing behind General Rand had deep enough pockets and military logistical forces capably trained for such endeavors. As far as David was concerned, he had enough to contend with—let Rand and his guys deal with that headache.

But first, David had some convincing to do. As Agent Jenks had made crystal clear at their initial, less-than-friendly meeting four years earlier in the Amazon, he ran the show. He had emphatically warned, "deviation from the mission is prohibited." So the very notion that David would balk now at his order to "stick to the script" could only spell trouble. David was a rebel—and Agent Jenks didn't like rebels.

59

THE PROPOSAL

Sunday, September 9, 2001

THIRD TIMES THE CHARM, David told himself as he tucked the diamond ring into his jacket pocket and headed out to his car. He felt good about himself now that he was on a viable path in his quest to develop Octane—despite the looming impediment of Agent Jenks—so the timing seemed right to move on with his life. He wanted this moment to be special, a memory Rose would cherish when she grew old, a story she would tell often and, of course, he wanted it to be a surprise. So as planned, Rose closed shop early and the two drove an hour north on the Interstate where he hoped, again, to pop the question.

"So where are you taking me?" Rose asked, no sooner on the road.

"If I told you, it wouldn't be a surprise," David said with one of his killer smiles.

Rose melted, then rebounded.

"Can you at least give me a hint?" she asked. "Have I been there before?"

"No, you have not, and no more questions," he admonished.

"Well, you can at least tell me if I am dressed appropriately."

David scanned her alluring figure seated next to him, adorned in a casual, cotton sundress and sandals. "Yes," he said, his breath catching at her beauty. "Now end of discussion."

Rose sank back into the convertible's leather seat, wind whipping and scenery flashing, but she was more than comfortable now, and more than ready for a wonderful day spent with David.

***

He backed his Corvette expertly into a tight parking spot and then scurried out and around to open her door and lend her his hand. "Welcome to Rockport, famous for its artist colony and galleries galore, ready to please your every desire, darling," he said, the two standing arm in arm on the sidewalk admiring the quaint coastal village.

"Oh David, I've always wanted to come here! I've heard so much about this wonderful place!" Rose swooned.

David beamed. "Anything to please you, Rose," he said as they headed off to explore.

A constant breeze skimmed off the ocean keeping the temperature pleasant and a salty taste in the air as they wandered from shop to shop. David marveled at Rose's knowledge of art. He loved to stand back and observe the confidence and ease with which she interacted with her peers or, dare I say, friends by the time she was through. She was a natural, completely within her element. He let her spend as much time as she wanted talking shop and moseying about, her passion clearly worn on her sleeve. It wore off on David, too, and he loved her for it—she made him feel alive. Each time she discovered an unexpected gem in a collection and her expression of surprise turned to pure delight, he couldn't help but smile, too. And then, of course, he'd pull out his charge card—the purchase his treat.

With the small trunk of his Corvette stuffed with her newly acquired possessions, their feet tired and dusk on the horizon, David knew the hour had arrived. "Before we stop for dinner, I have one more surprise," he told her. "But you must promise to keep your eyes cast down until I say to look."

Rose gazed back at him with a sparkle of childish wonderment. "I promise," she said.

"Good, then take my arm."

They walked together, slowly, down a gray, weathered pier out toward the calm, blue harbor. Rose could feel her excitement growing with each careful step. She had given herself over to David's guiding hands, feeling secure in their strength, her anxiety nowhere to be found. She felt like a young girl again exploring the possibilities of life—a feeling she had long forgotten but now, resurrected, one she found very much to her liking.

David brought her to an abrupt stop and grasped her shoulders firmly, positioning her for the big reveal. "You can open your eyes now," he said.

It was like a canvas awash with the setting sun—pastel shades of purple and pink cast onto white cumulous clouds and the rippling blue waters below. But the true gem in the picture was perched across the inner harbor at the end of a granite wharf—Motif #1, a modest red fishing shack, arguably one of the most painted buildings in the world. In the setting sun, against an ocean backdrop straight out of Hollywood, light and shadow cast their nets upon its unassuming architecture and, oh … how it took your breath away.

Rose gasped … and then tears followed.

"What's wrong, Rose?" David asked, his heartbeat quickening.

"Oh, sweet David, nothing is wrong," she laughed through her tears. "It's perfect … the view … so overwhelmingly beautiful."

David took her shaking hands into his and gazed into her warm hazel eyes. "Yes, I agree … the view is overwhelmingly beautiful."

His gaze locked with hers, a look that spoke of the depth of his love. And then he got down on his knee and withdrew a tiny box from his jacket pocket. He flipped its lid open. "Marry me, Rose," he said, presenting the diamond ring. "Spend the rest of your life with me. I promise to take care of you … to make you happy. You are my world, Rose. Without you, I am nothing. Marry me."

Rose had given herself time since Eugene, time to become the person she was meant to be. No longer stifled by his controlling personality, she was free now to spread her wings, to choose her own destiny. And as the tears flowed down her cheeks, her gaze hopelessly lost in the deep, blue depths of David's eyes, she was ready … oh so ready … to speak the one word David had longed to hear. "Yes," she said, "yes, yes, yes!"

60

—·—

A BIRD'S-EYE VIEW

Tuesday, September 11, 2001

ROSE, THOUGH EAGER TO reveal her engagement to Roxy, kept her ring hidden from her in her purse. She wanted the setting to be special when she told her daughter the good news. Then the opportunity arose to go to New York—just the two of them.

September in New York ... the best time of year in the most thrilling city—Roxy's exact words when her mother proposed their mother-daughter outing. Rose was delighted with her daughter's reaction, and right away the two began to plan their getaway. There was, however, one piece of business in the city Rose had to tend to first—and the primary reason for the trip—an early-morning appointment with Lori West at the Artistic Collaborative.

Rose was more than flattered when Lori approached her with a potential offer to join their board. Of course, the members wanted to meet her first, see if she'd be a good fit. Initially, Rose was hesitant to consider taking on more responsibility, what with her new business and all, but when she informed David of the possibility, he urged her to at least meet with them.

So this morning, mother and daughter hopped an early flight to LaGuardia Airport. It was a glorious, late-summer day—the clear sky a robin's egg blue with a balmy breeze blowing against sun-warmed faces—the kind of day that unwittingly transported your soul to a higher dimension, where strangers exchanged smiles reflexively as if their collective consciousness had been prompted by the universe to rejoice in its splendor and give thanks. Certainly, this was how Rose felt. Sitting on the plane, she reflected upon her life up to this very moment. Her dark days of the past were just that, the past. Here, now, in this moment, she had been graced with bountiful joy and much for which to be grateful. She was on the verge of new beginnings and could feel the excitement tingling through her like she was once again riding the wind on the back of her filly Star—the freedom of her youth returning, the reigns in her control and the choices hers to make … and now she chose commitment. She was ready to settle down again with a man—a man devoted to her happiness, a man who encouraged her, a man who would move Heaven and Earth for her. She never felt more certain of a decision. So when the plane landed and mother and daughter disembarked, Rose stepped out to the concourse with a spring in her step and a smile on her face that bespoke of the love in her heart and her optimism for the future. On this glorious day, she was ready to move on.

Manhattan, a spectacle of vibe and vigor, left most, if not all, who came here clamoring for more. No less for Rose and Roxy who, riding in their taxi, felt excitement building with each passing block. Fifth Avenue itself, the most famous street in Manhattan, was abustle with businessmen in suits and ties, camera-toting tourists, high-fashioned high-heeled women and sneaker-clad joggers all juggling for precious sidewalk space, while street traffic clamored with police sirens, trash removals, taxi horns and construction jackhammers. The cacophony of sights and sounds would be a sensory overload to those less acquainted, but for mother and daughter it was an exciting reprieve from their quiet life in a quiet neighborhood.

Their taxi pulled up curbside to drop Roxy off as planned before Rose would continue on to her appointment in lower Manhattan.

"When we meet for lunch," Rose said, "I have exciting news to tell you, darling."

"Mother, you're such a tease! What could be more exciting than the board accepting you?"

"You'll just have to wait and see," she said coyly, Roxy's eyes rolling at her mother's worn-out mantra. And then Rose leaned in close and gave her daughter a big hug. "I love you so much, darling," she said, before breaking free, allowing Roxy to step outside onto the sidewalk. "See you soon," Rose said, blowing a kiss through the window as the taxi took off, leaving Roxy waving into the air—and alone.

Her anxiety suddenly lurched. She knew it would. Desperate to tamp it down, she headed toward a bagel shop. *Just the fix I need,* she thought, her nose homing in on the smell of yeast and coffee wafting out the open door.

★★★

Inside, Roxy took a seat by the window; and while indulging in calming sips of hot brew, she distracted her mind with people-watching—an amusing pastime she and Zach had developed as low-to-no-income students frequenting coffee shops in Boston. They would each take turns picking someone out from the crowd and imagining who they were and what they did for a living. Remembering this now, remembering Zach, she felt a tug of nostalgia and wondered how he and Paul were doing in L.A. If her script had gained any traction. If Zach had found someone to replace her. She did miss him, but she had no regrets, not with a lifetime yet to explore on her own terms, and on her own time. Someday, if Mr. Right came along, she'd settle down; but it was a future yet too far off to contemplate and not worth the energy expended. She had more important things now to consider—like a view from the top of the Empire State Building. She checked her watch. It was time to go.

★★★

Rose exited the taxicab and just stood there, frozen in place, looking up. The towering skyscraper before her suddenly made her feel small and insignificant. She imagined that from one's perspective at its top, looking down, she'd appear ant-like, a mere black dot in the larger scheme of things. Perspective was everything, Rose knew, in painting and in life. How we chose to see ourselves and others determined the life we chose to live. Rose always chose optimism—turning life's hardships into opportunities, changing what she could change, letting go of what she couldn't—trusting God to be her guide. And though she stood there, feeling insignificant in this world, she gave thanks to God for her life and his blessings and asked Him yet to remain with her, to guide her on her next journey. And then, cradling her purse and the ring within, Rose inhaled a deep breath and strode into the building.

***

Roxy strolled over to The Empire State Building just off Fifth Avenue, made her way to the entrance and rode the elevator up to the observation deck. On this clear day, a bird's-eye view greeted her with 80 miles of panoramic vistas and landmarks like Central Park, the Brooklyn Bridge and the Statue of Liberty on Ellis Island.

She wished her mother was with her now, sharing this. But the two had made a pact earlier, a means of helping assuage Roxy's anxiety while Rose was gone, pledging to look out across the great expanse between them at the exact same time and know they were each thinking of the other. Roxy checked her watch—less than a minute to go. Her eyes scrutinized the landscape, searching the vista for the skyscraper where her mother was to be. It wasn't hard to find—one of the two tallest buildings looming over New York City's lower Manhattan skyline.

Then, like a floater detected in her field of vision, her eyes picked up on an object from out of nowhere, moving quickly across the sky. While her eyesight labored against the object's glaring reflection bouncing off the morning sun, her brain strained to make sense of its trajectory as she observed it moving from point A to the obvious and catastrophic point B. And though her brain ran and re-ran the data over and over, always drawing the same conclusion, Roxy fought it. But her body understood—a sudden racing of heart and holding of breath and clutching of grip on the rail for support as her frantic eyes beseeched her brain to say it wasn't so.

My darling Roxanne, I love you, the voice declared suddenly in her head, somehow straddling space and time—the only voice she trusted as a child, the voice that read her bedtime stories, the voice that called her by her given name. Tears streaming down her cheeks, Roxy stared at the tower across the great expanse, her heart finally coming to terms with what her brain already knew. "I love you, too, Mother," she cried back as the plane hurtled into the skyscraper, burst into a fireball and shook the earth.

PART FOUR

Five Years Later – 2006

TreesTales Publishing

61

—·—

GIRLFRIEND

Friday, August 18, 2006

With the sun soon to rise over Boston, Megan O'Malley sat next to the open window of her third floor Beacon Hill apartment in the cool, quiet darkness enveloped by the glow of her computer screen, the curls of her illuminated hair dancing rhythmically about her face with the breeze. Beneath her window, the sweet perfume of climbing jasmine wafted upward, intoxicating her; and like Dorothy in the poppy fields on her way to Oz, she was tempted to lie down to sleep, the brisk morning air all that prevented her from succumbing to her tiredness. Up all night consumed by her work, such ungodly hours were now routine in her life. Sleep would come later.

Inside her apartment, travel books and journals stacked table tops pyramid-style, casting otherworldly shadows about the darkened room. And although the framed photographs of people and places on all four walls might appear as specters in the night, by daylight they are revealed as old friends, relics of her journeys down roads little known and less traveled.

For the past five years Megan's robust career as a freelance journalist has transported her to faraway places—her award-winning work increasing publishers' demands and, in turn, her road trips. Though, if you asked her colleagues, they'd claim her own adventurousness seduced her to new sojourns; but within her restless mind resides the truth, and there she prefers to keep it.

At twenty-seven years of age the Irish lass still shuns a crowd. And although her natural beauty and spirited laughter often draw attention, there is still no significant other to mention in her life. In public, she laments the existence of a man capable of relishing a woman whose career sends her chasing shooting stars—but in private, she knows better.

Outside, on the street below, the start and stops of the newspaper truck announce morning deliveries to her neighbors' well-appointed dwellings. Soon, the street lanterns lining the brick-patterned walkways of Beacon Hill would dim with the rising sun. Megan hastened her fingertips on the keyboard, her deadline fast approaching.

Struggling with heavy eyelids, closing and then jarring open like window shades let loose, she typed her final sentence, then murmured, "That's all she wrote, folks." As if on cue with her click of the send button, nature's first light began to paint the room; and as all was called to life with the brushstrokes of dawn, Megan's head fell to rest upon her forearm, her computer down for the count beside her.

★★★

Somewhere off in the distance the sound of incessant ringing summoned her from peaceful slumber. Neck stiff, Megan slowly raised her head, eyes squinting in the bright light of day. She grasped the phone. "Hello," she said, dazed, her mouth as parched as a dry watering hole. Scrambling her free hand over a pile of notes, she reached for the dregs in last night's coffee cup—grimacing with her first sip.

"Hey girlfriend!" the voice on the other end said. "I heard you getting in late last night—I've missed you oodles! We've got lots catching up to do, sweetums. How about lunch? I'm preparing Veal Marsala, your favorite! Say around noon?" No mistaking the effervescent voice of Andre Soprastrano, second floor artist-in-residence, ready to offer up a shoulder to cry on, a meal for the weary, or both.

Glancing at her watch, Megan realized she'd slept away half the day. "Andre, great to hear your voice," she said through a yawn, "I've missed you oodles, too." Massaging the back of her neck, she stood and stretched. "Lunch sounds great. But I need to shower and check my messages first, then I'll be down."

"Sure thing honeycakes. I'll just whip us up some sweet dessert to swoon over! Take your time." Andre's line went dead.

Meagan hung up the phone, raised the cup to her lips for one final disgusting swig, thought better of it, and headed off to the shower.

★★★

"Meg, received your copy—fabulous job! Call me when you get this," read the briefly written email message from Roxanne Pendleton, now New York Editor-in-Chief at the award-winning travel magazine, Global Thrills.

Roxy's rise at GT was meteoric, the first woman to break through its glass ceiling. More than once her male counterparts had tried supplanting her; but they were clueless to her grit, honed from a childhood spent in survival mode. And it was her grit that earned her the unofficial nickname of Moxie Roxy by her male detractors—though none were ever man enough to say it to her face.

Megan occasionally wrote for GT, though the two women kept their friendship a secret. But when off the clock, their relationship reverted to their hallowed college days as roommates.

Hitting the speed dial button, Megan balanced the phone between shoulder and ear as she assessed herself in the mirror. She pulled a lipstick tube from her purse and, leaning in toward her image, expertly outlined the sensuous peaks of her upper lip.

"Roxy Pendleton speaking," the business-like voice answered.

"Rox, it's Meg," she said.

"Thank goodness you're back," Roxy answered, not bothering to hide her relief.

Megan had expected as much, considering tomorrow's date.

"Your story was enthralling," she said, regaining her business-like composure, "you never fail to impress me, Meg."

"Thanks, Rox. Coming from you, it means a lot," and it did, as Roxy always gave her honest opinion. "Are we on for tomorrow?" Meg asked, switching gears. After a long assignment away, she was looking forward to her decompression ritual—their usual get-together reminiscent of college days, two best friends gabbing well into the night over take-out pizza and beer.

"Absolutely!" Roxy said without hesitation. "There's a flight that should get me to Boston around eight. Sleep in, I'll catch a cab to your apartment and make you breakfast." Roxy treasured their friendship and would move the earth for Megan, their bond having grown even closer since the death of her mother. Time spent together provided her with a sense of security and relief, time when she could let her guard down and feel unconditionally loved.

"You're the best, Rox," Megan said, her appreciation apparent in her tired voice. "Tomorrow, girlfriend," she said.

"Tomorrow," Roxy echoed and hung up the phone.

Peering critically at her image in the mirror, Megan ran her fingers through her hair, her drooping curls momentarily displaced from her forehead. She smoothed her skirt and straightened the collar of her white linen blouse. Her reflection granting its approval, she grabbed her purse and headed for the door.

***

A mouth-watering aroma greeted her in the stairwell, her empty stomach gurgling. Fatigue having completely overridden any thoughts of food, she hadn't realized how hungry she was until now, her legs wobbling and body shaking with each downward step.

In her famished state, a door was all that stood between her and a satiated appetite. Megan raised her unsteady hand to knock, but before her fist could make contact, the door swung open. There towered her savior, Andre Soprastrano—a wide-grinning Italian with a glass of merlot in one hand and a tray of homemade bruschetta in the other.

Megan's first heaven-sent mouthful released an unsolicited moan, which was followed by a healthy gulp of wine and gasp for air before closing in on the second bite. This, of course, was modus operandi for Andre, who fondly anticipated their dining soiree upon each of Megan's return trips; and Megan absolutely coveted Andre's gourmet cooking.

Leaning in on his elbows at the kitchen counter, massive hands supporting an unshaven chin and a strapping frame obliterating the fuchsia stool beneath him, Andre was absorbed in her every satisfied mouthful. A smile never left his face. Having grown up in Boston's North End among a household of five sisters, Andre knew better than to interrupt a famished female; and so he waited patiently for Megan to finish chewing and come up for air. Straightening up on his stool, arms folded over his chest and desperately trying to suppress the grin growing on his face, he said, "Sugarplum, how do you manage to pack so much food into such a slim body?"

Megan laughed and returned his good-natured barb. "You know, Andre," she said, swirling the wine in her glass beneath her nose, "with cooking like this, I'm surprised some good-looking buck hasn't claimed you for his own yet."

"Oh, but creampuff, I told you we had lots to catch up on," Andre teased.

Megan gagged on her wine. "What?" she sputtered. "You mean you finally met your match?"

"Like bread and butter, sweetiepie! Isn't it great! I've been dying to tell you all about Nick!"

"Nick?" she queried.

"Nick Bennett. We met weeks ago at my gallery! He's an artist, too, you know—paints the most fabulous abstract oils! He's very well-known on the circuit. Anyway, one thing led to another, and he's agreed to exhibit his works at my gallery tomorrow night! You've just got to come to the gala and meet him, dumpling!" Andre said, eyes pleading as he grabbed Megan's hands. "I won't take no for an answer."

Nick Bennett. Why I'll be damned, she thought. *What's it been … five years?* Time had gotten away from her, always on the road. Her mind schemed. "Roxy's coming up in the morning …" she baited.

"The more the merrier," Andre interrupted. "The both of you have to come! And if you play your cards right, you might just find your next storyline in Brazil."

"Brazil?" she asked.

"The Amazon to be exact. Nick's brother David is a scientist. He researches herbal plants in the rain forest. He'll be there with Nick tomorrow night."

David Bennett … interesting, she thought. "But of course we'll come," she said, replying without further ado. And then fighting hard to keep a straight face, razzed, "Besides, how could we pass up a chance to meet the guy who's willing to put up with the likes of you."

Before she knew what hit her, Andre flew off his stool and wrapped her in a massive bear-hug. "Thanks girlfriend, you're the best!" he said. And then without missing a beat, releasing her arms-length, eyebrow cocked and voice sexy, proclaimed, "Time for dessert!"

62

MEMORY LANE

Friday, August 18, 2006

A SINGLE OIL PAINTING adorned one white office wall; the others remained bare. Mesmerized, his eyes slowly embraced the painted bloom, caressing the curve of each petal. Amazing, so delicate a painted flower wielded such power over him. But this did not surprise David—the painting had been a gift from Rose and now, with her gone, nature's grip, both fragile and powerful, had been even more unrelenting on his life.

"Afternoon!" came the exuberant greeting filtering in through the open doorway, jarring David from his reverie. "You wanted to see me boss?" Brad Parks stood outside of David's office, his head jutting in. The go-to man when a job needed getting done, Brad had early on earned himself the enviable position as David's right-hand man. And now his work ethics and patience were finally paying off.

"Brad my boy, come in. Take a seat," David said, now all smiles. "Two questions for you," he said, leaning forward in his chair. "First, will you be coming tomorrow night to Nick's gala?"

"Sure thing, boss," Brad replied, "looking forward to it."

"Good," David nodded, "Nick will be pleased. And second," he paused, "how would you like to accompany me down to Brazil next week?"

"Are you kidding!" Brad bellowed. "Fucking yes!"

David opened his bottom desk drawer and retrieved a bottle of scotch with two shot glasses. Filling each one to the brim he raised his on high and, passing one to Brad, offered a toast. "To Brazil," he said, "a trip well-earned and long-deserved."

"Here, here," chimed Brad to the sound of their glasses clinking, the savor of their swallows lasting but a celebratory moment before David eyes settled back onto his lone painting. It was how the man coped with life after Rose, a form of meditation that relaxed his soul. "Thanks, boss, for your confidence in me," Brad said, and recognizing David's state of reverie, deposited his emptied glass onto the desktop and left David to it.

Brad made his way back to his desk, the corners of his mouth upturned in a self-satisfied grin. It was like winning the lottery—finally going to the Amazon. And after five years and counting in his hunt for answers to the mysterious plant extract that he was convinced his boss had hidden, Brad was certain that the key to his quest would be found in Brazil.

"I'm heading out for some air … won't be back today," David announced as he abruptly left his office, an occurrence not uncommon these days. "See you tomorrow night at the gala," he said before exiting the lab.

Brad gave David a usual thumbs up and watched his boss leave the building. Then, leaning back in his chair, a smile forming from ear to ear, he thought, *Yup, Brad my boy, all roads lead to Brazil.*

★★★

The Boston Public Garden was abuzz with tourists and locals alike, all out for a leisurely stroll on a warm August afternoon. On the pond, Swan Boats paddled both youngsters and the young-at-heart across the placid waters, gliding beneath drooping willow branches and a suspended footbridge. David stood on the bridge watching as a Swan Boat passed beneath, his distorted reflection staring back in the concentric ripples that followed.

Five years since I last stood here with Rose, he thought, only it felt like yesterday. The Garden was one of her favorite places to come and set up her easel. *She loved painting the flowers, the swan boats, this bridge,* he reminisced. Staring at the water, his gaze passed through his now-stilled reflection as his mind passed through time.

It was still hard for him to process losing the love of his life. Hard to think back to the very short time they had together, time he would give anything to have back. He blamed himself for her death. He should never have urged her to attend that meeting in New York and wished he had pushed her to reveal the news of their engagement to Roxy here at home instead. Now, as things stood, news of their betrothal never reached her daughter's ears. No one, save David, would ever know. And that suited him fine. Sharing the news of a happiness that was never to be was too hurtful.

No good living in the past—that was a different lifetime; now is now, he thought and proceeded on with his routine walk.

Ever since the horror of September 11, David's attitude on Operation Octane had taken on new meaning. Despite his abhorrence of Agent Jenks, the idea of ridding the world of those who would harm innocent people like Rose had suddenly taken on more appeal. Now, as he passed the gallant statue of George Washington sitting astride his horse, he felt in good company with the commander-in-chief of the Continental Army as, David, too, was involved in a struggle for a cause greater than himself. And like Washington, he considered himself both a revolutionary and a patriot.

He sat down at his customary bench along the walkway, still lost in time. Moments later, a passing jogger sat to rest beside him. Outfitted in shorts and a Harvard Crimson T-shirt, the jogger's youthful face presented him as a bona fide collegiate. He was, however, General Rand's messenger.

"The garden's infested," he said, keeping his eyes straight ahead as he spoke the pre-arranged code between panting breaths.

David's heart skipped a beat. At long last Operation Octane was a go. He provided the instructed response: "The bugs need spraying." He couldn't help but smile at the irony of his words.

Five years ago, General Rand had green-lighted David's test trials of a water-borne bacterial disease, with small successes in various pockets of Africa. The logistics, however, were risky and cumbersome, having to infiltrate the hot spots with one of their own men for years. But, ultimately, the success of 'tainting' wells and watering holes produced the desired results—turning aggressive radicals into peaceful protestors, so to speak. Realistically, however, this method was unsustainable. A widespread airborne disease was still considered the paramount goal and now, five years on, General Rand's directive had been realized—David had finally produced a 'weapon of peace.'

The General's messenger bent down, fumbling with his shoelaces. David deliberately dropped his sunglasses and bent to retrieve them. "D-day: 9/11," the messenger declared, then, without another word, he stood and proceeded on with his jog. At first David was stunned, but then it seemed poetic justice that on the anniversary of the day his world fell apart, the day he lost Rose, Octane would launch. He stared after the messenger exiting the Garden, passing through the open wrought iron gates and jogging across Charles Street, melding in with the churning sidewalk crowd. Even after he was long out of sight, David sat staring, frozen in time—stuck in memory lane.

63

—·—

A SONGBIRD'S LAMENT

Saturday, August 19, 2006

WITH EACH INTERMITTENT BREEZE the drawn bedroom shades tapped the sills of the open windows, a soft light filtering in. On the nightstand, a china cup sat steaming with its ghost tail rising. Megan rolled over in her bed, drawn toward the Hazelnut scent like the nose of a hound. From her kitchen, a low humming took wing. *Roxy's here,* her brain told her. Megan sat up expectantly in her plumped-pillowed perch, hands carefully enfolding the cup and luxuriating in its warmth as she savored the aroma and her first long sip.

Humming a melancholic tune like a songbird's lament, Roxy entered the room ferrying a breakfast tray complete with vase and flower. Her sorrow was palpable.

"You spoil me, Rox," Megan said.

"You deserve it, and so much more," Roxy answered, placing the tray on a bedside stand. There was nothing she wouldn't do for Megan, her rock, who kept her life from crumbling to pieces after the wrecking ball crashed in on her world with her mother's death. And now, today, the 15th anniversary of the hurricane that damaged both of their souls irreparably, Roxy had once again sought refuge with her best friend.

Preparing to purge the knot that had been twisting her gut like an Indian rope burn, Roxy walked to a window and, releasing the shade, leaned into the fresh air, inhaling deeply. "Last night I dreamt he was still alive," she began. "I woke up in a sweat, my heart racing so fast, and then … such relief when I realized it was only a dream," she said, turning to face Megan. "You know Mother and I were forced to live in a house of horrors whenever Father decided to grace us with his presence. That day in the backwoods I had no choice—I had to protect her."

It was always the same lament with each anniversary of her father's death: Roxy replaying that horrible, hot August day over and over—the beatings she and her mother endured at the hands of her drunken, deranged father, the hunting rifle weighted against her bruised shoulder, her trembling finger pulling the trigger—and each time finding justification … but not forgiveness. For fifteen years there wasn't an answer to her best friend's torment, and Megan doubted there would be now.

But unlike Roxy, on this and every anniversary of her mother's death, Megan found silence best served her own torment, choosing to batten down guilty thoughts in the prison cell of her mind rather than lend oxygen to spoken words and give life to the voice of her demons. Besides, what good would it do? Her mother was dead and not coming back. But Megan understood that people struggle differently with their demons. And so, when it came to Roxy, she gave her best friend what she needed, lending both ears and an open heart, unconditionally.

Megan swung her legs over the side of the bed and patted the spot next to her. "Come sit," she said. Roxy acquiesced, wrapping herself in the safety of Megan's embrace, her tough exterior walls crumbling as tears welled in her eyes.

Retrieving a slice of buttered toast from the breakfast tray, Megan offered it up to Roxy's lips. "I've got a surprise for you tonight," she said, venturing a diversion as Roxy took a bite.

"A surprise?"

"Yes, but we have to go shopping first; you'll need a cocktail dress."

"A cocktail dress? Why? Where are we going?" Roxy asked, wiping a tear with her hand.

"Now if I told you that, it wouldn't be a surprise," Megan teased.

The moue on Roxy's face melted Megan's resolve. "Okay, okay. We're going to a gala," she caved, "but no more clues. Come on now, help me get dressed," she said, standing and pulling Roxy to her feet. "We can catch brunch on Newbury Street before checking out the boutiques."

★★★

"How's Andre doing?" Roxy asked as they descended the stairwell, passing his second-floor apartment.

"Oh … he's doing fine," Megan said, smiling inwardly, "just fine."

64

—·—

THE WILL

Girl Flashback

OTHER THAN FLYING TO *Washington D.C. for her father's annual 'Take-your-son-to-work day,' Girl had never flown anywhere else, fun destinations unheard of in the Pendleton household. But on this day, the ten-year-old was excited to be flying to South Carolina, despite the fact they were headed to her grandmother's funeral. Given the window seat, with her mother in the middle and her father on the isle, she couldn't take her eyes off the view. The take-off, itself, was always exhilarating, going from zero to over 180 miles per hour in less than a minute, but then, when she looked out of her window at the clouds below, well, her imagination took flight—her world catapulted into one of flying dragons and castles in the clouds, she a maiden warrior on the back of the biggest and most beautiful creature in the kingdom—her reverie only interrupted when the stewardess brought peanuts.*

Girl hardly knew her grandmother, she and her father had been estranged, never visiting one another. But she did receive birthday cards yearly with an enclosed check. And so it seemed strange to her, with her grandmother dead, that her father would now show an interest in going. She thought perhaps because he was an only child there was a duty expected of him to pay his respects, but then her father cared little about what people thought of him, and the duty of attending or not attending his own mother's funeral would not have mattered in his decision. But after the funeral ended, and her body was laid to rest, Girl found out the reason.

"Would everyone kindly gather in the living room," her grandmother's lawyer said, directing family and friends, now back at her home, for a reading of her will.

When everyone had taken a seat, her lawyer began. "I will read Mrs. Pendleton's wishes in the order in which she wrote them," he said. Clearing his throat, he began. "To my best friend, Sarah Johnson, I bequeath the English bone china set she so admired. Think of me dearie when you use it." Sarah smiled, clearly pleased. "To my delightful niece, Anne Pendleton, I bequeath my treasured art collection. May you find pleasure in its beauty, my dear." Anne burst into tears. "To my dear brother, Charles Pendleton, I bequeath my prized Cadillac. I know you will care for her like the baby she was to me." Charles chuckled, nodding his head in the affirmative. "To my cherished sister-in-law, Louise Pendleton, who was more like a sister to me, I bequeath all of my fine jewelry." Louise was speechless, dabbing the corners of her eyes. "To my darling granddaughter, Roxanne Pendleton, I bequeath the entirety of my remaining estate, placed in trust until age twenty-one, whereupon you are free to do with it as you will." The room filled with gasps. Girl didn't understand what had just happened, but before she could ask her mother, the lawyer continued. "And finally, to my son, Eugene Pendleton, I bequeath … nothing," her lawyer said squeamishly, but still carried on with the reading. "To give is to receive, son. In life you gave your mother nothing, not even a minute of your time … therefore, in my death, so too shall you receive nothing."

Shock, disbelief and then rage followed in quick succession as a red-faced Eugene bellowed incompetency claims at the lawyer, questioning his mother's state of mind at the will's signing which, in fact, came years well before the onset of her Alzheimer's. But in the end, he had nothing to contest. Everything was legal. His hands would never be able to touch Girl's inheritance—his mother had made certain of that.

The plane ride home was quiet, her father silently fuming at his reversal of fortune. Her mother, once again seated beside her, reached into her purse and retrieved a small envelope. She handed it to her daughter. On its surface, elegantly written in her grandmother's hand, was her name, Roxanne. Inside was a brief note:

My darling Roxanne,

In life, we never know what is around the next corner. When your grandfather passed on so early in our marriage, I was forced to face life on my own. Not all women in my situation were as fortunate to have been amply provided for, as your grandfather made sure I was, greatly easing my burdens of worry over rearing a child alone and paying the bills. The day may come, though I pray not dear, that you may find yourself in a similar position; and if you do, I hope your inheritance will help to see you through.

Your loving Grandmother

Girl folded the note back into its envelope and looked out of the window. Their plane soaring high above the clouds, she dreamed now of turning twenty-one and a life freed of her father's consent.

65

—·—

THE GALA

Saturday, August 19, 2006

ANDRE SOPRASTRANO WOULD NORMALLY stand out in any crowd—tall, dark and handsome. But tonight, dressed in black and white formal attire with a charming smile fit for the cover of GQ, the man was a showstopper. Though, to be honest, the only eyes he hoped to impress tonight belonged to Nick. All the same, business was business, and Andre had no problem playing second fiddle to his love interest. This was, after all, Nick's night. And, as the ever-gracious, charismatic host of this evening's event, Andre knew how to work a crowd, parlaying flattery along with accolades into huge sales and fat charity checks. Never did he doubt that the evening would be a success.

And that was all that mattered to Nick because, tonight, in honor of Rose, he planned to contribute one hundred percent of his sales to benefit art programs for troubled teens. His way of paying forward the goodness she had bestowed upon him because, if it were not for her, he'd be a nobody. That she believed in him helped Nick to believe in himself. She had been so instrumental as a mentor, her guidance and urging what prompted him to take chances, her confidence rubbing off on him. He missed her terribly. At first, her death didn't seem real. And, still, he can't stop seeing her in the places they frequented together, hearing her calming voice, feeling her presence over his shoulder as he endeavored to paint a canvas. And tonight, especially, Nick was never more adamant that her spirit was with him—certain she was smiling.

As the evening drew on at the posh Back Bay gallery, the crowd swelled, and the champagne flowed. David had arrived unaccompanied, as usual. After Rose, no other woman could measure up. He found himself a tucked-away corner where he and his champagne could party, for the most part, undisturbed. But when he heard a voice say, "So this is where you've been hiding," he knew the gig was up.

With a wide, gleaming smile, Brad Parks had snuck up behind him.

"Brad my boy, glad you could come," David said. "I see you've found the champagne."

"My second," Brad confessed.

"I've stopped counting," David retorted.

A pretty, young woman sauntered by, her eyes flirtatious. Brad returned the look. David hadn't bothered to notice.

"I think I'm being summoned," Brad said, and sauntered off after her.

All fine with David, preferring anonymity in the crowd. But then, a familiar figure approached, and David's body stiffened.

"David," Michael Campo said, extending a hand, "it's been a long time."

"Michael," David responded, shaking his hand, "yes it has."

Awkward is an understatement in describing the silence that followed, until Michael broke the ice. "I've been following your brother's career with great enthusiasm … you must be really proud of his accomplishments … and I'm sure if Rose were here, she would be as well … she took such great interest in his work … and she was such a terrific mentor, a terrific person," he said, all in one breath, a run-on sentence trying to fill the uncomfortable void, his voice shaken at the mention of her name.

David realized then that Michael hadn't known of his engagement to Rose, her untimely death pre-empting their joyous announcement. And despite the rivalry between them over her love, he could see the man was still hurting and didn't have the heart to rub salt into his wound. Of what good would it have done anyway—she was gone. Instead, he smiled and said, "Yes, Rose was terrific. And we were all lucky to have had her in our lives."

"Yes," Michael agreed, "we were lucky." And then, before another awkward silence could descend, he gave his one-time adversary a good-natured clap on the shoulder and said, "Well, take good care of yourself, David. Hope to see you around town sometime."

David nodded and then watched as another broken-hearted man retreated into the folds of the crowd.

"David," Andre called excitedly, making a fast approach.

No rest for the weary, David sighed to himself.

"There are two very attractive ladies here claiming to know you," he said, reaching David and pointing in their direction. Both women were engrossed in animated conversation with Nick, catching up on the past five years, everyone laughing and smiling like it was just yesterday.

One of them turned to face him. *Rose,* he thought, his heartbeat kicking into a frenzy.

"They wanted to surprise you," Andre said, "and from the look on your face, I'd say they succeeded."

Was he hallucinating? Too much drink playing tricks on his mind? Shit. He couldn't focus. His heart kept telling him one thing and his brain another. David felt his legs carrying him forward as if in a dream, voices and people around him a haze, only her smiling face all he could see.

"David," she said, kissing his cheek, "it's Roxy … Roxy Pendleton," she clarified, when he didn't respond.

"Roxy," he stammered, "you'll have to forgive me. I've had a few too many. You look … beautiful."

"You remember my friend, Megan," she said.

"Yes. Yes, of course," he said, without his eyes ever leaving hers.

"Well," Andre said, "I'm sure the three of you have a lot of catching up to do. Nick and I will leave you to it."

As soon as they departed, Megan, aware that three's a crowd, announced, "I'm off to find some champagne," and sprinted away.

Roxy turned to David. "How about some fresh air?" she offered, and accepting David's arm, he led her outside—smiling.

★★★

"So, are you a friend of Nick Bennett's or just a fan?" Brad said, snagging a glass of champaign from a passing server's tray and offering it to Megan.

Grateful for ending her protracted chase for the bubbly, she said, "Thanks, and both."

"Is that so? Interesting. How long have you known each other?"

"Since college."

"So you knew Nick before his celebrity."

"I guess you could say that."

"What was he like back then."

Megan felt uncomfortable with where this conversation was going. She didn't even know who this man was. "We haven't introduced ourselves," she said. "I'm Megan O'Malley," her hand outstretched.

"Pleased to make your acquaintance, Megan," he said, shaking her hand. "I'm Brad Parks."

"So, Brad," she asked, "how do you know Nick?"

"I work with his father as a research assistant."

"I see," Megan said.

"And what's your line of work, if you don't mind my asking?" Brad rounded.

"I'm a freelance journalist … just finished a piece for Global Thrills, a travel magazine."

"So you move around a lot?" he said.

"Just got back from Indonesia."

"Wow, half a world away. Where will your next feature take you?"

"I'm on hiatus. No assignment yet."

"Say … you ever been to Brazil? The Amazon to be exact?"

"Can't say that I have."

"Well, I'm going down with David next week. Maybe you'd be interested in tagging along. Could make an interesting story. Who knows, maybe you'd get to meet a shaman or two," he laughed.

The wheels rolled in Megan's head. *Is this a come-on or an honest offer?* she thought. *Maybe both.* "I'll give it some thought," she said, finishing her champaign and snagging another.

★★★

After her mother's death Roxy closed The Rose Art Gallery, sold the Cambridge home and said good-bye to the Bennetts, lodging for a while with her Grandpa Max at his horse ranch in Connecticut. Wanting to feel closer to her mother—her remains never recovered from the ashes—she moved into a condominium in Manhattan bought with her grandmother's inheritance. She'd made a pledge when she'd left Cambridge to move forward with her life and to never look back. Dwelling on the past wouldn't bring her mother back; but learning to be on her own, she knew, was what her mother would want of her. So, she secured a job as a freelance journalist with Global Thrills in Manhattan, her salvation, where she devoted all her hours and energy to rapidly moving up the ladder—all the while never considering a serious relationship. But seeing David now—his eyes catching hers and holding them tight—she was having second thoughts. They hadn't seen one another in five years, and during that time she had matured into a beautiful woman, uncannily resembling her mother. His gaze bearing down on her now unearthed long-buried feelings that raced through her wanton body. Back as a college girl he was off-limits, belonging to her mother. But now, with his deep ocean blue eyes diving deep into her soul, well ...

"How's life in New York City?" he asked, his body's proximity close, brushing against hers.

"I'm Editor-in-Chief now at a travel magazine."

"Impressive," he said, "though I'm not surprised. Rose always said you were a born leader." He smiled, his gaze suddenly growing distant.

"And you, David? How's time treated you?" she said, pulling him back.

"Ah ... life as a dedicated scientist eschews time, Roxy, paying mind only to the next discovery around the corner."

"So it's safe to say that your work has become your life?" she asked.

"Safe to say."

Not unlike me, Roxy thought, *but we'll see about that.*

***

"So tell me more about the Amazon and your work there," Megan said.

"Well, David's mentor, Dr. Benjamin Shaw, operates an herbal farm there," Brad said, their empty champagne glasses mounting up on a nearby tray. "We use the farm as a source for many of the cancer therapies we research."

"And these herb specimens have led to viable therapies?"

"Some, yes. But the true marvel of the Amazon are the yet-to-be-discovered plants that could lead to future treatments. The possibilities are endless."

It was obvious Brad wore his passion for his work on his sleeve. Megan admired this quality; it was one she herself possessed. And the more she and Brad talked, the more comfortable she felt around him—and the more she thought about his whirlwind offer to do a story on the Amazon. She knew from experience that sometimes the least expected opportunities brought the most reward. But if she were to accompany him on a trip to Brazil, she knew theirs must remain a strictly working relationship. After all, she was going after a story, not a boyfriend. She had no doubt she could manage the situation, despite any ideas Brad may otherwise have.

"Sounds like a fascinating trip," she said.

"Honestly, it will be my first time down," he said. "I can't tell you how long I've dreamed about this."

"And you think David would be okay with my tagging along?"

"How could he refuse such a beautiful, intelligent woman? Besides," he added, "his fifteen minutes of fame from your article could be instrumental in securing coveted funding. And what research scientist doesn't crave that?"

★★★

"The Amazon, you say?" Roxy's gaze locked with David's. "Such an incredibly beautiful and horrifically menacing place—how do you reconcile yourself to that?"

David laughed. "You prepare for the worst and hope for the best."

"My, how cavalier you are with your life."

"Well, it's not like I'm there on my own. I do have guides—two of the best—I trust them with my life."

"That is quite remarkable."

"What is?"

"Trusting strangers with your life."

"Not if you want to survive in the jungle," David said. "It's not a walk in the park, Roxy. There is real danger."

"There's real danger everywhere," she said, reliving the image of 9/11 in her mind.

"Yes, but not 24/7 like in the Amazon. You virtually need eyes in the back of your head, day and night. And the jungle isn't discriminatory with respect to its victims—no matter how well prepared you may think you are."

"So, knowing the dangers and your relative odds of survival, you still choose to go. Why?"

"Because it is a mystery—not unlike a woman—alluring, surprising, challenging. And once you've tasted of its sweet splendor, you ache for more." He smiled.

"Intriguing," Roxy said, falling silent to her thoughts.

***

"So this is where you two have been hiding," Megan said, all smiles, as she and Brad exited the gallery door on this balmy August evening and joined David and Roxy out on the sidewalk.

No rest for the weary, David thought once again, as he put on a smile and greeted the couple. "I see, Megan, that you've met Brad Parks, my ace research assistant," he said. "And Brad, may I introduce you to Roxy Pendleton ..."

"... my best friend and boss at Global Thrills," Megan interjected in a hushed voice, "but we try to keep that close to the vest."

"A pleasure, Roxy," Brad said, leaning in to exchange handshakes.

"We've just had a rather interesting conversation about the Amazon," Megan offered.

"What a coincidence—so have we," Roxy responded. "Go on."

"Well, as a journalist, I find the Amazon intriguing."

"My word exactly," Roxy said.

"I mean, can't you imagine the interest generated from a storyline about life in the jungle? It would make for great copy—you know our readers crave adventure."

"Now hold on a minute," David interjected. "No one's going to the Amazon."

"I am," Brad said.

"Yes, you are," David said begrudgingly, "but not Megan."

"David, I am more than capable of taking care of myself—I've traveled the world."

"I don't care how worldly you think you are, nothing can prepare you for the Amazon."

"I'd like to go, too," Roxy said, startling David into silence. "It would be a great opportunity to get back in the saddle and write something. Megan and I could share a byline." She meant what she said, but in the back of her mind lurked something more—a perfect diversion from guilt-ridden memories on this fifteenth anniversary of her father's death. And … she'd be with David.

He eyed her seriously. This was risky business, not some game. He'd be crazy to take them along. And his failure to protect Rose from harm still lived large in him. But Roxy's unexpected presence had stirred emotions long forgotten and a yearning to be with her, though he knew none of this wasn't rational. But then, when had his heart ever agreed with his brain when it came to the Pendleton women. Still, it was a decision he could live to regret—again.

Roxy touched his arm. "David, we put our trust in you and your intrepid guides to 'prepare us for the worst and hope for the best,'" she said, quoting his words.

"And don't forget, you'll have me along to help lend a hand," Brad added, his enthusiasm a little much.

David didn't like being put on the spot, nor being ganged up on. "This is craziness," he said. "Are you all out of your minds?"

"We'll do everything you ask of us," Roxy said, her pleading eyes penetrating his. "Please … just sleep on it."

Game over. David knew it. Even before he broke from her eyes, before Andre opened the door to bid them all enter for Nick's closing speech, before his head hit the bed pillow that night … he knew Roxy had won—and now come what may, there'd be no turning back.

***

When David got home from the gala, though it was late and he was tired, he picked up his SAT phone and dialed.

"Pretty late for you to be up, knowing how you need your beauty sleep," Doc said, answering on the first ring.

David smiled. "Thought you'd like a heads up. I'm coming down Monday and bringing guests with me."

"Oh," Doc said, "anyone I know?"

"Don't believe so. Two lady friends interested in your work."

"You don't say. Well, I look forward to their company."

"Doc," David said, turning serious, "how are you doing?"

"Fantastic … getting less cantankerous by the day," he said, chuckling. "I'm a whole new person."

"Still monitoring your DNA?"

"Yes, mommy. Just like a good little boy," Doc teased.

"And?"

"And all is good. The mutation is still holding firm."

David breathed a sigh of relief. It had been five years since Doc had offered himself up as a guinea pig for various trials of David's airborne 'weapon of peace', the last of which a year ago seemed to have taken hold. But David still harbored great worry and responsibility for his mentor's health. Although from the sound of things, Doc seemed to be holding up well. And Doc, for his part, figured a man had to die from something—better he dies trying for a worthwhile cause than to have wasted precious time twiddling his thumbs.

"Good. Then see you Monday," David said.

"Not if I see you first," Doc laughed.

★★★

Journal Entry, Saturday, August 19, 2006:

Megan said she had a surprise for me, but I never saw this one coming! David … after so many years, seeing him again … it was like being a teenager anew. Those same feelings resurfacing like they'd never been buried, flirting with my heart like I was flirting with him. But there was something there, in his eyes, like he felt something, too. Question is, who were those feelings for—me or mother?

66

LIVENING UP THE JOINT

Monday, August 21, 2006

THE SUN HUNG LOW, its last hurrah igniting the horizon before setting, though only glimpses penetrated the canopy. The mosquitoes buzzed—still hungry, still annoying. And the macaws circled in and out of the treetops, squawking at the top of their lungs like heralds announcing to all the arrival of royalty. Brad and the two women may not have been royalty, but their arrival at Doc's farm deserved some touting, having survived their first trip unscathed down the mighty Amazon and its connecting tributaries and then the laborious overland march through the jungle. Of course, kudos for their prosperity must be given to David and the cousins in running a tight ship, knowing all too well the crazy shit that could happen with the slightest of slip-ups in a place like this. Not allowing the inexperience of their charges to get in the way of a safe journey, they had hoped for the best and prepared for the worse.

"Welcome everyone! Welcome!" Doc said, a big smile crinkling the corners of his eyes as David and his entourage broke free of the brush. "Hope your trip wasn't too arduous."

David grasped his old mentor in a bear-hug and assured him, "We were well-cared for by Ramon and Bruno, but it's good to finally be here."

"And this must be Brad," Doc said, extending his hand. "Good to put a face to the voice on the phone. Glad you could make it, young man."

"Doctor Shaw, believe me, the pleasure is all mine," Brad effused, his handshake strong and earnest.

"Please, just call me Doc … no formalities here in the jungle." And then, eyeing the women, he turned to David saying, "And I presume these two lovely ladies must be my surprise guests."

"I'm Roxy Pendleton, Editor in Chief at Global Thrills, a travel magazine, and this is free-lance journalist Megan O'Malley," Roxy said, jumping ahead of David with introductions and not surprising him in the least with her take-charge attitude. He just stood there, smiling.

"Well, it's certainly a pleasure to make both of your acquaintances," Doc said, stepping forward to shake each of their soft, un-calloused hands. "I look forward to lively conversation as we all get to know one another better. But first things first. You must all be tired after your long journey. Ramon and Bruno will show you all to your cabins where you can refresh and rest yourselves before dinner. And, please, let me know if there is anything you need. We may be far from civilization as you know it," Doc smiled, "but we try our best to stock the niceties of refined living."

David hung back with Doc as the others proceeded on to their cabins. As he watched them go, his brain registered a familiar scent hanging on the heavy, humid air. His eyes scanned the premises for its origin, coming to a stop under the thatched-roof pavilion. There, a shadowy figure stared back at him, his lit cigar glowing. "What's he doing here?" David said.

"It seems Agent Jenks knew you were coming—you and your entourage."

"What?"

"He arrived yesterday."

"The guy's got eyes in the back of his head," David said, exasperated.

"Yeah, well, he wasn't too pleased you bringing strangers here just as the operation is readying to launch.

"He's over-reacting," David said. "No one knows anything."

"And he's here to make sure it stays that way. Listen …" Doc said, pausing, "just ignore the guy. I, for one, am looking forward to some feminine company and livening up the joint." Doc smiled his shit-eating grin and then, arm around David's back, led him off to his cabin.

***

It was strange how this jungle had become like a second home to David, each visit eliciting a certain comfort that came with familiarity, despite the dangers. But seeing Jenks here not only shot up his blood pressure but shot to hell any comfort level he'd expected to entertain.

While blazing torches stood sentry around the pavilion's perimeter, embers flickering into the blackness beyond, the two eyeballed one another across the long, wooden table. While Doc kept the dinner conversation as heady as the brandy—enthralling his visitors with personal tales of jungle adventure and danger—Jenks just sat there, an obvious lump on a log, noticeably detached and uninterested. Doc had introduced him to the gathering as a US Federal Agent with the Food & Drug Administration just making a quality control house call—believable, if not the whole truth. But the man's silent presence was unnerving—a feeling of 'Big Brother' watching pervading the party.

"So Brad," Doc said, pouring himself another brandy and clearly enjoying himself, "any stories of interest to share?"

"None that can be measured on the jungle life-and-death Richter scale like yours."

"Then just humor me, son. Tell me a story about your youth."

"My youth …" Brad said, thinking. "Well, I was always fascinated by science as a kid. My parents bought me those age-appropriate do-it-yourself kits to encourage my interests. But by junior high I had run the gamut available in the hobby shops and, bored, moved on to experiments of a more *explosive* nature, nearly blowing up the house trying to make a bomb." Everyone gasped. "It'd be an understatement to say that my parents weren't too pleased. But despite that, they never stopped me from following my passion—provided I did it in the backyard shed from then on," Brad said to laughter.

"Well, it sounds to me, Brad, like you did venture onto the Richter scale somewhat with that escapade," Doc said to more laughter.

Then he turned to the ladies. "Roxy … Megan, who'd like to share a story?"

Roxy spoke up. "Well, I doubt any personal story of mine could ever top one of yours, Doc … or even Brad's," she said, smiling. "But I am in the business of publishing stories of intrigue, and Megan and I would very much like to write one about you."

Jenks jerked his head in her direction, his eyes landing hard on her—his sudden movement noticed by all.

"I'm flattered," Doc said. "So tell me … what, exactly, would that entail?"

"Well," Megan stepped in, "we'd like to give our readers a taste of what it takes to live, work and survive here in the jungle. Incorporate your experiences here with tribal life … share a shaman's remedy or two?"

Jenks coughed loudly, choking on his own cigar smoke. Everyone turned toward him.

"Stories of intrigue, you say?" Doc said, liking the sound of it. He did regard his life's work in the jungle as intriguing, if not noteworthy enough to be recorded for posterity. "Why not?" he said, without further thought. "Consider me at your disposal."

"Wonderful," Roxy said, smiling. "When can we start?"

"Sunrise … meet me at the farm." Doc said. "And Brad, here, can tag along—just leave any explosives behind, son." More laughter.

Brad grinned broadly. "Sure thing Doc."

David looked over at Jenks, the man more sullen than ever …

Not a good sign.

67

—·—

PHILOSOPHICALLY SPEAKING

Tuesday, August 22, 2006

ROXY, FOR ONCE, HAD slept like a baby. The exhausting previous day's journey to Doc's farm combined with the heavily oxygenated air and enchanting rain forest sounds had lulled her into a deep state of repose. So deep, she had slept past daybreak and Doc's scheduled meeting at the farm.

David stood outside Roxy's cabin door with her morning cup of joe, not surprised she had overslept. He recalled experiencing the same unfathomable slumber with his initial visits to the jungle—but that was before Viper had given him his Sphatika … the quartz crystal possessing his nightly dreams and impeding his rest. He knocked on the cabin door, stirring her within. "Come in," she said groggily, sitting upright in her hammock, mosquito netting splayed about her. "Rise and shine," David said, pulling back the netting and handing her the coffee. Still star-struck at her likeness to Rose, he couldn't help staring.

"You're an angel," she said, taking both the cup and notice of his stare, though her eyes didn't let on, cast down as she sipped. "Please," she begged, "tell me I'm not late for my meeting with Doc."

"Not to worry," he soothed, "Megan and Brad are still out like lights."

"Doc will be displeased," she said, suddenly standing, her nightshirt exposing her long, slender legs.

"Not exactly," he said, her bare legs capturing his attention. "He never truly expected any of you up at the crack of dawn after your long journey yesterday. It's just a game he likes to play with newbies—a challenge no one has yet to meet."

"Really? That's a relief," she said inhaling more of her coffee.

"Oh, I wouldn't be too relieved just yet," David said with a knowing look.

"What do you mean?"

"You'll see," he said, smiling. "Now, I'll let you get dressed while I rouse the others."

★★★

Down on his old, achy knees among the contiguous rows of plantings, Doc was doing what he loved most, harvesting herbs. The jungle and this farm spoke to his soul. And, despite complaints about marauding mosquitoes and any lack of rain, this was where he was meant to be. And he especially liked sharing his affinity with nature with whomever would listen. So it was with great enthusiasm that he greeted his newest acolytes to his world, but not without some playful admonition first for holding up the start of his day.

"Good morning," he said, slowly standing, using his arm as a third leg. "Or is it good afternoon?" His smile was mischievous. "I did have high hopes that perhaps one of you would have risen to the early morning challenge. But, alas, the contest continues," he said wistfully. "No matter, we have a busy day planned. Full speed ahead."

Roxy looked over at David, his grin ear to ear. She wanted to poke him.

Megan, embarrassed, sheepishly avoided Doc eyes.

Only Brad let it fly, unruffled.

"Tell me Doc," he said, as they walked through the plantings, "do you have knowledge of the healing properties for all of these plants?"

"Every last one of them, son," he said. "I pride myself on learning all I can to record and preserve that knowledge for generations to come. Because, who knows, someday someone may find a beneficial application for one of these herbs that we haven't yet thought of."

This struck home with Brad, but a question nagged at him. "Doc," he said, "I'm all for discovering new remedies for the betterment of mankind but, philosophically speaking, what if a plant was discovered that could be used to its detriment? Would it be right to withhold its knowledge from the world? To wipe out any reference of it for all posterity for fear of it falling into the wrong hands?"

"That, son, is a loaded question. Now, I'm no philosopher, but as a scientist I am of the opinion that progress marches on, good or bad, no matter the outcome. Suppression of knowledge is only as good as those policing it. And, as we all know, man is not good at keeping secrets. Sooner or later, information leaks. And then, the best we can hope for is that sanity rules the day."

Brad's unexpected question and Doc's prescient warning in response stunned David. He stared at his mentor, dumbfounded. He had deemed himself sole proprietor and guardian of Octane's secret formula knowing that if someone like Jenks, the antithesis of a model citizen, got his hands on it, the genie would be out of the bottle and there would be no putting him back. Brad's question had brought the burden of this knowledge into the light of day, and it never weighed so heavily as now. Doc held David's stare, a secret knowing passing between them, and then continued with his tour.

An hour later, winding things up on the farm, Doc proposed a pilgrimage into the rain forest for his guests to experience jungle life firsthand. David, of course, was apprehensive, his fear of danger hardly unfounded. Of course, there was no way he could hold anyone back. They had come to see the rain forest and not even he could stop them. Best case scenario—well, there was no best-case scenario. Them not being here would have been the best-case scenario, but it was too late for that. Now, he was obliged to maintain damage control—to be an extra pair of eyes and ears—to make sure everyone was still breathing at the end of the day.

★★★

There was no sign of Jenks at the farm this morning. But David knew better than to hope the man had left. The thing about Jenks was his unpredictability. It kept David looking over his shoulder, feeling vulnerable—as if he didn't have enough to worry about.

David gathered his entourage together and performed backpack checks before giving each of them a thumbs up to proceed, the eagle scout in him resurrected to be prepared. Ramon and Bruno stood back, smiling as they watched David's antics. They had come to love David like a brother, his welfare always paramount under their watch. If performing inspections gave him peace of mind, who were they to argue. But they knew when push came to shove, David counted on them above all else; and they weren't about to let him and his guests down—the cousins ready, willing and able to provide the red-carpet treatment. So, as usual, Ramon took the lead while Bruno backed up the rear, bookending the group in a snaking, single file procession.

Brad was like a kid at Christmas, bursting with excitement. He fell in line behind Ramon and Doc as they headed back out into the brush. David observed him from the rear. He couldn't help but smile at Brad's enthusiasm, seeing something of himself in his young protégé. But he knew leaving the rain forest would prove a tough sell for Brad when it came time to return home, now that he'd gotten a taste of this place. Or maybe not—not if he was leaving with Megan on his arm.

Oblivious to Brad and his obvious attentions, Megan followed next, snapping pictures with a camera she'd dug out from her mother's belongings—one her mom used on her many assignments while in the Peace Corp—because now she was not only a journalist on an assignment, but the official photographer on this trip as well. And though the camera was old by today's standards, for Megan, its sentimentality outweighed modernity, and her mother's long-ago tutorage of its operations all came back like it was yesterday. She had forgotten how much she'd enjoyed sharing those days on the island with her mom chronicling the rising sun and rolling tides, photos of which now filled albums stacked and stored in boxes back at Megan's Beacon Hill apartment.

Roxy had all she could do to just breathe with David following so close behind her. Being here with him felt like deja-vu, the feelings she'd had for him as a teenager returning full force. And though she surmised his sudden interest in her was driven by her near-mirror image to her mother, she was okay with that. She could play the part—it was what she did best—how she survived. And, as long as David wanted her around, she'd more than oblige.

David brought up the end of the line, close on the heels of Roxy, his irrepressible feelings toward her, however misguided, undeniable. Was he selfish for bringing her to this bewitching and menacing place, absolutely. Could he live to regret his decision, without a doubt. But he was over-the-moon happy whenever she looked his way. Reality and reason had fallen off the map—David was operating now on a strictly emotional level. And if he wasn't careful—that could prove dangerous.

The procession passed within thirty feet of Doc's secret laboratory, unnoticed and buried within the jungles sprawling foliage. Even David had to look twice despite knowing its location. Its existence was always remarkable to him, and he often wondered about a time in the far future—what would be made of this anomalous discovery. A smile crossed his face as they passed, taking pleasure like a little kid with a secret.

It wasn't long before a burst of rain surprised them and the creatures of the forest, sending the toucans squawking and spider monkeys screeching. But the heavy spillage of rain onto the voluminous brush muffled their chatter. Megan tucked her camera into her backpack and yanked the rim of her safari hat further down. Brad, however, removed his hat, letting the cool rain wash over his heated body. David threw a rain tarp over Roxy and himself and nestled her body in closer with his arm. Doc, Ramon and Bruno simply marched on as if nothing had happened.

After the rain passed the mosquitoes came out en masse—and so did the bug spray, the three guests creating auras of mist about them as the others just stood back, grinning.

"What?" Roxy said, taking in their smirks. "Am I supposed to let them dine on me?"

"After a while you get used to it," David said. "And besides, you'll eventually run out of spray."

"Well, so long as I have it, I aim to give these little buggers a run for their money," she retorted with one final, dramatic squirt before pocketing her can of spray.

The crew rolled with laughter, its contagiousness soon sweeping Roxy up along with them.

The stop was a perfect opportunity for a break and, for Megan, some candid shots. She pulled out a bag of trail mix and stuffed a handful into her mouth as she worked her camera. "Smile," she said, capturing Roxy with a mouth full of crackers, while David held up 'rabbit' fingers behind her head and grinned. Stealthily, she snapped a shot of Brad engaged in animated conversation with Doc, neither of them noticing. Then she swung the camera at Ramon and Bruno off to the side, the two sharpening the blades of their machetes in preparation for the next leg of the journey. She took several shots, hoping to have captured at least one worthy of publishing. Then she turned her camera back onto the jungle, moving slowly and cautiously out into the brush—the sway of a tall fern the last indicator of where she'd once been.

68

—·—

THE ANTS GO MARCHING

Tuesday, August 22, 2006

THE RAIN FOREST SEEMED to call to Megan. She was intrigued—everywhere something new, something different for her lens to capture. And yet she knew from experience that her photographs could never capture the true essence of what it was like standing here in person under a canopy of interwoven branches, the light soft and filtering, the air heavy with the scents of both life and death. It was the same as it had been for her as a kid on Rocky Point Island in Maine accompanying her mother on photo shoots, the pictures failing to capture the salty ocean breeze that filled her nostrils or the feeling of soft mist alighting her skin. The memories suddenly overwhelmed her, tearing her eyes. She briskly wiped them dry with her palms and, conscious of a job yet to fulfill, moved on.

Focusing her lens on the copious flora and fauna inhabiting her surroundings, she continued with her intense picture-taking endeavor until her camera ran out of film, forcing her to stop and reload. Utilizing a decaying tree stump as a perch, she sat and popped open the camera's back, removed the spent roll, and dropped in a replacement. Her stomach growling in hungry protest, she fisted more trail mix from her backpack into her mouth and chewed as she sat in awe of her surroundings. Closing her eyes, she inhaled the rain forest's sundry smells and listened to its myriad sounds, allowing her sensory perceptions to fully experience the jungle to better write about it later.

It was then, with her eyes closed, that she felt the first jolt of pain from a powerful sting, followed by dozens more to her leg. The pain was so excruciating, it felt as if she had been shot multiple of times. She stood wailing like a banshee—and then passed out cold onto the ground.

They found her within seconds, Ramon and Bruno first on the scene. And what they saw terrified them. "Bullet ants," Ramon said, quickly swiping the insects off of her bitten leg with his bandana before he and Bruno dragged her away from the tree stump, the ant nest cozied up to its base.

Doc and the others stood back, horrified.

"What can we do to help?" Roxy pleaded, on the verge of tears.

"To be truthful, once the ants go marching, not a hell of a lot," Doc said. "Their venom will cause her extreme pain that could last up to a day. During that time, we can expect her to pass in and out of consciousness, experiencing a temporary paralysis of her leg. But the good news is that the venom doesn't spread—she will survive."

Megan moaned and came to, her body covered in sweat and violently shaking, her anguished wails resuming.

"Quickly, Ramon … Bruno, build a stretcher," Doc said, "we must get her back to the farm at once."

The cousins, devastated at their failure to protect Megan, rushed off. Falling unconscious again, Brad lifted her limp body into his arms and carried her in their direction.

★★★

When Megan awoke on the stretcher, her body tied down to keep her safe and secured, she wailed and cried and moaned in pain until blacking out again—a ritual she kept up for the entire journey back to the farm. It was difficult for all to witness; but for Roxy, powerless to help her best friend, it was two hours of mental torture.

David worried about both women, the weight of guilt coming down on him like a sledgehammer. All of this was his doing, his fault, and he took full responsibility. But if he wanted to improve the situation and redeem himself, he knew he had to take immediate action—something drastic to turn the tide. There was no anti-venom for bullet ants—only long, excruciating, tortuous time—but he had another idea, one that may or may not help. Still, he had to try. The only problem standing in his way was the cigar-smoking federal agent watching over his shoulder.

***

Back at the farm, Megan—still tied down to her stretcher—was situated as comfortably as possible in her tiny cabin. With the entire entourage standing there by her bedside, the small quarters became even tighter. Roxy took matters in hand.

"Everyone, shoo," she said, motioning for them to leave. "Go and make yourselves useful elsewhere. No sense standing around here. I'll sit with her." The men didn't argue, their unease palpable within the cabin's four constricted walls.

Doc and Brad headed out to the farm to join in with the harvesting, while David pulled Ramon and Bruno aside—he had a mission for them. But first, he had to search out Agent Jenks. It was odd that the man hadn't shown up to assess the commotion surrounding Megan. Very strange, indeed, considering the man's usual Gestapo-like tactics around David's activities. He found the pavilion empty—though an ashtray held the warm stub of a recently extinguished cigar. David gazed around, his attention drawn to the window of Jenks' cabin and movement within. *Good,* he thought, *just stay there.*

David hurried back to the cousins and the trio slunk off into the rain forest, hopefully before Jenks caught sight. David was never one for sneaking around. Even as a kid he disliked the vulnerability of hide and seek. But now he had no choice. He needed to do this for Megan … and for Roxy. And who was he kidding, he needed to do this for himself … to make things right.

Outside of Doc's hidden lab, Bruno stood guard against Agent Jenks while Ramon cut away the overgrowth covering the door—a more arduous process with Ramon forced to use a smaller blade, David unwilling to risk Jenks hearing the loud whomps of a machete. Minutes later, with the task completed and the door unencumbered, David opened it to reveal his secret world.

Sterile and bright under fluorescent lights, he moved about the lab with purposeful steps, locating the stored extracts from Pran. Remembering

Livingston's directions, he conjured a vile of the more potent elixir fed to him by the sinewy tribesman. With Megan's severe reaction to the ant venom, he assumed her system would require such a strong dosage to counteract the poisonous, painful effects—if, indeed, it worked at all. Recalling how amazing the elixir had made him feel, he hoped, at the very least, it could help allay some of her suffering. He worked quickly mixing the concoction and, once completed, capped the prepared vial and pocketed it along with a syringe into his backpack. So far, so good. Now to return undetected and administer the injection to Megan.

The cousins constructed a facade of branches and leaves to once again conceal the lab's door, and then the trio advanced with hushed stealth back to the farm. While passing through cool fronds of ferns that tickled their exposed skin, a sudden movement fifteen feet out brought them all to a dead stop. The ferns swayed and parted, exposing the long snout and giant body of an anteater poking through. Too busy foraging for insects, the hungry creature, possessing an excellent sense of smell but known to be nearly blind, couldn't have been bothered with the trio. Blind or not, they gave it a wide berth, not wanting it to catch their scent and stir up a commotion.

As millions of insects trilled in the forest, they moved silently on. David kept vigilance for two glowing eyes up in the canopy, not looking to become the main dish of a jaguar's next meal. He thought back to his first encounter with the jungle cat—when Livingston showed up with perfect timing to save the day. Now, if David was lucky, he hoped that it would be his turn to do the same for Megan.

69

—·—

DEEP POCKETS

Tuesday, August 22, 2006

Peeking through feathery ferns on the outskirts of Doc's farm, David scanned the open-air pavilion—not a shadow to be found of his nemesis sitting beneath its thatched roof. He thought for sure once Jenks had noticed he'd gone missing the little hound would have been on his tracks. *Where the hell is he?* David wondered, still looking over his shoulder. But the current whereabouts of his nemesis wasn't a priority, because now he had a mission to fulfill—a risk he was willing to take to right his mistake—and Jenks be damned. A chilling moan permeated the humid jungle air sending goosebumps up the back of David's neck. *Megan,* he thought, beelining it for her cabin.

Roxy had sat by her dear friend applying cool compresses and offering encouragement throughout her blackouts, though hardly sure Megan could hear a word of them, and then, during her agonizing, restless, waking moments, gripped her hand tightly. Now, sitting by her stretcher, Roxy rested her head upon her best friend's arm, eyes closed.

David attempted a soft approach, but the squeak of floorboards roused her.

She looked up, bleary-eyed.

"How's she doing?" David asked, gently massaging Roxy's shoulders with his hands.

"Still moaning," she answered.

"And you?"

"Tired, but I can't complain," Roxy said, "not compared to what she's been going through."

"Why don't you go and get some rest," David offered. "I'll sit with her."

"I don't know," Roxy said, "what if she worsens?"

"Then I'll come and get you," David assured. "Go on. You won't be of help to her if you're a zombie."

Roxy reluctantly acquiesced, her brain giving over to her body's urge to sleep.

Through the window, he watched her retreat into her cabin and then, like the hands of a compass, his eyes swept the farm's landscape for Jenks. The coast looked clear, but who could say for certain. David found it ironic that a greenhorn such as himself was recruited into the undercover business—the last occupation on the planet he'd ever have chosen … the risk and all. But here he was, feeling like a kid about to get caught with his hand in the cookie jar—his nerves shaky, palms clammy and blood pressure rising, thrumming in his ears. David inhaled several long, slow, calming breaths. He looked at Megan, the unconscious young woman emitting a long, low moan. What was he waiting for. Every minute he delayed was another she suffered. He unzipped his backpack.

Snap—a twig broke outside.

David froze at the sound.

Heavy, slow footsteps ascended the steps. The door swung open.

"Doc," David exhaled. "I thought you were Jenks."

"He's gone," Doc said, his demeanor serious. "Go ahead and give Megan the shot … then we have to talk."

★★★

"It was the right decision, son," Doc said, gazing down at Megan's body, hopeful the shot would work.

"You knew what I was up to?" David asked, not completely surprised.

"I knew."

"Then Jenks probably knew, too," David said, dejected.

"Hard to say. He was too busy dealing with General Rand."

"What?"

"You better sit down, son," Doc said, pulling him up a chair. David acquiesced.

Doc paced the room then stopped, his eyes latching hard onto David's. "I was returning from the farm, making my way up near Agent Jenks' cabin, when he stepped outside. Suddenly, his satellite phone began ringing," he said. "When I heard him say, 'General Rand, sir,' into the receiver, I figured it must be something important for the boss to call, so I snuck round the side of his cabin and lingered, eavesdropping on their conversation. From what I could tell, the General was blowing off steam with Jenks, ranting about Octane's launch site—seems he was pulling for the African continent over the Middle East. Then Jenks, seemingly trying to placate Rand, said, 'just because some Christian fanatics have deep pockets, it doesn't mean they get to run the show.' Well, son … that statement gave me pause. See, when it comes to U.S. Special Operations, there is one chain of command in the driver's seat … the President as Commander-in-Chief and his generals—period. The idea that some Christian fanatics would have control … no way. And deep pockets? … our country's security being sold to the highest bidder? Never. It's treasonous."

"So what are you saying, Doc?"

"I'm saying that we've been bamboozled—that Operation Octane is not legit—and that General Rand and Agent Jenks are Feds gone rogue."

"Jesus," David said. It was just what he feared happening—getting caught in a web not of his spinning. Now, in the eyes of the U.S. Government, he and Doc would be branded traitors if their participation in this illegal operation ever came to light. This was bad. Really bad. "So if the U.S. Government isn't behind this, then who is?" he asked.

"That's the million-dollar question … the answer to which I don't want to know."

"And where's Jenks now?" David asked.

"Returning to Manaus, I assume to meet with the General. He left with Rand's men—and if we're lucky, they get lost," Doc said, a smile softening his face. "Listen, David, I'm sorry for involving you in this mess."

"I'm a big boy, Doc. I could have said no thanks. As far as I'm concerned, we're in this together and we'll get out of this together."

"Well, I can tell you right now, I want nothing further to do with this illegal operation," Doc said calmly.

"These aren't nice guys we're dealing with—they mean business, Doc. And our knowledge of the truth of their operation could put our lives in danger. We must be careful."

"Understood, but I don't like being used, and nothing would please me more than to tell General Rand to fuck off," he said, smiling, his new self even less fearful than his old.

"Doc … don't do anything rash. Please, just give me some time to figure out our next move."

"Son, this old ticker of mine has only so many beats left," Doc said, hand over his heart. "I have valuable work to get on with here at the farm, and I don't plan to waste any more precious time on the dealings of unscrupulous men."

"I hear you, Doc … just let me think this through."

"Okay, son, but be quick about it. My tongue has a mind of its own," he grinned.

Right now, David wasn't so sure the new, calmer Doc was an improvement over the old, cantankerous one.

***

Outside of Megan's cabin, sidled close beneath her window, Brad crouched low—listening.

70

— • —

GOOD LUCK CHARM

Wednesday, August 23, 2006

DAVID COULDN'T SLEEP AT all last night, though not because of the quartz crystal now strung on a golden chain about his neck—if only that were so. No, his mind raced strategizing plan after rejected plan to protect him and Doc from the very real ramifications of their unsanctioned actions. His thoughts kept circling back to his double-crossing nemesis, Agent Jenks. He never liked the man to begin with, but now Jenks' betrayal felt personal because they were supposed to have been working on the same team. But David was enraged more so for Doc than for himself, knowing that his beloved mentor's patriotic pride had been taken for a ride.

But severing ties or not with Operation Octane proved a conflicting decision for him. When Doc had first approached him to create a contagion to remove aggression, David came on board solely because his good friend had asked for his help. But then the idea of eliminating hot-heads from hot-spots around the world took on steam when his dear Rose died at the hands of radical fanatics, cementing Octane's objective even more for him. Now, however, failing to sever ties would bind him and Doc to General Rand's illegal operation—and the real consequences of jail time if they were found out. It was a Catch 22 for which he had no answers as he tossed and turned in his hammock.

And then, of course, there was the situation with Megan further nullifying any chance of a restful slumber, his responsibility for her well-being and the need to get her safely home besetting his mind. If the Pran potion worked as he hoped and her condition improved enough by the morning, he'd consider her swift return to the States. But for now, all he could do was wait.

And, as if those worries cluttering his mind weren't enough, a third deterrent to any shuteye came in the wee morning hours in the form of an unexpected visitor—though you could hardly call what transpired a hardship.

"David," she whispered, entering his cabin, her silhouette shadowy in the darkness.

Startled, he sat upright. "Roxy," he said, her voice unmistakable, "what's wrong? Is Megan alright?"

"She's resting … Brad's with her now," she assured, moving closer.

David's eyes followed her spectral movements drawing nearer his hammock—her fingers working the buttons of her nightshirt, each one undone slowly, methodically, until the shirt slipped softly from her shoulders onto the wooden floor. She lifted his mosquito netting and slid atop him, naked, her tongue finding his in an instant.

David's mind blanked, totally engaged in the moment, his hands wandering her curvaceousness, cupping her ample breasts. His pulse quickened as blood rushed his manhood. Her loose, long hair spilt forward over their rhythmic bodies, eyes locking as he entered her, their moans unrestrained as she rode him. Though each was undeniably attracted physically to the other, and this union satiated both their desires, it wasn't love that drove this act. Deep within their haunted souls they both knew the truth—that their passionate refuge in each other's arms was solely an escape from their painful pasts … and that they had used one another.

Still, when the act was done, Roxy remained in his receptive arms, her fingers roaming his chest hair and the gold chain around his neck. "What's this?" she asked, stroking the crystal pendant strung there.

"My good luck charm," he answered, not willing to tell the truth.

Roxy smiled. To her, luck—good or bad—was something the universe bestowed randomly. But if David thought a crystal could channel good luck, who was she to criticize. After all, a Magic 8 Ball directed her life.

Before the sun rose, she dressed and returned to her cabin … leaving David, finally, in a deep state of slumber.

★★★

Journal Entry, Wednesday, August 23, 2006:

Sex in the jungle with David—how erotic it was!

But when I think of him with Mother, I doubt she allowed it to happen between them, not with her view on a commitment-first basis—absolutely influenced by an early pregnancy with me that forced her into a marriage she lived to regret ... although she adamantly emphasized dozens of times that she never regretted having me. But despite my honest belief she was in love with David, without his affirmation to a committed relationship, knowing Mother, I can see her remaining steadfast in her aversion to letting loose.

Such a pity.

71

—·—

THE GARDEN PARTY

Girl Flashback

THE GARDEN PARTY HAD just ended. An unusual event for the Pendletons who normally eschewed entertaining, unless there was something in it for Eugene—as was the case this time. They had entertained a group of deep-pocketed guests who would, hopefully, back Eugene's bid for the Republican nomination to the office of President of the United States. Not only were prominent CEOs from across the nation in attendance, but also the Vice President of the United States. No small coup. The dinner could have been hosted at a major Manhattan restaurant known for extravagant dishes, where each guest paid an outlandish sum per plate to attend. But Eugene would hear none of it. His idea of a fundraising venue, ironically, was one with a welcoming family atmosphere, a place where a person was inclined to greater generosity if he didn't feel like he was being forced to pay for his meal. Indeed, a home-cooked meal was just the ticket, especially when the two women in Pendleton family were more than up to the task.

Of course, neither Rose nor twelve-year-old Girl had a say in his decision. But neither would have objected. Such excitement in their lives was a rarity, and they craved a little excitement. Besides, cooking together had not only been a bonding experience for the women, but a joy. They loved watching all the popular, televised cooking shows and experimenting with recipes using all the latest cookware and gadgets in their own test kitchen. And though they were used to preparing a meal for three, the idea of cooking for scores more didn't rattle them. No, mother and daughter relished planning the event as if they were staging a high-society wedding in their well-groomed gardens. Of course, cost meant nothing to Eugene; rather than diminish reserves from his own campaign war chest, he was more than willing to spend his wife's inheritance. And he readily approved of their plans, not once doubting that they could pull this off. In fact, the closer the date came, the more his mood lightened. He seemed almost … joyful. So self-assured was he of a successful fund raiser, (and, in fact, by evening's end an additional six-digit dollar figure had been promised to his treasury), that he had already moved on mentally to planning the next move on his political chess board—gaining his party's nomination.

It was not a done deal. There were uncommitted congressmen and caucuses to cajole and convince with promises he wouldn't keep, and seeds of doubt to sow about his competition through innuendo and false rumors leaked to the press. Eugene played hard ball—no apologies given. Anyone willing to challenge him knew the score. Still, he expected the usual suspects to step up to the plate—the millionaire outsider looking for a new play toy, or the power-hungry career politician, like himself, who knew the ways of Washington. But he was ready for them, more than ready, and by God, the nomination would be his.

It was late evening when the last guests departed. Rose sent Girl off to bed while she helped the waitstaff hired for the occasion with cleanup. She was feeling proud of how well the event had gone. And though her husband never voiced his appreciation, the fact that he didn't complain said enough. And so, when the last vestiges of the garden party had been packed up and hauled away, Rose headed for bed, exhausted but content.

Eugene had retired earlier to his study, bourbon in hand. And as she approached his open door, she had hoped to pass unnoticed, not wanting her mood spoiled. But several yards beyond it, when she thought herself in the clear, Eugene emerged from the room, another bourbon in hand.

"Rose, what's the hurry?" he called out, his words stumbling over themselves. "Come join me for a drink."

Rose froze, turned with a smile and retraced her steps.

"Have a seat," he said, indicating the chair opposite his as he opened a desk drawer and retrieved a second shot glass, its crystal prisms flickering beneath the lamplight. He filled it to the brim and pushed it across the walnut desktop. "A toast," he said, holding his glass high to the air.

Rose didn't feel like drinking, but she knew better than to object and raised her glass.

"To the 42nd President of the United States," he said, and downed his shot. Rose took a sip.

"Come now, you can do better than that for your future president," he said. Rose downed it.

"Better," he said, pouring them each another shot and then, sinking back into his leather chair, began his intoxicated rant. "Son of a bitch Randy McDougall threatened me tonight," he fumed. "Said he'd withdraw committed funds to my campaign if I didn't get his client's bill passed … turncoat no sooner retired from congress than became a money-grubbing lobbyist … forgets our friendship, the leadership positions I got him … ingrate thinks he can just waltz in and take control of my purse strings! Who does he think he's dealing with? Well, I set the bastard straight. Told him blackmail was very unbecoming, and if he wanted to do business in the future, he should forget we ever had this conversation—and then you know what that yellow-bellied bag of shit did? Put his fucking tail between his fucking legs and hide-tailed it out." Eugene laughed and downed his drink.

Rose was silent, looking down at her drink. When she looked up Eugene was smiling at her.

"Come on, Rose. Finish your drink and then come with me to bed," he mumbled.

Rose did as told, then stood. Eugene escorted her down the hall to their bedroom, his legs unsteady and head beyond woozy. When they reached the bed, he pushed her down upon it and then fell in beside her. Rose turned her face away.

Girl stood silently outside her parent's door and waited, counting the seconds as usual. This time she hadn't even reached ten when she heard his snore. Her mother safe, she crept back off to bed.

72

—·—

THE EYES OF A WOMAN

Wednesday, August 23, 2006

MEGAN AWOKE TO find Brad asleep in the chair beside her. "Brad," she called, her voice weak.

Brad's eyes cracked opened.

"Morning," she said, smiling.

"Megan, oh my God, Megan," he exclaimed, bolting to a stand, "you're okay." He ran to the cabin door, opened it, and yelled out to all who could hear, "Everyone … she's okay … Megan's okay," before rushing back to her bedside.

"You had us all scared shitless," he blurted, his heart beating wildly. "I'm so glad you're back. I missed you, Megan," he said, his feelings fully exposed.

She went to reach out and touch him but then realized, with some confusion, she couldn't. "Why are my arms bound?" she asked.

Embarrassed, Brad tried to explain. "I'm so sorry for all this, Megan, I really am, but you could have hurt yourself if we hadn't restrained you. You were flailing with the pain. We had to keep you still for your own good," he said, his fingers fumbling now to undo the wrappings.

Just then, Roxy stormed the one-room cabin.

"Meg," she said, bursting into tears as she hugged her best friend.

"I'm okay, Rox. Really. Don't cry," Megan begged.

Doc and David entered next and at the sight of her, David breathed a sigh of relief. "Are you feeling any pain, Megan?" he inquired immediately, forgoing any pleasantries.

"No. Just groggy … and really tired." Megan looked around at everyone standing at her bedside. Confused, she asked, "What happened to me?"

"You disappeared into the forest taking pictures," Brad volunteered. "We found you lying by a tree stump infested with poisonous bullet ants. They attacked you … dozens of them."

"Strange," she said, considering this, "I only remember pain … and the eyes of a woman."

David's breath sucked in. "What did you say?" he heard himself ask.

"I can't explain it, but somehow these beautiful eyes spoke to me, calmed me … eased the pain."

Lanya, David thought, as he recalled injecting Megan with Pran. Was it possible the potion linked the two? After all, he and his brother had seen Lanya's eyes after experiencing Pran. His head was spinning with what this meant—the danger it could pose if Megan became a conduit of visions, too, and Jenks learned of them. David shuddered at the thought of his nemesis on the trail to discovering Lanya and the hidden Moksha village and, worst still, Pran's location. But as long as he and Doc were the only outsiders who had knowledge of Ramati—the garden otherwise known as Paradise—he'd have control over Pran's use. But if it were to fall into Jenks hands … he didn't even want to think about it. Then again, David understood that for Megan's visions to continue, she would have to possess a quartz crystal worn permanently on her body or receive additional doses of Pran, and he was hell bent that neither would ever happen.

Doc spoke up. "Enough talk for now. Megan's been through a lot and her recovery requires nourishment and rest," he said, remembering how he felt after surviving his snake bite. "Roxy and Brad, would you kindly tend to her needs?"

"Sure thing," Brad said, a silly, love-struck smile consuming his face.

"Of course," Roxy added, her eyes catching hold of David's, passion still burning.

"Well then," Doc said, "we'll leave her in both of your very capable hands."

Directing David out the of cabin door and descending the porch steps, he asked, "Coffee?"

"You read my mind," David replied, as the two headed for the pavilion and the steaming pot of morning brew they knew Carlos would have waiting for them.

***

"Pretty good romp in the old hammock last night," Doc said, flashing his shit-eating grin as he sipped from his mug at the long, wooden table.

David mirrored him back with a wide grin himself, not bothering to deny the truth.

"Oh, to be young again," Doc sighed.

"Being old and wise has its advantages, too," David said, his cup of Joe helping to sooth his nerves.

"Well, for just once I'd like to be young and wise."

Doc's words transported David's thoughts to Lanya, her youthful appearance belying her actual age—that is, if Doc was to be believed about Pran eliminating sickness and, thereby, extending one's life. But if that were so, perhaps it was possible to be both young and wise.

"Doc," David said, hesitating to go there, "what do you make of Megan's vision?"

"You mean seeing Lanya's eyes?"

"How'd you know they were Lanya's eyes?" David asked.

The flabbergasted look on his protege's face made Doc laugh. "Son, you forget I experienced Livingston's potion and the years I've known Lanya. Surely, by now, it's obvious to me whose eyes they are."

David wasn't laughing. "What if Jenks finds out? Bad enough he learns we gave her Pran, but to discover her vision, too … that's a slippery slope. I'm worried, Doc," he said.

"Don't be. The vision is just a one-off. Won't be repeated. And like I said, it's highly unlikely he knows about Megan's injection, what with his tail in a spin over General Rand's call."

"Well, I'd rather not take any chances," David said. "If she's up to it, we'll leave in the morning."

"Don't forget Agent Jenks is with General Rand in Manaus," Doc said. "You could cross paths."

"And if he returns to the farm, we'd cross paths here. It's a chance I'm willing to take."

"You know that the man most likely knows everything about her by now—including her home address," Doc said. "It will be impossible to keep her under wraps."

"I've considered that."

"And what about the operation? You know I want out."

"Doc," David said, his head throbbing again, "just let me get Megan home safely, and then I'll figure it out."

Doc reached across the table and patted his friend's hand. "Okay David," he said, even toned, "I'll leave it with you, but don't take too long … I'm no man's fool."

★★★

Brad watched Roxy head out to the kitchen to round up breakfast from Carlos for the three of them; and when she was out of sight, he sat back down next to Megan and tenderly took hold of her hand. Leaning in close he said softly, "Your vision's intriguing … tell me more."

73

—·—

HOMEWARD BOUND

Thursday, August 24, 2006

D ROPLETS OF MORNING DEW trickled down the canopy leaves, spilling softly onto the heads and shoulders of those trekking below. At sunrise David and entourage had emerged from their cabins and, having relayed their goodbyes and thanks to Doc at the farm, started back into the jungle, homeward bound. David's guilt weighed heavily on him. This trip had hardly turned out the way he had hoped—in fact, it had proven to be a nightmare, his culpability exacerbating a growing sense he was drowning in quicksand without a lifeline. And he was not alone. His steadfast guides, Ramon and Bruno, still burdened with guilt from their failure to protect Megan, were adamant they'd carry her on a stretcher until they reached the river, both unwilling recipients of any further self-blame. But guilt can be a motivating factor and, if nothing else, all three were determined to get the women home safely.

Brad wiped his face of water droplets. In Ramon's place as point man, he eagerly led the group with machete in hand clearing a path as they went, each swing conferring satisfaction in doing his part to help. The physicality of it was a workout but, despite the protests of his upper body muscles, he kept at it, stopping only to catch his breath and wring out his headband of sweat. The rhythmic machete whomps and the jungle's ceaseless song faded to background noise while he hacked a path forward and mulled his thoughts. The past two days had presented him with bits and pieces of information he desperately wanted to fit into a larger picture. There was a connection, he felt sure, between Megan's vision and the knowledge he gleaned from eavesdropping on David and Doc. And all those bits and pieces of information put together seemed, to him, to spell trouble for Megan. Beginning with her injection. What was in it? Did it have anything to do with the mysterious plant extract back at the Cambridge lab? And did this substance cause her vision? And why did 'the eyes of a woman' in her vision elicit a measured reaction with David—which Brad was keen to detect. And Agent Jenks—who, exactly, is this shady character and, more to the point, what is Operation Octane and how are David and Doc involved? The answers to these questions, Brad was certain, posed a risk to anyone who sought them; but he had fallen hard for Megan and, sure she was somehow caught in the spinning of this tangled web, would do anything now to protect her.

As Megan, ferried along by the cousins, kept losing her battle with exhaustion, falling in and out of a state of drowsy consciousness, Roxy kept a close eye on her as she and David brought up the rear of their troop, everyone trekking onward in silence, their perspiration percolating with the rising heat.

Pushing forward through the jungle brush, Roxy contemplated this trip and her disappointment in its early termination, though she would never fault Megan for this outcome having witnessed the poor girl's suffering. But strange as it seemed, she found the challenge of survival in the jungle not unlike that perpetrated upon her as a child—the chaos and uncertainty of both being familiar territory, where a strength of will was paramount to staying alive—a valuable lesson for which, unfortunately, she had her father to thank.

By mid-morning they arrived without incident at the first of several tributaries and, once settled into two of Doc's long, wooden motorboats beached along the banks, both crews shoved off. Brad gladly volunteered to accompany Megan, with Ramon directing the tiller in one boat; while David rode along with Roxy, Bruno in the driver's seat of the other. All morning, they wound through connecting waterways, passing under low-arching branches and around narrow bends. It was dry season once again in the Amazon basin with water levels reduced but still navigable. The mosquitoes were biting, of course, but by now all were immune to the nuisance as an accepted part of jungle life—and complaints were nowhere to be had.

Megan, despite her pledge at the outset of this journey to keep her relationship with Brad one of strictly business, failed to reject his zealous attentions as he catered to her every comfort in the boat—cushioning her with blankets, offering her copious amount of water, engaging in comical conversation to make her laugh. Perhaps it was her vulnerability as a captive audience in a time of need responding to his kindness, or maybe her recent trauma had somehow altered her outlook on life. Whatever the reason, she had let her guard down, leaving Brad to construe her response as a positive step forward in their relationship. Now, only time and she would tell.

As their boats meandered the gentle-flowing waterways Roxy felt at ease, greatly because Megan was doing better, but also because she was with David in this mysterious, primal place. Their relationship had temporarily appeased her addiction to a life-long craving of escape—vital to her very existence. Like a drug she could not live without, he represented an indispensable distraction from reality and all its painful unpleasantries. And if David's steady presence in her life meant having to live with the ghost of her mother, then Roxy was content to do so, albeit with her calling the shots, because she had no doubt that David would do anything she wanted—all she had to do was ask.

David had plenty of time to think while meandering the tightly woven tributaries, the damp earth and murky waters a calming balm of familiar scents that helped to clear his head. He looked over at Roxy, whose return smile gave him the resolve to find a way out of the tangled mess his life had become so that he could simply live in peace with her. He thought about Operation Octane and the dangerous predicament in which he and Doc now found themselves. It was clear to him there was no easy way out, not if they valued their lives. But for now, he could only handle one problem at a time. First, he had to contend with Jenks. If the man had made it back to Manaus, David knew that encountering him must be avoided lest suspicions or questions arise regarding Megan. But realistically, if the guy was onto something, David knew trying to keep him at bay would prove futile. His only hope was to disembark at the pier and catch their flight back home unnoticed. Did he have faith in such providence—hardly. But it was all he'd come up with.

When, by late morning, their boats finally broke free of the dark, twisting waterways and were discharged into the sunlight and onto the wide Amazon River, it was as if they'd been emptied into open seas.

"We're on the homestretch now," David said, leaning towards Roxy, the wind tousling their hair as their boats picked up speed, heading towards the great river's divide. Despite the hornet's nest he might be stepping into in Manaus and his heart heavy with worry over Doc, having Roxy with him lifted his spirit. If nothing else was certain, the one thing he knew for sure was that, now that he found her, he would never let her go. She had resurrected his life; and like the phoenix rising from the ashes, she had resurrected Rose, too. Though this was a minor detail David tried hard not to think about.

When, at last, the great confluence came into view—the Amazon splitting into the Rio Negro's black waters and the sandy-colored Solimoes—David knew it wouldn't be long now. Both boats turned up the Rio Negro, heading for Manaus, the main transport hub for the entire upper Amazon basin.

Soon they motored past the familiar shanty towns built high up on stilts along the riverbanks, signaling their approach to the city. They got in line with a hodgepodge of river boats heading up the waterway towards the busy port. When finally reaching the dock, the cousins maneuvered each motorboat carefully between the larger cargo transports before securing their small crafts alongside the pier.

It was late afternoon when all had safely disembarked. David's eyes scoured the port. The place was still bopping with activity, and his hope soared that they just might make it through unnoticed in the crowd. But then his eyes landed on a small motorboat docked nearby, its wooden side emblazoned with the name, "Brandy," and his heart sunk.

74

—·—

THE PLAN

Friday, August 25, 2006

WHEN THEIR PLANE TOUCHED down on the tarmac, it was the wee hours of morning and still dark in Boston. Connecting flights following on the heels of a long day in the jungle yesterday had everyone wiped out. And David had yet to lay eyes on Agent Jenks. True, he could never feel completely confident of not being shadowed, but why would the man wait to pounce this long when he could have done so in Manaus? No, David was optimistic that Jenks was unaware of Megan's experience with Pran and even more optimistic he'd stayed behind in Manaus. And so, too, had the cousins. And if, by chance, Jenks had spotted Ramon and Bruno at the dock, their excuse for coming into port to stock up on goods for Doc was legit, if not the whole truth. So now, when Roxy declared she'd stay at Megan's until she recovered, and Brad insisted on escorting them, David backed off from his protective stance and acquiesced, choosing to head home instead.

★★★

He fell both into bed and a trance-like sleep, his mind delving deeply into a kaleidoscope of ever-changing dreams. When he awoke, it was with a start, eyes wide and heart throbbing. His dreams had become more vivid over the years since his wearing of the quartz crystal, though they remained nonsensical—their meaning and where they'd lead only Lanya knew. He got up from bed and walked into the bathroom, splashing cold water onto his face at the sink. In the mirror his dripping, confused reflection looked through him. *Lanya,* he thought, her eyes still with him upon waking. David couldn't deny the strong connection they shared, nor could he deny her pull on his rational, scientific mind—the paranormal slowly becoming less uncertain, though its acceptance still uneasy. Quickly, he wiped his face of the wet and uneasiness to find his old, lucid self staring back in the mirror.

David checked the clock. One-thirty in the afternoon—he had slept the morning away. Jet-lagged and exhausted, he dragged himself down to the kitchen for a cup of joe. With Annika no longer in his employ since Nick's recovery and his move to his own place in South Boston, the house seemed quiet and empty. Most mornings he loathed it, but today the silence beckoned him to think. He took his coffee over to the table and sat. By the time he finished his second cup, he'd strategized a plan on handling General Rand's rogue operation. His scheme put Doc's sole safety first because, as much as he tried, there was no scenario that managed to get them both off the hook. So, without disclosing his new-found knowledge of Operation Octane's illegitimacy, David's aim was to convince General Rand to release Doc, an old man, from any further commitment, while he would stay on to complete their deal. After all, Doc had provided a plant to eliminate aggression and recruited a genetic scientist to create an airborne disease—his services were accomplished. How could Rand balk at that?

Still, he knew what this decision meant for him personally if he got caught by the U.S. Government. But he had no choice. Even if Doc had agreed to stay on, if things went sideways and they got caught, how long would the old man last in prison? At least a man of David's age had a fighting chance at survival and maybe even to find a way out of this mess given time. But time was something Doc had in short supply, and his work was too important to chance being caught.

David got up and retrieved his satellite phone from the counter. It was time to call Doc.

75

—·—

GOING PUBLIC

Saturday, August 26, 2006

THERE WAS AN INCESSANT ringing in the background, too far away to be annoying until a loud, effervescent voice message recording suddenly filled the airwaves, jarring Megan awake: "Good afternoon girlfriend. Heard you getting in before the chirp of birds this morning … and from the shuffle of footsteps, it sounded like you have company? Not looking to intrude, honeycakes. Just checking if all is okay, and if I should whip us up dinner later. Let me know. Chow!" Beep, the answering machine shut off. With Andre Soprastrano's voice still echoing in her eardrums, Megan opened her eyes to find Roxy lying in bed next to her—and staring back.

"Damn that Andre," Roxy said, cursing the rude awakening and then emitting an expansive yawn.

"Yeah … but he makes a wicked Veal Marsala," Megan countered. Both women burst out laughing.

"What's so funny?" a voice inquired from the living room.

"Brad," both women said in shocked unison, having forgotten his insistence on staying the night.

Megan swung her blankets off and legs onto the floor, throwing on her bathrobe. "My protector awaits on the sofa," she whispered to Roxy, smiling and not the least bit annoyed by an interested suitor.

Roxy smiled back at her best friend, wondering whatever happened to the college roommate who'd shut down, posthaste, the slightest interest shown her by the opposite sex. There was a definite shift in her mindset ever since Brazil. But then … Roxy could say the same about herself.

★★★

"Divine, absolutely divine," Brad murmured between mouthfuls. "Where did you ever learn to cook like this?"

"Italian genes," Andre said. "Here, help yourself. Might as well finish it off."

Brad only hesitated as long as it took the two women at the table to nod their concurrence before accepting the remaining Veal Marsala onto his plate.

"So now, sweetpea, tell me more about the article you two plan to write," Andre said, leaning in on his elbows toward Megan with anticipation. "Will you include your experience with the bullet ants."

"Oh yes, most definitely. The jungle's dangers are integral to our storyline."

"And your vision? The woman's eyes—will you mention them?"

"I haven't decided yet," Megan said, her voice uneasy.

"Whether we include it or not," Roxy assured, "the article, combined with Megan's wonderful photographs, of course, will absolutely intrigue our patrons."

"Well, I, for one will be looking forward to reading it," Andre said, rising from his chair. "Coffee anyone?"

"Only if it comes with dessert," Megan teased.

"Whenever has it not, sweetums?" Andre retorted, making his way out to the kitchen.

A strange foreboding at the thought of Megan's vision going public gripped Brad. As a scientist whose work required evidence-based explanations, no room was allowed for gut feelings. But hard as he tried, he couldn't expunge the bad feeling building inside him. Perhaps it was due to the secrecy surrounding Megan's injection and David's questionable dealings with shady characters. All he knew was that he had to shelter Megan from a danger not of her making. And then he had a thought.

"Megan," he said, "after all you've been through, won't you consider a well-deserved pause in your work schedule … allow your mind and body to rest now so that later, when you are recharged, you'll think more clearly."

Megan looked at Brad, an intensity in his eyes seizing hold of her. She did not answer right away, pausing to consider his entreaty. "I am tired," she finally said, exhaling long. "Maybe some time off would do me well."

"Of course, Meg," Roxy said, jumping in. "Take all the time you need. The article can wait."

Brad sat back in his chair, breathing a bit easier. He'd won a small reprieve in an even smaller window of time to figure out what the hell was going on. He could only hope he'd managed to pause the clock long enough to keep Megan from getting hurt.

Andre emerged from the kitchen bearing a silver dessert tray and a delectable smile. "Coffee and cannoli, anyone?"

76

—·—

GONE

Sunday, August 27, 2006

DAVID WAS BESIDE HIMSELF. Doc wasn't answering his satellite phone. He'd been trying to reach him for two days now and his nerves were wearing thin. On this warm, summer evening he sat in his home office peering out the window, the sunset coloring the sky in vibrant shades of pink and orange. But David didn't notice the sky, staring through it and beyond contemplating the worst. How could he not? Knowing Doc's mindset, he never should have left him there. God only knows what he may have said or done. But then, he couldn't have deserted Megan and Roxy in their hour of need, could he? Second guessing was doing him no good. He picked up the phone for the umpteenth time and dialed again.

"Ola," the unexpected voice answered.

"Hello," David said, taken aback. "Who is this?"

"Senhor David, that you?"

"Ramon? ... Where's Doc?"

"Not here ... gone."

"What do you mean ... gone?"

"Farm workers say he gone since we go to Manaus. Cousin Bruno and me come back, look in cabin, find backpack and phone still there ... but no Senhor Doc ... he never go any place without them."

David's mind spun in a panic.

"Ramon, call me if you hear anything more. I'll be in touch," he said, hanging up so he could think. He knew something bad had to have happened for Doc to disappear without a trace, leaving behind everything vital to his survival in the jungle. Ramon was right—he would never do that … unless he was forced to. *Jenks,* David thought. But how was that possible? The dirty crosser was in Manaus … he'd seen Brandy docked at port. Although, he realized with sudden clarity, he'd never actually seen hide nor hair of the man himself. And then came the eureka moment: What if it wasn't Jenks who brought the boat to Manaus? What if Brandy was a decoy used by General Rand's men to cover Jenks' tracks still back at the farm—lying in wait for us to leave to ambush Doc? David covered his face with his hands with the realization the bastard was on to them. "Oh, dear God," he lamented, "what have I done?"

What he'd done was left Doc alone to voice his mind at being used, giving Jenks and Rand the upper hand now that they were aware David and Doc knew the truth of things. There was to be no bargaining advantage for Doc's safety. No under the radar release of Octane and a quick exit for David. That was over. Now all that was left was his forced finish of the mission and, he feared, the finish of his life. But wait—why should he even complete the mission if they were just going to kill him anyways? And then a cold terror like no other coursed his veins with the answer—because they'd threaten to harm Nick.

***

The sun down now, David threw on his jacket and headed out to his car in a panic. He needed to see Nick, to make sure he was safe. They hadn't spoken since David's return home. But now, his brother wasn't picking up his phone either.

When first he'd slid in behind the wheel, David thought he'd smelled smoke through his open windows. Now, the cold barrel of a gun lodged in the crook of his neck, he knew he hadn't been hallucinating. "We've got to stop meeting like this," he said, zero levity in his shaken voice. The gun withdrew from his neck, but its coldness remained on his skin.

"Funny guy," Agent Jenks said straight faced, then he walked around to the passenger side and got in, his pistol blanketed beneath a sport coat draping his lap. "Drive," he said, as if instructing a cabby, cigar gritted between his teeth.

David put his car into gear and pulled out from his driveway. At any other time, he would have enjoyed the ride through Cambridge—he loved the city, its vibrant pulse coursing the streets like lifeblood through veins—but today the only lifeblood he was concerned about was his own. Oblivious to his surroundings, David was on autopilot, his body taking him in one direction while his mind took him in another.

Minutes passed in silence before Jenks spoke. "Something on your mind you want to ask me, Bennett?"

David's head felt nauseous, and it wasn't from cigar smoke. He swallowed hard. "Where's Doc?" he said.

"Let's just say he's indisposed," Jenks snarled, leaning in closer to David's ear with a fresh stream of smoke delivered through gritted teeth. "You know Bennett, all you and Doc had to do was follow orders. I thought I had made myself perfectly clear there were to be no deviations from the mission … no compromising our cover. Did you think I was joking?"

David said nothing, scared speechless.

"Gifted artist, your brother," Jenks said. "Would be a shame for the world to lose such a talent."

David found his voice. "Keep my brother out of this, Jenks," he said, his hands shaking on the steering wheel, "You'll get your Octane."

Jenks exhaled one last puff of cigar and flicked the stub out of the window. "Stop here," he said, his unblinking eyes meeting David's. David pulled up curbside. Jenks leaned in. "If you ever want to see your brother alive again, you'll do exactly as I say."

David couldn't breathe.

"Tomorrow night. Seven o'clock. The Boston Brahmin Club. Bring an envelope with ten grand … and mind you … be discreet. And oh … gentlemen's attire required," he said, his lips curled into a strangled smile. Then, his jacket still draped over his gun, the cold barrel of the pistol thrust once again into David's neck, he warned, "Not a word of this to anyone. Your brother's life depends on it."

The cold traveled down David's neck and spread throughout his body, a frozen terror holding him hostage as he watched Jenks exit the car and walk away, disappearing into the night.

***

The salty ocean air flowed through the open windows of David's Corvette as he sped through South Boston's Seaport District. Even a well-seasoned New Englander like himself could find the harbor's pungent odor objectionable at times. Though tonight, its presence went unacknowledged, neither good nor bad, his frantic mind elsewhere.

Ahead on Sleeper Street a row of converted warehouses jutted out before him—home now to successful and struggling artists alike. David pulled his vehicle haphazardly into the first available parking space along the stretch and abandoned his car, jumping out and running down the narrow, cobbled street to Nick's building. Within the entry a converted freight elevator awaited, its iron-grated doors wide open. David rushed inside, slammed the doors shut and impatiently pressed the button several times before a slow, nerve-wracking ride delivered him to the third floor and came to a stop. Exiting, he fumbled with the spare key his brother had given him to the loft until its door finally opened.

David stepped inside, hoping against hope to find Nick standing behind the stainless-steel counter of his state-of-the-art kitchen smiling at him, the smell of percolating coffee permeating the open space. His eyes searched the room with its ceiling-to-floor windows and rooftop skylights, remembering how Nick had declared this place an artist's dream when first he saw it. But now the exposed aluminum ducts, vintage brick walls and wide pine-planked floors seemed of little significance—because the one person it mattered to wasn't here. David's heart sank, pulling him down to the floor and onto his knees ... a cry like a wounded animal barreling up and out of his throat.

77

BOOGEYMAN

Monday, August 28, 2006

WITH HIS fiRST STEPS into the old Boston Brahmin Club David had all he could do to keep from turning around and walking out, the tobacco fumes overwhelming his lungs and stinging his eyes. The pungent smoke swirled in ethereal formations, masking the club's more palatable scents of aged wood and alcohol. It took David several seconds to adjust to the room's darkness with its mahogany-paneled walls and single-bulbed sconces. All around him timeworn sofas and chairs arranged in cozy vignettes bade patrons to sit and linger and, indeed, some tarried beyond their original intent once ensconced. David wasn't interested in tarrying. The sooner he and his lungs could escape this dirty business, the better.

He scanned the room's shadows for his evening rendezvous. In a secluded corner a man sat alone at a table, the flick of his lighter exposing his image like a lightning bolt revealing the landscape. David recognized his face. He maneuvered his way over, past velvet-draped windows and patina-framed portraits, to an awaiting wing chair, its worn cushion sinking under his weight and his stature taken along with it. Suddenly, David felt small … and vulnerable.

Across the table a heavy-set man, sporting a conservative pin-striped suit and forgettable tie, stared into David's reddened eyes in a game of blink. His mouth slowly opened as if to speak but, instead, spewed pent-up smoke like a crater releasing lava from a volcano.

David blinked. "That habit's going to kill you," he said, coughing.

"Why don't you let me worry about that and you concentrate on your own problems," Agent Jenks snapped.

David shifted in his seat, his Armani suit evincing more confidence than his face.

"You've got something for me," Jenks stated rather than asked.

David surveyed the room before reaching into his inner breast pocket. With great reluctance he removed an envelope, slipping it between the folds of a newspaper nestled on the tabletop. With the finesse of a magician's hand, Jenks scooped up the print and hocus-pocused the hidden envelope to within his suit jacket.

David was sickened with worry over Nick being held hostage through no fault of his own. And it pissed him off big time paying Jenks' bribe to keep his brother alive, though not because of the money, but because of the man's total lack of decency. But then the little shit clearly had no morals, or loyalty—as evidenced in his double-crossing, double-dipping, on-the-side extortion scheme showing zero allegiance to his superiors. David surmised that if they caught wind, things wouldn't play out too well for the little bastard enriching himself at their expense. But now, enough was enough. Fed up with the man's arrogance and profiteering, David's disgust and anger trumped his being scared shitless. "I'm guessing you won't be sharing any of that with General Rand … or those religious fanatics in charge," he spat.

Jenks' face blanched with surprise but then morphed beet red as he held in his anger, though his eyes shot daggers across the table. "You know, Bennett, I'd be careful if I were you," he said, his hand stroking the polyester fibers of his jacket and the lumpy payoff beneath. "People in high places aren't too happy right now. If it weren't for me," he said with false magnanimity, "your brother would be dead already." He released one long, slow puff as if to add drama to his words.

"By the way, have you read today's news?" Jenks said, flipping the newspaper open, his stubby finger pointing to a sidebar article.

Jesus, Mary, and Joseph … David's brain reeled as his eyes skirted past the print and landed on the accompanying photo. Its caption read: "Renown Harvard biologist, Doctor Benjamin Shaw, missing in Brazilian Amazon." David stared with incredulity at his beloved mentor, his chest tightening with each breath as if wrapped by an anaconda.

Jenks stood, hovering, and then leaned in close to David's face. "No funny stuff," he warned, his words exhaled in a final puff of smoke, "you wouldn't want to end up like Doc." He jammed his cigar stub into the ashtray with such finality that David flinched, spooked like a kid by an imaginary boogeyman, only … this boogeyman was for real.

78

— · —

OH, SO EASY

Tuesday, August 29, 2006

I T WAS POURING OUTSIDE, a gloomy, gray morning, matching Roxy's mood as she lay awake listening to the raindrops pounding the roof, her best friend still sound asleep beside her. Day three since returning from Brazil and, thus far, Megan had shown no inclination to write their article. Roxy, though remaining steadfast by her side, was slowly losing her sanity—some to boredom, but most to dire thoughts about David.

Something was wrong. He wasn't returning her calls. Had she misinterpreted the hold she had over him, or rather, that of the spirit of her mother? David certainly hadn't given her that impression with his warm embrace and protracted kiss before they went their separate ways after landing in Boston. So now it seemed odd not to hear from him, and more than a bit unsettling. *Well,* she thought, fighting feelings of dejection and depression, *worse things have happened to me.*

Roxy rolled over and quietly got out of bed, headed for the bath. She pushed the shower curtain aside and turned on the faucet. Waiting for the water to warm, she disrobed, catching a glimpse of herself in the fogging mirror. *Who am I?* she thought. Usually, the answer depended on the circumstances of the day—who she needed to be to survive. But this time, when she stared into her reflected eyes, there was no answer, only tears. She sat down on the edge of the tub and, for the first time in a long time, wept. Pretending, it seemed, was tiring. But it was the only way she knew how to live, and she had lived that way for so long now that the woman staring back in the mirror was no longer recognizable.

The tub full, Roxy slid in beneath the warm water, her head totally submerged and soon seeking breath. But she did not take one. Did not want one. It would have been easy … oh, so easy … to just let go. She would have. Only … Megan walked in.

"Beat me to it again, Rox," she said.

Startled, Roxy broke the water's surface. "I'm done," she said, breathless. "All yours."

"Don't let me rush you," Megan replied.

"It's okay," Roxy said, suddenly feeling nauseous. "Please … hand me my towel."

"Are you alright, Rox, you look a little pale?"

Roxy wrapped herself quickly and stepped out of the tub. "I'll be fine," she said, grasping her stomach. And then the feeling moved higher. She ran for the toilet just in time.

Megan held back the long, wet strands of hair while her best friend bent over the basin—and retched.

79

—·—

DIG DEEPER

Tuesday, August 29, 2006

IT HAD BEEN TWO days since Brad had departed Megan's apartment under the pretext of work, though not entirely untrue, as he was anxious to put on his detective's hat and sleuth for his missing puzzle pieces at the lab. And with his boss missing in action the entirety of yesterday, Brad had put to good use his gifted time, right up until David walked in through the door this morning. One look at the man, and he knew something was off.

"Morning boss, how's it going?" he said, noting the dark circles beneath David's eyes and his disheveled appearance—mussed hair and a wrinkled shirt incongruous with his usual fastidiousness. "Still jet-lagged?" he offered.

David looked at him bleary-eyed, like he'd been on an all-night binge. God knows he wanted to confess everything, to liberate his burden and share his misery. But at what cost? Hadn't he ruined enough lives already without dragging Brad into this? The answer was clear.

"Still jet-lagged," he said, turning into his office and closing the door behind him.

Brad watched his boss sit at his desk, head cupped in hands—the look of a defeated man—so unlike the admired scientist sought after for his clarity, a man always in control. He wanted to confront David, tell him what he knew ... that he had connected the dots ... that the mysterious plant extract he'd found hidden in the lab, when analyzed against that salvaged from the spent syringe David had used on Megan in Brazil—and left in his backpack abandoned in her cabin—was a definitive match. But this information, on its own, did little to fill in the blanks: Was it responsible for relieving Megan's pain and hastening her recovery? Did it enable her vision—the eyes of a woman—that seemed to elicit a barely restrained response from David? And what did her vision mean, if anything? Also, how did any of this connect with Agent Jenks and his secret mission—Operation Octane? There were too many questions still in need of answers. And without those answers, confronting his boss might make matters worse for Megan. So, for now, Brad decided to let it ride … and dig deeper.

David sat listless at his desk, his mind and body toast. He had been so wrapped up with concern over Doc and then Nick, that he had completely forgotten about the women—until his eyes coursed his white walls and landed on Rose's painting. *Roxy,* he suddenly thought, and sprinted from his chair like a man on a mission. "Heading out," he said to Brad, exiting his office and not bothering to elaborate.

Brad gave him the thumbs up and watched him leave the building. *Great,* he thought, *back to digging.*

80

—·—

BETWEEN TIME AND SPACE

Tuesday, August 29, 2006

"I HAVEN'T BEEN ABLE to reach Nick for two days. I'm worried, David. Have you heard from him?"

David hadn't given any thought to Andre. But now here he was cornered by the man on the narrow stairwell to Megan's apartment, totally unprepared as how to respond.

Andre had heard footsteps approaching his second-floor landing and hoped it was Nick when he prematurely opened his door. The disappointment on his face was unmistakable.

"We spoke when I first returned, but not since then," David said, his nerves shaken as he struggled to steady his voice. "Probably deep into one of his paintings. You know how single minded he gets when he's painting."

"That's what I thought, though still," Andre said, "it's not like him to not check in."

"I wouldn't worry. I'm sure you'll hear from him soon," David said, continuing the climb up the stairs to Megan's flat, his heart racing.

"I hope so," Andre said, his voice uneasy as he stepped back into his apartment and closed the door.

David arrived on the cramped, third-floor landing a wreck. He stood outside Megan's door trying to catch his breath, pearl-like beads of perspiration clinging to his forehead. As of late, his life had become a clusterfuck, and now he hadn't a clue how to manage Andre. The clock was ticking, and he knew it wouldn't be long before answers would be demanded. God, he was tired and wished for nothing more than to rest from his troubles. But when the door opened to his knock, the face that greeted him looked as downtrodden as Andre's. "Megan ... what's wrong?" he asked.

"Oh David, I'm so glad you're here. Roxy's not well."

She led him into her bedroom, shades down and curtains drawn. "Rox hasn't been herself. Maybe a virus?" she said, retreating into the living room and leaving David to stumble his way over to the bed in the dark.

"Roxanne, darling," he said. He called her Roxanne—only her mother ever called her that. Her eyes fluttered open at the sound.

"David?" she said. "Is that you?"

"Yes, my love, it's me. How are you?" he beseeched.

"Better ... now you're here."

"Go back to sleep, my love. I'm with you," he said, sitting next to her on the bed, his fingers gently smoothing her hair.

Roxy closed her eyes and drifted off. David settled back against a pillow, his eyelids heavy, worry and exhaustion having caught up with him. Sleep followed quickly—and so did Lanya's eyes.

***

Somewhere between time and space he saw them ... but this time was different—there were no dreams, only an unsettling sensation like the weight of the world suddenly thrust upon his shoulders. He felt encumbered, frightened. But then, like a child soothed by his security blanket, her eyes calmed his fear before fading away.

"David," Roxy whispered.

Startled awake, his gaze fell softly upon her face.

"David," she said ... "I'm pregnant."

81

A MOTHER

Wednesday, August 30, 2006

"I CAN'T BELIEVE YOU'RE going to be a mom!" Megan squealed, ecstatic at the news.

Roxy couldn't believe it either, but between a missed period and morning sickness, she was more than certain. What a difference a day had made. Now, when she looked in the mirror and asked herself, "Who am I?", for the first time the answer that flowed off her tongue wasn't just another of her fake and transient cast of characters but something real and lasting, a title she could own, a 'mother.' A simple word and, yet, so transformative, instilling a purpose—a reason to live.

"Rose would have been so pleased," Megan said.

"Yes, she would have," Roxy said, smiling at the thought of her mother being a grandmother. Oh, if only she could have shared it all with her. But who knows, maybe Rose had something to do with it, sending her a child as a salve in her hour of need—the thought did pass Roxy's mind, because that would be so like her. But the reality was Rose was gone from her life … and now she had David. And though she was unsure, at first, as to his reaction of the news of fatherhood, once the shock of it had passed, his smile lit up the darkened room and his kiss said it all. It was to be a new beginning for Roxy, becoming a mother, and she was determined not to screw it up.

"So will you take time off from work?" Megan asked.

Roxy hadn't given it thought. "Perhaps," she said, though now the idea of calling it quits with her high-pressure job and becoming a stay-at-home mom, and still writing on the side, began toying with her mind. She was ready for a change in every aspect of her life, ready to move on to exciting new ventures, and with David by her side, she had no doubt such things would come to pass.

"Speaking of work," Roxy said, welcoming the opening, "you feel up to writing our article?"

"I am if you are ... Mom," Megan said, a huge grin plastering her face.

***

Journal Entry, Wednesday, August 30, 2006:

Is this how you felt, mother, when you found out you were pregnant with me— overwhelmed, afraid, excited? You were a wonderful mother. I can only hope I'll be like you with my daughter. Yes, daughter. For some reason, it feels like a girl—maybe she'll be you reincarnated ... coming back to give me a taste of my own medicine! I would welcome that, Mother. I miss you so much! But, somehow, I can't help feeling you will be watching over us. I hope so, mother. I really hope so.

82

WHAT'S GOOD FOR THE GOOSE

Wednesday, August 30, 2006

MOST PEOPLE LACK TIME and patience—and Brad proved no different. He felt the pressure of the clock ticking off the hours as he searched in vain for answers to better protect Megan. Despite no empirical proof, the trepidation he felt in his gut was real, certain that something was about to give. So, in his desperation to understand Megan's reaction to her injection, he concluded only one viable option—injecting himself with the matching plant extract found in the lab.

"What's good for the goose is good for the gander," he said, rolling up his sleeve and plunging the syringe's needle deep into his arm.

The sun had been down for hours now, the lab long emptied of workers and the building quiet. Brad settled back into his chair, closed his eyes and waited. It was strange, this vantage point of a scientist-guinea pig perspective. He wasn't sure what to expect, how he'd react. So now, at the mercy of a foreign substance he'd allowed to invade his body and the moment of truth upon him, he had no idea of the Pandora's box he was opening.

He had tried drugs before—psychedelics to expand his mind—but this trip surpassed those experiences. His mind flowed like rushing wind, weightless and invisible, free of boundaries yet connected to a cosmic consciousness. And it was then, in that blissful state of knowing when he saw them—those beautiful eyes. They pierced his soul and delved deep, her essence mixing with his, the two joined in a timeless universe.

Minutes passed in this transcendent state, but when Brad awoke, it had felt like hours.

As moonbeams pierced the glass windows of the laboratory and illuminated the darkness surrounding him, he sat motionless in his chair, a calmness upon him. His understanding of Megan's experience was absolute now. He had witnessed those eyes of a woman, the same beautiful eyes she saw, and felt their mystical connection. But there was more—a seed of revelation had been implanted deep within his brain. And as he sat illuminated in moonlight, he felt prompted as if by the universe to voice it, a single word of whisper: "Ramati."

83

—·—

TICKET OUT OF DODGE

Thursday, August 31, 2006

Roxy caught an early morning flight home. She flew first class, David's gift of comfort to the mother of his child. He was seated beside her. Escaping to New York City was his ticket out of Dodge because, right now, he couldn't face Andre, whom he knew would soon be looking for answers to Nick's disappearance, not to mention Megan, whom Andre would surely turn to for help and who, without a doubt, would consult Brad—all three a slippery slope he must avoid, because the less they knew the better to keep them and his brother alive. And then, of course, there was Roxy—a wrench thrown in the works complicating his plans with fatherhood. Now she and his unborn child were of major concern, because God knows the depths of depravity to which Jenks would sink if he learned of her pregnancy.

Roxy peered out the plane window as they flew in and out of cumulus clouds, though her gaze didn't see the sky because her mind was focused elsewhere. When she turned to face David, a smile lit her face.

He loved seeing her smile.

"It was wonderful working with Megan on our article and finishing it just under deadline," she said with obvious satisfaction in her voice. "I hadn't realized how much I missed writing. Maybe I'll quit my job as Editor-in-Chief and go back to journalism," she said, throwing it out there for his reaction.

"Darling," David said, "you should do whatever makes you happy."

"What makes me happy is being with you, David, and having your baby."

"That makes me happy, too," he said, reaching out and taking hold of her hand. "Don't worry, darling. Everything will work out, you'll see," he said, his words spoken to convince himself as much as for Roxy's sake.

She settled back in her seat and closed her eyes. David watched her with worry thinking, *What have I gotten her into?* But he had no choice, not now that she was with child—his child. He was going to have to confide in her, tell her everything, because it was better to be prepared for the enemy you knew than to be caught off-guard by his shadow. As the drone of the plane's engines pervaded his ears, he settled back and closed his eyes, impersonating a restful state though his inner mind never ceased to spin.

★★★

Roxy's condominium, bought with her grandmother's inheritance, was in lower Manhattan, situated just blocks from Ground Zero, the site of the terrorist attack that took her mother's life five years earlier. She chose to live where the fallen ashes of destruction had dusted the neighborhood like snow cover, because only in this quasi-graveyard of missing victims did she feel close to her mother.

David rubbed her bare feet as they sat side by side on her tufted, velvet sofa. But as his fingers worked her tired muscles, his eyes roamed the surrounding walls bedecked with oil paintings.

"Mother's art," Roxy said, answering his unasked question. "I've filled every room with it."

Suddenly overwhelmed, David dared not speak lest his voice betray his emotion. But Roxy could tell by the look on his face that her mother's ghost was once again supplanting her.

"Ten days from now will be the anniversary of her death," she said, her voice solemn.

Ten days from now Octane will launch, David thought. What he had once considered a noble cause executed in honor of her memory had otherwise turned into a devious act. It left him feeling duped, angry, confused. He had wanted to feel like her death had meaning, like some good could come of it. And it pissed him off to no end that Jenks took that from him. It seemed all that man did was take—his money, his mentor, his brother. Well, he'd be damned if he'd let the little shit take the woman he loved and the child she carried—his child.

"I failed miserably at protecting Rose," he said suddenly, his statement startling Roxy.

"What do you mean?"

David shifted in his seat and took her hands into his. "Roxy … do you trust me?"

"With my life, David."

The irony of her answer didn't escape him, for it had come to that.

"Darling, there are bad people out there. People who want to hurt us. Sometimes we can't stop them—and we lose the ones we love."

"What are you saying, David?"

"I'm saying … I know things. Things that some bad people want kept secret. Things that have put me, and by extension you, our baby and Nick's lives in danger."

"You're scaring me, David."

"Darling, you're strong … strong enough to handle the truth … and I need to tell you the truth."

★★★

The tale she was told seemed surreal, like a science-fiction novel. And yet, the gravity of it sat like a weight in the pit of her stomach, the danger all too real.

At last, after a stretch of silent contemplation, Roxy responded, "So … Doc is dead?"

"There's just no way to know for sure. His body hasn't been found," David answered, his voice cracking. "But if he is dead, the likelihood of finding his body in the Amazon is zero."

"And Nick? What of him?"

"My brother's too valuable a cash cow to kill," David scoffed. "He stays alive as long I play along and pay Jenks his blackmail."

"And when the operation is completed? What then?"

David had been haunted by this very question since Nick's abduction. His eyes met Roxy's with undaunted determination. "I must rescue him before then."

"How? You don't even know where he is."

"I have a plan."

"And where do I fit in this plan?"

David looked at her with longing in his heart, torn between keeping her close under his watchful eye, or sending her away. Bringing her with him back into the perilous Amazon would magnify her danger exponentially but sending her away wasn't without risk of Jenks finding her. Either way, her life would be in jeopardy; but he chose the lesser of two evils. "Darling, I want you to go stay with your grandfather at his ranch. It will be safer for you there."

Roxy gave it thought. She hadn't told Grandpa Max about her pregnancy yet. She was sure he'd welcome her visit, and the news. Still, she worried about leaving David. "I'd rather us be together."

"We will be, darling, when this is all over. In the interim it's important to stay undercover and out of reach—for everyone's sake. Can you get time off work?" he asked.

She nodded yes, recalling all the vacation days she'd refused to take—fearful of an untended mind traveling to dark places. But now it was time; and she decided if she was going to do this, to secretly bear the burden for them all, then she was entitled to some answers. "This plant that Doc discovered in the Amazon, you say it eliminates aggression. How?"

"When humans ingest the plant's genetic material, it exposes their DNA to a gene-altering bacteria, stopping the aggression gene from being expressed by virtually turning it off. Then, without aggression, fear is eliminated. And without fear, all negativity ceases to exist—creating positive, peaceful connections between people."

Long ago Roxy had yearned for a world without fear—always a pipe dream. But now, the prospect of such a possibility being within reach made her lightheaded. *Could this be true?* she thought, sitting back suddenly, resting her head against the sofa, her hands on her stomach.

"Darling, are you okay?" David asked.

"I'm fine … just a little woozy," she said, rubbing her belly as her mind raced with the thought of raising their child in tranquility. And then it crystalized. "David," she said, abruptly sitting forward, "imagine a world banished of hatred and cruelty—rid of the pain and suffering they cause—imagine living in a world without fear," she said. "It's possible … you're telling me it's possible?"

David was never more certain of the truth of Doc's theory, that Pran would transform the world. His own brother's DNA was living proof, test after test indicating a mutated aggression gene, and the metamorphosis of his emotional well-being was undeniable—not to mention Doc's own documented transformation as well.

"Yes, my love," David answered, "It's more than possible."

"Then you must do it," she said, "release the bacteria."

David looked into Roxy's eyes, and like Eve with Adam in the Garden of Eden, her words tempted him with the possibilities.

84

LIVING UNDER A ROCK

Friday September 1, 2006

"SOMETHING BAD HAS HAPPENED to Nick. I just know it," Andre said, pacing Megan's living room floor. "He hasn't answered any of my calls in days so this morning, in desperation, I drove over to his apartment. From outside, everything appeared dark through his loft windows. Even so, I ventured up and rang his bell. When that didn't work, I pounded his door. Nothing. No signs of life."

"What did David say when you told him?" Megan asked.

"That's just it, sweetpea, I can't reach him either—all of my messages are going straight to his voicemail."

Megan turned to face Brad seated next to her on the sofa. "When did you last see David at the lab?" she asked.

Brad tethered to her gaze. Having partaken of the mysterious plant extract and having experienced the eyes of a woman as she had, though he'd never tell her he'd done so, he felt a mystical bond between them. And while his visit this morning to her Beacon Hill apartment was made with her welfare in mind, an undeniable spark ignited deeper passions between the two once cozied up together on the couch—but that was before Andre showed up in tears.

"Three days ago," he answered, the tether unleashed. "The man looked awful, like the walking dead. I figured he was still jet lagged from the trip home. He hung around ten minutes max and then left in a hurry, like he had a plane to catch. No sign of him since."

"And this doesn't worry you?" Megan asked.

"It's David's lab, he comes and goes as he pleases … and since Rose died, he hasn't been himself."

"And now," Andre said quite innocently, "I suppose it doesn't help much with Doc missing in the Amazon."

"What?" Megan and Brad pounced, their eyes staring back at him, horrified, like they'd seen a ghost.

"I assumed you knew," Andre said, startled. "It was reported in the newspaper. The article said he's been presumed dead … though no body's been found."

"That's not possible … it can't be," Megan said, her voice shaking.

"Andre, do you still have that edition?" Brad asked.

"It should be bundled up for collection with the rest of the week's newspapers. I'll get it for you." He stood and quickly left the room.

The idea of harm coming Doc's way, death even, shook Brad to his core. He had come to like and respect the old man and his work at the farm. His sudden disappearance, Brad realized now, would help to explain David's shocking appearance when last seen at the lab. And he could only surmise now that his boss had withheld this grave information to keep him from snooping and out of harm's way. And though he wished there was a way to help David now, the situation was beyond his control. All he could do was protect Megan. But living under a rock since returning from Brazil, with his focus usurped by the mysterious plant extract, had sidelined reality. Missing the news of Doc's disappearance was the kind of slip-up he couldn't afford, not if he wanted to keep Megan safe. Struggling to find meaning to this horrid new piece of his puzzle, he sensed that the dire, tectonic shift of events that he'd been expecting ever since learning of Operation Octane had duly arrived. Brad always knew it would just be a matter of time before the shit hit the fan. The only question was who, if anyone, would be left standing when it did? To be honest, he'd never figured Nick into the equation. Though, as he thought about it, kidnapping him—which now seemed more a likely possibility—made sense if David was to be forced to comply with a criminal act. But what, exactly, was the criminal act? Brad needed to know to complete his puzzle.

"I'm calling Roxy," Megan announced on the verge of tears, her voice shaking with all the uncertainty surrounding her friends. She dialed her number and listened to an incessant ringing. "She's not answering," she said, and tried again, her panic increasing exponentially after a half dozen more unanswered attempts. Brad gently removed the phone from her trembling hands and put his arm around her. "I hope she's okay," she said, nestling into his shoulder, "I worry not reaching her—especially now that she's pregnant."

"Roxy's pregnant?" Brad said, taken aback, the weight of the rock he'd been living under suddenly heavier. "Who's the father?"

"Why … it's David," Megan said. "I thought he would have told you."

Brad's head spun. Too many surprise puzzle pieces coming together at once.

Cradling a stack of old newspapers within his arms, Andre burst through the apartment door and hurried over to the wooden coffee table, dropping the bundle with a thud. The room fell silent as his nimble fingers sorted through the stack and swiftly located the desired edition. He turned page after crinkling page until landing upon the article, his slender finger directing Brad's gaze to the story.

The article was brief. Other than the fact that Doc had been reported missing, there were no conclusive findings—only a brief, sensationalized story masquerading as good journalism. Brad checked out the byline. "The article was written by a Drew Dexter," he said out loud to the others. Their heads shook with zero recognition.

"Maybe it's time we call the police," Andre suggested.

"No … no police. Not yet," Brad said. "First I need to pay this journalist, Mr. Drew Dexter, a visit. See what I can find out." His adrenaline was pumping full speed while his mind considered the rabbit hole he was about to go down. "Will you two be alright until I get back?"

"We'll be fine … won't we sugarplum?" Andre said, his forced smile displayed for Megan's sake. "I'll make us something to eat. Nothing like food to help calm the nerves."

Megan didn't respond, her attention focused on Brad. He leaned in and kissed her lips. "Don't worry, sweetheart," he said, "we'll figure this out." And he really did believe so—he just wasn't certain who would be left standing when he did.

85

— • —

A CHARMER

Friday, September 1, 2006

THE BOSTON NEWSROOM BUZZED with the tension of worker bees trying to make deadline—telephones ringing and dozens of voices conversing all at once. The worn, wooden floors of the century-old building creaked under foot as Brad advanced between rows of antiquated desks heaped upon with sundry papers and stained coffee cups. A studious-looking young woman leaning against a co-worker's desk, pencil behind her ear and eyeglasses supporting her hair back from her face, stopped her banter as he approached. Brad, obviously lost and looking out of place, welcomed her smile. "Can I help you?" she asked.

"Yes, please. I'm looking for Mr. Drew Dexter."

She turned and pointed to a senior gentleman in the far corner of the room. "You mean Old Timer," she said without malice, "the guy with the plaid vest and bow tie. Hard to miss him."

"Thanks," Brad said, and made his way over.

Upon approach, Mr. Dexter's appearance exuded that of an honest, seasoned reporter, one who had mastered the art of landing a good story over years of experience. But looks can be deceiving and, as any shady businessman will tell you, honesty is open to interpretation when it comes to the bottom line.

"Hello, Mr. Dexter," Brad said, towering over the older gentleman now seated behind a crammed, paper-strewn desk. The septuagenarian glanced up from his work, taking a moment to refocus the bifocals half-way down his nose.

"My name's Brad Parks," he continued, hand extended. "I'd appreciate a moment of your time, sir."

The veteran reporter beamed and shook Brad's hand. "Please," he said, "take a seat young man," though the only nearby chair was careening with papers. "Oh dear," Mr. Dexter said, laughing affably at the obvious dilemma. "I keep meaning to clear that," he said, and slowly pulled himself up out of his chair, scooped the pile with what seemed a well-practiced skill, and added it to the precarious stacks already lining his desktop. "Now then, tell me," he said, sighing from the effort and sinking back into his chair, "how can I be of assistance?"

"I'm inquiring into a piece you wrote concerning Dr. Benjamin Shaw's disappearance in the Amazon."

"Yes, yes … I know the one."

"Seven days ago I was with Dr. Shaw in Brazil, so you can imagine how shocked I was when I read your piece. Now I'm just trying to make sense of it. In that vein, sir, could you tell me who provided you with this information?"

"Why, young man, a good reporter never reveals his source."

"Yes, I respect that fact, sir, but could you at least tell me how the doctor's missing person report was verified by your source?"

"Well, young man, without divulging the name of my direct source, let's just say that if you can't trust the U.S. Government's verification, then whose can you trust?"

Brad stopped breathing. Jenks. Had to be. He was with the government's Food and Drugs Administration and their most likely connection to Doc.

"Son, you all right?" Mr. Dexter inquired. "You look like you've seen a ghost."

Brad considered the older gentleman in the plaid vest and bow tie, a relic of his time—born of a generation of professional reporters faithful to a high work ethic and moral code, men who dealt in the truth—or so Brad wanted to believe. But then, again, was there a nefarious reason for Mr. Dexter to readily give up the U.S. Government as the connection to his direct source? Could it be Jenks wanted to be found out? That he wanted this story to be a blatant warning to any hound dog sniffing up his trail to back off or end up like Doc? Indeed, maybe the two were in cahoots together with a handsome payoff from Jenks padding Mr. Dexter's palm for writing the story. Or, maybe, Mr. Dexter truly was just an innocent pawn Jenks played like a fiddle in this dangerous cat and mouse game. But, no matter Mr. Dexter's innocence or guilt, Brad had few qualms there was more to the article than what was reported.

"I'm fine, sir," he said, rising. "Thank you for your time."

They shook hands.

"The pleasure was mine, young man," Mr. Dexter said. "Come back any time."

Brad walked back through the newsroom caught up in his thoughts, retracing his steps between the rows of antiquated desks and busy bee workers in a daze, blindly passing the studious-looking young woman sitting at her desk.

"Old Timer's a charmer, yeah?" she called out after him with a smile.

Brad turned and smiled back. *A charmer, indeed,* he thought, a vision of Mr. Dexter in a turban playing a punji flute flashing through his mind—the snake in a basket swaying to his movements, readying for attack.

★★★

After his visit with Mr. Dexter, Brad found himself still floundering for facts he could bite his teeth into. He returned to Megan's apartment empty handed and dejected knowing that just beyond her door she and Andre were waiting in hopeful anticipation.

Andre's eager eyes looked up at Brad as he entered the room, following him as he walked over to an overstuffed armchair and, sighing, sank into it.

"Let me get you some coffee," Megan offered.

Leaning forward on the sofa opposite Brad, Andre couldn't wait a moment longer to ask the question nagging at him. "So, did you find out who was the source of the story?"

"Yes and no," Brad said.

Megan returned and handed Brad a cup of steaming joe. He took a careful sip.

"From what I could gather," he said, "someone within the U.S. government verified Doc's missing person report. But Mr. Dexter refused to identify just who." And Brad wasn't about to divulge his best guess either.

"The U.S. government …" Andre said, mulling it over in his head, "well I suppose a missing U.S. citizen in a foreign country would warrant investigation by the Feds. Did he offer any further information?"

Brad shook his head.

The disappointment on Andre's face only intensified Brad's guilt over not coming clean with what little he knew, tempting him to tell all. But spilling his guts right now wouldn't help anyone. He still needed more information.

"I was just hoping that there might have been some connection to Nick, what with the coincidence of the timing of their disappearances. You'll have to forgive me," Andre sighed, "I'm just a huge ball of worry right now … especially that Nick's missed his medication all this time."

"Medication?" Brad said. "What medication?"

"Oh …" Andre said, realizing he'd let the cat out of the bag, "Nick asked me not to tell anyone."

"Andre," Brad said, leaning forward, "I promise, anything you tell me stays in this room."

Andre paused a moment to give it some thought, then said, "All I know is that he drinks some plant potion every night to prevent his cancer returning."

"What plant?"

"Not sure. But he's been growing it in the greenhouse at David's place. Some experimental drug his brother put him on."

Oh, how the wheels in Brad's head spun. *Of course,* he thought. The answer to Nick's miraculous remission from his cancer had been growing in his boss's own backyard this whole time, clearly out of Brad's reach and sight. But why hide it from him?

"Thanks, Andre," Brad said, making a mental note to pay the greenhouse a visit later.

"Not sure I can do this much longer. Maybe it's time to bring in the police," Andre said.

"Not just yet," Brad countered.

"Why not?" Megan said, staring him down as if she could read his mind. "What aren't you telling us?

"I have a hunch that needs following up. Give me another day. If nothing materializes, I promise, we call the cops."

86

PICTURE PERFECT

Friday, September 1, 2006

IN THE AFTERMATH OF Rose's death Roxy finally gave in to her mother's wish and procured a driver's license. Now, as she drove her own car down the dirt road and under the curlicued, wrought-iron signage heralding Triple Crown Ranch, she recalled her stay with her grandfather back then, before she branched out to build a life on her own in New York City. It had been months now without seeing him, she busy with work and he busy with his horses—if not training them then off to the races. She wondered if he'd even be at the ranch now, not having bothered to call him ahead of her visit. She had wanted it to be a surprise, and her pregnancy announcement as well, which didn't seem right done over the phone.

The sweeping beauty of rolling hillsides with swaying grasses spilling down into the valley and nestling her grandfather's ranch caused her to suddenly pull her car over and get out. The vista captivated her as a child and still did. If ever there was a picture-perfect, bucolic setting, this was it. But it dawned on her now the oddity of this scene failing capture to a single painting by her mother after taking up the brush in her later years. Of course, Roxy had no way of knowing that all subject matter to do with the ranch was much too painful a reminder to Rose of her father's coldness and, thus, capturing such images on canvas for posterity was strictly taboo. So, unaware of her mother's history with Grandpa Max, she took one last, lingering look and then slid back behind the wheel and continued down the dirt road to the ranch, the thought now vanquished from her mind.

She spotted him right away, his still lean 69-year-old body propped against the track fencing, observing a young stallion rounding home-stretch. When her car pulled up next to the stables he turned to look, grinning wide as she got out.

"Roxy," he shouted, moving quickly toward her, "what a wonderful surprise."

The two hugged, Roxy sinking into his comforting, flannel-shirt embrace, her nose seeking out and finding the familiar scent of his Old Spice aftershave.

"Why didn't you call?" Max asked.

"Figured I'd surprise you."

"Well, that you surely did," he said, still beaming. "You look absolute-ly radiant," he said, taking full measure of her now as he stepped back.

"Sunshine does wonders," she said, not wanting to spill the beans on her pregnancy just yet. "How goes it?" she asked, nodding toward the racetrack, changing subjects.

"This one's a contender," Max said.

Had Rose been present, she would have rolled her eyes and thought, *same old story*. It was hard for her not to be jaded when it came to the horses, formidable competitors for her father's love. But to Roxy, her grandfather's horses posed no such threat. Instead, they provided what she needed most—a temporary reprieve from fear and a sense of security whenever she rode. Rose could only have wished as much for herself.

"Come watch," Max said, walking Roxy, arm in arm, over to the track.

★★★

As flames crackled and sparks sputtered within the fieldstone hearth on this cool September evening, grandfather and granddaughter shared its warmth ensconced in two aging, chintz-covered chairs—telltale leftovers from Roxy's deceased grandmother. Though worn around the edges, the ranch house looked much the same after all these years, still fostering a welcoming coziness with its rustic-beamed ceiling and log-cabin walls.

But time marches on not only for places and things, but for people as well.

Roxy observed her grandfather in the warmth of the fire's glow; he appeared tired, more so than she'd last remembered, chalking it up to the natural aging process and years of hard work overseeing the ranch. But if Max cared to share the truth, he'd admit his decline as a direct result of Rose's death and the tsunami of guilt that followed.

Mesmerized by the flickering flames, Roxy recalled her childhood spent here on horseback riding the wind, free to be herself, free to breathe. Her gaze then fell softly upon her grandfather, the only father-figure she could ever trust, and her heart suddenly filled with gratitude.

"Grandpa Max," she said, breaking their silence, "I don't think I've ever thanked you."

"Thanked me for what?" he said.

"For letting me come ride as a child … for providing distance from my father."

Oh, the guilt that rose up like bile in his throat—guilt that had stalked him ever since his daughter married that conniver; guilt at having failed miserably as a father to protect her; guilt at having allowed Eugene to control him like a puppet. And oh, how easily he gave in to the savvy manipulator—the very threat of Eugene's powerful connections shutting down his horse farm enough to silence any further protests over Rose's mistreatment. The shame ate him alive.

"Your father was a bastard," Max spewed, as if the words were rancid. "He thought he was a force of nature, lording his power over everyone. But in the end, Mother Nature showed him who was master. Poetic justice—and good riddance to him."

Roxy was shocked. She knew her father was an evil man, but had no idea of the contempt, the loathing, Grandpa Max held for him. In that instant she felt vindicated. No one, not even her mother, had ever spoken such words. All her life, unable to forgive like Rose, she had felt alone with her feelings, burdened by hatred. But now … now, to hear her grandfather voice what she always felt … it was liberating. She got up from her chair and fell to her knees at his feet, her head coming to rest upon his lap and her tears flowing.

Hesitant, Grandpa Max hovered a stilted hand over Roxy's head before lowering it slowly to gently stroke her silken tresses. A moment later, emboldened by her acquiescence, he bent closer her ear and whispered the words long denied his own daughter: "You're welcome."

87

— · —

COLLATERAL DAMAGE

Friday, September 1, 2006

I N THE COOL OF the morning, Brad followed the stepping-stone path alongside David's house and pushed open the arbored gate, passing beneath its overgrown blooms of roses on his way to the backyard. As evidenced by the once manicured flower beds and lawn now growing unruly and rambling, there hadn't been a caretaker on the premises for some time. And save for himself, and the chirping birds on wooden houses dangling from Japanese maples, there were no other obvious signs of life—not that Brad had expected to find either of the Bennett brothers home. He spotted the small greenhouse tucked in the backyard corner and made his way over. Its door jammed shut, he yanked it open and was immediately overcome by an intense wave of humidity laden with sweet perfume. "Ramati," he said out of nowhere, eyes transfixed on the mini-jungle of blooming flora stretching skyward—but, with the sudden dispensing jolt of a downward misting spray, the word of revelation from his vision was quickly forgotten.

As Brad literally soaked in the coolness, it was obvious to him that the plants' nourishment was dependent upon a timer, in lieu of human assistance. Also obvious was a need had been felt to keep these plants alive when no one was here. Clearly, then, these plants were valued—but valued for what, exactly? If his gut proved right, the extracts from these plants were one and the same as that of the extract he had found hidden in the lab. And if confirmed, it would mean that the extract used by David on Megan, and the one Brad had used on himself, would be identical to that used in Nick's cancer potion—all originating from this one specific plant species that almost certainly originated in Brazil.

But if this plant was responsible for the cure to Nick's cancer, why hide such a discovery? After all, such a finding would have meant a huge scientific coup for his lab, personal financial security, and an unimaginable benefit to mankind. Brad realized there could be only one answer. David couldn't tell anyone because lives were on the line. And Brad's gut told him this healing plant was at the heart of everything—the mysterious and illegal Operation Octane that he'd overheard David and Doc speak of, rogue FDA Agent Jenks' involvement, Doc's disappearance in Brazil and now the kidnapping of Nick. But for what purpose could such a benevolent plant be used by malefactors? That was the million-dollar question. Brad grabbed one of the potted plants for later analysis and hurried from the premises.

★★★

Megan was in turmoil. Andre no better. So when she received an unexpected phone call from her father, with whom her relationship and past visits home had been stressed by hidden guilt, a strange urge overtook her emotions, and she made a split-second decision.

"Dad," she said, "I'd like to come home for a visit."

"Lass, yer nu de dure is alwus open."

"Might I bring a friend along, too … if that's alright."

"De more de merrier.'

"Thanks Dad. And Dad …" she said, swallowing the lump in her throat, "I love you."

"Oi love yer, too, lass."

When the call ended, Andre stared at Megan.

"You don't have to come with me," she said, "I just thought …"

"Sweetiepie, once Brad returns and we call the police there won't be anything more to do, and being here alone will drive me out of my mind. I'm coming with you. Give me ten minutes to pack my things," he said, and left.

Within a short time, a knock came at Megan's door. She answered expecting Andre. Brad stood there instead. Her arms flew around his neck and, he, of course, reciprocated, wrapping her body within his.

Andre came up behind them with his duffle. "Going somewhere?" Brad said, noticing the bag.

"He's coming with me to Maine … to my dad's," Megan said. "We just need some time away from all this craziness."

"Can we talk before you go?" Brad said, mentally processing this surprise turn of events.

"Of course," Megan said, and once again the trio returned to their seats in the living room.

"Well, did your hunch prove out? Did you learn anything more?" Andre asked.

"A dead end. Sorry," Brad said, not wanting to get into a discussion about the miraculous plants growing inside the Bennett's greenhouse.

"So I guess this means we can contact the police now," Andre said.

"Listen, you two go on up to Maine, and I'll file the missing person's report with the police. Better to keep you both out of this," Brad said.

Andre was hesitant. "You'll let us know the instant they find out anything?"

"Of course," Brad said. And then, leaning forward to stand, his eyes fell upon the coffee table and a stack of printed papers resting there. The bold typeface on the top sheet caught his attention: **The Mysterious Amazon**. "Is this what I think it is?" he asked Megan.

"Yes, the final draft of Roxy's and my article," she affirmed, nodding her head.

"May I?" he said, eager as all get out to peruse its pages, hoping against hope that a certain phrase had been omitted.

"Be my guest," Megan smiled.

His eyes skimmed the article until the words he had hoped not to see glared back at him: "… the eyes of a woman …"

Ever since she and Roxy interviewed Doc in Brazil, Brad was sure that rogue FDA agent Jenks would be on the lookout for the article. Would the man know the meaning of Megan's vision, Brad had no idea, but her vision was a calling card just begging for investigation. And if the mystical plant extract used in her potion was involved with Operation Octane, as Brad now believed, and Jenks linked Megan and her vision to it, then her knowledge would be considered a security risk to their mission, and she a dangerous liability destined to become collateral damage. Of course, so too would Brad. But he pushed that thought aside, Megan his prime concern now.

Brad swallowed his fear and asked, "When will your article be published?"

"Within days," Megan answered.

Days. That's all the time he had before Jenks got his hands on it. "I'll wait to read it then," he smiled, returning it to the coffee table. "No need to hold you two up now."

Megan grabbed her suitcase and Brad walked them outside. Her car loaded up and ready to go, Andre sat in the passenger seat waiting as the lovebirds stood on the sidewalk embracing.

"I'll join you next weekend," Brad said, hating to leave her, but someone had to watch the shop in David's absence. "Don't worry. We'll get through this."

Megan wasn't so sure, but she smiled despite her misgivings, wanting badly to believe him.

Once she was settled behind the wheel of the driver's seat, Brad closed her car door. Window down, she pulled him in close and kissed his lips, hard.

"I'll call you if I hear something," he said, and then backed away, waving briefly as he watched her car pull out from the curb and merge with the traffic. Relief washed over him, their retreat to Maine a godsend because it was imperative she got to a safe haven, NOW. What with the article soon to be published, the further he could distance her from Jenks the better. And until he could join Megan in Maine, at least she would have Andre and her father as protectors, though his heart was torn at leaving her.

So, with the serendipitous timing of their departure to Maine and an ever-increasing sense of doomsday's advance, Brad, once again, donned his proverbial investigator's hat and, with his greenhouse plant snuggled safely on the floorboards of his car, drove back to the lab ready to dig deeper—and with absolutely no intention of calling the police.

88

TICKLED SILLY

Saturday, September 2, 2006

D AVID CAUGHT A THURSDAY evening flight out of New York for Manaus. By Friday morning he was on a motorboat cruising the Amazon River with the cousins and back at the farm before nightfall. Now, Saturday morning, time was closing in with t-minus eight days to Operation Octane's launch. He had a checklist in his head warranting his attention before then, but first the matter of Agent Jenks needed tending to.

The cousins' familiar whomp whomp of machetes cut through the thick, oxygenated air as well as the tangled vines and ever-encroaching brush blocking the lab's hidden door. Oblivious now to the strangeness of its existence within a jungle, David entered as though going to work in Cambridge, his mind set on the job at hand, uninfluenced by his surroundings.

You might say he was a man ahead of his time, a man who discovered the key to a wondrous secret—so unimaginable, so tantalizing, so dangerous—the control over which no mere mortal could expect to maintain. But David was a soul possessed, set on a path only those driven by madness would seek. Though he hardly considered himself mad. No, he believed he and his mission were of noble calling. After all, he was about to save the world.

Screw Agent Jenks, he thought, taking charge of his destiny via the one weapon over which he had control—Pran. Standing now behind the stainless-steel laboratory table, he concocted Livingston's potion. Tired of that lowlife toying with him and feeling helplessly tangled in a web not of his doing, it was time now to turn the tables—time to strike at his foe's Achilles heel—to use the man's one weakness against him.

David opened his backpack and removed a box, not just any box, but one containing a dozen Cuban cigars. He had made the purchase during his stopover in Manaus, part of his plan to coax Jenks into spilling the beans about the truth of Doc's disappearance and Nick's whereabouts and who exactly was funding the illegal Operation Octane. With a potion-filled syringe in hand, he lifted each brightly banded cigar from the box and injected it with the odorless, tasteless elixir. After a few cigars, David figured the lowlife should be tickled silly to provide his much-sought-after answers; and by the time he finished off the entire box, well—Jenks would be under his spell. At least that was David's hope. It was a long shot, but the only shot he had.

***

David's call went through on his first try using Doc's satellite phone. After several rings a disgruntled voice answered, "This better be good news, Bennett."

"Agent Jenks … always a pleasure," David said, controlling his sarcasm.

"Skip the bullshit, Bennett."

"I'm in Brazil, readying the payload."

"About time," Jenks said. "Already on my way. Be there by supper time," he said abruptly and hung up.

***

Beneath the thatched-roof pavilion Carlos had provided a sumptuous meal by jungle standards—roasted duck, fried green plantains, wild yams, mangos and melons. But such delicacies were a waste on Agent Jenks, a strictly red-meat-and-potato guy.

David poured two Cognacs, Jenks' brandy of choice, and handed one to his nemesis. "I know we got off to a bad start," he said, "but I want you to know, Jenks, I've been on board with this mission since day one—and more so after 9/11. Ridding the planet of trouble-making fanatics is not only noble but right, and I want nothing more than to complete the mission successfully, get my brother back, and get on with our lives." Ironically, despite his brother being held hostage by Jenks, David believed every word he said. "So," he continued, "in the hope we can put our differences behind us and move forward toward finishing this important business, I present you with a peace offering." David reached beneath the long, wooden table and retrieved the hidden cigar box, sliding it across to Agent Jenks.

The surprise on Jenks' face was followed by a look of genuine pleasure as the recipient of such a generous gift, though no words of appreciation were voiced. He opened the box of Cuban cigars, each one affixed with its trademark black and gold Cohiba label—a top-notch brand that went for top-notch dollar. David watched in silence as Jenks removed one cigar, handling it like a precious treasure as he stripped the outer leaf wrappings and summarily cut its tip. Then, with perfect timing, David reached across the table with his lighter, flicking it as Jenks leaned in, cigar between teeth. "You know, Jenks," he said, laying it on thick now, "the more I think about the mission, the more I admire the courage of those in charge. I mean, it takes really huge balls to pull off an operation of this magnitude." Jenks drew several small puffs as David cleared his throat and raised his glass. "I propose a toast," he said, "to huge balls and a better world."

Jenks didn't bother to meet David's glass. Instead, exhaling smoke, he downed his drink in unison.

Aware of Jenks' proclivity for disloyalty to his superiors as evidenced by his bribe, David hoped the words he next spoke would cut through to the bastard's ego enough to start him talking. "Must be vexing, though, a smart guy like you ending up taking orders from the General," he said. "I mean, you're the one running the show from the trenches. Seems to me you should be the one in control at the top."

Jenks, gritting his cigar, looked straight at David. "Rand doesn't run the show," he said, "though he thinks he does."

"Well … if Rand doesn't run the show, who does?" David said, holding his breath.

Jenks' judgmental eyes seized upon David's as if sizing up his worthiness of such knowledge. His decision made, he declared, "There are some things better left unsaid, Bennett."

David caught his drift—if he valued his life, he had best not stick his nose where it didn't belong. What was he thinking, pushing Jenks so hard? It was way too early in the evening for either Pran or the booze to have taken hold. But patience wasn't David's virtue. Now he was forced to recalibrate, take a step back and slowly plod through the sludge of building trust before venturing back again into those murky waters. It was going to be a long night.

★★★

Atop the long, wooden table a drained brandy glass lay prone against Jenks' resting head, the man down for the count. David had managed to remain awake, but just barely. He checked his watch—minutes after midnight. He was perturbed with himself, more than perturbed—angry. For hours he had held court with this asshole, listening to his bloviating on about his powerful role at the FDA, his control over the approval of drugs while holding the pharmaceutical bosses hostages to his whims, each willing to pad his palm. These little nuggets of information he offered without prodding as David nodded along as if interested, stroking his ego, awaiting the right moment to pounce with his queries. All for naught. Once again, David had miscalculated, realizing all too late in the game that he had plied the man with much too much alcohol, rendering Jenks barely comprehensible even before his succumbing to the drink. Just another instance of David's over-eagerness at work, too impatient to bide his time for Pran alone to do the job. So now, with a new day on the horizon, he was forced to wait for Jenks to sober up—and enjoy a few more smokes tomorrow.

89

SUSPICIONS

Sunday, September 3, 2006

GRANDPA MAX HAD BEEN observing his granddaughter for two days now, her voracious appetite only increasing. He had his suspicions ever since her arrival to the ranch, but a man learned never to ask if a woman was pregnant, lest he was wrong, and she took offense. So he sat back in his ladder-back chair at the kitchen table, silent but amused, and watched her eat.

Feeling the intenseness of his stare upon her, she looked up from her near-empty plate and said, "What?"

"What do you mean, what?"

"You're staring. I hate when people stare, especially when I'm eating," she said.

"Mea culpa," Max said, "it's just that you're so beautiful, I can't keep my eyes off of you."

"You're full of bullshit, Grandpa, you know that?"

"Look in the mirror, honey … beauty is beauty. Your mother had it, and so do you."

Roxy was well aware of her mother's beauty and her likeness to her, perhaps never so much than when with David. But she didn't like to think about it, because then she'd have to confront the true motive for his loving her—a truth she couldn't bear knowing.

"So tell me," Max said, his curiosity cutting to the chase, "is there anyone special under your spell?"

Her fork full of pasta, she paused it mid-air, her thoughts scrambling as she returned her grandfather's scrutinizing gaze. "As a matter of fact, there is," she said, the last forkful finding its passage into her mouth.

"Well don't keep me in suspense," he said, as she continued chewing. "Who's the lucky guy? Anyone I know?"

Roxy swallowed. "I doubt you know him," she said. "His name is David Bennett. He's a Harvard geneticist with a lab in Cambridge, but right now he's in the Brazilian Amazon researching plants to cure cancer."

"The Amazon. Now that's a place of wonder and intrigue … and more than a tad scary," Max said, cringing at the thought.

"I found it beautiful."

"You've been?" he said, surprised.

"Yes, with David. It's like his second home."

"Impressive. He sounds like a smart guy. So, you two serious?"

"Yes, Grandpa, we are."

"And he makes you happy?"

"Incredibly happy. Happier than I've ever been."

"Well then, that's all a grandfather could hope for."

Roxy smiled and, in an instant, she made a decision.

"Grandpa," she said, "how would you feel about becoming a great-grandfather?"

★★★

Journal Entry, Sunday, September 3, 2006:

Family. Grandpa Max is all I've got now. All I've ever known, other than my parents. So how wonderful, now, for my family to grow. And Grandpa Max couldn't be more pleased. You'd think he never had a kid.

90

— • —

XANADU

Monday, September 4, 2006

I T HAD BEEN TWO days since Agent Jenks' arrival at Doc's farm, and though David had readied Octane's payload prior to his nemesis' arrival, he'd falsely portrayed the effort as still needing tweaking so as to delay its handover while he waited for the tainted cigars to take effect. Not that waiting bothered Jenks any. He was content, laid back, dare I say even patient for David to complete his task, enjoying his precious cigars as he whiled away the hours, feet kicked up in his hammock. But for David, the angst and impatience bore through him like a knife. However, there was a silver lining in biding his time—after two days and an untold number of smoked cigars later, Jenks' current condition rendered him devoid of all interest in the details of Octane's manufacture or the hidden laboratory itself. The man had his cigars and little need for more as his mind slowly drifted off to Xanadu.

Lolling in a hammock on his cabin's stoop, David approached Jenks and pulled up a seat on the steps. By now the man's mood was more amiable. He actually smiled, well—smirked—at David, but that was a big improvement to being outright ignored. With the temperature yet cool from the early morning dew and a cup of Joe in his hand, David was in an upbeat mood, ready, once again, to broach the much-desired-but-failed conversation he'd earlier attempted.

"Morning Jenks," he said. "How's it going?"

Jenks turned his head slowly away from his rainforest view and looked him straight in the eye. "Hell of a morning, Bennett," he said, "all mornings should be like this." He took another slow puff of his cigar and shifted his focus back onto the jungle, eyes fixed in a glazed stare.

"The payload should be ready in a day or two, just working out some minor bugs," David said, checking for his reaction.

"No rush, Bennett. I'll be here … not going anywhere," he said, still staring off.

It was the stressless, recliner-chair reaction David was counting on—Jenks' body planted firm, his mind loose. Encouraged, he pressed the man a little further.

"I'm sure General Rand will be pleased to receive it—not to mention his superiors."

"His superiors," Jenks said, a nerve hit, "will fucking lick your ass, Bennett. They've been having wet dreams about this for ten years."

"Ten years?"

"Ever since the formation of E.D.E.N."

"Eden?"

"Bennett, pay attention here," Jenks exhaled in frustration, David's ignorance an intrusion on his tranquility. "E … D … E … N …," he said, each letter spelt out in slow motion. "'Eradicate Dissidence—Equanimity Now.' The consortium's fucking joke of an acronym."

"The consortium?" David said, his blank stare forcing Jenks to elaborate further.

"My fucking superiors are the consortium, moron."

"Your superiors are a consortium?"

"Didn't I just say that?"

"Eradicate Dissidence …" David said out loud, more to himself, giving the phase thought, "so that's where Octane comes in."

"The guy's quick on the uptake," Jenks said to no one in particular.

"And Equanimity Now … the desired end result?"

"Give the boy a star."

"Makes sense, the acronym. Why do you consider it a joke?"

"Didn't you learn anything in Sunday school, Bennett? The Garden of *Eden*?" Jenks teased. "A peaceful paradise … before that bitch Eve tempted Adam with an apple," Jenks said, puffing his cigar. "Eden is the goal of the consortium—bringing it back on Earth."

"Just have to rid the world of its troublemakers first," David said, the puzzle pieces falling into place.

"So they believe."

"And you don't?"

"'Ours is not to question why; ours is but to do or die.'"

"Well, if you don't believe in their objective, then why commit to achieving it?"

"Pays good."

Those two simple words confirmed David's long-held view that Jenks missed the boat when loyalty and integrity were doled out. But the lowlife had a point about the money—everything about this secret operation reeked of it … including Doc's hidden lab and its expensive equipment. Follow the money, David's brain told him.

"Yes, money's a consideration," David said, attempting assuagement. "And I imagine it takes a lot of it to finance an operation like this one."

"Not a problem for those bastards. They're the movers and shakers of international society—the world's rich and powerful."

Deep pockets, David thought, the phrase Doc had overheard Agent Jenks say to General Rand coming back to him.

"Sounds like a devout group, wanting to re-establish Eden on Earth," David said, pushing harder.

"Naw … just a bunch of elitist Christian radicals on another crusade to eliminate the competition," Jenks scoffed.

"The competition?"

"You know—other religious fanatics—those supposed troublemakers who, they say, spew hatred and intolerance into the world in the name of God. Now it's the consortium who thinks they've got the lock on the one true religion, and everyone else is wrong."

David's mindset as a scientist always precluded any notions of religion—formal or otherwise. But now, having experienced Pran and Lanya's eyes, perhaps this new-found mysticism could be considered a religion, too. And like any religion, there was a lot about it he questioned. But the loss of Rose sent him spiraling, and it was his connection to Lanya that kept him from hitting bottom. People cling to beliefs that work for them, he learned. Who's right and who's wrong? Religious wars since the beginning of time have yet to determine the answer.

"Bennett, you're ruining my Zen with all this talk," Jenks said, leaning his head back and closing his eyes. "Leave me be—those beautiful eyes of a woman are beckoning."

David was taken aback, though he always knew that the Pran potion injected into Jenks' cigars posed a risk of him seeing Lanya's eyes. But it was a necessary risk. And so long as the man thought them nothing more than a dream-like hallucination, David wasn't concerned. He did wonder, though, if Lanya's eyes had provided Jenks with visions, like her eyes had always done with him. And if so, what those visions were. Nevertheless, he was convinced that of the two men, Lanya knew he was the good guy. After all, he had walked with the Moksha in another lifetime and had returned for a greater purpose. She had to be on his side—any other thought was simply ludicrous.

91

INSTINCT

Monday, September 4, 2006

I T WAS JUST BEFORE dusk on Rocky Point Island, the colors on the water a mirror image of the setting sun. Andre couldn't stop raving about how beautiful the oceanscape was, memorizing the image for a painting later. Megan's dad had just motored the two over from the mainland and had helped them to safely disembark. The lighthouse beams were just beginning to project themselves upon the encroaching darkness as the trio made their way up the stone-strewn path to Sean O'Malley's cottage.

The place hadn't changed in the fifteen years since Kathleen O'Malley's death. Sean kept his wife's memory alive by leaving things exactly where she had placed them. And though the carpet and curtains had long ago worn, they were kept swept and washed and respectable enough for his liking. Now, as Megan once again stepped foot inside, it felt like she'd never left.

"Make yerselves at 'um," Sean said, throwing another log on the fire to ward off the early evening chill. "Yer two must be starvin'. 'elp yerselves ter sum lamb stew warmin' on de cooker."

"Thank you, Mr. O'Malley, for welcoming me into your home," Andre said.

"Tis gran' ter 'av yer as a guest. Keeps me from blatherin' ter meself.' An' please, call me Sean."

The three settled at the small, wooden dining table, steaming bowls of stew before them, the familiar smell transporting Megan back in time to her mother standing at the stove preparing her favorite dish. She looked across the table at her father. "It's good to be home, Dad," she said, smiling.

Sean saw in his daughter's face something he hadn't seen in decades—contentment.

"It's gran' ter 'av yer 'um, sweetheart," he said. "Nigh ayte up an' tell me everythin' you've been up ter."

The dinner conversation first touched on Brad, how he and Megan met and visited Brazil together with the others. She, of course, failed to mention her attack by the bullet ants, not wanting to cause needless worry after the fact.

Sean saw how her eyes sparkled at the mention of Brad's name and presumed their relationship the source of her contentment. His heart was uplifted, filled with happiness for a daughter long-suffering the loss of her mother.

Later, when the conversation got around to Andre, Sean took particular interest in his painting. Having always admired his wife Kathleen's passion for photography and his daughter's for writing, the passions of others sparked great interest in him. But when the conversation turned to Nick, and the seriousness of the situation unfolded, Sean understood the unprompted visit by the two.

It was late when Andre stood to make his way to the guest bedroom, clearly exhausted. Megan provided him a bath towel and soap to wash up and then returned to sit with her father at the table.

"Dad," she said, "I need to talk to you about mom—I need to tell you something."

"I'm listening, lass," Sean said, a loving, father-confessor tone in his voice.

To be sure, she did feel like a penitent, ready to unburden her soul and make amends, ready to accept a father's unconditional love. And so she spoke the words long vowed to secrecy, "Mother was pregnant when she drowned."

Sean looked at her quizzically, silently mulling her words, and then he reached out across the table and took her hands into his, softly stroking them with his thumbs. "Aye, she wus, lass," he said.

Confused, her eyes searched his for meaning as he continued to speak.

"She didn't tell me outright, but dare were signs of mornin' sickness," he said. "She'd been throwin' up for a week before de storm ... but oi didn't nu for sure 'til de doctor's bill arrived after 'er death. Whaen oi foun' oyt, oi didn't 'av de 'eart ter tell yer, love, knowin' waaat a siblin' wud 'av meant ter yer. Loosin' yisser ma wus enoof for yer ter 'andle. But it seems yisser ma got ter share 'er joy witcha, an' i'm glad she did. Only … why didn't yer tell me yer knew?"

"I couldn't," Megan said, her voice overcome with sorrow. "It was my fault she died, and because of me you lost a child. I couldn't bear to add to your grief."

"So you've carried dis guilt raun witcha al' dees years," Sean said, recognizing the enormity of her burden. "My Bejasus, lass, it wasn't yisser fault. Waaat 'appened oyt dare in de storm wus nature's doin', not yers. If de shoe wus on de other foot, don't yer tink I'd 'av gone after Princess in de 'urricane? Dat filly wus family. Yer acted on instinct lass—ter save a loved wan. Yisser ma acted on instinct, too. 'Tis waaat family does, who we are. Family cums first—alwus 'as an' alwus 'ill."

***

Returning to the island had never been easy for Megan after her mother's death, each trip home bringing with it a resurfacing of guilt. But this time she sensed things would be different, though unaware as to the reason why. What the Pran potion had begun in the Amazon, the gradual diminishment of her self-imposed guilt, her father now finished—his words the permission long sought to forgive herself … to love … and to be loved again.

92

— · —

RO-RO

Girl Flashback

*I*T WAS THE WEEKEND *Girl had been waiting for, time spent with Grandpa Max, just the two of them at his ranch. She was seven now, a big girl—certainly taller—better able to ride a horse, she thought. Unfortunately, her father had to drive her there as Rose had a commitment with the church, over which Eugene had seethed his contempt. And as if driving her wasn't bad enough, he'd then have to face Max, certainly no love fest between the two arch enemies.*

When they pulled into the ranch, Max was waiting by the corral watching a new stallion in training. Girl opened her door and, her backpack bobbing, ran to him; but Eugene neither stepped from his car nor acknowledged Max's presence with a wave. He simply backed up and sped off, dust flying behind him.

"Hello sweetie," Grandpa Max said, down on one knee and arms thrusted out. She fell into them, secure in their tender embrace, always a soft caress—never hurting. But then she stepped back and eyed the stallion.

"He's handsome," she said, "but too big for me."

"Well, don't you worry about that," Max said, recalling the fiasco a year earlier when he was absent from the farm and Eugene had his evil way with the two women he loved most. "Grandpa has one just the right size for Goldilocks."

Girl laughed a contagious laugh and then said, "Show me."

They entered the stable and walked to the third stall where a beauty of a filly was munching on hay. "Oh Grandpa," was all she managed to say, her mouth hanging open.

"She is something, that's for sure," Max agreed.

"What's her name?"

"Ro-Ro," he said, grinning, "named after my two most favorite girls, Roxanne and Rose."

Girl laughed that laugh again, and Max ate it up, thankful she still had laughter in her.

"Want to ride her?" he asked.

"You betcha," Girl said.

So Grandpa Max saddled Ro-Ro up and walked her out to the corral, passing a ranch hand now leading the stallion back to his stable. Girl remembered the stallion she had ridden with her mother the year before—he was much too tall and ran much too fast for her liking, but Buck was still a good boy.

"Alley-oop," Max said, lifting Girl up into the saddle. "You ready?"

Girl assessed her grandfather with all the trust in the world. "I'm ready," she said, and the laughter rolled out from her as they made the first round.

93

SWEET DREAMS

Monday, September 4, 2006

GRANDPA MAX SAT QUIETLY in the early morning darkness by his granddaughter's bedside watching her as she slept. Her moans had drawn him into her room—the same room that had belonged to her mother as a child. He'd made it a point to avoid this space, the open floodgate of memories it unleashed too much to bear. But now, as if they were his own, each of her moans elicited an uncomfortable shift in his chair and a fervent prayer that her discomfort was due to pregnancy and not to sinister dreams the likes of his—their dark, disturbing thoughts badgering and tormenting, unbidden, night after night. Either way, he was powerless to help her. All he could offer now was his presence and unconditional love, and he intended to give her both so long as she needed.

With hours until dawn, and Max nodding off in his chair, Roxy awoke suddenly to the sound of her own screams, quick-fire heart palpitations thrumming her chest, and a perspiration-soaked nightgown clinging to clammy skin. Startled awake, Max hastened to her bedside and took her hand. "It's okay, sweetheart. I'm here," he said, "I'm here."

"Grandpa," she whimpered, tears rolling over her cheeks and down her neck.

"Shush now, rest," he said, stroking her hair. "Everything will be fine." Yet, in his heart, he knew the futility of his statement. The two had never shed their victim's mantle, their rage and humiliation from the past still alive and kicking, festering in their minds. Max, who was too old and tired to fight it anymore, looked with compassion upon his beautiful granddaughter's face, wanting better for her. He bent over her and gently kissed her forehead. "Go to sleep, my darling," he whispered. "Sweet dreams."

94

HUNTER AND PREY

Tuesday, September 5, 2006

IT WAS EARLY EVENING when General Rand's men showed up at the farm—unannounced. Come morning, they were to escort Agent Jenks along with the Octane payload out of the jungle to General Rand and an awaiting flight out of Manaus. Though their arrival was unexpected, David was ready for them. Now his only concern was to extract from Jenks the vital information concerning Doc and Nick before the man left.

Jenks was doing just fine—more than just fine—he was David's new-found friend. Still enjoying his cigars, his arm now wrapped about David's shoulders, the two sat on the steps of his cabin's stoop, bud-dy-buddy. The guy, having lost his aversion to everything social, was now a talking machine. Such closeness to his nemesis was repugnant to David, and not just because of the cigar smoke tearing his eyes. But he was on the homestretch and, never losing sight of his end goal, forced himself to stay focused as he leaned into Jenks' shoulder, giving the bastard every opportunity to confide any and all tidbits of relevant information.

The sun had just set behind the canopy and the torchlights were lit—the sounds of twilight life taking over the jungle. It was a bewitching hour, David's favorite, one he used to fear. But now he welcomed it as he merged with the shifting worlds, his senses heightening in anticipation of predatory activity—the irony not lost on him that hunter and prey on this night sat huddled side by side, though their roles as yet undefined.

"Bennett, good buddy," Jenks said, squeezing David's shoulder for emphasis, "you and I are a lot alike. Drugs are at the center of our work—you at your lab creating them and me at the FDA approving them. Think what this world would be like without them? Without us? We do the world a great service. People will always need drugs, will always need us—we're indispensable."

David thought about Doc's theory, that Pran prevented people from getting sick, and if it proved to be true, the day would come when all drugs worldwide, and both their respective jobs dealing with drugs, would become obsolete. Of course, he kept this thought to himself.

"You know," he said, pivoting, "Doc's farm is a repository of future pharmaceutical discoveries. He did a hell of a job bringing it together, preserving the knowledge of ancient rain forest plants for generations to come. Only now … without him …"

"Doc was a loose cannon with a short fuse who couldn't be trusted," Jenks said, his unexpected words a jarring interruption. "Now I ask you … what was I to do?"

That was the million-dollar question David had long-needed answered, and Jenks was in a talking mood.

"I knew he eavesdropped my conversation with the General. I faked ignorance at the time, but the situation was problematic—he had to be dealt with," Jenks said, grateful for a captive audience with whom to vent his frustration. "So I had Rand's men take the boat to Manaus while I secretly stayed behind watching you and your guests leave, waiting to get Doc alone. He wasn't surprised to see me—in fact, it was like he was expecting me. He smiled and then called me a fucking piece of shit. Said he was through taking orders from me and Rand. I reminded him that deviation from the mission was prohibited. He said "Bullshit," that the General had tricked him, used their past stint together in the Army to worm his way into his trust. Kept going on and on about loyalty and honor … and our lack thereof. The man had a point." Jenks grinned. "But the General had a mission to accomplish using whatever means to justify the end—with no apologies. Doc wouldn't accept that. Said he wanted nothing further to do with the operation—to count him out.

"Now, I was actually fond of the old geezer … he had balls," Jenks continued. "So I gave him a choice, to either keep his mouth shut and finish the mission, or to outrun my pistol. Said I'd count to twenty … give him a head start. Of course, the hard ass chose the latter."

Jenks exhaled several small puffs from his cigar, though David hardly noticed the smoke clouding his face, totally engrossed in the unfolding mystery surrounding Doc's disappearance. "Don't leave me hanging, Jenks," David said, pushing the envelope for all it was worth, "what happened?"

Jenks gave it less than a second's thought and let the beans spill. "The guy moved fast for an old timer," he said. "I fired several shots after him into the brush—if I hit him or not, I didn't bother to find out. Figured if my shots didn't get him, the jungle would."

For the first time in a long time, David felt hopeful. If anyone was resourceful enough to survive in the Amazon, it would be Doc. It all made sense now, Ramon and Bruno returning from Manaus to find Doc's satellite phone and belongings still in his cabin with no sign of the man himself. Sent running for his life, there was no time to retrieve them. David wouldn't even entertain the thought of his mentor suffering a fatal shot. No, he told himself, his friend survived the assault—escaped. But to where? And then it hit him. He stifled a smile. *Okay,* he thought, *now for Nick.*

"Jenks, what happened with Doc was unfortunate," David said, "but I kept my part of the bargain. Now, with the operation coming to a close, tell me what you've done with my brother."

"Your brother is back in the States, though at the moment I don't know where."

"But you can find out?" David pushed.

"Not possible."

"Why not possible?"

"Let's just say they lost him."

"Lost him?"

"Bennett, buddy, believe me when I tell you it was out of my control. The General's men took him hostage. Hid him in an empty storage container in South Boston. When they came back to check on him, they found the lock broken and your brother gone—no one's seen him since."

David felt the air knocked out of him. *Who could have possibly taken him?* he wondered, his mind scattering in a thousand directions. He sat there speechless, feeling helpless but not hopeless at the possibility his brother was alive and safe.

Jenks yawned and flicked his cigar stub into the dirt, snubbing it out with his boot. "I've enjoyed our little chit chat, bud, but tomorrow's a big day, and it's time I called it a night," the rogue FDA agent said, pushing himself upright and climbing the cabin steps to his awaiting hammock without another word.

But David wasn't ready for bed, his mind now wide awake. He stood and, with purpose in his steps, headed toward the campfire to where Ramon and Bruno sat relaxing. "Be ready come morning," he said standing over them, determination in his eyes. "Once Jenks leaves—we find Doc."

95

IN FOR LIFE

Wednesday, September 6, 2006

T HE DAY HAD finally arrived. While Rand's men prepared to exit camp with Octane's payload, Jenks was on his stoop, sitting upright in his hammock enjoying a final cup of joe along with a magazine, flipping through the pages as David approached.

"Interesting magazine Rand's men brought from the States," he said, holding up the cover of Global Thrills for David to see. "And a fascinating article your lady friends wrote on Doc and the farm. Too bad he's not here to read it."

Jenks' words hit David like a strong wind, slowing his steps—the article by Roxy and Megan having fallen completely off his radar.

"It seems that Irish lass experienced a vision similar to mine … talk about a weird coincidence," he said, falling silent to his thoughts. Then he gave a chuckle. "I tell you, the more time I spend in this place, the stranger things get," he said, placing the magazine down on his hammock and gingerly standing upright. "One thing's for sure, good buddy … I'm gonna miss lying here enjoying those top-notch cigars you gave me. This one's my last," he said, indicating the stub he now gritted between his teeth. "Well, time to get moving," he said, Rand's men awaiting him. He descended the steps and then stopped, turning to David. "Just between us, bud, you know this isn't the end of business between you and the General. Like the Mafia, there is no 'free and clear' of the consortium. Once you're in, you're in for life … just saying." Jenks fist-bumped David's shoulder and then joined the General's men transporting the payload, the orderly lot slipping into the flora and out of sight like a line of ants under leaf cover.

Jenks' parting words were of little significance to David—he was through doing the bidding of Rand and the consortium. If they tried coming after him, well … bring it on. He wasn't fearful, not if the future worked out as he planned. Today, with the cousins bookending him into the rain forest, machetes at the ready, David's only focus was his quest to find Doc. And in this God-forsaken place, he knew there was only one sanctuary in which Doc could find refuge—with the Moksha.

★★★

As the day's heat intensified with the arcing sun, and bodily pores dripped like open faucets, the trio pushed forward in an unbroken clip, aiming to put as many miles as possible behind them by sunset.

There was no place more evident of nature's never-ending cycle of death and rebirth for David than the ancient grounds of the Amazon, exemplified in the stumbled upon remains of a bird's nest, scattered and laid to waste by a predator. This was all part of life's transient cycles, he knew, as he bent to retrieve a small feather cast among the broken eggshells. But what if life's cycles could be altered—life prolonged and death delayed. Would nature's balance adjust? Would the fittest survive and thrive? Would the planet give birth to a new world order? He didn't have the answers, but Doc's theory on Pran's potential to ultimately eliminate disease excited the scientist in him. Though, if he were honest with himself, he would have to admit that the unknowns about Pran made everyone on the planet vulnerable—including him. Though that part of the equation he had failed to compute.

While navigating the never-ending terrain of flora, fauna, and pesky insects, David's mind continued navigating his thoughts on Pran and its use in Octane—the bacterial concoction of his own making capable of unimaginable consequences and zero possibility of reversal once released. This forbidden fruit, long sought by E.D.E.N., would be the most impactful weapon known to man since the atomic bomb ending a violent world war, because it would permanently alter the trajectory of mankind's DNA and eliminate world violence forever. Yet, despite this outcome, an outcome he readily approved of, David couldn't abide letting General Rand and the consortium off the hook for what had happened to Doc and his brother. For that … they had to pay.

As for Agent Jenks, it pleased David to no end to have gotten the upper hand with his tainted cigars. But he wasn't exactly happy about his 'good buddy' experiencing visions of Lanya's eyes, in large part due to his fear of Jenks connecting the dots to Megan and her injected potion, but also due to his jealousy. He had become addicted to Lanya from their very first meeting of minds under the waterfall and with his obsession kept alive to this very day through Viper's gift of a quartz crystal—his Sphatika. To be sure, he craved their otherworldly union like sex, though their coupling of minds was infinitely more satisfying. And now, the idea of sharing her with Jenks was anathema to his being. But the good news was that his cigars had run out, and David could only hope Jenks' visions would end along with them.

When the three amigos finished setting up camp for the night, hammocks erected and provisions warming over a campfire, the sun began its descent in the tropical skies. David sat by the fire staring into the flames.

"Senhor David, no worry about Senhor Doc," Ramon said, astutely interpreting his friend's concern. "He wise, old man—learned from village elders survival in forest … what plants safe to eat, what plants medicine."

"I agree with you, Ramon. Doc's a tough cookie, alright, but I worry about him being alone. Look what happened before—the effort it took to save him from a snake bite."

"Senhor Doc strong in here," Bruno chimed in, holding his gut.

For sure, the septuagenarian had guts, the most important ingredient to survival in this place and, without which, most would wither and die under the strain. Doc was definitely a tough pill for this jungle to swallow, and he would survive, David knew, if only to throw it back in his protege's face.

"Tomorrow, we find Senhor Doc," Ramon said. "You see."

David settled into his hammock, millions of trilling insects a background serenade to his thoughts. As usual, he bedded down with his Sphatika upon his chest, the finger-wrapped crystal embraced in readiness of his mental soirée with Lanya and the vision she would impart. But David had been mistaken all these years in his interpretation of her visions as snippets of his past life with the Moksha, when actually those seemingly disjointed scenes were visions of the future, of a life yet to come, yet one for which Lanya was preparing him—the reason for his return. But such preparation required patience and time, because her gift of knowledge—wisdom—could only be received when one was ready. Had David realized his mistake, perhaps he would have slowed down, thought things out, waited for better understanding; but unfortunately, his blunder only caused him further impatience and confusion … especially when he considered the oddly familiar vision experienced in last night's dream.

At first, its familiarity baffled him, unable to place it, until his mind dredged up an uncomfortable recollection he'd thrusted aside post haste almost a decade ago: That of a dark, dank cave encroaching upon him. He was there with the cousins—fire-lit torches illuminating quartz stalactites and stalagmites; Ramon playing three drum-shaped crystals and the cave vibrating; Ramon touching the Sphatika between David's eyes and asking, "Have question?"; and then heat like a fireball traveling up his spine to the crown of his head, bursting into a brilliant vision. "See answer," Ramon had said, though the image David saw had made no sense to him then at all. It still didn't. But he realized now, with absolute certainty, that his vision of long ago was one and the same as the vision Lanya had revealed last night … and, unbeknown to him, one he was yet to experience.

And the question Ramon had invoked at that time, and for which David had sought an answer, stemmed from the perplexing comment Doc had made—that David had returned to the Moksha for a greater purpose. He no more believed that then than if told the world was flat. But coming from Doc, it stuck in his craw. And so, when Ramon asked, "Have question?", the involuntary query formed in his head.

If his vision, the answer, did in fact hold the key to his greater purpose in life, he needed to understand its meaning. Now, as he lay eyes closed in his hammock awaiting his soirée with Lanya, he re-hashed the vision repeatedly in his mind. But each instance revealed no more meaning than had its predecessor, just a do-loop of a future he was yet to experience projecting the same vision over and over again—of a man in a shimmering white robe.

96

— · —

AN OSCAR NOMINATION

Wednesday, September 6, 2006

Finished with her ride, Roxy dismounted one of Grandpa Max's horses and led him into the stable. Her bad dream had changed their grandfather-granddaughter dynamic and now, every time he looked her way, all she saw was pity in his eyes. Riding was her only escape, and so she would ride for hours at a time, trying to avoid his uncomfortable gaze.

When she walked into the ranch house, he was speaking on the phone, his back to her. Hearing her enter, he turned, saying to the party on the line, "Hold on, please. She just walked in." He handed her the phone and said, "a friend of yours … Zach Tanner."

Roxy didn't speak at first, her brain wrapping itself around this name from the past. Then she smiled into the receiver and said, "Hello Zach."

"Hey Rox! How the hell are you!" he said, his voice pulling her back five years to college and feeling like it was just yesterday.

"I'm great," she said, picturing his corona blond hair and crystal blue eyes. "How's things with you?"

"Super! Just super! You know you're a tough person to reach," he said. "But then I remembered you once mentioning your grandfather's ranch in Connecticut called Triple Crown and, voila, I found you!"

"Well, it's nice to hear your voice, Zach" she said. "What have you been up to?"

"That's why I'm calling, Rox," he said. "I'm proud to tell you that Paul … you remember my friend Paul Revere … Paul and I made a film together, and it's premiering next week in Boston! We used your script, Rox—it was amazing! Got funding right off the bat, it was so good. Paul produced it and I played lead male. It's gotten a lot of buzz and there's even talk of an Oscar nomination!"

"Congratulations," Roxy said, trying to instill enthusiasm in her voice as she recalled the script drawn from her past and the torturous hours spent writing it. A tremble rippled through her.

"We owe it all to you, Rox. And now I plan to keep my promise—I'll have two tickets waiting for you at the box office as a guest of honor. Bring a friend if you like."

She could see his sexy smile through the phone. "I'd be honored to attend," she said.

"Good. I left all the particulars with your grandfather. I can't wait to see you, Rox."

"Likewise, Zach. Thanks for calling."

"You bet," he said, and then the line went dead.

Roxy stood dazed from this blast from the past, as if stuck in a parallel universe. The last time she saw Zach was their college graduation. Her mother was alive then and her future uncertain. Now Rose was dead, but Roxy was never more certain that her future was with David. *If only he would call,* she thought, her anxiety starting to rise; but then she caught herself on the slippery slope and switched her focus back to Zach. She realized now she hadn't asked him the film's title. Back when she wrote it she hadn't named it, hard enough to have finished it. *Better he named it,* she thought now, not wanting further ownership. But she was curious to see it, if anxiety's ugly head didn't rear. Only, who would she bring as a guest—certainly not Grandpa Max. With enough on her mind already, she postponed any decision for later. And with that thought, her grandfather appeared from the kitchen.

"Supper's on," he called.

"Coming," she replied, trying not to look in his eyes.

★★★

Journal Entry, Wednesday, September 6, 2006:
    What a blast from the past!

Zach Tanner—the sun-kissed surfer boy from California, raised by a normal family, with big hopes and dreams … one of which you now apparently achieved.

We had some fun times together, but we could never have made a success of it. We were from different worlds … you and me. You never could have understood who I was and where I came from; and I had all I could do just to survive—let alone dream.

Until now.

97

A FAVOR

Thursday, September 7, 2006

THE DAY BROKE WITH a light shower. "A good sign—God give us blessing today," Ramon said, packing up his gear.

"We need all the blessings we can get," David acknowledged, the worrisome journey ahead top of mind. Backpacks fastened and the campfire extinguished, he eyed the site one last time as they headed out. "Did you remember to turn off the lights?" he joked with Ramon, looking to break the tension.

Ramon smiled. "No, but I did put out cat."

They all laughed at the old, private joke Ramon learned from Doc, and it felt good to laugh, given the stress of the day. David thought about living in a stress-free world. Without fear and anger and the hatred both fomented, the world could be such a place. But the fate of the world left to the likes of Rand and the consortium, men he had reason not to trust, turned his stomach. A secret weapon as powerful as Octane shouldn't belong in the hands of untrustworthy men.

"Senhor David," Ramon said, interrupting David's thoughts, "we find Senhor Doc … then what?"

"We'll cross that bridge when we get to it, Ramon. First, let's find him."

✦✦✦

The sun sat high when they stopped streamside for a break. A man could lose his mind in these jungles if he weren't careful, the heat and dehydration the devil's willing assistants. But the trio knew better, splashing their sweat-streaked faces as they drank and refilled canteens, readying themselves for the next leg of the trip.

Background chatter of forest creatures swelled on the hot air. Ever aware of being watched by the animals, David was no longer bothered by their vigilant eyes. He was an interloper on their home turf, after all, and their scrutinization came along with the territory. He could handle their surveilling him. What he couldn't handle was being spied upon by his own kind. It went against the natural order of things—man was supposed to be at the top of the food chain, the hunter … not the hunted. But ever since leaving the farm, he couldn't stop looking over his shoulder, always expecting a tail by Rand's men. He knew he couldn't live a life beholden to the consortium and needed a way out. But the answer still wasn't apparent. "Let's head out," he said, anxious to make it to the Moksha village before sundown, once again glancing over his shoulder as they left.

"Senhor David … look." They hadn't gone far when Ramon stopped, pointing to the ground.

David bent to observe more closely. Footprints. Two sets in the dirt—one of boots, the other human feet.

"I see you found us out," an old, familiar voice shot out from the brush.

When the three men looked up, Doc and Livingston were pushing through the ferns, grinning from ear to ear.

You would think they had all hit the lottery, such carrying on of hugs and back slapping. But in a way it was a huge payoff finding Doc early in their search—and alive.

"Livingston knew you were coming, and I just had to tag along … couldn't resist the look on your faces laying eyes on the walking dead," Doc said, his own eyes twinkling. "Of course, he knew when I was coming, too. The man never lets me down." He patted Livingston's back with affection.

The Moksha native, a man of few words, smiled.

"But now, son," Doc said, quickly dispensing with pleasantries, "we've got some serious catching up to do."

The same old Doc, David thought, thankful to have him back.

"First, there's something you should know," Doc said, pulling out a SAT phone from his backpack.

"Wait? What? Where'd those come from?" David snapped, knowing the cousins had found Doc's things abandoned in his cabin.

"Emergency supplies I stashed by the lab in a hollowed-out tree trunk—made a pitstop there on my run to the Moksha."

"So why didn't you call me? Let me know you were okay?" David demanded, hurt.

"Because I wanted you to believe I was dead," Doc said.

"But … why?"

"Because I needed to stay dead. And I needed you to complete the mission."

"Since when did you care about completing the mission?"

"Since it meant the safety of your brother," Doc said.

David's face blanched.

"Jenks was waiting for me after everyone left the farm. He knew I was on to them, and I understood from Jenks my days were numbered—men like Rand don't leave loose ends. But they needed you to finish the mission; and to guarantee that you did, I realized Nick would have become their insurance policy … and the albatross hung around your neck for all their future endeavors," Doc said, pausing to let his point sink in.

"So after I escaped from Jenks, I knew I didn't have much time. I called an old army pal who owed me … asked a favor of him with no questions asked," Doc said.

"What favor?" David said, his voice wary.

"To protect Nick. To get him to safety. Only … he was a step behind Rand's men in reaching Nick's apartment, arriving just in time to witness his abduction. But not to worry," Doc quickly interjected, "he trailed their vehicle to a storage facility, watched them secure Nick inside one of the units and then leave. That's when he made his move and broke Nick out."

"So where's Nick now?" David asked, holding his breath.

"At a safehouse in Maine," Doc said, lifting his SAT phone and punching in some numbers. A voice answered on the other end. "I've got someone here wanting to talk with you," Doc said into the receiver and then handed it to David.

David's hands shook as he took the phone. "Nick," he said, his voice trembling, "is that you?"

"David … I'm so glad to hear your voice! Are you alright?"

"I'm fine, Nick. I'll explain everything to you real soon, just stay put until I can get to you. And bro, I'm so sorry you got tangled up in this mess. But I'm taking care of things now. Everything will be fine."

"It's okay, David," Nick said, accepting his brother for his word—never having reason not to. "Take care of yourself."

David handed the phone back to Doc. "Thank you," he said, his voice cracking.

Doc nodded.

"Okay then," David said, clearing his throat, "let's head back."

"No, son … I'll be staying," Doc said, his voice tender. "Safer they think I'm dead. Besides, my home is with the Moksha now."

"But what about your farm?" David queried.

"Let the natives run it. Besides, you and I both know Pran will make every one of those plants obsolete, given time."

At the start of David's journey, Pran's influence in eliminating aggression had been just theory, one he viewed with ample skepticism but, nevertheless, one he humored for his mentor's sake. But his years of painstaking research had proven Doc right. Now his mentor's theory that, given time, Pran would also be a panacea to all disease no longer seemed an outrageous reach.

"Son," Doc said, his gaze steady on David's, "you remember your first encounter with the Moksha, the entire village celebrating your return to this lifetime with their firelight dance? You were confused, skeptical even, of your greater purpose to being here. Well, now that purpose is playing out."

Livingston, silent within the circle of men, moved forward and grasped David's forearms. "David walk with Moksha," he said.

Once, those words had stirred great angst in the scientist; but now, he grasped a connection. The line he'd once drawn in the sand between science and the paranormal had blurred, understanding now that science only went so far; but his connection to Lanya had eliminated all bound-aries—took him places he never knew existed.

The wiry little man clasped the Sphatika strung from David's neck and held it up before the scientist's eyes. "Have question?" he said, touching it to David's middle forehead. "See answer."

He understood Livingston's gist. His Sphatika would provide the an-swer to his quest—the meaning for his life—through Lanya's eyes, of course. Only, his patience was wearing thin, his understanding of her visions still found wanting, and his fruitless search for purpose was leaving him tired and vulnerable. He nodded at the Moksha native, who took his leave.

"Here's my phone number and Nick's," Doc said, handing David a slip of paper. "Stick it in your boot."

"Doc," David said, encircling his mentor with a bear-hug embrace, "thank you."

"Let me know how things work out. And once things settle down, come visit." Doc smiled.

David smiled back, despite his sadness at leaving him behind. "You know I will," he said.

★★★

All the way on his trek back to the farm David's mind spun like a spider weaving its web, creating a trap to capture its prey. He had time enough to consider the ramification of his actions, the dangers posed to those he loved and the consequences of doing nothing. But he refused to allow men like Rand and his E.D.E.N. cohorts push him around, even if he agreed with the principle of their mission. So just before sunset, when the trio had made it back to the farm, David's mind was made up.

He pulled out his SAT phone from his backpack and punched in several numbers. The voice on the receiving end answered: "Federal Bureau of Investigation."

98

—·—

ONE HUNDRED LIGHTBULBS

Friday, September 8, 2006

BRAD WAS AMAZED AND totally befuddled by the plant he'd absconded with from Nick's greenhouse. In his rush to escape the spray descending upon both him and the specimens, and to return post haste to Megan's apartment, he totally missed seeing it. But now, back at the lab exactly one week later, he still didn't know what to make of this anomaly, wonder, freak of nature—this unheard-of species in the plant kingdom capable of reproducing itself via both seeds and spores. His eyes weren't hallucinating the white seeded blooms on tall, thin stems nor the spores lining the undersides of its broad, green leaves—home to thousands of them. Brad struggled to understand it, let alone classify it. But as he ran, and re-ran, his analysis of this oddity, it confirmed his suspicions. Its extract was identical to the one he'd discovered hidden at the lab, as well as to that left clinging to Megan's vial from Brazil. And now, there was its potential link to a cure for Nick's cancer. If indeed it proved the common denominator, of what significance was this mystery plant to the larger picture? How did it square with this secretive Operation Octane and its potentially lethal dragnet of victims?

It had been a week since Brad had last seen Megan and was no closer to solving the disappearing act of Nick and Doc. Frustrated with his trail growing cold, he reconsidered the one person who had shed any light on the subject—the one person who knew more than he was willing to say. And as if one hundred lightbulbs went off in his head, he grabbed his car keys and bolted from the lab. It was time to re-pay a visit to Mr. Drew Dexter.

★★★

In a fortunate stroke of serendipity, just as Brad entered the parking lot, Mr. Dexter was exiting his newspaper's workplace and walking to his car. In a split-second decision, Brad pulled into an empty parking space and watched the elder gentleman settle into his vehicle, a vintage 1958 blue and white Chevy Impala that looked like it had just rolled off the assembly line, exuding refinement and unmistakable flair—not unlike Mr. Dexter himself, attired in his plaid vest and crisp bow tie. He could have confronted the man at his car, but his inner voice whispered, *Wait.* So he let Mr. Dexter pull out of the lot and then lagged behind, well hidden. Glancing down at his gas gauge he sighed with relief, grateful his tank was full, because now was not the time to lose his tail for a refill stop, not when so many questions still needed answering. Though for all he knew, this could simply be a jaunt to the local grocery store or the corner dry cleaners. But when Mr. Dexter's Chevy Impala departed the neighborhood and turned, instead, onto the Interstate heading north out of Boston, Brad had to consider the possibility that this outing wasn't a usual errand run.

After an hour and a half on his tail, Mr. Dexter's car exited the highway via an off-ramp for Kennebunkport, Maine, and then proceeded on a slow, meandering drive through the small coastal community, past elegant oceanfront properties with sweeping beach views. After lazily drinking in the shoreline vistas, and in seemingly no apparent hurry, he drove into Dock Square, the town center, where quaint boutique shops pitched their final sales during these last warm days of summer. He did not stop there, however, continuing on through the tourist hubbub to the quieter outskirts of town.

By this point Brad was beginning to feel like he'd literally and metaphorically been taken for a ride. Maybe Mr. Dexter was simply enjoying some sun and fresh air on a day trip to Maine, or perhaps he was headed to conduct an interview for the newspaper. As these and other scenarios played out in his head, the Chevy Impala suddenly made a slow and careful turn off the rural road they were traversing and disappeared through a hedgerow of arborvitae. Brad rode on by, passing a narrow driveway so well concealed by the greenery it would have been easily missed had he not observed Mr. Dexter's turn. Quickly, he pulled his vehicle off-road, dispatching it lickety-split before making his way back to the inconspicuous entrance. Slipping between the evergreens he emerged onto a winding, graveled track lined with evenly spaced hydrangeas, their fifteen-foot heights creating a perfect shield. He proceeded with quiet stealth moving forward like a jaguar on the prowl, down on his haunches behind blossom-covered branches, springing from bush to bush ever closer his prey. Up ahead he could just make out the Chevy Impala through the branches. He heard its car door slammed shut and observed Mr. Dexter mounting the porch steps to a country-cottage-styled home. Making his entrance, the front door swung open with a yawning squeal and, from within, a muffled voice escaped on the breeze but then was abruptly silenced with the door's firm closure behind him.

Brad's curiosity peaked. With soft footfalls he climbed the porch steps and, his backside hugging the cottage walls, inched his way toward the nearest window. His heart pounding with both excitement at discovery and trepidation at getting caught, he stood glued aside the windowpane for several calming seconds before cocking his head and venturing a look in. Mr. Dexter's back was to him obscuring the person to whom he was speaking, their conversation inaudible through the glass. Brad leaned back, forced to wait until Mr. Dexter physically moved aside to visibly reveal the stranger.

Several impatient seconds later, when he chanced a second peek, the elder newspaper man had shifted his position, allowing Brad a clear view. But what his eyes saw, his brain could not compute. Confused, his mind a jumble of thoughts, Brad moved as in a trance to the front door and slowly opened it.

"Well I'll be damned," Nick said. "Will you look what the cat dragged in!"

***

"Have a seat, son," Mr. Dexter said, pointing the obviously bewildered young man to a chair at the dining table. "I'll get you some water."

Nick dragged a chair up beside him. "It's really good to see you, Brad," he said, beaming with delight. "I can't believe my luck—first Mr. Dexter and now you, just when I was hankering for some company. Sure beats sitting alone reading paperback novels all day … nothing against novels," he said, grinning as his eyes passed over the fully stocked bookcase tucked up against a floral-papered backdrop.

Mr. Dexter returned with the water and placed it in front of Brad who, after taking several healthy gulps, looked from Mr. Dexter to Nick and back to Mr. Dexter again. No one spoke. Finally, in exasperation, he snapped, "Will someone please explain to me what the hell is going on—why is Nick here?"

"Ah, the million-dollar question," Mr. Dexter retorted, pushing up his bifocals. "I'm afraid I don't have a full answer to that one, son. But I can tell you what I do know." He pulled out a chair on the opposite side of the table and slowly eased himself down onto it. "Doctor Benjamin Shaw, whom all of us affectionately call Doc, is an old Army pal of mine. Prior to his relocating to Brazil, we'd gather weekly for a few rounds of poker and drinks with the boys. But after he left the country, our communications became sporadic—eventually breaking off entirely. I hadn't spoken with him in years until his recent phone call asking me for help," he said. "Understand, son, we were like brothers during the Korean War. He saved my ass more than once. So when he asked me to protect Nick, I couldn't refuse."

"Protect Nick from what?" Brad asked.

"The bad guys," he said. "Honestly, I don't know who they were, and Doc never said. Probably figured better I didn't know. Anyways, they kidnapped Nick and locked him in a storage unit in South Boston. Luckily, I was on their tail and managed to get him out once they left. Then I brought him here, to what was my childhood home and now my summer retreat … when I can manage to escape work to get here."

"Then what?" Brad said, impatient.

"Once I had Nick safely tucked away, I called Doc back on his SAT phone. That's when he asked me to write the article for the paper."

"For what purpose?"

"All he said was it was better if anyone looking for him thought he was dead."

"Why?"

"Again, he didn't say."

"And what about Nick? What was the plan?"

"To keep him here and wait for his call, which came yesterday—and David was with him … there in Brazil."

Brad took a moment to catch his breath and absorb this welcome revelation. They were both alive—together in the Amazon.

Brad turned to Nick. "What did David say?"

"That he was okay and was taking care of things and would explain everything soon … and to stay put."

The wheels in Brad's mind turned trying to work things out. "So the source of your article was Doc, not the U.S. Government," he said.

"Correct. Doc only told me to say that if anyone actually came looking."

"A cover story," Brad said, ruminating. "And was I the only person to come looking?"

"So far, yes."

Brad thought about it. If Jenks did happen to come across the article, he would have figured the locals reported Doc missing—nothing suspicious there. And if he had actually visited the newspaper and was fed the cover story by Mr. Dexter, the fact that the U.S. Government would have followed up on a missing American citizen wouldn't have surprised him in the least—a masterful touch by Doc in covering his tracks. Brad felt a modicum of relief that Jenks hadn't shown up—yet.

"Now I'd like to ask you a question, Brad," Mr. Dexter said. "How did you find us?"

"I followed you."

"But how did you know that I'd lead you to Nick?"

"I didn't … just followed my instincts."

"Well, let's hope the bad guys don't have your instincts," Mr. Dexter said, his face sober.

The room fell silent, all but for the tick tock of an antique grandfather's clock. Brad drank his water and took in the surroundings of Mr. Dexter's childhood home—the delicate, hand-crocheted table scarf; the fine English bone china display in the pine corner cabinet; the chintz floral swag draping the dining room's sunny bay window and …

"How's your health, Nick?" Brad asked unexpectedly, his eyes having fallen to rest upon the window's sill—and Nick's greenhouse plant set there.

Nick's eyes followed Brad's to the plant. Now he understood the tenacity his brother valued in the guy. He smiled. "I'm great … but let's not avoid the elephant in the room," he said, aware the gig was up. "You know about the plant."

"Yes I do, Nick … and I'm glad for your health," Brad said, laying a reassuring hand on Nick's shoulder. At that moment he wrestled with divulging his own experimental use of the plant's extract, and how it had healed Megan's pain from the bullet ant bites, and how the two had experienced the 'eyes of a woman' while under its influence—and he wondered whether Nick had experienced them, too. But now was not the time or place for such discussion, not with Mr. Dexter present. The less the elder gentleman knew, the better if Jenks came looking.

Brad finished his drink and stood to go. "Looks like we're at a stalemate until David's back in touch" he said. "In the meantime, I'm heading to join Megan at the lighthouse. Andre's there with her."

"Andre's there?" Nick said, surprised.

"Yes. They were both beyond upset when you and Doc went missing—thought maybe a change of scenery would take their minds off things."

"I want to come with you," Nick said.

"Your brother asked you to stay put," Brad reminded him.

Nick smiled. "I know that my brother has my well-being at heart, and I've abided by his wishes all of my life, including that I sequester here. But I did it to allay his fears—not mine," Nick said. "You see, when I had cancer, I worried 24/7 about my mortality. Then, when the cancer left my body, strangely, so did my fear, and not just of dying—but of everything. And with fear's departure, the void it left in me was filled with an inner peace the likes of which I have never known. I love my brother, Brad, but his fears, real or perceived, no longer hold sway over me. I see things differently now … and right now, I want to see Andre. Mr. Dexter," Nick said, turning to the elder gentleman, "could you get word to Doc for me? I'm sure he can reach my brother. Let him know where I'll be?"

"Will do my best, son … and if you need anything, you know how to reach me."

Nick retrieved his plant, tucking it under his arm and, along with Brad and Mr. Dexter, exited the front door.

"Good luck to you both," Dexter said, standing back on the porch as they descended the steps. And then, like a concerned father, he called out after them: "Watch yourselves."

★★★

When they reached Brad's car, Nick unloaded his plant onto the rear floorboards and then hopped up front, Brad already in the driver's seat. Their windows down, a scent sauntered in on the undulating breeze—*cigar smoke?* Brad thought. He shook it off as his imagination, started the engine and pulled out.

99

— · —

ROAD TRIP

Friday, September 8, 2006

D ESPITE BEING WITH GRANDPA Max, Roxy was lonely. She understood for her safety, however, David silencing not only their communications but all contact with the outside world until he completed the operation, at which point he promised to call. But the wait had made her anxious. And to worsen matters, ever since her hysterical and embarrassing outburst from her nightmare, she couldn't bear the look of pity in her grandfather's eyes. So she made an executive decision, one that went against David's wishes to stay incommunicado. She called Megan.

"Where the hell have you been? I've been calling you for days now—why haven't you answered? Don't you know how worried I've been?" Megan ranted at her best friend, tears trickling down her cheeks.

"Oh, Megan, I'm so sorry to have made you worry. Everything's okay. Honestly, I'm fine. I've been staying with my grandfather, out of touch, for a while. I'll explain everything when I see you," Roxy said.

Megan swallowed a sob. "I'm with my dad, too, on Rocky Point. When can you come?"

"Today, if you like. I can head out now and be there near sundown."

"Dad will be waiting at the dock," Megan said. "And Rox … I'm so happy you're coming."

"Me too, Meg."

With her bags packed and a promise to bring David back for a visit before the baby was born, Roxy bid good-bye to Grandpa Max and drove out through the valley, back up through hills of rippling grasses, and away from Triple Crown Ranch—her childhood memories in tow. She looked at her watch—five hours and counting on her road trip to Maine.

★★★

As they drove out of Kennebunkport following the coastline north, Brad glanced over at Nick. For someone who had just been kidnapped and then squirreled away from the bad guys for days, he certainly gave the impression—slouched comfortably in his seat with the breeze mussing his once meticulous hair—of an unburdened soul, as though nothing bad had happened.

The same could not be said of Brad, wound tight like a top, grip clenched on the wheel and foot heavy on the accelerator, his eyes darting from road to passenger and back again.

"Go on," Nick said, reading Brad's mind like tea leaves, "say what's on your mind."

"At Mr. Dexter's there was more to the story than I chose to tell," Brad said, his words freed like air released from a valve.

"I thought as much," Nick said. "Always figured David kept you in the loop, if not me."

"Well, I'm afraid this time he kept me in the dark just like you—left me with only crumbs to follow. But I kept digging."

"Of course you did," Nick smiled.

"Long story short—somehow, I believe that plant of yours is at the center of all that's happened."

Eyeing the plant in the back seat, Nick said, "David had once asked me to keep it a secret."

"That begs the question, why not tell a world weary of cancer the welcome news of a cure?"

"I'm guessing you think there's more to this," Nick said.

"Has to be. Something about this cancer-curing plant was deemed worthy enough of your kidnapping," Brad said, looking over at Nick and gauging how much more to say. "You knew nothing of David's work with Doc … of their involvement in what they thought was a secret government operation?"

"What secret operation?"

"An illegal one is all I know ... one that seems to have left them holding the proverbial bag."

"You're saying they got played?"

"Precisely."

"By whom?"

"Rogue agents of the United States Government."

If Nick was shocked, it didn't register on his face. "How deep are they in?" he asked.

"From the sound of things, up to their necks."

Nick was silent, contemplating the situation. Then he faced Brad. "I trust David," he said. "Somehow, he'll pull through."

Brad admired Nick's confidence in his older brother and wished some of it would rub off on him; but, truth be told, he didn't think things looked good for his boss.

★★★

The sun had set, and the dark skies were blacker still from a swell of thunderclouds threatening rain when Roxy pulled into the harbor parking lot. She exited her car and strained to see the island, but all that was evident were the sporadic beams from the lighthouse cutting through the gloom. Sighing, she headed down the ramp to the dock.

Ahead, a lantern burned bright, illuminating the ruddy-faced, scarlet-haired behemoth of a man sitting in his motorboat. "Mr. O'Malley," Roxy called out, approaching with slow and methodical steps, not looking to breach the water thinking it the landing.

"Careful lass, take me 'an'," Sean said, directing her safely into the boat. "Tricky time av day ... de devil's 'our," he said.

Though the air was balmy, a chill ran through her.

"Got room for two more," a voice rang out from the darkness.

Roxy knew the voice and, when he stepped into the light, she exclaimed, "Brad ... what a wonderful surprise!" But then another face emerged from the shadows, and she blanched as if seeing a ghost. "Jesus," she said, "is that really you, Nick?"

"In the flesh," he said.

"Cum, de two av yer, git in," Sean said. "Time enoof ter blather whaen a roof is over our 'eads from de comin' storm."

★★★

Megan and Andre burst into tears at the sight of their missed loved ones walking through the door, everyone hugging everyone, voices overlapping and questions flying.

"People, make sum room ter breath," Sean O'Malley said, stepping into the mayhem and directing people to the cottage's sparse seating. Nick placed his plant, carried from car to boat, now onto the windowsill next to Roxy, who sat herself down onto a rocker and watched the spattering raindrops trickling down the outer glass. Brad shared a bench with Megan, who clutched his hand and that of her best friend in the rocker beside her. Nick joined Andre on a cushioned wicker sofa, arms wrapped tightly about one another, while Sean went to boil water for tea.

Nick was all smiles, loving the attention, especially after days of confinement, his demeanor calm like the eye of a storm, despite the madness swirling about him.

"Where have you been all this time?" Andre asked, his voice both demanding and full of love.

"In hiding," Nick said.

"Who on earth from?" Andre asked, confused.

"The bad guys who kidnapped me," Nick answered.

A tirade of emotion erupted within the room.

"Look," Nick said, unruffled, "I don't have specifics on who or why, or even how Doc knew I was kidnapped, all I know is that he contacted a friend who rescued me out of a storage facility and brought me to a safe house in Maine where Brad picked me up and then brought me here."

Andre internalized Nick's statement and then said in a somber tone, "So I assume your being here now means you are out of danger?"

"I'm fine," Nick said.

"I didn't ask if you were fine," Andre said.

"Don't worry, Andre. My brother was just being overprotective."

"So you've heard from David?" Andre said, still badgering for answers.

Roxy jerked her head back from the rain and set her steely gaze on Nick.

"Yes," he said, "once … while I was in hiding."

Roxy was crushed. And jealous. David had called Nick and not her. Of everyone in the room, only she knew the whole truth of the matter, David having confided everything to the mother of his child, preparing her for any surprise attempt on their lives. But, despite the hurt, she kept mum on it all.

"Where is he now?" Andre asked. "What did he say?"

"He's in Brazil and said he'd explain everything later."

"And Roxy, you've not heard anything from David?" Megan inquired.

"No," she said, shaking her head, her heart bruised.

"None of this makes any sense," Andre said, frustrated. "Maybe we need to get the FBI involved."

"There's no need," Nick said with authority. "David is taking care of things. Have patience."

On the ride over, Brad had shared all he knew of the situation with Nick, the two agreeing to say nothing of the illegal, secret operation David was caught up in or of Brad and Megan's experience with the miracle plant potion. Too much information would only complicate things and lead to more questions, of which neither were willing to entertain. And certainly, neither wanted David's activities put under a microscope by the FBI. The key to everything was to remain calm and have patience—easier for Nick to say than anyone else.

Sean O'Malley entered the room carrying a tray of tea-filled mugs. "Ah," he said, "nathin' loike a warm cuppa durin' a storm." Outside, now, the rain was pouring.

100

THEY'RE ON TO ME

Friday, September 8, 2006

IT WAS EARLY MORNING. David was in a deep sleep, his body spent after yesterday's exhausting trip. A whomp-whomping sound in the distance barely stirred his consciousness, his mind ignoring the intrusion as he rolled over in his hammock. It was only when, shortly thereafter, an exchange of unfamiliar voices ever increasing in volume encroached upon his cabin that he was jostled into full awareness. Outside, a squad of men outfitted in fatigues and brandishing rifles had infiltrated the farm. David quickly threw on his clothes and exited his cabin, looking for someone in charge. Twenty feet away, a man turned to face him. He looked strangely familiar. And then it struck him—three weeks prior at the Boston Public Garden, he was the youthful-faced jogger in a Harvard Crimson T-shirt who sat on the bench beside him and relayed the General's green light for Operation Octane.

"David Bennett … Special Agent Seagram, FBI," he said, his gun pointing, "General Rand requires your presence."

What was happening? David struggled to make sense of things as he was surrounded by gun-toting men. And then it clicked. Seagram was another of Rand's men working rogue within the federal government, just like FDA Agent Jenks, the two having gone over to the dark side to join Rand's operation.

Fuck! David thought, *my anonymous call to the Bureau … of course, Seagram must have caught wind. And when he informed E.D.E.N., they would have known I was the whistleblower—who else would have knowledge of their fanatical plan to release a biological weapon into the world. Fuck! They're on to me! Fuck! Fuck! Fuck!*

David had been confident his plan would have worked. Turning the FBI onto Rand and their trailing him to the consortium's members was supposed to be David's way out. With one stroke, E.D.E.N. would have been dismantled, David would have been freed from their grip and Octane would have been removed from their untrustworthy hands. What became of Octane after that—well he had a plan. But now …

"Step to, Bennett, we haven't got all day," Seagram said, his pistol pointing the way as his prisoner moved out, hands cuffed in front of him.

Passing familiar grounds, the troop marched him beyond the wooden cabins, over the footbridge crossing a shallow stream and out through the jungle's fringe to a clearing nestled within a ring of forest—Doc's herbal farm. The natives, who were normally busy working the harvest, were nowhere to be seen. Instead, plunked down dead center, crushing numerous plantings, a military helicopter sat waiting.

"Move, Bennett," Seagram said, while the squad assisted David up and in below the whirring rotary blades. All men on board, the chopper lifted higher and higher and, as it did so, David looked down at the farm and saw two familiar figures running into the clearing. Helpless now, all Ramon and Bruno could do was look up. *Adeus amigos,* David thought just before the chopper darted out of sight.

★★★

The helicopter followed the snaking Amazon River, an amazing view from David's perspective and one he would have enjoyed if not for his circumstances. Instead, he was listening intently to the soldiers' small talk, trying to pick up any useful tidbits, though his understanding of Portuguese, as ascertained through Ramon and Bruno, was limited. Agent Seagram was useless to the cause, hardly uttering a word. David sat across from the youthful-looking agent wondering how he ended up working for the likes of Rand. But then, Seagram could be thinking the same of him. For some, like Jenks, David knew the answer was money. For Doc it was patriotism. For David, it was loyalty (to Doc).

But where did Seagram fit in? If he had to venture a guess, he would say power—what man didn't like power?

The chopper banked right and swung over the Rio Negro, moving inland toward a military airport. David assumed the soldiers riding with him were hired mercenaries, bought and paid for by E.D.E.N. Their uniforms bore no insignia, though everything about them shouted money, especially their shiny new weapons and boots. Against such men, he didn't stand a chance. And as the chopper hovered down onto the landing pad, David's heart sank with it. Seagram had taken control of his destiny and left him vulnerable—and David hated being vulnerable.

101

LOYALTY

Saturday, September 9, 2006

DAVID COULDN'T SLEEP A wink last night after he was dumped unceremoniously into an empty six-by-eight-foot storage closet located within a huge, metal airplane hangar. More like a cell than closet, someone had thought to furnish it with a tattered mattress stinking of body odor and a metal pot to piss in. The windowless room belied the time of day—minutes indistinguishable from hours, adding disorientation to David's confusion and fear. Only when someone opened his door and slid in a breakfast tray did his brain finally reset. Cereal, toast, coffee—certainly not room service at the Ritz Carlton, but it was more than he expected. Still, his stomach tied up in knots, he lacked appetite. He drank the coffee—strong but doable.

When Special Agent Seagram entered the room twenty minutes later, David, his body jittery and heart racing from both the caffeine and adrenaline coursing his veins, knew he should do something but couldn't muster the strength or courage. Instead, he sat on the mattress terror-stricken, looking up at the man with a gun like a capsized sailor who can't swim.

"Rise and shine, Bennett," Seagram said. "We've got a plane to catch."

His hands re-cuffed, the soldiers pushed him forward, out into the cavernous hanger, it's monstrous doors now wide open and a private Cessna jet parked at the ready, its steps down awaiting passengers.

"Move," Seagram commanded.

David obliged, his pace hastened along by Seagram's pistol at his back. When they reached the boarding stairs, Seagram and his men followed David up onto the craft, then the stairs retracted and the door latched, leaving any chance for escape behind.

"Sit," Seagram said, indicating the seat opposite his across the aisle, where one of his goons then cuffed him to the armrest.

David looked around, taking in the plane's newness, an obvious recent purchase and an extravagant one at that. *Follow the money,* he thought, knowing without a doubt that E.D.E.N. was its benefactor and not the U.S. Government.

"Where are you taking me?" David questioned.

"You'll know when we get there," Seagram said.

David spoke no further the entire flight. Tired and his body aching from the previous night's lack of rest, he shrunk back into his seat and closed his eyes. Sleep soon followed. A respite before the storm.

★★★

Hours later the Cessna landed—just where, David wasn't sure, not because of the heavy rainfall shrouding the window view outside, but rather because of the mask covering his eyes. Three black SUVs awaited the passengers. Still hand-cuffed, David was shuffled off the plane and into the second SUV, strategically placed center in the motorcade. Approximately a half-hour later, all three vehicles pulled into an underground parking facility. Only Special Agent Seagram and two of his men in the second SUV accompanied David into an elevator. David could feel it ascending, and when its door opened, he was led down a long corridor before coming to a halt. Someone knocked on a door and a voice responded, "Enter." The two soldiers remained stationed outside the door, while Seagram entered with his prisoner.

"David Bennett, we finally meet," Rand said.

Seagram removed David's mask and, when his eyes refocused, he knew it was the General, recognizing him from an old picture Doc had: Large jaw, square shoulders, crew cut—your cartoon stereotype, only real.

"Sorry for the inconvenience," Rand said, indicating the mask. "Precaution ... you understand."

David understood nothing—only that his life was in this man's hands.

"Sit down, Bennett," the General said, spoken more as a command than with magnanimity.

David moved to a chair facing Rand, the man's eyes like a hawk's studying his prey from across his desk.

"Seems we have a problem," the General said, leaning forward onto his elbows. "You see, above all, what I expect of my men is loyalty."

David squirmed in his seat.

"Now that phone call of yours to the FBI is not what I would term loyalty. I expected better of you, Bennett. You're a smart man—some say brilliant even—but that was a boneheaded maneuver. Luckily for all of us my man, Seagram here, intercepted it, so no harm done. Still, E.D.E.N. wasn't happy. Too close for comfort, if you catch my drift. So here's what's going to happen, Bennett. You are to be given a second chance to prove your loyalty."

David stared at Rand, not liking the sound of things.

"After much debate," the General continued, "the consortium has decided to change the target site of Octane's inaugural launch. Rather than focusing on isolated, bit players in Africa or the Middle East, we have decided to switch to a bigger stage offering a more expedient bang for our buck—the political landscape of Washington, D.C." Rand had David's attention, and the General knew it, so he continued his grandstanding.

"Consider the U.S. Congress," he said. "Removing aggression from a man's sensibilities removes his capacity for anger and outrage. So instead of a hostile Congress, imagine one devoid of resentment—think of the bipartisan work that could be accomplished, the laws written and passed that promote our cause. By targeting the political leaders of the most powerful and influential country in the world we can seismically shift domestic and international policy toward Christian values and doctrine. Aiming for influential lawmakers instead of two-bit troublemakers, we can affect world policy change not only on a grander scale but on an accelerated timeline, thereby attaining E.D.E.N.'S realization—a peaceful world—in our lifetime." Rand paused to let his words sink in, while David hung on each one of them.

"Now, getting back to your loyalty, Bennett."

Fuck, here it comes, David thought.

"In two days' time, Operation Octane will launch on the U.S. Capitol. You are to be its sole facilitator. But understand this, Bennett ... should you be caught in the act, I will leave you hung out to dry with complete deniability of your existence. After all, who would believe a mad scientist over the General of the Defense Intelligence Agency." Rand smiled. "But, to be sure, you will be watched. And if you fail to deliver, you will not only pay the price with imprisonment for treason, but you will do so risking the lives of your brother and girlfriend."

David gasped before he could stop himself.

"Yes, we have them under surveillance as we speak, ready to move in—if necessary."

Was Rand calling his bluff? Did his goons locate Nick and Roxy? *Oh God,* David thought. *Oh God.*

102

—·—

A THUNDERCLOUD'S COMING

Saturday, September 9, 2006

Sean O'Malley was in a chipper mood on this rainy Saturday morning, the unexpected company a delightful change to days usually filled with solitude and contemplation. Up before everyone, he got to work preparing an Irish breakfast feast. "'Ope everyone 'as a 'earty appetite," he said cheerily, presenting a spread of bacon, sausage, fried eggs, hash browns, toast with butter and, of course, tea. "Not up ter me usual standards as bein' last minute an' al'," he said apologetically to incredulous moans of, "are you kidding?", "smells delicious," and "you can cook for me anytime." Sean beamed and poured the tea.

By contrast, Roxy sat staring out through the living room window at the continuing rainfall, the gloom pervading her mood. Still not hearing from David, she was desperately attempting to hide her anxiety. The close quarters of six adults forced to share overnight accommodations didn't help matters either. And it didn't help, too, that she alone knew what David was up against and could share none of it. Of course, she thought the worst by now—and if he was dead, what was to become of her and their baby. Round and round her thoughts went, a despondent carousel ride that never ended.

"Ye comin', Roxy?" Sean called out to her. "Git it while it's 'ot."

Roxy, her do-loop of gloom interrupted, arose and joined the others.

After breakfast, dishes cleared and put away, the men settled down at the dining table for a game of cribbage. Megan cornered Roxy. "Let's take a walk," she said, noting something was up with her best friend.

Donned with umbrellas, the two walked out toward the lighthouse and tumbling waves, seagulls crying overhead and the smell of salt in the air.

"So are you going to tell me what's going on with you?" Megan asked.

"Nothing," Roxy said, attempting a poker face. "Why do you ask?"

"Because you didn't answer my calls for days … you were with your grandfather whom you rarely visit … and you arrived here a nervous wreck."

"It's that obvious?" Roxy said, a slight grin acknowledging her best friend's astuteness.

"This has to do with David, doesn't it?" Megan said.

"Yes … I'm worried about him," Roxy said, wishing she could divulge more.

"Stands to reason, as no one seems to know what's happening with him," Megan said, exasperated herself with the whole situation. "So is that why you went to your grandfather's?"

"Partly … I also wanted to tell him in person I was pregnant."

"I bet he was thrilled!" Megan said. "Knowing your grandfather, that child of yours will be riding a horse in no time."

"No doubt outfitted in a cowboy hat and snake skinned boots," Roxy said, the two of them laughing.

"But, seriously, Rox, tell me," Megan said, "why did you wait so long to call me?"

Roxy told her a partial truth. "I've been depressed, Meg. Not up to seeing anyone."

Even me, Megan thought, looking into Roxy's eyes. But she understood. She knew the look. "Yes, I could tell."

"And you, Meg? What brought you home?" Roxy asked, knowing the mental stress that always accompanied her trips back.

"Honestly? I felt like it would somehow be different this time."

"And was it?"

"Yes, surprisingly so. I made up with my dad, Rox. All these years of carrying guilt around was for nothing—he knew, Rox … he knew my mom was pregnant. But he didn't know that I knew, too. And now … it's so good to be free of it, to be able to breathe and not hurt inside anymore."

Roxy was shocked. The bond that had held them together, the guilt, the pain, was no more. She had sensed a change in Megan, could see it in her face, but couldn't define it. Now it all made sense. And Roxy was crushed— and never felt more alone.

"Let's get back to the house," she said, looking up at the sky, "looks like a thundercloud's coming."

★★★

Journal Entry, Saturday, September 9, 2006:

Meg and I are worlds apart now. Our bond is no more. She crossed a barrier that still holds me back—freed herself of the demons that still haunt my dreams. I am glad for her, but sad for me. And though I haven't lost my best friend, it feels like it, because Meg is forever changed.

103

VIGILANCE

Sunday, September 10, 2006

AFTER A DECADE OF planning and dealing with the egos of men with means, General Arthur Rand was finally ready to officiate the grand mission. For the first time ever, the members of E.D.E.N. would gather under one roof to celebrate the execution of their brainchild. It was no small undertaking and Rand, more than tired of their bickering and arrogance, finally would be able to put it all to rest with a successful launch.

He had placed Special Agent Seagram in charge of security. With the change of launch site from a small hot spot to the biggest player on the world stage, he depended on the man's vigilance to pull this off. There was no room for error. They had worked too long and too hard to fail, and failure, for either of them, did not bode well.

And now, of course, was the added twist of David Bennett thrown into the mix. Rand felt confident that he had put the fear of God in him with his little speech, but then he remembered the scientist's rebel streak with FDA Agent Jenks, forcing a demand for an anti-venom delivery in the jungle. Would have to keep a close eye on that one, to be sure, but that was what Agent Seagram was for.

Rand checked his watch. The first of E.D.E.N.'s members should be arriving soon.

★★★

Agent Jenks checked his watch, then picked up his 2-way radio. "All Units report," he said. Static. "Unit 2 … all quiet." Static. "Unit 3 … holding steady." Static. "All Units hold your positions," he ordered, before disengaging. A minute later his phone rang.

"What's your update, Agent?" General Rand said, looking for a surveillance report from Jenks.

So far, the job had been easy. Once Roxanne Pendleton and Nick Bennett had arrived, they hadn't left the island. This suited Jenks just fine—the more simple and less complicated an operation, the better. Still, his experience had taught him how things can change on a dime. Vigilance in his job was key.

"Sir, no change. All quiet and under control," Jenks said.

"Good. Let's keep it that way."

"Yes sir."

Dead air.

Jenks considered Rand and men like him as fools with their grandiose desire for status and power. Nothing lasts forever in this business—someone was always looking to edge his way up the ladder and step over you. He knew how vulnerable his boss was right now and didn't envy him one bit. No, his lower-rank, less-hassle position, with a cigar thrown in, kept Jenks a happy man.

His car inconspicuously parked among the other vehicles in the harbor lot, Jenks lifted his binoculars and peered through the rain-splatted windshield. The island drew him in—its isolation and surroundings of great beauty and peril not unlike the Amazon. And with that thought, his mind latched on to those beautiful eyes of a woman—and Megan's article. It was all so very curious to him—the connection they both seemed to share, the strange coincidence that had no answer. Still, the idea that someone else had seen those eyes meant he hadn't been hallucinating … that he wasn't losing his mind. And as long as she was alive, she was proof of his sanity. He tucked that thought into the back of his mind and lit another cigar.

104

LAUNCH DAY

Monday, September 11, 2006

G ENERAL RAND STOOD AT the head of an oversized conference-room table—E.D.E.N.'s members fully assembled, voices hushed—the definitive hour at hand.

"Gentlemen," he began, "today is launch day and, with it, Operation Octane will mark the beginning of a new world. Mankind's previous efforts to quell global aggression through diplomatic negotiations, sanctions, military force—all have failed. It has been a steep uphill climb, but now, finally at the mountain top, the view of a peaceful world is within reach. Today, with Octane's release in Washington, D.C. and its global spread thereafter, mankind's exposure to this ubiquitous virus will facilitate a change so gradual it will go unnoticed and unchallenged until, at last, all byproducts of aggressive behavior are forever wiped from the face of the Earth. Today, gentlemen, we have the power to save the world from itself—and we will do so."

To resounding applause, General Rand left the room, leaving the consortium members to their breakfast and bluster while he attended to the day's important business of a successful launch, now complicated by an unexpected hurricane spinning nearer the Capital's doorstep. Even nature couldn't cut him a break.

***

Agent Jenks, stiff-legged from lodging overnight in his vehicle, stretched as best he could in his seat. Through his rain-spattered windshield, he observed a fog-laden island. Jenks rather liked the inclement weather, kept him on his toes, forced a more 'eyes-peeled' approach to his job. But today he rather doubted anyone would be inclined to depart the island in conditions like this. He reached for the dashboard and turned on the radio.

" … and it looks like a stormy day ahead for the folks in our Nation's Capital, the hurricane taking an unexpected turn in trajectory this morning, defying all weather models projecting its track safely out to sea. Instead, heavy rains and high winds are expected to linger in the D.C. area all morning as the system skirts north along Maryland's coast before clearing out by afternoon. Stay tuned for all the latest updates on the storm's development," the announcer said, before the station returned to its regularly scheduled programing and Jenks switched off the dial.

"Fuck," Jenks said, mulling the situation, glad he wasn't Agent Seagram who now had one more curve ball to deal with. But nature was calling with his own emergency so, foregoing any further thoughts on the hurricane, Jenks stepped out from his car into the fog and took a long, satisfying piss.

***

Inside the cottage Sean O'Malley, having been eaten out of house and home by his unexpected guests, prepared the only fixings left in the pantry for breakfast—a large pot of Irish porridge. But with his icebox empty and lunch soon to roll around, he informed his daughter he'd be making a grocery run to the mainland.

"Let me come with you," Megan said.

"Naw, love, yer stay wi' our guests. Oi won't be long."

Donned in his yellow slicker, Sean yanked its hood up over his head and, with a lit lantern, ventured out the door into the thickening fog and wind-blown rain. His footsteps careful on the wet stones, he followed the slippery path down to the dock and his awaiting boat. Climbing on board, he started up the motor and pulled out slowly, riding over the rocking waves to the shrouded mainland practically by heart.

From inside his vehicle Agent Jenks first heard the motor's drone over the tussling waves before he caught sight of a light bouncing upon the water. Staring into the fog, he observed a boat breaking from its murkiness and then mooring dockside. A lantern in hand, its skipper disembarked the vessel, picked his way through the gloom up the ramp to the fog-cloaked parking lot, entered his car and slowly drove off.

Jenks caught a brief glimpse of the man's face in the lamplight—luckily, not one of his wards, but still … so much for the island's inhabitants staying put because of weather.

***

David had been assigned surprisingly decent sleeping quarters, still a small room without a window but with an attached bath and a comfortable bed. Such accommodations, however, didn't induce anything close to a restful state, as he tossed and turned all night, the fate of his loved ones foremost on his mind.

Launch Day arrived without fanfare for David as Special Agent Seagram entered his room without knocking. "Time to move, Bennett. Put these on," he instructed, tossing him an FBI regulation windbreaker along with a fake id. After David complied, one of Rand's goons re-cuffed his wrists and blindfolded his eyes, pushing him out the door.

While navigating the twists and turns of several long corridors, a door swung open without warning in front of them, ushering out a throng of unexpected voices. One of Rands goons held David back as two men exited the doorway. *Foreigners,* David thought, from the sound of their accents and of those that were loudly emanating out from the room. It took a few seconds to register, but then it hit him—E.D.E.N.'s members were here. Of course, they would want to be present for Octane's inauguration after a decade's-old love affair with this project. David suddenly felt the enormity of his task and the burden of their eyes trained upon him, knowing that if he screwed up … those same eyes would seek revenge.

A hand protecting his head, once again he was lowered into the back seat of a vehicle taking him, he presumed, to the U.S. Capitol, a building so well-secured after the dire events of 9/11 that he began to doubt his ability to pull off the plan.

As his vehicle emerged from the underground parking garage, straightaway it was buffeted by a one-two punch—first by strong gusts, swaying it into the oncoming lane, and then by pelting rains, hitting the roof and surrounding glass windows with the reverberant ferocity of a pellet gun. David instinctively ducked.

"Fuck," Seagram swore from his front passenger seat, mimicking the driver who struggled for control.

"What's going on?" David ventured to ask.

"A hurricane, Bennett—a fucking hurricane."

David wondered about the implications. Would the operation be aborted? Postponed? He got his answer without having to ask.

"Take off his blindfold," Seagram directed Rand's man riding shotgun in the back seat before he looked David directly in the eye. "Let me explain something to you, Bennett, in case you were hoping otherwise—no storm will terminate the execution of E.D.E.N.'s mission." Then he picked up the two-way radio and issued the following instructions to all units: "Operation Octane's a green light … I repeat: Operation Octane's a green light." Then he looked back at David and said no more.

The familiar sights of D.C. whizzed past as David scanned the blurred landscape. On a normal Monday the crowds who returned for the start of a new workweek, along with busloads of visiting tourists, would have overflowed the streets. Now, most were deserted. Instead of life as usual, this sudden, unexpected storm forced the closure of some rain-swelled roads and the shut-down of many businesses, as well as sent the stunned and stranded public scurrying for cover, with many sheltering in place—including the lawmakers in the U.S. Capitol. *Virtual sitting ducks,* David thought. But then, he knew, so was he.

Amazing how easily rogue Special Agent Seagram infiltrated the Capitol. He simply drove up in his government-issued black sedan and flashed his Bureau identification badge—no one stopped him. And, of course, no problem gaining inside access with a biological weapon because the inside man was one of his own. The entire bogus ensemble just walked in like they belonged there. If David had any doubt about overcoming security heightened since 9/11, he didn't now. At this juncture, it was obvious to him just how deeply E.D.E.N. had embedded itself within the U.S. Government—and it troubled him.

"Let's get to work," Seagram ordered.

★★★

Roxy was the first to learn of the hurricane's approach. She was washing dishes in Sean's kitchen and had turned on his weather radio. *As if things couldn't get any worse,* she thought upon hearing the dire projection of its trajectory up the Eastern seaboard, as far north as Maine by tomorrow morning. She had no idea where David was at that moment. No one had heard another word from him since he'd last called Nick four days ago. She couldn't even say if he was alive or dead. And now, a hurricane was bearing down on them—and she was hurting.

Since childhood, Roxy had learned to stay strong by fighting her pain and yet, paradoxically, it was the pain that kept her strong—the two inseparable. But she was tired of fighting and tired of the pain, longing only to be weak in David's arms. But that was impossible now, because now she had a child to fight for. So she had to be strong—strong like David had said she was when he told her she could handle this situation, strong because she had no other choice—until the promise of a better world was fulfilled.

"It won't be safe for us to stay on the island," Megan said, speaking from personal experience. "As soon as my Dad gets back, we'll ferry you all across to your cars."

"And your dad? Will he evacuate?" Brad asked.

"He most certainly will, even if we have to carry him kicking and screaming," she declared.

It seemed to Megan the only one showing little regard for the oncoming storm was Roxy, once again occupying the rocker by the living room window. Megan looked over at her, worried. She could sense a wall had gone up between them ever since their talk two days earlier, when she spoke of her mended relationship with her dad. More than anything she wished for Roxy the same liberation from guilt. But now any discussion on the subject was immediately shut down, and all other interactions between the two had become stilted and less than engaging. Still, Megan wasn't about to give up trying. No matter what, Roxy was her best friend, and she would stand by her.

***

Outside the fog had lifted, but incessant showers continued to coat the windshield of Jenks' car. From the corner of his eye, he caught the movement of Sean O'Malley's vehicle pulling back into the lot. With full grocery bags loaded in each arm, he made his way down the ramp to his boat and, once again, set out across the choppy waters. Jenks watched his retreat then rolled down his window and lit another cigar. Depending on how things went with Operation Octane, whether a successful launch or not, would determine how the day would end for him, and for his wards—Nick and Roxy. He was itching to get moving, one way or the other. But the slow passage of time only intensified his obsession with Megan's vision. It was all he could think about now.

***

Special Agent Seagram had done his homework. From what David could tell, he'd studied the Capitol's floor plans and schematics, especially those of the electrical grid and ventilation system. All that remained was for David to do his part, which Seagram summed up as quick access, quick release and a quick withdrawal. Sounded easy but David knew reality always threw curves.

"We need to talk outside of cameras," Seagram said, veering David left into the men's room, while Rand's man stood posted outside—a deterrence to any desperados seeking a piss.

No prying eyes in here, David thought, as he scoured the walls, ceiling and stalls.

Seagram rested a briefcase he'd been carrying across the sink and opened it. "Put these on," he said, retrieving a watch and a GPS ankle monitor, tossing them to David. "You'll be observed and tracked, Bennett. So don't even think about pulling a fast one."

The thought of being stalked turned his stomach, and now, standing alongside toilets and sinks in a less than noble setting for the launch of a world-changing mission, he questioned how he got here. But here he was. And in his moment of distress he wondered, knowing what he knew now, if he could start over again, would he have made the same choices. Of course, the answer was obvious—the scientist in him could never have resisted the powerful lure of Octane's potential.

"Now for the piece de resistance," Seagram said, lifting up a false bottom of the briefcase, widening David's eyes. Secured in place was the payload David had provided Agent Jenks.

Seagram smiled. "Show time."

★★★

"I'm not leavin'," Sean O'Malley declared, depositing his grocery bags onto the kitchen counter as his face grew red with irritation. "I've lived on dis islan' for de better part av me life through theck an' thin. Oi won't be leavin' nigh."

"Dad, either you go or I stay," Megan said with a stubbornness inherited from her father. "Which will it be?"

"Nigh love, don't be loike dat. Yer go wi' Brad an' de others. I'll be gran'."

"The last thing I want to do is stay on this island in a storm, Dad. You know that. But you leave me no choice."

Sean sighed heavily in resignation and then, exasperated, said, "For 'eaven's sake, someone tend ter de groceries before they spoil."

Brad dutifully emptied the bags while Megan stored the goods away, their growling stomachs foregoing a home-cooked meal in lieu of a quick departure.

"Put some hustle in it, people," Megan said, as everyone gathered up their belongings, anxious to be leaving well before the storm had a chance to bear down on them. By tomorrow morning she wanted to be well inland, away from the giant swells that swallowed her mother.

They exited the cottage in a snakelike column cautiously weaving their way down to Sean's boat in the burgeoning rains. It took some doing for all seven to climb aboard, their footholds precarious with the up and down roller-coaster motion of the waves. And then, once safely onboard, possessions snuggled tightly upon laps and wind-swept rains stinging faces, Sean's boat broke through crest after crest of the turbulent channel as he headed toward the opposite shore.

All was going well until the appearance of a fast-approaching vessel, its lights glaring and its bullhorn blaring, "U.S. Coast Guard, return to the island … I repeat, U.S. Coast Guard, return to the island." It was more than unsettling, it was frightening, especially maneuvering an about-face turn in the rough waters. The patrol boat escorted Sean's back to the island where everyone disembarked before the vessel pulled in port-side and a familiar figure of a man jumped down from its deck onto the dock to join them—his pistol drawn.

"Everyone do as I say and no one gets hurt," Agent Jenks said, using the cliched line of bad guys. "Move … up to the lighthouse."

★★★

Outside the Capitol Building the storm raged while, inside, life carried on as groups of stranded tourists made the best of the situation gathering within the Great Rotunda and Statuary Hall, taking in the Nation's history while waiting out the elements. David wove his way through the crowds on his way to the Capitol's south wing to the Hall of the House of Representatives and its gallery situated on the upper level. There, the press and public were allowed to sit and observe the Legislature at work in the chamber below; however, passes were required for all visitors. Again, David's fake FBI badge worked wonders as he walked past the long line of tourists and breezed right in. He moved to the centrally designated position directly below an air vent, his ankle chafing against the monitor while his whole being chafed at being hijacked—feeling like a leashed dog under Rand's firm grip undergoing obedience training. But there was little he could do now about the way things turned out. Best case scenario was to just do as told so that Roxy and Nick would escape the crosshairs of Rand's target.

Though he had visited the Capitol before, this was his first time in the gallery. It was an interesting perspective of Congress at work—party members huddled below like two opposing football teams with two opposing strategies, both looking for a win. But he knew with Octane's release that this worldview would be relegated to history, and in its future place—governance requiring zero effort under a unified legislature with a unified platform. But before such cooperation could be manifested, his directive must be successfully executed.

Everything in life was about timing. Special Agent Seagram had been specific about this, explaining the on-off cycling of the chamber's air conditioning system every fifteen minutes. This was vital to the tampering of the electrical grid by a Rand operative, virtually shutting down all lighting within the Hall of the House of Representatives precisely when the air conditioning system kicked back on. It would be then, the blackout timed with the resumption of air flow, that David, stationed beneath the critical vent, would complete his mission.

In position now and steadying himself, the a/c system above him cycled off. David checked his watch. Fifteen minutes until launch time.

***

Frightened and confused, Sean O'Malley and troop did as told, pushing against wind gusts and annoying rains in their forced retreat back over slippery rocks, all lugging possessions and Nick with his plant, up to the light house.

Upon reaching its door, Jenks said, "Inside ... all the way to the top."

"What's the meaning of this?" Brad demanded, outraged, refusing to budge.

"Just be a good boy, Brad, and climb," Jenks said, directing the pistol at him.

Round and round the abductees ascended the ninety-foot tower's spiral staircase, finally reaching the lantern room at the top.

Megan approached Roxy. "Are you and the baby okay after such a trying climb?"

Roxy, still catching her breath said, "We'll be fine."

Jenks' ears perked up. The exchange caught him off-guard. He had to hand it to David, hiding Roxy's pregnancy from him, though he did recall their passionate cries of ecstasy like wild animals echoing in the jungle night. Now the pregnancy made her an even more valuable hostage. He made a mental note to never underestimate his 'good buddy'.

"On the floor," he ordered.

Exhausted from the climb up, no one argued.

"Phones in here," he said, kicking a small empty box over to Brad. When everyone had unloaded their cell phones, Jenks kicked the box back out of their reach. Then he pulled up a lone stool and sat, his threatening pistol in clear view resting against his lap.

"I don't understand," Megan said, the first to speak and clearly confused. "I thought you were an FDA agent. Why are you holding us hostage?"

"Don't blame me. I'm not responsible for your unfortunate circumstances," Jenks said, actually sounding sympathetic. "I just follow orders."

"Orders from who?" Andre asked, staring Jenks down, seeking some long-sought answers as he pulled Nick in closer.

Roxy answered. "General Arthur Rand, head of the Defense Intelligence Agency."

All heads turned in her direction, jaws dropped. Even Jenks'.

"Well, well," he said, "will wonders never cease."

"Roxy, who told you this?" Megan asked.

"David did," she said, abandoning her vow to him of secrecy for safety's sake, pointless now that Jenks had captured her and Nick.

"Roxy, what else did David tell you?" Brad asked, sensing the long road to finding answers was finally at hand. "We need to hear everything."

★★★

David stood with his back against the gallery's wall, heart-pounding palpitations throbbing in his ears. He looked around at the scattered crowd, mostly silent as they observed the congressmen working in the chamber below. He eyeballed the legislators' attendance at about ninety percent, sure that the consortium would relish his nailing this majority in one fell swoop with the legislators never knowing what hit them.

With the throbbing in his ears crescendoing and his breaths coming short and fast, David knew by his watch he had mere seconds to go. When cries of surprise elicited forth from all directions at the chamber's sudden blackout, and the whoosh of air flow resumed strong above his head, David withdrew from inside his FBI jacket an air pistol, aimed the loaded barrel high and pulled the trigger.

All the hopes and dreams of E.D.E.N.'s members rested with his discharging pellets of powdered bacterial spores—too small to see, smell or taste—that float like dust motes out onto the air, circulate with the current into the respiratory systems of all who inhale and alight onto surfaces everywhere, clinging for weeks in a viable state awaiting the human touch.

David's hopes and dreams rested upon his not getting caught. The deed done, he quickly pocketed the air pistol back within his jacket and moved briskly among the agitated crowd to the nearest egress, exiting out from the dark into the light.

"Capitol Police … stop right there," an officer said, confronting David with the barrel of his gun. "You're under arrest. Hands in the air."

David, stunned, looked around for Seagram. He was nowhere in sight.

***

"Let me get this straight," Brad said, "you're telling us that Doc was approached by this General Rand to find a plant in the Amazon capable of removing aggression, with the ultimate goal of eliminating militant hot spots in the world. And then, when Doc found such a plant, that's when he enlisted David to do the actual work of creating this airborne 'disease.'"

"Correct," Roxy said.

"But you're saying during that time neither of them were aware that the General and Agent Jenks, here, were bad actors in a covert scheme, operating under the false umbrella of the U.S. Government?"

Jenks listened intently. Smiling at being called a bad actor.

"That's right," Roxy said. "Doc was doing what he thought was his patriotic duty, and David wanted to help him out—you know how he admired the man. But when they realized that this clandestine operation was illegal and not what they had signed up for, Doc wanted out. But David, knowing the truth of things, was afraid to show Rand their cards. Thought it safer to go along and complete the mission, despite the fact that if they got caught, they'd be charged with treason," Roxy said. "And then Doc and Nick disappeared."

"So our disappearances were tied to this covert operation," Nick said, intrigued.

"Yes, it seems so. Both were meant to scare David into completing the mission, but with the added bonus for Agent Jenks, here, to take advantage of your kidnapping by blackmailing David for money to keep you alive."

"You dirty bastard," Brad said. "What kind of man are you?"

"One who likes money," Jenks retorted shamelessly.

"Go on Roxy," Megan pressed.

"There's not much more to tell," she said. "When David left to complete the mission in Brazil, he had no idea what had become of either of you ... and I haven't heard from him since," she sighed.

"So this airborne 'disease'," Andre said, still poking, "tell us how it works."

Agents Jenks, who had once adamantly prohibited discussion of the mission outside of Rand's circle, now seemed untroubled with compromising the mission's cover—David's tainted cigars having effectively mutated the bluster right out of him. Instead, his mellowed self leaned forward with keen interest to learn of Octane's inner workings—the secret of which David had kept from him.

"It's a bacteria that turns off the aggression gene in people's DNA," Roxy said. "And then, without aggression, David says fear and all the negativity it creates disappear. People's natures turn positive and peaceful."

"But is it contagious?" Megan asked, wary. "Will it spread beyond the targeted hot spots?"

"Yes, I believe it can," Roxy said. And then she ventured out on a limb. "But if turning terrorists into pacifists requires the entire world to change as well, then I am more than a willing participant if a peaceful world comes of it."

Megan gasped. "Rox, you can't mean that."

"Meg, don't you remember 9/11? What they did to my mother and thousands of others? David would be righting a wrong by doing something noble for mankind."

"Rox, there is nothing noble in a vengeful blindsiding of humanity. People have a right to self-determination," Megan argued.

"David and I lost my mother … we hurt," Roxy said, her weary eyes fixed on Megan's. "All we seek is a peaceful, more perfect world in which to live."

"Don't kid yourself, Rox," Megan scoffed. "Our world could never handle perfection—not in Eden, and not now. The bad comes along with the good, that's just the nature of things. Mess with that and you mess with God's plan."

"Don't talk to me about God's plan," Roxy admonished. "What did your *so-called* God ever do for me? Bless me with a wonderful father? Is that what we need more of in this world—people like him?"

"Don't use your father as an excuse. Just because bad things happen doesn't give anyone the right to decide how people should act—like some Stepford society. It's insane," Megan said, her voice agitated.

"On the contrary, Meg, it's the sanest thing I could ever be a part of. I have a responsibility now to my baby," Roxy said, her hand rubbing her belly. "I want her to live in a world free of violence. Imagine a world rid of angry people."

"What if I want to be angry?" Megan threw back at her, her voice rising with the realization that, if Roxy got her way, she could never cry out in objection again. "What right is it of anyone's to determine how I should feel?"

"Try to understand, Meg. Mankind won't miss emotions they can no longer feel. It will be the end of all pain—the path to freedom."

"Freedom?" Megan said, incredulous. "Look in the mirror, Rox. You're still that frightened little girl caught in a hurricane. All these years you've let your guilt eat you alive. It's time you forgave yourself and let it go—that's the path to freedom, not this."

"Forgive myself?" Roxy said, her laughter haunting. "What good is forgiveness when I can never forget the pain? Forgiveness won't set me free—only memories that no longer hurt."

"Your mother believed in forgiveness," Megan countered.

Roxy stiffened. "Mother was always trying to save sinners from themselves with her loving forgiveness. She could forgive Father. But I'm not like her," she said, a sudden chill in her voice. "Don't you see? The day I pulled that trigger, Father won. I became like him—a monster."

The lantern room fell silent to the cries of soaring seagulls and swelling waves crashing high against the lighthouse in the brewing storm. Roxy exhaled a deep sigh and with a sorrowful look at her best friend, said, "I'm tired of fighting the pain, Meg. I just want it to end."

"Rox … you're not a monster," Megan said, her voice soothing. "When you pulled that trigger you were an innocent child who had lived through unfathomable horrors. No one could ever fault you for trying to save your mother. And no one understands better than me what it's done to you, but Rox … this isn't the answer." Then she turned to the others in their stunned silence and said, "We have to stop this."

Sean O'Malley spoke up. "There's nathin' any av us can do, love."

"He's right," Agent Jenks said, having heard enough and ready now to switch the subject to one of a more personal nature. "Besides, it will all be over soon, so why don't we just relax and enjoy some civil conversation … a re-do of our little gathering in the jungle, perhaps," he said, shifting on his stool to get more comfortable.

Nick and Andre exchanged questioning looks, clearly out of the loop.

"Maybe this time we could trade stories about dream experiences … visions. Megan, why don't you start," Jenks said, coyly. "Your article in Global Thrills said you experienced a remarkable one … of a woman's eyes."

"Don't engage him Meg," Brad shot back in protective mode.

"I saw them, too … several times," Jenks admitted, "while I was in the Amazon waiting for Bennett to complete the payload. Each time, they conjured up a different vision; but their effect was always the same—calming," he said. "The last one I had was of these tall, exotic-looking blooms—oddly similar to that one," he said, his gaze landing on Nick's specimen but then, paying little mind, continued on with his story. "But just as the vision was leaving me, those eyes planted a word in my brain: Ramati."

Brad sucked his breath in and froze. Ramati—the same word he recalled from his own vision after a self-injection of the plant extract.

"I know that word," Megan said. "Before I traveled to India on assignment, I studied Sanskrit. Ramati is Sanskrit for paradise."

Jenks started laughing hysterically. And when he finally calmed down enough, wiping the tears from his eyes, he said, "Fuck … the irony is just too much."

"What are you talking about?" Brad said, annoyed.

"The whole point of this operation was to re-create Eden, the perfect world that existed before the Adam and Eve fuck up. Get it—Eden … aka Paradise." He started laughing again. Then his eyes landed a second time on Nick's plant, and he sobered up. "Why do you carry that around with you?" he asked.

Nick had nothing to hide anymore, and he wasn't afraid to speak the truth. "This plant is my medicine … a miracle plant that removed my cancer … removed my fear. And if I were a betting man, I'd wager David used it to create the payload for your mission … to remove aggression … to re-create Eden."

Nicks words voiced what Brad was thinking: the plant was the key all along to connecting the dots—from the hidden extract he'd found at the lab to David's gene-altering bacteria—the first and last pieces to the puzzle. After all of his digging for answers, he never felt more certain he'd found them. And, of course, the idea of a cure for cancer excited him, but he couldn't let that excitement get ahead of him. His boss needed to return safe and sound first.

***

As Monday slowly rolled into Tuesday, the endless hours spent locked up in the lighthouse were agonizing, everyone anxiously waiting for Jenks to hear back from General Rand. But, in the pre-dawn hours, instead of a phone call materializing, a hurricane rolled into Maine full force. Inside of the lighthouse may have been the safest retreat on the island from the storm's rage, but its position on the ocean's edge was directly in its line of fire. There was no getting away from the boom of an angry ocean pummeling its outer facade or the unsettling howls of tempestuous gusts hefting crested waves out of their depths and tossing their salty spray onto the lantern room windows. And the beacon's Fresnel lens was like a pulsating strobe in the blackened skies, its flashes every ten seconds both eerie and annoying. The entire scene was like a bad horror movie where there was no escape, only a slow and torturous ticking of time to an inevitable doomsday finish. Of course, none of the six innocent inhabitants of the lighthouse wanted to give credence to the fearful wanderings of their minds, instead rationalizing a happy storybook ending, because no one ever believes the unthinkable can happen to them—until it does.

Megan sat squirreled up, knees to chest. All her previous outrage stifled by fear, her eyes locked in a stare that saw nothing. Sean, along with Brad and Roxy, took turns sitting with her, offering words of encouragement and a gentle embrace, as she relived her worst nightmare.

Andre stayed by Nick's side, taking quiet comfort in his partner's steady calm. But yesterday's revelation of a contagious disease changing his DNA had left him confused and unnerved. Yet, he had to wonder, would such a thing be all that bad considering the positive nature of the lovely man he had fallen in love with. And when he looked at Megan and the fear written all over her face, the idea of a gene-altering disease that would take that from her now seemed more a mercy than a threat.

Jenks, impatiently awaiting the much-delayed phone call from General Rand confirming a successful mission, turned his thoughts to what Nick had said regarding his plant, how it had helped to cure his cancer; and if, as Nick had suggested, it was true that this plant was used in the creation of Octane, too, well … he had to admit to the brilliance of the man behind it all. And a guy as smart as that could certainly pull off the inaugural launch of Octane without a hitch—at least that's what he told himself. But the longer the call was delayed in coming the more discontented he'd become in the beacon room's humid environment, his trigger hand dampened and fingers cramped from his incessant hold on his gun. Needing relief for his stiffened joints, he momentarily switched hands with his weapon. And that was all it took. A few seconds of human frailty for Brad to rush him, knocking him off his stool and sending his Glock skittering across the lantern room floor, coming to a dead stop beside Roxy. Surprised, but without hesitation, she retrieved it—and directed its barrel at Jenks, spread eagle on the ground.

"Tie him up," she said, quickly coming to her feet.

Sean ran for some rope he had stashed aside.

"Take it easy, Roxy. You don't want to accidentally fire that thing," Jenks said, considering her to be inexperienced.

"You don't need to worry about that, Jenks. I know how to handle a gun. And believe me, if I shoot you … it won't be an accident."

Brad took the rope from Sean, yanked Jenks' arms behind him and laced and knotted his wrists. Finished, he pushed the man to the floor.

"Don't move," he said, and then looked over at Roxy. "I can take that from you now," he said, reaching out for the gun.

Roxy looked at him, then stepped back, away from everyone. "I'm sorry," she said, "but I can't let you call for help … I can't let you stop David's mission."

Megan came out of her trance. "Rox," she said, "give Brad the gun."

"I'm sorry Meg. I never meant to hurt you … any of you," she said, picking up the box of cell phones and backing toward the stairs. And with one last lingering look at Megan she said, "You may not believe it now, but one day people will thank David." Then, nothing more to say, she turned and retreated down the spiral staircase—walking out on her best friend, on any further discussion, and on any chance to change her mind.

★★★

"FBI—hold it right there," the agent hollered into the wind as Roxy exited the lighthouse, the world outside wild and chaotic with both nature and government officials vying for control. The flash of the lighthouse beacon exposed a round-up in progress, the good guys indistinguishable from the bad in the pre-dawn darkness. "Back inside," the agent yelled, confiscating Roxy's gun and escorting her in. Several more agents followed. "Wait here," he said, a single guard posted with her as he and the others bounded up the staircase. When they reached the very top, the call of "FBI" reverberated all the way back down to her.

Tired and confused as to what was happening, Roxy sat down on the bottom step, the box of phones resting on her lap. Fifteen minutes later, Agent Jenks was being hauled down the stairs in handcuffs. He passed her without a word. "You're free to go," the agent told her before closing the door behind them. But she remained seated there, alone and scared—frightened of what Jenks' arrest forebode—not wanting to face the prospect of a future living in fear. Then, her footsteps masked by the storm, Megan silently approached from behind and joined her best friend on the step, wrapping her within her arms. Roxy began to cry.

"I'm here," Megan said, Roxy's head on her shoulder. "I'm always here."

★★★

The walls were closing in around David, at least that was how he felt after hours spent in an isolated holding cell overnight and now sitting alone in a small, gray interrogation room with only his panicked thoughts. His eyes scanned the space, noting the absence of a two-way mirror and just one ceiling camera mounted into the adjacent-facing corner. He stared at it, wondering who was staring back. Then the door opened and FBI Special Agent Seagram walked in, alone. He looked up at the camera. David followed his gaze to the flickering red light, which suddenly went out. Seagram bent to remove David's ankle monitor, then handcuffs, and when done, sat down across the table from him. "The camera's been turned off," he said. "What we say in this room stays in this room. Understood?"

David swallowed hard and nodded.

"I'm not who you think I am," Seagram said. "I work as an undercover agent for the FBI. For the last decade, ever since E.D.E.N. hit our radar, I've been infiltrating their ranks, patiently waiting to expose its charter members in the act of biological warfare. Today, we hit pay dirt, cleaning house all the way down to the lowest levels—thanks to you," he said, his youthful face exuding a rare grin.

David was floored, unsure what this meant for him.

"First off, I want to apologize for my rough treatment of you, but it had to look legit. I needed your reactions to be authentic. Didn't want to send the wrong signals to the wrong people. Hope you understand.

"Second, I want to thank you for your phone call to the FBI alerting us to the payload's movement. Timing was critical and your call enabled us to take possession of the goods and make a switch without notice, thus preventing the release of the actual bacteria."

David stopped breathing.

"That's right," Seagram said, "the U.S. Government safely retains the original payload. Now … we understand by your phone call you wanted no part of this illegal endeavor and that you had been forced under duress of your brother's kidnapping to do so. As your actions aided in the successful termination of a terrorist biological threat, our government has deemed to nullify all charges against you and thanks you for your service to your country. You are free to go."

David shook with relief, hardly able to believe what he was hearing, but then a cold fear descended upon him. "What about Roxy and Nick?" he said, panicked for their safety.

"The situation has been neutralized—they are no longer in danger," Seagram said. Then he pulled out a burner phone and handed it to David. "Maybe there's someone you want to call," he said, and shook David's hand before leaving the room.

★★★

"Hello," Roxy said, having pulled her ringing phone out from the box and answering, her voice shaky from crying.

"Roxy … is that you?"

"David … oh David," she said, and began to cry again.

"It's okay, darling. I'm well. We're all safe now."

Through her sobs, she said, "I'm with Megan at the lighthouse," and squeezed the shoulder of her dearest friend still sitting on the step beside her.

"So your grandfather told me. Sounds like a nice guy. Says he's looking forward to meeting me."

Roxy laughed through her tears.

"I hear Nick is with you, too?"

"Yes, David. He's well. We all are … baby, too."

"I can't wait to see you all, darling, but I have to go now. I'll be home tomorrow. Tell Nick I love him, and I'll call him then. And darling, can you meet me tomorrow in Boston at the Public Garden … noontime on the bridge? We can talk about everything then."

Roxy swallowed a sob and, smiling, said, "Nothing could keep me away."

105

SAFE PASSAGE

Girl Flashback

THEY EXITED ROSE'S BELOVED garden just as the eye of the storm had passed from them, providing safe passage out from the backwoods to their home before the hurricane's wrath was resurrected. Mother and twelve-year old Girl, bruised and broken, still entwined in each other's arms, staggered toward their country manor. Pressing forward through the returning headwinds and renewed rains, they reached the manor's battered door and pushed inside, struggling against the revived tempest to close it behind them. Yet wrapped in each other's arms they sank to the floor, zapped of strength. And then began the flow of tears—of relief? … of happiness? … of sorrow? … of regret? It was improbable that Rose or Girl could have labeled their emotions right then, all of it so overwhelming.

When at last Girl was able to reach a phone and dial 911, an ambulance appeared an hour later on the heels of the retreating storm. Mother and daughter were whisked away for a hospital stay that lingered longer for Rose. The truth was finally out about Eugene. Rose could no longer point to an innocent home injury as the cause of her trauma, her battered body irrefutable evidence. Eugene's body was retrieved a day after the storm by the authorities and cremated thereafter. Later, when Rose was up to it, she and Girl had his ashes interred into a single cemetery plot, having no wish to be buried beside him. And no grand headstone marked his grave, just a simple plaque secured flush with the ground duly engraved with his name and dates of birth and death, without any mention of a beloved husband and father inscribed on its face.

Back from the cemetery, the weight of the day finally taken from them, mother and daughter sat across the kitchen table from one another, each with a soothing cup of tea.

"What do we do now, Mother?" Girl asked.

Rose looked at her daughter with all the devotion and love in her heart and said, "Live, my darling. We live."

106

—·—

LOOSE ENDS

Wednesday, September 13, 2006

D AVID REACHED BENNETT LABORATORIES before the sun had risen, due to an early arrival into Boston on a private jet, courtesy of Uncle Sam—Agent Seagram's way of making things up to him and saying thanks. It had seemed a thousand yesterdays since he'd stepped foot into the lab, seen the flicker and heard the hum of fluorescent bulbs overhead coming to life, smelled the familiar chemicals of experiments underway, or felt the sensation of a cool stainless table brushing up against warm hands. But after a few minutes, David was on autopilot and, except for his presence, the building was dead, which was exactly as he wanted it.

He entered his fish-bowl office, flicked on the lights, and walked to his desk. Sitting down, he opened the left bottom drawer and withdrew a bottle of scotch with a single glass. After he poured himself a shot, he sat back in his chair and rested his eyes upon Rose's oil painting hung upon the opposite wall. He used to love admiring it, the single rose captured on canvas, her favorite flower that just so happened to be her name. He smiled and raised his glass. "To Rose," he toasted, downing his shot. Finished, he stood and walked over to the painting, reaching behind its frame to remove a key taped there.

Back in his office chair, he used it to unlock the right bottom drawer of his desk, then pulled it ajar and removed a small box. He didn't bother to open it. Instead, he tucked it safely within a pocket of his jacket and abruptly stood, leaving the building. Outside, a taxi was waiting to take him home to a long-anticipated hot shower and a fresh change of clothes before his rendezvous with Roxy.

***

Roxy drove like a bat out of hell down the Maine coastline toward Boston, glad to be free of pitying eyes, though everyone had forgiven her crazed actions given her obvious duress over David and the pregnancy, not the least of which to mention the storm instigating nightmarish memories of the hurricane fifteen years ago and her father's death. But now none of that mattered to her, only seeing David. She knew his mission had likely failed, given that Megan and the others had gleaned as much from the FBI agents who had raided the island and arrested Jenks. It was not the outcome she had hoped for, certainly not the outcome she had desired for her baby's future. But she was strong, and if life had taught her anything, it was how to endure pain. Only now, she wouldn't be alone in her struggle—she would have David and their child.

***

David arrived early at the Boston Public Garden, walking its flowered pathways, taking time to slow down and reboot his mind. His life had taken on a fantastical popcorn-movie quality as of late, and now he was looking for the part where the leading man gets his girl and has a happy ending. But before such a welcome conclusion, he had loose ends in need of tying up.

He sat down on the bench where collegiate-looking Agent Seagram had jogged to a stop three weeks earlier, dispatching the go-ahead code for Operation Octane's launch on September 11—the five-year anniversary of Rose's death. Then, as now, David didn't want her death to be the summation of her existence, how she died to overshadow the remarkable contributions she'd made in this life to helping others. She deserved better. And it was this steadfast determination to honor her life that spawned his crazy but gutsy plan—

He called the consortium's bluff.

He had already validated to General Rand and the consortium his competence as a scientist with his creation of an effective waterborne contagion proven to have removed aggression. Why, then, would they have need to question the veracity of his airborne contagion? Check its contents? Substantiate his word? They didn't. And so all their hopes and dreams of establishing a new Eden went up in proverbial smoke because not only was the payload that shot from David's air pistol a fake supplanted by Agent Seagram and the FBI, but the original air pistol he'd delivered up to Agent Jenks had never been loaded with the authentic gene-altering bacteria in the first place—which meant not only was Congress never infected, but that the virus now in the possession of the U.S. Government was an imposter. All to David's liking, as he'd never trusted the unworthy likes of Rand and his lot with the most powerful weapon in the world, nor did he want the government's prying eyes discovering the vital functions that made Octane tick. And just as importantly to his liking, this was payback for the pain and suffering of his loved ones. But now, with E.D.E.N. and the U.S. Government out of the picture, he could focus his attention on completing his plan by dealing with those loose ends—and honoring Rose.

★★★

Roxy spotted him on the bridge. A swan boat had just passed beneath, and now he was staring into the water's dark, rippling depths watching something he'd dropped in sink. She ran to him.

David looked up as she called his name, his brilliant smile and opened arms greeting her. The two locked in a passionate embrace, their hungry mouths seeking one another's as time stood still. When they finally broke for air, David stepped back arm's length and, holding her hands, took full measure. "You look wonderful, darling," he said, and gently, he placed his hand on her abdomen. "And the little one?" he asked. "How's she doing?"

Roxy beamed. "She's incredible. Strong like her mom."

"No doubt," he said, kissing her tummy.

"David," Roxy said, her curiosity getting the best of her, "What did you drop into the pond?"

"Well, darling, if you must know … it was my good luck charm," he said. And when she looked at him questioningly, he said, "You're the only good luck I am ever going to need from now on."

It had been time for David to say goodbye to his Sphatika—and to Lanya. His life with Roxy was beginning anew, and his heart couldn't abide two mistresses. Lanya had brought him to realms he had never known existed, piercing the veil of illusion and connecting him to all of creation; but his relationship with her had been otherworldly, untouchable, beyond his reach. Roxy was here, grounded in the present, more than willing to share his love and to whom he could give his heart. She would be his world now—and forever.

Roxy smiled.

"Speaking of luck," she said, looking out over the pond, "I've been thinking a lot lately about becoming a mother … of the important decisions that will have to be made for our child … and I realized something about myself—I've lived a lie. All my life, I convinced myself life was a crap shoot dependent upon luck, so why not base decisions on some random pop-up answers of a Magic 8 Ball. But now that I am going to be a mother, I know that that was just a bull-shit excuse I told myself to avoid hard decisions. Now it's time for me to stop hiding from responsibility," she said, "time to grow up." She reached into her satchel and pulled out her Magic 8 Ball. Facing the pond, Roxy held it out over the water and let it go, watching it fall into the dark, rippling depths with a kerplunk. "Not to say that I don't believe in luck sometimes," she said, looking back at David, smiling. "I was lucky to have found you."

David kissed her forehead and then gently took her arm. "Come, darling," he said, "let's walk."

The handsome couple promenaded the colorful gardens, now vibrant in the glorious noontime sun. As David had planned, upon reaching a rose patch he halted their walk. Stooping to retrieve a small bud on the ground, his gentle and protective hands lifted it to his nostrils, whereupon he inhaled its intoxicating scent.

Roxy observed his far-away look and knew his mind's wanderings. Saying nothing, she let him be with his thoughts.

"Darling," he said, pocketing the rosebud, his mind returning to her, "I assume you know my mission was aborted." He didn't wait for her to reply. "I know how disappointing that must be for you. It is for me, too. But I'm going to make it up to you."

David got down on his knee. "Say you'll marry me, Roxy, and I promise … you will never live in fear again."

Roxy looked down into his dark, ocean blue eyes. Tears forming in her own. "Yes," she replied, her lips trembling. "Yes, my love."

David reached inside his jacket pocket and retrieved the small box. He stood and slowly opened its lid.

It wasn't what she was expecting.

"Accept this as a symbol of my everlasting love and loyalty," he said, "a promise to cherish our love into eternity." And then he removed the small, glass vial within and pulled out its stopper. "Breathe in, my love," he said holding it beneath her nose. She complied. He did the same. Then, to honor Rose, he turned toward the roses and emptied the vial's contents over the bushes. Just then, a gentle breeze swept the air like a broom, shooing the bacterial spores on their way to the far corners of the Earth.

Such a difference a day makes, the hurricane of their yesterday's now a passing storm, replaced by the promise of sunny tomorrows.

"Let's celebrate," Roxy said with a sudden uplift of voice and rapturous glow, embracing David.

"Anything, my darling. Your wish is my command."

"Make love to me."

"Delighted to," David said, and he kissed her with all of his heart.

★★★

As they set off, arm in arm, into the downtown neighborhood, a crowd was gathering on the opposite sidewalk outside of a theater. "Look at all those penguins," David said, referring to the men dressed in tuxedos. "Must be a premiere."

Roxy, shocked at her lapse in memory, jerked her head in time to catch a glimpse of Zach's corona hair glistening in the sun. And then her eyes rose and noted the marque: 'Hurricane.' She gave a laugh.

"What's so funny?" David asked.

"I don't think I'll be seeing that one."

"Oh? Why is that?"

"Because … I've already lived it."

★★★

Journal Entry, Wednesday, September 13, 2006:

This will be my last journal entry. It's time to say goodbye to you, Father—and to fear. Your grip on me was always tight and determined, painful and controlling, your cruelty a constant, and all because you wanted a son—but you got me.

Here's the thing, father—the pain made me strong, just like you always wanted me to be … and mother, too. You underestimated us, our strength to keep going on—in spite of our fear. You were the weakling, father, the bully who had to make himself seem big. But your shadow could never overcome us. Mother had placed her faith in God, and I placed my faith in Mother—and together, we stood tall.

EPILOGUE

200 YEARS LATER

I T WAS IN THE year 2206KC, at the infancy of a new era decreed as Kingdom Come, during the bicentennial celebration commemorating Earth's return to Paradise when the incident happened. The family of the House of David sat in the front row as honored guests, rapt with attention and unaware of what was about to befall them. Though, had Rose been alive, the ironic timing of events would not have surprised her because she never did believe in coincidence.

The first speaker took to the podium. "Blessed Brothers and Sisters," he began, the audience hushing, "two hundred years ago our Savior stood amongst mere mortals, His calling unknown to the masses but ordained by God. He lived in a time foreign to many, a time we reference as The Dark Opposites, when human emotions existed called negatives—most notable amongst them, hatred and cruelty. But, in fulfillment of the scriptures, the miracle of His work expunging all negativity from the world cleared the promised path to eternal love and kindness and the return of Paradise on Earth. And so, Brothers and Sisters, let us stand now to give honor and glory to our exalted Savior." Thousands rose to their feet and, with uplifted heads and arms, all hailed in unison, "Praise be David Bennett, Son of God."

Now, had Rose been present, she would have told these misguided followers that the David she knew was a mere mortal, an imperfect soul lost like all the rest in search of a path home. Although, as it turned out, this mortal's soul was impatient and his path unconventional. He rejected the wisdom of lessons learned through the arduous unfolding of time. Instead, he sought a quick fix—and so he chose to play God. But scripture has it: For what man knows God's counsel, or who can conceive what our Lord intends? Rose would well agree, and she most assuredly would add that only the Heavenly Father knows the day and hour of the Lord's return. But David's work had freed mankind from two hundred years of negativity. If, during those two centuries, life wasn't Paradise on Earth, what was? And if he wasn't the savior, who then?

To be clear, David never started out to be a savior. All he ever wanted was to help mankind and, in the end, was convinced his greater purpose was to release his bacteria upon the world. But what he failed to understand was that nature wasn't ready to receive it—and nature always wins. And so, the incident happened …

Honored with a front row seat and preoccupied with her baby doll, three-year old Rosie sat nestled between Roxanne Pendleton-Bennett and Megan O'Malley-Parks, her eighth-generation grandmother and 'auntie', respectively. Quite content in her doting-mother role, Rosie was oblivious to the multitudes bestowing praise upon her eighth-generation grandfather. And it wasn't until David, the spurious Son of God himself—clothed in a shimmering white robe—took center stage to united cries of "Thy Kingdom Come, Thy Will Be Done," that Rosie's attention was diverted from her doll onto a tiny black ant encroaching on her space. Curious, she slid nearer her seat's edge, legs dangling and gaze steady. And then, overcome by feelings she could not define, she did something so out of character, so entirely foreign, so utterly inconceivable—

She stepped on it.

Acknowledgements

This book is not only the end product of many years of determination on my part, but also the amalgamation of efforts by friends and family to help me see it through. So, it is with heartfelt appreciation that I thank the following people: my writer's workshop instructor, Margo Ball, for your insightful knowledge and recommendations when this story was still in its infancy; my cover designer, Tim Barber of Dissect Designs, for your wonderful interpretation of my book's setting and essence; my sister and biggest fan, Catherine Wright, for your hawk-eye editing and multiple readings in preparation for publication; and my husband, Jim, for your perceptive eye with regard to clarity of plot and your constant encouragement and help to the very end. I am eternally grateful to all.

ABOUT THE AUTHOR

Theresa McNeice is a believer in the idea that one can find meaning in dreams—her debut novel is a case in point, having awakened one morning with not only the idea for her story, but the book's title! The idea may have come quickly, but the novel's completion took eleven years of tireless and patient devotion.

Her New England upbringing imbues her storytelling ... as does her penchant for the mysterious unknown. A contributor to her community college newspaper and a small-town writer's workshop, she has long enjoyed the craft.

When not writing, she enjoys oil painting, time spent with her family and travel. She lives with her husband in Massachusetts.

Photo: Kate Carlson Photography